THE WRONG KIND OF SPY

RHIANNON BEAUBIEN

The Wrong Kind of Spy
Rhiannon Beaubien

Copyright © 2023 by I Write With Inc.

Cover artwork by Auni Milne
Interior design by Yvonne Parks at PearCreative.ca
Map by Christine Fenske

All rights reserved. No part of this publication may be reproduced, distributed, or transmitted in any form or by any means, including photocopying, recording, or other electronic or mechanical methods, without the prior written permission of the author, except in the case of brief quotations embodied in critical reviews and certain other non-commercial uses permitted by copyright law.

ISBNs
Paperback: 978-1-9992989-3-7
Hardcover: 978-1-999-2989-4-4
E-book: 978-1-999-2989-5-1

For my grandmother Jean Beaubien
1926–2010

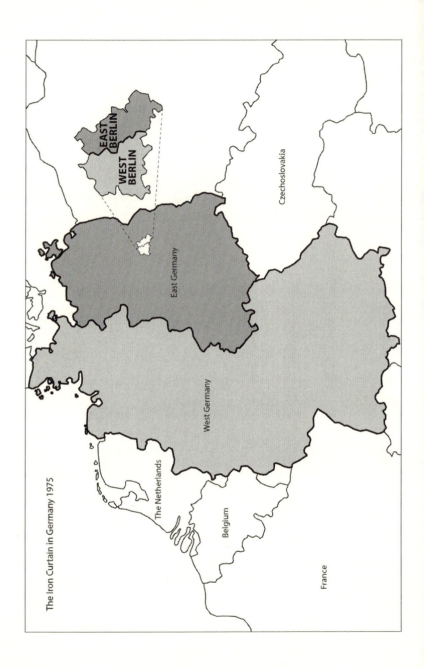

PROLOGUE

Tom sat back in the car, smoking a cigarette and letting the heat wash over him. He'd been back for two weeks, and he still hadn't knocked on the door. He just sat in the car every day, smoking the cigarettes he'd given up long ago, and watched the faded turquoise wood. Sometimes it opened. People went out. Less often new people went in.

He didn't know what he was waiting for—what would make him get out of his car, walk the fifteen or so steps to cross the street, and bang his knuckles on the wood. But it was part of the reason he was here. So he also knew he wasn't leaving until he figured it out.

The street hadn't changed much in the few years since he'd been here. The same dirt road. The same one-story houses lining it, once bright colors faded under the sometimes relentless sun.

He'd come here to make amends, but to whom, he wasn't sure. Maybe just to himself.

He didn't even know if her husband and kid were still here. They could have moved. They could have died. His check got cashed every month, but that didn't mean anything.

He remembered when he'd first met Isabella. He'd been roaming around, looking for contacts while focused on Carlos, on proving himself. It had been hard to find anyone who was willing to run agent on Carlos. Most people didn't want to get involved. The rest didn't want to help the American.

Isabella hadn't exactly volunteered. Not right away. She disliked her cousin Carlos, was wary of him and what he brought into her life, even if just on the fringe. She was married. She had a son. There was no reason for her to help the CIA. But Tom had kept on her. Partly because she was a good contact. And—although he hadn't admitted it to himself until he was dragging her out of a pool of her own blood—partly because she had the most beautiful eyes. Looking into them made him realize he was alive. Every time she smiled at him, eyes crinkling at the corners, his heart tripped over itself. He pursued her relentlessly because it was a lifeline when the rest seemed to be drowning him.

When Isabella died, he'd had so many regrets. Mostly that he'd been selfish. Her information had been okay, but nothing that changed anything. Once she started, however, she was all in because to be any other way, she'd said, would have been more dangerous. There was no point in just wishing for a better life for her son. Things didn't change by accident. They changed because people cared.

He hadn't understood that then, but he'd used it. Let her go on because it was better for him.

He stubbed out his cigarette. He guessed he had his own patterns. Falling for women who cared about things they have no business caring about.

His hands gripped the steering wheel. He could just sit here until he rotted. Jillian was safer without him, as safe as anyone could be in Berlin. He needed to forget Jillian and do what he came here to do. He didn't want to end up standing over her dead body too.

He started the car, pulled out onto the empty road, and inhaled to focus until the rest fell away. He was here to put a bullet in Carlos. That was the best thing he could do for Jillian. And maybe, just maybe, it was the one thing he could do to put the memory of Isabella to rest.

CHAPTER ONE

Jillian sat on the terrace tapping her fingers on the tabletop as she watched the sun set behind the buildings. She was nervous. She hoped she wasn't being paranoid. Her fingers moved faster as her patience ebbed. Where was James?

He was supposed to meet her here at eight, well after his shift on the base ended and more than enough time to change into his off-duty clothes. James, her only confidant in West Berlin, was the one person who could tell her if she was being crazy. It was a weird feeling, that she hoped that's what he thought. She'd rather be a lunatic than know she was being targeted.

It had been such an intense year for her. She'd taken this assignment in West Berlin because she wanted to travel, to do something different. She hadn't wanted to spend her whole life in Ottawa doing the same job day in and day out, then waking up thirty years later not noticing that time had passed. She wanted to do meaningful work, but she also wanted adventure. A signals intelligence assignment in West Berlin had seemed like the answer. She could use her skills, her knowledge, to help her country, but do it on the front lines.

Overseas assignments weren't that common for SIGINTers. She'd had to fight for this one. The last year had given her more than she bargained for, and even though she would trade some of it away, she knew there was no going back to the person she'd been. She was more cautious now, but also more committed. She wanted to see her mission through to the end. And she wanted to take everything she'd learned and do something useful with it.

Where is James? He's supposed to be here by now. He's not usually late. The anxiousness about what she wanted to tell him was making her heart pound. *Hopefully he's just been held up at work. Hopefully he isn't being targeted as well.*

Jillian took a long gulp of her beer. When James got here, she could order another one. West Berlin was beautiful in September. It was still warm enough to walk around in short sleeves, and the light was almost golden. Everything had a crispness to it, like it was all coming into focus before it disappeared into winter.

She breathed a sigh of relief when James loomed over the table before taking the seat opposite her.

"Sorry about being late. I lost track of time at the end of my shift. We got a new shipment of records in today."

James was a radio broadcaster for the British military. Officially called psychological operations, or psyops, he was winning hearts and minds over in East Germany one rock-and-roll song at a time.

"It's fine," Jillian said. "I missed you last week. Don't let it go to your head or anything, but I get lonely when you're not here."

James grinned. "That's not the first time I've heard that."

Jillian rolled her eyes. "You know what I mean."

"Aye." He sighed. "I suppose I do. Would replace me in a heartbeat, wouldn't you, for that spook you're still dreaming about."

She knew he was teasing her. She and James were friends—the best of friends after what they'd been through, and she wouldn't trade him for anything. But she missed Quentin too. Missed him in a way that made her heart ache, which scared her. Quentin—real name Tom, which she was never supposed to use—employed by the CIA, had left her in West Berlin to go deal with his past. Her rational self thought it was better that he'd gone. She knew she should let him go. She barely knew who he really was. But the less rational part of her admitted she wanted desperately to find out.

The three of them had been through so much that she felt bonded to both of them, James and Quentin, in ways that neither time nor distance were likely to erase.

"No need to look so sad, Jillian," James said. "It was just a bit of a jest."

"I wouldn't, you know. Replace you. You're stuck with me now."

He smiled. "Just what I need, then."

"It'll be good for you. Being around me will stop you from turning into an impossible, cantankerous old man."

"I'm not sure how you're going to manage that. But it might be proper fun to watch you try."

Jillian waited until he got himself a beer, with another one for her. She leaned in closer, so she could lower her voice for a little more privacy. "So, you know, I don't have any self-esteem issues."

James looked confused but didn't interrupt her.

"What I mean," she continued, "is that I'm fine with the way I look. I don't really even often think about it. But at no point in the history of me have I ever been asked out three times in one month."

"You've got a bunch of blokes chasing you, then?"

"Guys I don't know. That I've never seen before. These are not students at the institute that I see in the hallways. Three times—once when I was just sitting in the Tiergarten reading and twice when I was having a coffee at a café close to campus—these guys have just appeared out of nowhere and asked me out."

"And you don't think it's real? You aren't a bad-looking lass, you know."

"I'm not fishing for compliments. I'm telling you something is weird about it."

"What, then? You think the Stasi are trying to honeypot you?" James asked.

"Would that be so farfetched? After what happened? You warned me they might get interested, and Frank was surprised I hadn't already been detained, which is why he forbade me from ever going back east."

James took a slow sip of his beer. "It isn't outside the realm of possibility. The Stasi could very well be curious about you.

We don't know what that man Victor Smith told them, and we also don't know if Lisa's father had to give something up about you to help his daughter get out of the country."

Jillian didn't know what to do, and she was sick of not knowing what to do. These assignments should come with a manual. That spring, when her friend Lisa had disappeared into East Berlin, Jillian had risked a lot to find her. Risked her career. Risked being detained by the Stasi. Risked being tortured to give up everything she knew about Western signals intelligence, including the copied satellite collection she was currently processing out of the West German Science Institute.

Every time she'd made a decision while trying to help Lisa, she'd been told by Quentin, James, or her old boss Frank that she was making a mistake. It was a mistake to help anyone. The sensitivity of her mission meant she was supposed to lie low, not attract any attention, and stay well out of reach of the East Germans or the Soviets.

Except she hadn't. At first she'd been terrified that Lisa, who knew what Jillian really did for a living, would give her up. Then she'd been scared that Lisa needed help and no one else was going to offer any. Jillian had made it out of that situation by the skin of her teeth. Yes, the ending had been happy, as in Lisa had survived. But Jillian knew she'd raised a bunch of flags with the adversary, and her position in West Berlin had become precarious. She'd also made an enemy of ex-CIA officer Victor Smith by exposing his fraudulent activities, and she had no idea if there were going be repercussions.

With Quentin gone and Lisa home, she'd hoped she could just focus on her job and not attract any attention. Now she was nervous that it was too late for that.

"What do you think I should do?" she asked James.

"I don't know why you keep asking me about stuff like this. I didn't have a bloody clue when it was the American spooks all over you, and I certainly don't have a clue now."

Jillian sat back in her chair. "Well, how do we get one?"

"What?"

"A clue."

"What is this 'we' business?" James asked.

"Oh, come on," Jillian said. "I hang out with you all the time. Anyone interested in me is going to wonder about you."

"I'm tired of being your friend."

"No, you're not. I keep your life interesting."

"Too bloody interesting." James scowled. "I wish you'd be after asking me for something I could actually help with. A walking tour of the history of Berlin. How to use a microphone."

"What about you?" Jillian asked.

"What about me, what?"

"Have any beautiful women hit on you recently?"

"Are you serious?" James's eyebrows shot up.

"Why not? You're a good-looking guy."

"That I am."

"So?" Jillian asked.

"Have I got a bunch of East German trained honeypots crossing my path all the time?"

Jillian rolled her eyes. "What I mean is, have you been getting hit on more than usual? Even someone as charming and attractive as you must have an average."

"Well, Jillian, this is certainly new territory for us."

"Look, I think you should take this seriously. As for the rest of your romantic life, I don't really care. But it would be better for me if you didn't have an affair with a Soviet."

"Aye, I can well appreciate that. It might take everything I have to resist someone so well trained, though."

"Fine. You clearly want to be all mysterious. Suits me. I don't ever have to meet anyone you sleep with. As far as I'm concerned, you can be as chaste as a priest."

James laughed. "That I'm most definitely not. But you are a right pain. Now I'm going to be suspicious of any attractive woman I see."

"From my perspective," Jillian said, "that's not all bad."

"How you live like this, I don't well understand it."

"You don't have to. But now you have me curious. What was your last girlfriend like? What attracts you in a woman?"

"One who talks less than you. And who doesn't get attention from the Stasi or the CIA every five minutes."

Jillian smiled. "So I'm not your dream date. I can live with that. But since I'm supposed to be keeping busy these days with innocuous stuff, setting you up with someone might be something to do."

"You wouldn't have the first clue who I'd be interested in," James said.

"I don't have to knock it out of the park on the first pitch."

"Ah, I see you've been brushing up on your baseball knowledge in case your spook comes back."

Jillian didn't want to think about that. "You're changing the subject."

"Let it alone, Jillian."

"No. Tell me something. You must have a romantic past."

"You really are a tenacious pain in the arse."

"Something we all found out earlier this year."

"Well, since you're looking for something to do, I'll leave it to you to figure out what you can."

"How am I supposed to do that?" she said.

"It's not any fun if I tell you everything in one night over a couple of beers."

"Okay, tonight I get one question. A start. Tell me the name of the first woman you loved."

"Daisy."

Jillian laughed. "Let me guess. You were both sixteen, and it was when you had her shirt off in the back of your car that you realized you were in love."

James returned her smile. "Fair guess, but too much like a movie."

"Behind the barn? In the back of the church?"

His laugh boomed around the restaurant. "Fine. We were fifteen, and it was her smile. She used to smile at me like she wasn't sure if she should, and I couldn't imagine there was any better feeling in the world."

Jillian looked at James. Like, really looked at him. His gray eyes, the stubble filling in his cheeks, his large hands curled around his pint glass.

"What in the hell are you staring at?" he asked.

"I wasn't expecting that."

"What? That I have a past?"

"No, that you are so sweet."

"Are you planning to make everything awkward, then?" He sighed.

She smiled. "Fine. But I like you. That was a really beautiful thing to share."

"You're welcome, then."

Jillian felt the temperature cool as the setting autumn sun dipped lower in the sky. "All that aside, I mean it, James. I really believe that someone's gotten curious about me. So watch yourself."

"Does it ever end?" he asked.

"Not for me. Not until I leave, if you want to take a break from hanging out."

James shook his head. "No, Jillian. You're stuck with me as well."

She felt her anxiety ebb. West Berlin in 1975 was a difficult place to be in her line of work, and it meant so much to her to not be alone here. She wasn't sure she'd be able to do it otherwise. She wasn't a spy, not in the traditional sense. She had no proper training in human intelligence. She was an engineer tasked with collecting signals intelligence. The problem, as she'd learned all too well, was that out in the field, there sometimes wasn't that much difference between the two.

CHAPTER TWO

Frank looked up. He hadn't had a visitor in three weeks. This woman must be lost. Except she was carrying a box and looked angry, so maybe she knew exactly where she was. Frank sat there, inhaling through his cigarette, and decided to wait it out. She put her box down on one of the empty desks and stared at him. He wondered who would break first.

"Veronica Raeburn." She extended her hand. "We work together now."

Frank ignored her hand and leaned back in his chair. "Are you supposed to help me liaise?"

"I'm supposed to work with you to find common projects," she said, dropping her hand and stepping right up to his desk.

"Do you know much about it?" he asked.

"What?"

"Liaising."

She stared at him. "I know what the word means."

"Great. I had to look it up in the fucking dictionary, and after three weeks here, I still don't have a clue."

She obviously didn't know how to take that. "Don't you have an assignment?"

"No. I've been put out to pasture, which makes me wonder who you pissed off to end up here."

She paused. "It's quite a long list."

Frank laughed. "You from HR?"

"No. I'm an IO, meaning that I did the training. I haven't had an assignment yet."

Frank stood up and walked around his desk. An intelligence officer. It must be a long list indeed. He took a drag of his cigarette and looked her in the eye. She was almost as tall as he was. Frustration seeped out of eyes almost the same color as her black hair. "You here to babysit me? Make sure I don't go to the press or the Soviets?"

She looked genuinely surprised. "No. I'm here because I don't have a penis."

"Neither does most of the RCMP."

A smile touched her lips.

"So what have you done since you made intelligence officer?" he asked.

"Media monitoring."

"That it?"

"Yes."

Frank leaned against the desk and considered her. She was angry, and she had something to prove. This might be interesting. "What do you want to do?"

"What the rest of my cohort is doing: developing contacts, getting leads, contributing."

"I wouldn't overestimate what anyone here does," Frank said, stubbing out his cigarette. "Most of them are as useless as tits on a bull. Who do you report to?"

"Technically the supervisor of Rest of World. That's what you and I are supposed to be doing—figuring out some opportunities outside the Iron Curtain. And the Middle East, and China, and everywhere that might be of interest. It's where they put IOs who they think are unhinged or who can't cut it."

"Which one are you?"

Her jaw clenched. "Neither."

Frank regarded her. "You know, it's not a bad place to be. No one expects anything, and there's little competition, so when you come up with something, it'll be pretty easy to blow them away."

"I want to be closer to the action," she said, and he could hear the frustration in her voice.

"The way I understand it, you don't have much of a choice. They aren't going to let you anywhere near Moscow or Berlin."

"And?"

"You've got to find your own action. There's shit happening everywhere. Where would you start?"

She looked at him for a few beats. "Seriously?"

"Yeah. You and I have to find one source to exploit anywhere in the world the Canadian government isn't already looking too hard. Where would you start?"

She thought for a moment. "The Arctic."

"What?"

"We're steps away from the Soviets if you're up at the pole. There must be tons of information you could get from up there."

"Yeah, and that's what they do in Alert. I'm not freezing my ass off hoping to run into some sober Siberian. Next."

She pursed her lips. "Are you for real?"

Frank stood up and grabbed his coat. "Tell you what. Look me up. Ask around. Figure it out. And then, if you're interested in doing something other than sitting here gathering dust, spend some time thinking about where you'd go. Forget the budget, forget permissions. If you could go look anywhere, where would you start?"

He could feel her eyes on him as he walked out. He wondered if she was up to the task he'd set her. Maybe not. But Christ, he couldn't spend the next five years just sitting here. He had to find something to do.

Frank headed down the hall, determined not to feel like a pariah. He'd spent almost thirty years here. He still had friends who knew he had value. He made his way into the cafeteria and looked around for Howard, but he didn't see him. So he bought his coffee and sat down. He had to be old news by now.

He'd reached a count of fifty-seven gray flecks in the porcelain of his coffee mug when the table shifted a few inches. He looked up to see his old colleague trying to arrange his bulk on the other side.

"Frank," Howard said as he settled in with his fried egg sandwich. "Nice to see you."

"Yeah."

"How's the RCMP treating you?"

"Believe it or not, they have better coffee. The rest isn't much, but the coffee is good."

Howard chuckled. "Doing anything yet?"

"Working on this liaising thing."

"What does that mean exactly?"

"Find something that would be interesting for both agencies that no one is doing and no one wants to do."

Howard raised a brow. "Right."

Frank took out a cigarette. "So listen. A couple months ago, Kate Croswell in political targets gave me some information. It was an article from one of those diplomatic papers in the UK. Photo ops and how they're improving the world and all that. There was this guy in one of the photos, all chummy with some external affairs types. He's Cuban, but shows up everywhere our adversaries do. So I'm not quite sure what he's doing in a picture with the British."

"And?" Howard asked.

"I want to know where he is now."

"Is he a target?"

Frank smiled. "Funny you ask. He's relevant to a human intelligence operation."

Howard smiled back. "And which one would that be?"

"This new liaising thing we're trying to start with the RCMP. Our first joint target."

Howard finished up his sandwich and took a drink from Frank's coffee. "Sounds good. You know how I like to be on the cutting edge of things. Send me the info. Cubans always make for good intel."

"Thanks, Howard. I owe you one."

Frank sat back, in no rush to get back to his empty desk in the windowless, dismal room. The Cuban had left Berlin, of that he was pretty sure. If he'd headed to Moscow, Frank wouldn't be able to get near him. But if by some chance he'd gone back to his roots, there was a possibility Frank could do something interesting with this dead-end assignment they'd forced on him.

CHAPTER THREE

Aside from the potential honeypot issues, Jillian's life in West Berlin was the calmest it had ever been. She collected her signals, got them home, and spent the rest of her time quietly being a regular person. She went to cafés and walked the streets, soaking up as much of the atmosphere and the history she could. She went to different neighborhoods and contributed to the graffiti by leaving smears of pink nail polish at various places along the massive concrete wall that split the city in two. It had been up for fourteen years, this artificial divide, and Jillian knew so many Germans were hoping it would come down.

Other than James, she had her friend Madeline, a lifelong Berliner who was horrified at what had happened to her city. Madeline told wonderful stories and helped Jillian discover even more nooks and crannies. They went for picnics or to classic cabaret shows, and despite everything that had happened to her here, Jillian was grateful for so much of the experience of being in West Berlin.

Tonight she was going over to Madeline's apartment for dinner. Jillian thought that Madeline's cooking was more inventive than great, but it usually tasted okay and was more than made up for by the conversation.

Madeline lived in Wedding, a part of the city that Jillian was coming to know well. It was full of parks and interesting places to eat, and those five-story row buildings that were jammed up against each other. It seemed very European. Walking to Madeline's, Jillian reflected that West Berlin was starting to feel like home.

She was early, as usual, but she rang the bell anyway. Madeline never seemed to mind.

"Ah, Jillian. How lovely to see you again," Madeline greeted her.

Jillian followed her up the stairs, smelling cinnamon and vanilla. "Thanks for inviting me over. How was Bremen?"

Madeline took the bottle of wine Jillian held up and steered them both into the kitchen. "Oh, it was fine. I love that part of my country. And next week I'm off to Munich. I have decided it's time to catch up with a few people."

"Old friends?" Jillian asked.

"Yes, some of the women who worked at the cabaret for my mother during the war."

Madeline had one of the most fascinating histories that Jillian had ever encountered. Jillian had spent many evenings in this apartment hearing stories about the cabaret during the war. Part of it was glamorous, but mostly it was complicated. Having lived through that time, Madeline always emphasized how it was about survival. The cabaret was also a place where

Nazi officers would bring their collaborators, and they would often be set up with dancers, who would then spy on them. Jillian could barely appreciate what it would have been like to live that life. To her it was something out of a movie.

"Are many of those women here in Germany?"

"Some," Madeline said. "The war was horrible. And then, as I've told you, the years right after were in so many ways worse. So many people left because they had to. There was nothing here but rubble and cold and hunger. People wanted to forget, so they changed their names and they disappeared. But some of us, we faced up to it as best we could. I do not pretend one way is better than the other, but for me, it does no good to try to forget. There are some things that can never be forgotten." Madeline poured them each a glass of wine and set out some cheese. "But many of them ended up doing well. There are some good memories from the cabaret, and also most of the women loved my mother very much."

"It makes it sadder, doesn't it? What happened to your mom after the war. She had done a lot of good in the midst of all the craziness."

Madeline sighed. "Yes, she started drinking and never stopped. When she died ten years later, I felt there was so much I still didn't know. Even though I was there."

"Oh, Madeline, I'm so sorry."

"It is one of those things. She tried hard during the war to protect me, to protect the women working for her. And in that she was successful. We survived and always managed to eat. But she had to make so many compromises to do that. Spying for the Nazis made her sick, but this is the problem with collaboration.

It is usually so many small steps, until one feels there are no more choices. My mother was not rich or powerful. Perhaps we should have left before it started, but she decided to stay, hoping, like so many other people did, that the war would be over soon. After it began and the Nazis started to slice away the humanity of our country piece by piece, my mother decided she would focus on protecting what she could, which was everyone in our little cabaret. She took in some women who had nowhere else to go. She procured new identities for three Jewish women and employed them. She tried to protect those clients who were not supportive of the Nazi cause.

"There were little bombs everywhere, because some of the dancers, they didn't mind the Nazis. Sometimes all morality gets pushed aside in the face of wanting to stay alive. But my mother tried, as much as possible, to create a safe haven for the women in her employ. Of course, that meant working with the enemy. I look back on it and am amazed how she managed.

"At the end, whatever had made her hold herself together through the war, it collapsed. She felt she had made many wrong choices. Then our country divided, and she wasn't sure what it was all for. She started drinking and never stopped."

Jillian felt her heart get a little heavy. "Every time you talk about the war, I can't imagine how complicated it was to exist in the middle of it."

Madeline got up to stir something simmering in one of the pots on the stove. "I think this is why Germany—or at least the west side of it—why we keep throwing open the doors. Exposing everything we can is our way of atoning for it. At the bird's-eye view, as you say in English, the badness is obvious.

Hitler was evil. Himmler, Goebbels, Göring. There were so many people who twisted themselves beyond any recognition. But they alone did not fight the war. There were so many who participated with so many compromises along the way."

"My dad says that about the Allied alignment with the Soviets. He calls it our great moral compromise. In order to beat Hitler, we had to work with Stalin, who was in many ways equally terrible."

"Yes," Madeline said. "There are no winners in war." She pulled two bowls out of the cupboard. "I hope you like kidney stew. My doctor says I need to eat more organ meats. So I try this. I don't know how it will be."

Jillian had tried kidneys exactly never. But if she could sneak over to East Berlin, she figured she had the courage to eat kidneys.

The rest of the evening passed in interesting conversation. Jillian always maintained her cover as a student at the West German Science Institute with Madeline, and time had helped her feel less deceitful about it. And she was honest in all the ways that mattered about her likes and dislikes, the books she was reading, and her ideas for the future.

After dessert, Jillian insisted on doing the dishes. Madeline fought her every time, but Jillian felt it was an easy compensation for the dinner.

"Are you very busy with your schooling these days?" asked Madeline. "I know it is right in the middle of fall term, but I am not sure if you follow the traditional schedule."

"I don't," said Jillian. *Because I'm not really a student.* "I'm working on my PhD. I am an assistant to two classes and mostly just crunch data and try to work on my thesis. So except for times like holiday breaks, one week looks much the same as any other."

"I was wondering then, or hoping, if you would like to help me with a project?"

Jillian was intrigued. The feed she was collecting at the institute—the copy of a West German intelligence BND feed that Communications Branch of the National Research Council was making clandestinely—was in good shape and left Jillian with a lot of spare time. It might be nice to have something to do that didn't involve spying, worrying about being spied on, or thinking about Quentin.

"Possibly." Jillian smiled.

Madeline returned the smile. "Yes, I suppose it would help if I told you what I need. When my mother was running the cabaret, one thing she insisted on was keeping a record of everything we collected for the Nazis. A lot of it was handwritten, although by the end there were recorders in some rooms. My mother, she made a copy of everything."

"Really? Wow."

"Yes, well, at the time, she considered it a necessary protection. She wanted to be able to prove to the Nazis that she helped and also to be able to prove to anyone else that she was coerced."

"Makes sense," Jillian said.

"After she died, I didn't know what to do with everything. I didn't know if they had any value, but I also wanted to give myself a chance to heal. My mother was a difficult woman, but I missed her so much. Now though, I think it is time to go through everything. I'm sure the value is historical. The Nazis kept such meticulous records; as far as who did what, I think that has all come out. But the cabaret is a moment in history that I lived, and, well, I've been thinking of writing a book about it."

"Oh, you should," said Jillian. "Your stories are amazing. They humanize the war, and I think the everyday experiences are important to share."

"I'm happy you say that. Where I would like your help is making a catalog of everything my mother kept. There is so much. And it is such a big part of the story."

Jillian thought about it for two seconds. "I would love to. I'm not bad at analysis, and I'm great at organizing. And, very selfishly, I would love to read some of it."

"Thank you, Jillian. Your offer of help, I appreciate it so much. If you are free next Saturday, I will take you to the garage where I rent space to store everything. You can see what I have, and we can make a plan for how to do this. I have to say, I find it daunting. All those bits of paper and recordings. I have tried to take care of them, so I think it will all mostly be in good condition. But it's never been organized in any way."

It did sound daunting, Jillian thought. But it also sounded fascinating. And it was true that it wasn't entirely out of her main skill set.

"Yes, I can meet you next Saturday. We'll take a look, and then I'll help you start to organize it. It sounds like it will be incredibly cool."

"I hope so. For you. For me, it might be more sad. But like I said, there are some things that shouldn't be forgotten."

THE WRONG KIND OF SPY

CHAPTER FOUR

Frank sat looking over the memo Howard had sent him. Carlos Honouras was alive and well and working with the Sandinistas in Nicaragua. It seems he had gone back, if not to his roots, then at least to his past. Maybe it was just a continuation of his anti-American sentiment. Maybe he missed the food. But something didn't sit right with Frank. He couldn't make the connection between Carlos the revolutionary and Carlos the friend of British diplomats.

He heard the door unlock and looked up to see Veronica come in. She hung up her coat and dropped her bag on her chair.

"So," she said, sitting on her desk.

Frank raised a brow. "So?"

"I've asked around about you."

Frank looked at her. She wouldn't be able to tell him anything he didn't already know.

She appeared nervous, like the bravado that she'd had on the other side of the door hadn't quite made it all the way into the office with her. Frank almost felt sorry for her. Almost. But she wouldn't be of much use if she couldn't tell him people around here thought he was an asshole.

He folded his arms and leaned back in his chair.

"You haven't made many friends in the RCMP," she ventured.

He didn't respond.

"But neither have I," she continued, "so that's not saying much. Except you've been around a lot longer than I have."

He took out a cigarette.

"The one thing I found interesting is that everyone I spoke to here has the same opinion about you. You think signals intelligence is more important than human intelligence. And so you made everyone work their butts off to get anything out of CBNRC that they wanted for an op."

"Do you need me to explain why?" Frank joined the conversation.

"I know you don't want to be here. And I know you don't have any time for intelligence officers."

"Are you getting to a point?" He took a drag of his cigarette.

"Therefore, the impression I got is that you may be an asshole, but you're an equal opportunity asshole."

Frank almost smiled. "Is that a compliment?"

"What I'm saying is, I think you'll treat me like crap because I'm an IO, but I don't think you'll treat me any differently because I'm a woman."

"I've asked around about you too, you know."

"And?"

"And no one knows who you are."

She glared at him. "I told you how it's been for me."

"Yeah. It also makes you the ideal partner."

He could tell she hadn't been expecting that. "No one cares about you, so we can do anything we want. I'm not going to spend the next five years sitting in this room. All I really know how to do is collect SIGINT. They put you with me because neither you nor I have any field experience, so they think we'll have to go over old reports looking for something interesting. But what that idiot Bob Cranton in Personnel Security forgot when he pushed for my punishment is that in order to collect signals, you have to go out and find them. And that's how we're going to get out of here."

She stared at him. "What?"

"You heard me. Now, did you do your homework? Where should we go looking for some signals that would be of interest to an intelligence operation at both the RCMP and CBNRC?"

"You're serious."

"Aren't you? Yesterday you told me your sob story about not getting a fair chance since you got here. No one in your chain of command is going to send you anywhere, not if they've put you with me. All they think you're good enough for is a babysitting job. You want to get out in the field, you'll have to do it with me, and I can only go where the potential signals collection is useful. We also can't go anywhere our agencies are already active. But because we're Canadian, thus part of an outfit with a small footprint and not in too many places, we actually have a shitload of options. So what did you come up with?"

"You really think our superiors are going to let us go somewhere?"

"Yes, in my case to ease their conscience. Yours we might have to work on."

She smiled at him.

Frank held up a hand. "Don't thank me. I'm just working with what I've got."

"Okay," she said, "then so will I."

She moved to sit at her desk. "The way I understand it, we can't go to the Soviet Union or any of the countries behind the Iron Curtain. Allies of any sort are definitely out, which removes much of Europe. But Asia, Africa, and the Americas south of Mexico are wide open. That's a lot to choose from. But my top three are Panama, Chile, and Nicaragua. Panama's involved with a variety of revolutionaries, including the Castros. Pinochet's creating more problems than he's solving in Chile, and the Sandinistas in Nicaragua are getting very organized."

Frank contemplated her for a minute. "And where's the value to the RCMP?"

"All these countries deal with Castro. We are all over Cuba. We work with the Americans, because they're perpetually interested, but from what I've been able to pick up, we have great access in Cuba. That's why, of the three, Panama's my first choice. It's the easiest one to link to a Cuban operation in Rest of World."

"Any other reasons?"

"Yes. I can blend in easier in those countries on account of my coloring. And I speak Spanish."

Frank's head snapped up. "You do? Why?"

"I...I like languages. They're fun for me. After Russian, I wanted something simpler. Spanish has a similar structure to French, and half the world speaks it."

Frank was happy for the first time in days.

"It's not in the budget," Davis Johnson said.

Frank wished he'd brought his cigarettes. Veronica's boss was making him desperate for a hit of nicotine.

"What?" said Veronica.

"I don't have the money to send you to Central America. If you're interested in that region, you're going to see what you can find out from here."

"In Ottawa?" Veronica looked confused. Frank felt sorry for her, having this guy for a boss.

"We just want to go to the embassy," she continued, "to evaluate what kind of intelligence we could collect."

"We have someone doing that for us. That's the defense attaché's job."

"But we aren't getting much, not from Panama or Nicaragua. Isn't that the point of this new CBNRC liaison effort? For us to systematically evaluate where we could improve the signals intelligence we collect to support some of our operations?"

"I don't know what the executive wants out of having him here"—Davis pointed at Frank—"but my focus is on intelligence that's relevant to what might go down on Canadian soil."

Frank couldn't believe this guy had a job.

"But we know that Panama is becoming a meeting place for different revolutionary groups," Veronica continued, "and there is a lot of instability in the region. There could be recruiting happening here. And what if we could get something the Americans don't have? We could have leverage for one of our weak spots."

"The Americans are all over down there. You're not going to find anything they don't have. You're more useful here."

Frank figured he'd better say something before this guy gave him a stroke. "No, she isn't. Not if she's working with me. CBNRC has a foreign signals intelligence mandate. We can't easily collect anything on Canadian soil. It's a complete hassle if you don't know what you're looking for. The Americans have good coverage, but they aren't gods. They can't be everywhere; even they don't have the manpower for that. These countries have a different relationship with Canada, which means we have a different presence. We want to explore that."

Davis shrugged. "Like I said, I don't have the budget."

"What you don't have is the vision. What the fuck did you think she and I were going to do? Play Parcheesi in that dump you gave us for an office?"

"Now wait just a minute—"

"No thanks. You had your turn. We're supposed to be looking for new exploitation points that will produce intelligence that benefits both our organizations. We sure as shit can't do that in Ottawa." Frank stood up. "If you aren't interested in finding new sources, I'll damn well find someone who is."

Frank nodded at Veronica, who quickly followed him out of Davis's office.

"I can see where you get your reputation," she said.

"This organization is losing its way. There's too much pull by the criminal investigations. No one around here even knows what intelligence means anymore." Frank shook his head. "Not in the budget. What a joke."

"Where does that put us?" Veronica asked.

"Leave this with me."

"I want to know what you're going to do."

"I'm going to get you a new boss."

"What?" She looked startled.

"I report to the head of SIGINT. As my liaison partner, you should be reporting much higher than the supervisor of Rest of World."

"And you're just going to tell someone that?"

"Yeah, my boss. Either they get serious or they fire me."

"How do you know he's not going to fire you?"

"For the same reason they stuck me here. I was the director of access. I know too much. They want to keep me away from the action until my knowledge becomes old news. Until then, they want to keep me happy. Having me out of their hair and hanging out at the embassy in Panama or Nicaragua is a dream come true. I'm getting some sun and nowhere near anyone to find out the latest CBNRC plans. They want me to go, and I want to take you with me. So you need a new boss."

Veronica stared at him.

"The day they assigned you to me," Frank said, "will end up being either the best day or the worst day of your career."

"I think you might be right."

Frank hated flying. It never sat right with him, this metal tube jetting through the air and staying in the sky on account of the air pressure around the solid metal wings. He felt trapped and exposed at the same time. Thank God he could smoke. He figured a pack should get him to the landing in Managua.

Veronica was farther up in a seat by the window. He could tell that she was excited to be doing this—an actual mission off Canadian soil. It wasn't a true human intelligence operation, but she didn't seem that disappointed. Intelligence was intelligence, and she'd told him that supporting signals intelligence collection overseas was enough for a start.

He hadn't told her about Carlos yet. All he really had were a bunch of questions and an inkling that the Cuban was playing multiple sides of whatever he was involved in. He wasn't sure they'd be able to find Carlos, let alone get close to him. Frank had been in the intelligence business for more than twenty-five years, but he only knew signals. He didn't speak Spanish, he didn't have a network, he didn't know how to run an agent, and he didn't know how to move around Nicaragua looking for a renegade Cuban who had pissed him off six months ago.

But it also wasn't the first time he'd faced impossible problems. Collecting signals intelligence was often an exercise in trial and error, best guesses, and random luck, so Frank knew the one thing he had on his side was his ability to persevere.

They were showing up at the embassy on an information exchange mission. They had been set up as being from a new trade initiative. Their cover was more about obscuring their real role from the Nicaraguan government. They weren't on diplomatic passports. They weren't staying in a diplomatic residence. They were simply two civil servants looking to explore avenues for sharing commodities information. The setup was good. They had no official jobs and thus no official responsibilities. Frank could get a look around, see if there were some decent signals within range of the embassy. He could take a look at the current collection and offer ideas for improvement. He could find out who the main targets were of the defense attaché and offer some advice.

But more importantly, he and Veronica could explore the city and countryside. They would attend some meetings in different office buildings as seat fillers. They could go to tourist attractions and get lost along the way.

Frank wasn't leaving Nicaragua until he'd found out something about the Cuban. It was more than just morbid curiosity about the man who had both had an affair with and kidnapped Jillian—although that alone would make him interesting. The British connection was legitimate and didn't make any sense.

In West Berlin, Carlos had been working for the Red Army Faction. From what Frank got from Jillian and the few reports he could find, Carlos Honouras was heavily anti-American in all his activities. He had recruited for the Castros, had spent a lot of time with the Soviets, and was now helping out the Sandinistas. There was no obvious British diplomatic connection. Carlos appeared to be on the wrong side.

But after turning it around about a thousand times from a lack of having anything better to do for weeks, Frank realized that one thing he didn't know from the reports was how successful Carlos was. How many people had he actually recruited for the other side? Maybe every third one was a British plant. Except that nothing in Carlos's background suggested he'd be at all sympathetic to a Western democracy, let alone one whose colonial activities had included the violent suppression of people who would have rather governed themselves.

Whatever the British had set up with him, the Americans were definitely not in the know. Jillian's experience had made that clear. So had the reporting he'd been able to get from NSA. Carlos Honouras was an American target—someone they tried to keep an eye on and someone they definitely did not trust.

Surely the British knew all of this.

Frank had been in this business long enough to know that not everyone committed to a side. For some, playing the idealogues against each other was both fun and lucrative. It was possible the Cuban was working for the British. It was possible his loyalties were more with the Soviets. And it was equally probable that he cared about neither, keeping them both on the line and taking whatever money they were willing to pay.

Of course, that last option was the most dangerous. Having no friends made one completely expendable.

Frank had a legitimate reason to be curious about Carlos: the Cuban was the only adversary who knew Jillian. He hadn't figured out what she was really doing in West Berlin, but only because he hadn't looked. Carlos knew she was connected to the CIA, which made her situation precarious, depending on who he decided to tell. And despite his current disgust with the CBNRC for kicking him out the door to the RCMP, Frank didn't want anything to happen to that beautiful feed he'd set up in West Berlin. Of course, he didn't want anything to happen to Jillian either, but some risks came with the job. He couldn't stop her from getting into trouble if she was determined to find it.

Frank was also interested because if he could find out something unexpected, then he'd have leverage—to do what, he wasn't sure. But he had no intention of cruising to retirement in this ridiculous liaising role, buried in the basement of the RCMP.

CHAPTER FIVE

Damn it. Jillian was making him paranoid. Well, not her exactly, but all the shite she kept getting herself into.

Twenty-one years in the British Army, and up until six months ago, his life had been fairly sedate. He'd done the regular tours, the ones in Northern Ireland being no picnic, but still, it was just the usual guns and bombs. He was in the army. He expected those weapons. And in some sense he didn't mind them. They were overt.

But this covert spy stuff was really turning his head. It was so obscure James didn't know how any of them managed it without their heads exploding—having to be suspicious of everyone, parceling out information in little bunches so you got more than you gave, compartmentalizing who you were from who you were pretending to be. It was bloody exhausting.

He wanted no part of it. He didn't find it fascinating or intriguing, and he wasn't sure how much good any of it was anyway. He was sure some of the reports they produced were interesting. But earlier in the year, in June, he'd watched an intelligence officer named Claire get her head blown off by a Soviet who felt she was in the way. No reporting could be worth that.

He'd come to care about Jillian. Didn't want to see her get her head blown off either. James had spent his whole career trying to win hearts and minds. The best way to get people to give up their guns and their bombs, he felt, was to make them want what you wanted. And he didn't want to watch people die.

So now he was stuck with Jillian. Mostly it wasn't that bad; she was fun. She could be entertaining. She was different from many of the people he spent most of his time around. But he was worried that her suspicious outlook was rubbing off on him.

He couldn't blame her for being paranoid. One year ago he reckoned she would have been better categorized as a naive ingénue. Then she moved to West Berlin and started sleeping with a Cuban spy, which got the CIA interested, which in turn got her kidnapped by said Cuban spy, which was enough to make any woman suspicious of men for the rest of time.

James sat on the small balcony off the living room of his third-floor apartment. He didn't live on the base. This was unusual, but not unheard of. He didn't fight for much at work, but living in the city amongst regular people was important to him. He had sold the idea to his superiors as a necessity—how could he design psychological operations if he didn't understand the psychology of the people he was trying to reach? Three tours ago his commanding officer had agreed, and the precedent was set and that was that.

It was around seven o'clock, and the sun was starting to set. James sipped at his beer and watched the focus of his new and uncomfortable paranoia walk up the street.

She was a new tenant in the same building, having moved in about six weeks previously, in the middle of August. The first time he saw her, James thought she was just visiting someone. But then he saw her a few more times and realized she'd moved in. They'd progressed to saying hi when James saw her in the hallway. He couldn't tell what her mother tongue was, but he didn't think she was native German. That was no big deal, since West Berlin was a unique place that attracted a variety of people intrigued by what it would be like to live in a free city surrounded by walls. Six months ago he wouldn't have thought anything of her. She was attractive and held eye contact, and he would've asked her out. Now he wasn't so sure.

It was making him grumpy. He hadn't dated anyone in a while, and he was in the mood for that type of adventure.

She stopped a few steps away from the front door of the building and glanced up at his balcony. He continued to look at her. She offered a tentative wave.

Oh, sod it. What are the chances the Soviets or East Germans rented an apartment in my building and planted her here to seduce information out of me? Besides, he knew very little of value, and he also knew how to keep his mouth shut. *Maybe this is best seen as an opportunity. If she really is willing to shag for her country, who am I to stand in her way?*

James decided to finish his beer and go knock on her door. There was a much higher probability that she was just a normal person who was looking for the same thing he was.

Her door opened, and James got his first in-depth look at her face. She had tiny brown freckles scattered across the bridge of her nose that matched the dark freckles in her blue eyes. She gave him a hesitant smile, and he was sunk.

"Hiya," he said.

"Hi," she answered. He couldn't tell if she was just being polite, but at least she didn't shut the door in his face.

"I live upstairs. On the other side of the hall. You moved in not too long ago?"

She leaned against the doorframe. "Yes. I've seen you. You are not easy to miss."

His heart beat a little faster. "Would you like to get a drink, then?"

She let his question hang in the air for a moment, smiling at him. "You are Scottish?"

"For the last forty generations. Have you ever been out with a Scot before?"

"No," she said.

James could not stop staring at her. It was, he decided, a positive sign for the evening ahead. "We are, as a general rule, excellent drinking companions."

"Who can say no to that? Let me get my coat, and then we can go and I can find out."

He stood at her door, feeling inordinately pleased with himself. Successfully asking a woman out never stopped feeling fantastic.

She returned, pulling her arms into a dark blue jacket. "I am Jennifer, by the way. I think maybe it's a good idea to know my name?" She was turned away from him, shrugging into her jacket and adjusting the pink shirt she wore underneath, so she didn't see his expression falter for a moment.

James suddenly realized he had changed in the last year of hanging out with Jillian. He had always been sensitive to nuance. It's what made him excellent at his job. He studied people closely and built an understanding based on all the pieces he observed. It's how he knew what music to play, or what words to put on the leaflets, or how to describe the West without sounding patronizing.

But now those same nuances shook him. Instead of being curious, he was hesitant.

He knew right away that this woman's name was not Jennifer. She was at least thirty, and no one was naming their daughter Jennifer back in the 1940s. It was popular now. Also, he could tell that English was her second language. Or her third. It was perfect and slightly formal, not the way native speakers sounded. There would have been a few more "yeahs" or "sos" and conjunctions, "you're" instead of "you are." He had to give her and her teachers credit, though. She wasn't an amateur.

He wasn't quite sure what to do. He was attracted to her, and he was pretty sure he could sleep with her without compromising some nation's security. But he also knew that it was possible she wasn't genuinely interested in him. She wanted Jillian. And James had no intention of putting Jillian in any more danger.

"So," he asked, "where are you from, then?"

She paused for a moment. "Yugoslavia. Belgrade. For the last fifteen years. My mother is American."

"Ah, the grand national experiment. What brings you to West Berlin?"

She pulled her door closed and slid her key into the lock. "A change of scene. Work. And, I admit, curiosity. It's very different, this city."

They started to walk down the stairs, and James realized why spying was such a dangerous game. She could be from Yugoslavia. He doubted it. A Serbian named Jennifer? The thing was, though, the Eastern Bloc was really good at espionage—too good to have such a muddled backstory. If she had been trained by the Soviets, she would have spent the last five years watching *The Brady Bunch*. Hell, they would have called her Marcia. She would have been from Nebraska and sounded exactly like they do on TV. She would have been on the cheerleading squad and in West Berlin to pursue her dreams of being an artist, on a one-year leave from attending Bryn Mawr—the average, all-American, upper-class girl. She would have batted her eyelashes at him and put her hand on his arm and tried to be every man's fantasy. She would have been everything typical that one expects an American woman to be. At least, that's what he assumed a proper Russian honeypot would be like.

But this woman, she was none of those things. Jennifer. Yugoslavian. American mother. It was messy. Had they not had time to put together a proper backstory? Why the rush? Or, because he wasn't in the espionage business himself, did they think they could send a honeypot from the B list?

He knew that at least half of everything that had come out of her mouth was a lie. Yet he didn't know what to do.

Part of him wanted to turn around and bury himself in his living room with a few more beers, but he wondered if they would just keep coming at him. Jillian reckoned she'd been hit on three times in the last month. Maybe they *were* targeting him. Maybe they would just keep sending women his way until one clicked. If he and Jillian rejected everyone, surely they—whoever they were—would get frustrated or impatient and send someone far less lovely.

If he were a spy, which he wasn't, he supposed that knowing she wasn't who she said she was gave him the upper hand. He could play along. Keep it going. Give her nothing. Hope everyone would eventually lose interest.

And she was very attractive. It certainly wouldn't be a hardship to look at her for a while.

So James fell comfortably into step beside her, directing them to a quiet bar that poured generous pints. He would see where the night led and decide tomorrow if there was a better decision to be made.

CHAPTER SIX

"Is this what you really do when you're collecting intelligence?" Veronica asked.

Frank stood in the middle of the roof and systematically moved his dish degree by degree. He made notes after each one, but he was almost through the full 360.

"Yes. It's signals intelligence. You have to find a signal. The only way to do that is to see which ones are hitting a position where you could reasonably set up a collection point."

"So I guess it's clearer on the roof."

"Yes. Audio signals, whether from radio or basic voice, are best with no interference. It's a little-known fact, but obvious when you think about it, that each country tries to choose as its embassy location a place with the clearest signals access."

"To collect intelligence."

"Yes," Frank said. "One of the primary functions of embassies, actually. They're expensive and complicated, and yes, occasionally the diplomats do something useful and we get a good price for lemons or something. But one of the main reasons each sovereign nation goes to the trouble of setting up an entire protected office and residences in every other sovereign nation is to collect intelligence to, among other things, get a better deal for those lemons."

Veronica sat on a ledge that had been built beside a vent. "I feel like I should have known that."

"Not necessarily," said Frank. "Although I think it's damn obvious, it's pretty heavily classified stuff. Joe Q. Public is meant to believe that we all hang out with each other because we're trying to make the world a better place."

"Aren't we?"

"I am. That's why I try to collect SIGINT. But there's a reason why embassies are exempt from national laws. It's not so the diplomats can smuggle home the local specialties. It's because we're all spying on each other."

"So what are the signals like up here?"

Frank smiled. "Not bad. Whoever set up what they've got running downstairs wasn't from CBNRC. They're missing at least two interesting feeds. And look at this: see those wires running up there? Those are phone lines that happen to go to the Nicaraguan Ministry of Agriculture, and I don't think they've been intercepting anything from there. I'm sure I can set up a tap on those."

Veronica stood and walked around the roof. After a couple rounds, during which Frank managed to check out another thirty-five degrees' worth of signals, she came up to stand beside him. After a few more minutes during which she said nothing but continued to stand there watching him, he turned to her.

"What?"

"I'm sorry," she said.

"Don't apologize. I hate that. Spit it out."

Veronica was silent for a moment. "These are normal for you? The signals, I mean?"

"Ah. You thought it was all going to be bugs planted in office telephones."

Veronica smiled. "I never thought much about it, but yeah, that's a little closer to what I had in mind."

"I can set one of those up if we ever need to. But that's not true signals intelligence. We like to collect a whole bunch of intercept and then do our targeting. Radio. Radar. Commercial phone lines. Satellites now. We have a small team at CBNRC looking at fax. It's you guys who bug your targets."

"It seems a little tedious. I mean, I get why, but…"

"The setup is tedious. So is going through all the intercept. It's a giant haystack. But the way the targeting works, you can look for more than one needle at a time. So it's a tradeoff."

"You find a couple signals up here, and then you set up a way to intercept them. And then you make a copy of everything you capture. And then you hope there's something interesting in it."

"That about sums it up," Frank said. "Do you want some advice?"

"Sure."

"SIGINT or HUMINT, both require patience. Yes, checking the signal every degree over an entire circle is boring. So is approaching fifty people who work at the Nicaraguan Ministry of Defense in an attempt to find one who will run agent for you. This business is nothing like what you see in most books about spying. It's slow and mostly painful, but once in a while something clicks. When it does, you exploit it for everything you've got."

"Thank you, Frank."

"Jesus. It must've been bad for you at headquarters if you think that's worth thanking me for."

"There hasn't been anyone else who's told me anything I can trust."

Frank made some notes on the paper he kept stashed in his pocket. "Why do you stay there? There has to be something better for you somewhere else."

Veronica didn't say anything for a long moment. "I just don't think someone's dreams should be limited by their biology. Boys watch James Bond movies and they get excited, they want to be him. But you know what? Girls do too. They don't want to be the helpful Moneypenny or the vulnerable Russian who ends up in bed with him. They want to have agency, take the risks and make the difference. I know this job is nothing like what James Bond does in the movies, but I don't understand why I should give up on what I want because the world decided it's only suited for someone with a penis. I hope that doesn't make you uncomfortable."

The sun shimmered between them, the heat reflecting off the rooftop. Frank was beginning to sweat, but it didn't bother him. "This is the most fun I've had in a long time," he said. "Being the director of access, I haven't been out trying to find a source in ages. It's important, I think, to remind yourself every once in a while about what you're actually doing. It's easy to let the budget reports and the corporate policies and the politics obscure it all. So yeah, I get that it doesn't matter what equipment you have below the belt. Interesting is interesting."

"There was one other thing I heard about you," Veronica said after a few moments. "After you showed up at the RCMP and I was told I was supposed to work with you—like I told you, no one had much good to say except Marlene in records. I got to know her when I was doing the media monitoring. She was one of the only people who had anything to say to me, nice or otherwise. But anyway, she said that you deployed a woman on a SIGINT assignment. She didn't know much about it, but Marlene said it was a first."

"She was the best person for the job."

"Okay."

Frank was suddenly uncomfortable. He had no idea that Jillian's deployment had been talked about. He knew it had been epic for the three layers of executives and political officials he'd had to convince. But he'd had no idea it might have meant more than that.

He finished on degree 360. There were some good signals up here, and that telephone line was a bonus. It wouldn't be hard to make himself useful while he took a more comprehensive look around.

"I didn't think about Jillian being a woman when I picked her for the assignment," he said as he began to pack up his equipment. "Other people did, and it pissed me off. Not on behalf of all women, so don't put me on a pedestal. But I want to win, and to me she was the best person to put us in a successful position. She spoke the language well enough, she's a damn good engineer, and the setup she's monitoring is pretty damn unique. I don't think anything should come before the mission. Not politics, not agendas, not international relations—and certainly not someone's physical attributes. People who let their biases influence those kinds of decisions, they're just limiting the potential for success."

He stopped and looked at Veronica. "I'm not blind. I can see that ninety-five percent of our agencies are men. I don't think that's right; it makes us vulnerable. There are a lot of places where we want to get intelligence where no one likes or trusts Western men. Not putting women in the field just means we're missing a lot of opportunities."

Veronica picked up one of the bags of equipment. "You aren't an asshole, you know."

"Yeah, I am. Most people annoy the shit out of me."

"But only because they don't put the mission first."

Frank smiled. "You learn fast."

"Damn right I do." They started to walk toward the door that would take them back into the embassy. "So why did you pick me? I've got no experience. If you put the mission first, then how come I'm here?"

Frank thought for a moment. There was, he supposed, nothing wrong with telling her some of the truth. "Because you have something to prove, you don't trust anyone in your own agency, and you speak Spanish. I'm not just here for rooftop signals. There's a Cuban somewhere in the city that I'm interested in."

Veronica started. "So we're not in Nicaragua just because I suggested it?"

Frank held the door open for her. "No. I was always going to come here. You made it easier on many fronts."

Veronica was silent for a few steps. "What if I had pushed for the Arctic or suggested Indonesia?"

Frank snorted as he began to go down the stairs. "We were never going to go to the Arctic. That's a whole different kind of mission. As for the rest of it, I don't know. I needed someone who could help me here. The plan only really formed after I met you. Like I said before, I'm good at working with what I've got."

"And if I didn't want to come?"

He shrugged. "I would've explored my options."

Veronica appeared to mull all this over. Frank had thought about it more than once in the last few days. The only thing that would have made her a better partner for all this would have been if she'd already had contacts here.

He knew that Bob Cranton in Personnel Security had done what he could to orchestrate Frank's situation in the RCMP. In Bob's view, sticking him with a woman who had no field experience and no friends was a punishment. Frank had always thought Bob was an idiot, but this was the first time he'd been thankful for it. Bob's estimation of the worst partner was actually the dead opposite. Frank meant what he'd said to her: the fact that she had no field experience just made her determined to prove herself. And the fact that no one was looking out for her made it easy for her to shift her loyalties to Frank. The Spanish was just a random stroke of luck.

They were almost back at the closet where they would lock up the equipment. The hallways were empty, given that it was getting late in the evening on a Saturday.

"Are you going to tell me about this Cuban?" Veronica asked.

"I need a shower first. Then a beer. Then we can have a chat."

"Should I be nervous?"

"No. You're trained as an IO, and we've got a legitimate target. What we find out, it could make both our careers."

"Or it could get us both fired."

Frank shrugged as he put the equipment away. "Anything's possible, but I doubt it. We have a broad mandate: find out something that's interesting to both agencies. And this Cuban has the potential to be very interesting."

Despite not having traditional field experience, Frank was comfortable navigating in foreign territory. At the moment, he was looking for the right place to sit and have a beer and tell Veronica some of what he wanted her to do here.

He was looking for somewhere they could sit outdoors with nothing blocking their sightlines. He was also looking for somewhere no one would care who they were. Usually that meant nice, noisy family restaurants. Parents with young kids were always too busy and too tired to pay attention to what other people were saying. Plus, the screaming kids were good at obscuring conversation.

They were close to the embassy on the west side of Managua. Frank knew they'd had a bad earthquake here three years ago, and a lot of the city was still a mess, full of empty buildings, gutted and broken. There was no real downtown anymore, and most of what was being rebuilt was being done away from the center. The odd old building remained standing, like the Teatro Nacional, but it was surrounded by a wasteland of rubble. The disbursement of the rebuilding meant a lot of driving, but that worked for him, as it was a great excuse to get the lay of the land.

Life went on, he supposed. People still needed to eat. And get out. And live.

It felt really different, being here. He hadn't been out in the field in ages, but it was more than that. He wasn't here with any expectations. There was no interception setup to protect. There was no massive budget expense to justify. There was almost nothing to prove. Success hadn't exactly been defined, but neither had failure. If he and Veronica returned to Ottawa next month with nothing to show for their time here, no one would care. There would just be a shrug of the shoulders. No viable sources. Move on. It happened in SIGINT all the time. Sure, there were signals everywhere, but not all of them could be intercepted clandestinely. They always explored more possibilities than they could exploit.

In the two months since he'd stopped being the director of access for the CBNRC, Frank could feel himself shifting his perspective. Looking back, he wondered if he'd been holding on a little too tightly. He'd loved his job, but now he could see that every day had been such a battle. Keep the executives happy. Keep finding new sources. Troubleshoot all the technology issues. Follow all the corporate directives and policies and remember to tick all the boxes and fill out all the forms.

Here in Nicaragua he was under far less pressure. His boss would be happy if he stayed here awhile. The embassy was overjoyed that he had improved one of their current feeds. They'd be ecstatic if he did anything more. There was a weekly report to send home, and if all it contained was "still evaluating the situation," no one would be upset.

He missed his wife a little, but it was still her tennis season. After twenty-three years of marriage, they could easily enjoy a little time apart. It always made him appreciate how amazing Livia was when he was away from her.

Frank supposed that the stress of the last few years had taken its toll on his personal life as well. Working in this business was hard on relationships to begin with. That's why there were so many affairs within the CBNRC. Not only was the job intense, but if your spouse didn't have the same clearance, you couldn't talk about it at home. So a bad day often drove you to someone you could share it all with, and sometimes those connections turned into something more.

Livia was a painter. She'd managed to turn it into a decent income after raising their three children, but she'd never worked for the CBNRC. The only thing he'd ever told her was that he couldn't talk about his job. It was sensitive. Lives could be lost. So she'd never asked, but she was there for him always. He wouldn't trade how he felt around her, even after all this time, for someone who could share the gory details of a blown access operation. It wasn't those details that were interesting anyway. She didn't need clearance to be able to understand the frustration of pointless meetings or asinine colleagues.

Frank hoped that Nicaragua would be good for him. That he would go home a better husband and better person to be around. God knew Livia deserved that.

They turned a corner, and Frank saw exactly the kind of place he'd been looking for: a small, shack-style restaurant with a large outdoor dining area. The place was busy, there were lots of kids running around, and the beer looked cold. Perfect.

He steered Veronica toward the entrance, and then he followed as she got them a table.

"Do you want me to tell you what's on the menu?" she asked after they'd sat down.

"I know how to say cerveza," Frank replied.

Veronica smiled. "I know. I saw the grocery clerk teach you on the first day we got here."

"What was that thing with the potatoes I had the other night? At the place by the apartment?"

They were staying in one-bedroom apartments on the same floor of a three-story building a short walk from the embassy. They were like large hotel rooms, and the whole place was full of Canadians or Australians who were in Managua on diplomatic-related business. He figured that the embassy regularly swept for bugs but that the Nicaraguan cleaning staff put them back in with the same frequency. So he and Veronica didn't talk much when they were there.

"Nacatamales," said Veronica.

Frank looked at the list of dishes. "There it is. There are a lot of other words in the description."

"You can add different ingredients. Like vegetables."

"I hear the judgment in your voice."

Veronica shook her head slightly. "I don't know what you're talking about. It's just that you can ask for it to include vegetables, not just potatoes and meat."

Frank snorted. She sounded just like his wife.

"Are you ready to order?" he asked.

"Yes."

"Fine, then." Frank waved the waiter over. After ordering his cerveza and nacatamales, he settled back in his seat and lit a cigarette.

"Do you want to hear the story about this Cuban?"

"Absolutely," Veronica said.

"It's an edited version because some of it has to do with an ongoing SIGINT operation, but that part isn't particularly relevant to what we're doing here." Frank told her the parts of the story he thought she needed to know. He mentioned that Carlos had an affair with a deployed SIGINT officer, but he didn't mention where.

"I needed to know about him because he might have been targeting my officer," he continued. "It turned out he wasn't. It was just random bad luck. But then, after he left the scene and I stopped thinking about him, an analyst brought me a publicity newsletter. And there was the Cuban, all chummy with some British diplomats."

He stubbed out his cigarette and took a large swallow of the beer that had just arrived. He waited a moment for the waiter to engage with another table before he continued. "So, as I'm sure you can appreciate, I got curious. He's Cuban, and American reporting told me he'd spent some time recruiting for the Soviets. What's he doing in London, close enough to whatever diplomat to get into a photo op?"

"And now he's here?"

"So says reporting."

Veronica looked at him, clearly thinking it all over. "What do you hope to get out of it? What's the outcome here? We find him, and then what? We prove he's working with the British? Or a double agent? If you know that he sometimes works with the Soviets, then presumably MI6 does as well. They just haven't told their home office?"

"I've got no idea. It could be nothing. It could be something that everyone knows about but us. I do know that if he is working with the Brits, the Americans have no clue. He's on their enemy list on account of some stuff that went down in this very town. I couldn't get access to details, but I did have a friend confirm that Carlos is not a friend of the USA."

"So you think the British are double-crossing the Americans?"

Frank shook his head. "No. I don't think that the British, as a country, are double-crossing the Americans. But I do wonder if one British diplomat is an agent using Carlos to pass info to the Soviets. Whether it's state secrets or misinformation, I have no idea. But, you know, since they're allies, we'd be remiss not to find out."

Veronica thought for a moment. "Who were the diplomats in the picture?"

Frank started. He'd been so focused on Carlos it never occurred to him to identify the other people. "I don't know."

"I think it might be useful to find that out."

"Damn right. I completely missed that myself."

Veronica smiled. "Different types of intelligence."

"So they did teach you something at IO school."

"Do you have a plan for how to find Carlos? I don't think we're just going to run into him."

"Not a plan exactly. Just a mandate to collect signals and see where they lead us."

Veronica looked skeptical. "How long were you thinking of staying in Nicaragua?"

Frank shrugged. "Now that you know what we're looking for, you can help me out."

"Okay, then. How about we talk to our defense attachés a little more. We've been focused on the signals so far, but we have a dual mandate. Let's ask them what they're focused on and what they would like more of when it comes to contacts in the city. My guess is that it might not be hard to find Carlos. The Americans will certainly know where he is; we just need to get them to tell us."

"That," said Frank, eyeing the waiter coming with their plates, "sounds like a great idea."

CHAPTER SEVEN

Jillian sat back on her heels as she began to sort through the contents of another box. Helping Madeline was proving to be interesting, unsettling work. Each box contained hundreds of pieces of paper. Some were just slips with a hastily scrawled sentence. Others were full pages describing the details of an entire conversation. Most of the time it felt like reading a play or notes for a novel. Then there would be a reference to a battle or a concentration camp that Jillian would recognize, and she would be filled with a profound sadness as she was reminded she was reading the description of lives. Lives that were tragic and messy and painful.

As she placed each piece of paper into a folder, all labeled neatly based on the catalog system she had devised for Madeline, she felt that seeing these notes of individual conversations brought home the reality of the war in a way that nothing else ever had. It wasn't like reading a history book or some arm's-length description of events. These were people's conversations had in bed during a brief respite from the turbulence surrounding them. A lot of these people were torn up, confused, scared, and desperate. Some were believers who were looking forward to a future they thought was going to be brighter, and some were looking for a way out of the chaos.

Because the cabaret was patronized by Nazis and their supporters throughout the war, all of the spying by the women was aimed at learning the sympathies of the patrons. Thus Jillian knew that not all of the notes could be taken at face value. Madeline's mother had kept a record of what was reported, so it would stand to reason that some of the content was false. Depending on the sympathies of the women themselves, they might easily report false information, either to protect someone who was kind or to cast suspicion on someone who was cruel.

It would have been complicated. The cabaret employed between ten and twenty women over the course of the war. They were very likely not a homogenous group themselves in the eyes of the Nazis. Madeline said her mother hid three Jewish women, but she could only do so by procuring false papers and not confiding in anyone. Her mother knew that some of the women enjoyed their roles as informers for the Nazis and wouldn't hesitate to turn in the three Jewish women. Other women were more uncomfortable with the role and did their best to protect the men who didn't wholeheartedly support the cause. Jillian couldn't even imagine the tension of living in an environment where friends could turn to enemies quickly.

She was caught up in reading when she heard a clearing of a throat. She had left the garage door open halfway to let in some fresh air. The October day was warm and sunny, a day for short sleeves and sitting on patios. She planned to do that later, but for now the light from the door cut the gloom of the storage space. She looked up, seeing the outline of a man's legs standing at the threshold. The boxes of notes were being stored in an unused storage garage belonging to a friend of Madeline's. Jillian didn't know the friend, or much else about the property. It was on a side street off Lindower Strasse in the Wedding area of Berlin, close to where Madeline lived. The entrance itself was isolated from people passing by, but Jillian could still hear traffic and other city sounds.

Jillian stood, placing the paper in the box, and crossed to the half-raised door. She ducked under and emerged in the brightness.

"Hallo," she said.

"Hallo," the man replied. He was an older gentleman, with pure white hair and impeccably dressed in a charcoal suit and blue paisley tie.

"Can I help you?" Jillian asked in German.

"Oh, I am just stopping to say hello," he said. He pointed to a four-story apartment building across the street. "I live there," he said. "I see you come often into the garage, and I am an old man with not much to do, and I am curious. That is all."

She didn't know what to say. Madeline was due to arrive in half an hour with lunch, and Jillian wished the man had waited until then to introduce himself.

She gestured to the door. "Just a lot of papers. I'm helping a friend organize her life."

He tilted his head and looked at her. "You are not German. American?"

Jillian smiled. "Canadian. I'm a PhD student at the West German Science Institute."

The man looked at the garage. "Your friend is a student too?"

"No. She's a native Berliner, and a lot older than I am. If we were cataloging my memories, there wouldn't be nearly as many."

"So there is much to go through? These memories?"

"Yeah." Jillian nodded. "A lot of it is from the war. I don't think she's been ready to go through it before now."

"I see," said the man. "Like many Germans. Memories from the war have been shoved away, out of sight." He seemed lost in thought for a moment, then held out his hand. "Hans Gohl. Perhaps I might meet your friend when she comes."

Jillian took his hand. It was firm but papery. She figured he had probably been alive during World War I as well. "Sure. Why don't you come back in an hour or so? Madeline should be here by then."

"Yes, thank you. I will go for my coffee and then return," he said, tipping his head to her before heading in the direction of the bakery down the street.

Jillian watched him walk away. He was probably lonely. She'd noticed he wasn't wearing a wedding ring. It couldn't be easy, living a life where the biggest excitement was an open garage door.

Madeline arrived on time carrying pastries and coffee. "I did not know which flavor you liked, so I bought two of each," she said, setting down the box of food.

Jillian dove in, selecting what looked like raspberry strudel. This was Madeline's idea of lunch. Jillian was too hungry to care that she'd probably go into sugar shock by three p.m.

She had half of the strudel in her mouth before Madeline had unwound her scarf.

"Oh, Jillian, you are making such good progress. You have already sorted so many boxes."

"I'm happy you think so," Jillian said, swallowing pastry. "I keep getting caught up in what I'm reading. I think it's a good idea that we're sorting them by dancer first. I think the men would often choose the same woman if they came back. So later, when we read through everything, we'll probably be able to put together some narratives. Maybe even relate them to some historical events."

Madeline slowly sipped her coffee. "It is so wonderful that you are helping. I'm sorry if it does not seem like I'm doing a lot. Some of this, it is very hard to read. It brings so many memories rushing to the surface. I didn't realize how much I have saved."

"I can stop if you just want to close the door and leave it all buried. I'm sure it was a scary time."

Madeline sat for a moment, silently contemplating the boxes. "No. It does no good to run from the past. And this, these memories, they are a part of history too, I think. Maybe no one will ever be interested, but after we are done cataloging and making notes, as I said, I think I will put it all together in a book."

"I was actually wondering if you think a museum might be interested. Or the history department of a university," Jillian said. "This kind of source material is so amazing for researchers."

"Maybe," Madeline said. "The idea of a book was hard enough. I suppose it depends on what we find. I want to be careful too; these are people's lives. And, you know, many of them are still alive."

Jillian thought about that. "Have you ever told anyone what you have here?"

"Yes. But only in passing, and only to friends. It's not something I keep secret, but I also don't remember it much. When my mother died, I was more focused on missing her."

"Madeline," Jillian said, "are you sure you shouldn't be working with a museum or some other official organization as, well, protection? What I mean is that, could there be any stories in here that some people might be upset about if they came out?"

"Oh no, I don't think so. We did not entertain the leaders. There were other, better places for those interactions. I think what you will find in all these records is a microcosm of everything that is already known about the war—how some people were committed, some confused, and most scared. But it is interesting that you might think there could be something dangerous."

Jillian shrugged. "Honestly, I hadn't thought about it until you mentioned that a lot of the men would still be alive. But I read the papers. I know there are a lot of people who are…uncomfortable about the ex-Nazis who have ended up in positions of power in West Germany."

Madeline regarded her. "Yes, I suppose you may be right. For me, the war is such a long time ago I can barely believe it was part of my life. Berlin in 1945, '46, seems like something from a movie. But yes, it is true there may be some who could easily be hurt now by what happened then."

Jillian stood up. "I haven't seen anything yet that I would classify as…incendiary. But you might want to reach out to someone you can trust who would help you make all this public without it hurting you."

Madeline was quiet as she read through some of the papers that Jillian had already sorted. After a while she came over beside the box where Jillian was working. "I have been meaning to do this for so long. The days pass, and then the years, and I never seem to get to it. But I think having it done might give me some peace."

Jillian shivered a little. "It's not over, is it? In so many ways, the war really isn't over."

"Not for many people. That is why I've always confronted it—and why I should have sorted through all this a long time ago. People think it ends with the ceasefires and the peace treaties. But the effects go on and become part of new events, and so over time they contribute to the shaping of our world. As for the people who lived through it directly on the front lines, or in the bombed cities, or in the camps, I imagine that the war only really ends when life does." Madeline stood up and crossed the space to open a new box. "This is why war should be avoided at all costs, because the effects ripple outward."

Jillian nodded and picked up some more papers. "Oh, I meant to tell you—this older guy stopped by earlier. Apparently he lives in the building across the street. He is clearly retired and was curious about what we're doing here. I didn't tell him much because I wasn't sure how much you wanted to broadcast this." Jillian didn't add that she was used to keeping secrets and tended to default to protecting the confidentiality of everything. "Anyway, I told him you were in charge so he should come back when you were here."

Madeline smiled. "I'm not surprised we are attracting attention from the neighbors. This is a quiet area, and I've been renting this space for twenty years. It stays the same while the rest of the neighborhood changes around it. Seeing the door open must be big news. It's nice we've started while the weather is still warm. Soon we will have to keep it closed all the time, and then no one will have a show."

That was fine with Jillian. She liked keeping her exposure minimal.

CHAPTER EIGHT

Frank sat under the awning nursing his second beer. At home, he was a whisky man. But he was particular about his whisky, and it wasn't any good here. Lucky that he wasn't so particular about his beer. As long as it was cold and not too dark, it was fine.

He hoped Veronica was getting on well, meaning that he hoped she was getting some useful information. He knew that her confidence was shaky, but he also knew that the only way to build it was to jump right into the fire. She'd either figure out how to be a great IO, or she'd decide that she'd be better off switching professions.

He'd decided not to get in her way. As much as he knew about human intelligence work, he only ever bothered to pay attention to how it related to SIGINT. He figured she had the training, so they'd see if she could use it.

Frank had spent the last week improving the collection in the embassy. It hadn't been hard. A couple feeds came in better on a different frequency, and tapping the line for the Ministry of Agriculture had made the trade people happy with the inside scoop on oranges or something. It had created a few quick wins that had earned him the trust of the people in the building.

Since he had way more experience than a first-year tech, this was just the beginning. Cleaning up the reception on what they already received was basic stuff. Frank thought there was an opportunity to do some proper intercepting. There were a few embassies close by who weren't on the friendly list. And the Nicaraguan government, corrupt as it was, surely was collecting something that would be interesting to know. Frank had been doing signals a long time. Driving around the city, it wasn't that hard to spot the places that were in the same business he was.

He looked around. It was the end of the workday, and the streets were busy. He liked it here. He liked the pace, and he liked the people. He couldn't imagine what it was like to live in a country in such turmoil. You go out and get groceries, and celebrate birthdays, and raise your kids, but in the background, your country is in turmoil. It was something he'd never experienced. In Canada, the biggest fight was about how to develop the public healthcare system. No one was questioning democracy itself.

But here was the example that no matter what was going on with governments and ideologies, day-to-day people just get on with living their lives. The two old men drinking beside him, Frank imagined they'd be doing the same regardless of who was in charge of the country.

The sun dropped lower as he worked on his beer, but the night stayed warm. He saw Veronica coming down the other side of the street, and he waved at her. She looked a little flushed and a lot excited as she dropped into the seat across from him.

"So, did you get an address for me?" he asked.

She looked hesitant for a second. "No. Of course not. I doubt Carlos has an address."

"Jesus, would you relax a little? I told you, there is no better virtue in this business than patience. I was just kidding."

"Oh," she said, then a smile infiltrated her face. "But I…I think I'm making progress. I've made contact with a woman who is willing to talk to me a little. Not much, but a little. She's a friend of the man Phillip introduced me to." Phillip was the junior defense attaché at the Canadian embassy who had introduced Veronica to a couple of his contacts in Managua to get her started. "I don't figure she knows Carlos—that would be exceptional—but I thought we just need to start making contact with people who aren't in the Somoza government. People are cautious here. It makes me think there's a lot happening beneath the surface."

"So what's your angle? These people aren't going to bring a foreigner on the inside. That'll take years."

"I know," Veronica said. "I'm not here for political reasons. I'm a woman looking for a man I knew intimately in Moscow when I was stationed there."

Frank looked at her. "Not bad. But they know you're associated with the Canadian embassy."

"Exactly. Which is why the 'stationed in Moscow' story is perfect. I speak Russian. No one here is going to know about the politics of who Canada stations in the Soviet Union."

"And why would they think you'd be at all sympathetic to an antigovernment cause?"

Veronica paused for a moment. "Because I am. Somoza is a tyrant."

"Yes, but the official position—"

"Frank, I'm not an idiot. But Canada is a democracy that supports global freedom. It's why we climbed up Vimy Ridge and why we landed at Dieppe and Juno Beach. We can't be choosy about where we support democracy—not here, and not at home."

Frank regarded her for a long moment. "It makes it harder, you know, when you have your own sympathies."

"The mission comes first. If you don't trust me about that, then we should go back to Ottawa right now. I don't agree with what the Soviets are doing behind the Iron Curtain either, but the world isn't black and white."

"You think I don't know that?"

"The way I see it, learning more about Carlos is good for Canada and bad for the Soviets. That's good enough for me. But Canada can do better than just beating the Soviets. That's what I care about. Being slightly better than the worst is no big accomplishment."

"You can't actively help any antigovernment groups, especially anyone associated with the Sandinistas. That will piss off the Americans, which is one thing guaranteed to smother your career."

"I won't. Not deliberately. But we'll see what risks I might have to take."

Frank arrived at the embassy early, partly by force of habit and partly because he hated getting to work sweaty, and the days in Managua warmed up fast. He found it amusing that October was usually one of the cooler months. He'd probably melt in May.

He made himself a coffee on the way to his desk, which was really a folding table shoved up against a wall in a corner no one used. He was in the same room as the two defense attachés, and their desks weren't much better. Technically he shared his desk with Veronica, but she wasn't coming in much these days.

He set his coffee down and picked up the note that had been left for him. The amplifier he'd requested had been delivered and taken to the basement. That was good. He was going to add it to the setup on the roof.

Frank looked up as Mark Huesman, the senior defense attaché, walked in.

"Morning, Frank."

Frank lit a cigarette to go with his coffee.

"Jeannine Davis was looking for you yesterday," Mark continued. "Apparently, the stuff we're picking up from the Ministry of Agriculture is getting the cultural attachés excited. The minister is planning some big shindig, and now we've got an in."

"That's exactly why I came down here," Frank said. "To get us party invitations."

"Parties are great," Mark said. "Free food and booze, and the lips get looser as the night goes on. You've been in signals too long if you don't get excited by a good government party."

"So you go to them?"

"As many as I can. You never know when you're going to pick up something interesting for defense intelligence. There's a lot of antigovernment activity here. Since the earthquake, people are enraged at how all the relief funds have been siphoned off into Somoza's wallet. The suspension of constitutional rights with no end in sight just adds fuel to the fire. The Sandinistas seem to be building support, so Somoza's projecting as much as he can that it's all business as usual."

"Except it's not?" Frank said.

"Last month three bodies were found in a field outside of the city. Best guess is that they were pushed from a helicopter. The more the government cracks down, the more the pressure builds. People are risking their lives every day to challenge the government. And from what I gather, the Sandinistas, a lot of them, they aren't amateurs. They've got support from Cuba, Panama, and the Soviets. Somoza chases them out, and they just go to Mexico or Costa Rica and buy guns and write press releases. They've got sympathizers everywhere."

"Are you one of them?"

Mark looked at Frank for a long moment. "What are you asking me, Frank?"

Frank took a long haul on his cigarette. "Not officially, but what's your take? Like, if shit goes down, who do we want to win?"

Mark nodded. "It's a mess. The Americans seem to prefer the devil that you know instead of the devil you don't. They seem to think Somoza's better for their national interest, which makes him better for ours. But at some point, do you really need the friendship of a third-rate dictator? Plus, Nicaragua isn't exactly rolling in it. But the Sandinistas, they'd kick us all out—or at least that's what everyone thinks, on account of their friendship with Castro."

Interesting, Frank thought. It was pretty much the same feeling Veronica had. "I'm beginning to think the biggest problem the Soviets created was a world with two teams. That means we get stuck with all the extreme right-wing assholes just to prove a point. Democracy versus fascism was so much easier."

"Yeah. Hitler's one positive quality: he made moral ambiguity impossible."

"Except for the Swiss."

Mark laughed. "The Swiss. I love how they throw up their hands and say they were neutral. I bet you half of what the Nazis stole is sitting in Swiss bank vaults."

Frank couldn't agree more. One of the only countries in the world he had no patience for was Switzerland. You can't launder money for war criminals and call yourself neutral.

"Thanks for letting Veronica tag along with Phillip," Frank said. "It's helping us evaluate if there are any possible exploitation points."

Mark shrugged. "No problem. I think Phillip's enjoying it. He's not the newbie anymore."

Frank hadn't told Mark about Carlos, nor did he ever intend to if he could help it. As far as Mark knew, Veronica was looking for contacts who knew something about what signals the Nicaraguan government was already collecting. This was partly true, because that was their official raison d'être. Frank loved intercepting the interceptors, West Berlin being one of his biggest successes on that front. The Carlos thing was a side mission. He could explain it if he needed to, but he didn't want to—at least, not yet. He didn't want to set any expectations, nor did he want to be told to stand down. So that situation was between him and Veronica for the time being.

"Frank?"

Frank leaned into the receiver. "Veronica?" She sounded breathless.

"Frank, something's happened. I...I don't know what to do."

"Are you okay?"

"Yes, it's just...Can you meet me for a drink?"

"On my way. I'm going to walk through the park with that fountain we found the other night. Can you meet me there?"

"Yes."

"Okay." Frank hung up. He wasn't worried yet. She hadn't sounded panicked or distressed, just confused. He left the office quickly.

He'd been sitting by the fountain for fifteen minutes when she arrived.

"So?" he asked.

"I met with Estephania this morning. You know, that woman I told you about, the poet who's friends with this other woman who's from this wealthy family and writes political commentary? Anyway. It doesn't matter. I was walking home, meeting over, when this man started walking beside me. It threw me off, but before I could say anything, he started talking.

"Frank, he was American. And he wanted to know why I was looking for Carlos. I told him the Moscow story, and he said, 'Bullshit.' I elaborated with a bit of that backstory you gave me, about how I knew him as this Italian artist named Marco, and Frank, I swear to God, this guy turned pale. Paler than he already was.

"He grabbed my arm and stopped us both and demanded how I knew about Marco. I stuck to my story, but I could tell he wasn't buying it. 'Do us both a favor,' he said. 'Stay the fuck away from Carlos. If I see you again, I'll tell him who you are, and trust me, you won't want to be in Nicaragua if he finds that out.' I didn't know what to say. How does he know who I am? Or how did he know I was lying?"

Frank was as surprised as she was. "The Americans will mostly definitely know who you are. Since you've been hanging around Phillip, it wouldn't be hard for any of our allies to figure it out. But even if you were getting in some IO's way, it would more likely be settled by a call to the embassy, reassert the territorial lines or figure out how to work together. Let me think about this."

Frank was glad he'd brought his cigarettes. He lit one and stared out thoughtfully, going over what Veronica had told him. Who the hell would be threatening her like that? Finally, he stubbed out his smoke on the concrete wall that surrounded the fountain.

"Veronica, what did this guy look like?"

"Tall, but not too tall. Five-eleven, maybe six feet. Dark hair. Pale. The shadows under his eyes were so prominent he looked like he'd been punched."

"And it was when you mentioned Marco the Italian artist that he really reacted?"

"Yes. Do you know who he is?"

"I have an idea."

Veronica waited a few moments. "Are you going to tell me?"

"Not yet. Let's go back to the embassy. I have to make a call. But if I'm right, it's someone I've actually been dying to meet."

"Are you going to let me in on this?"

"Most definitely. I'll need you to stop me from punching his fucking face in, but only because he's the one other person in this country who's looking for Carlos. And he's going to be much better at finding him than we are."

CHAPTER NINE

James sat on his balcony enjoying the warm fall evening. It would be winter here soon enough, which had its charm, but it did not lend itself to sitting outside with a pint. He was feeling good. He knew it was on account of the sex and the accompanying fancy that he was in love. It was a bloody fantastic feeling.

He knew it would end soon enough. It always did. At some point it would get hard and involve details that he really wasn't interested in. He'd been through enough relationships to know to take his time and stretch this part out for as long as he could.

Jennifer was in the shower. He wished he could ask her real name. Jennifer didn't suit her, and it sounded so awkward. He felt like a fraud every time he said it, and he was sure she could tell that he avoided using it.

He supposed one of these days she was going to get down to business and tell him what she really wanted. So far she hadn't bothered. Maybe she was enjoying the sex as much as he was and didn't want to rush to the next stage, which in their case might not be a mutual breakup but some other request James couldn't quite guess.

She came out onto the balcony with her hair wet and her body wrapped in his bathrobe. He found it erotic, how comfortable she was with her body. She sat opposite him, tucking her legs underneath her butt while the V of the robe slipped low. It was clear she was naked beneath. It was amazing to him, her total lack of shyness.

She lit the cigarette she'd brought out with her. They sat in silence for a while, enjoying the colors cast by the setting sun and watching the people down on the street.

"Sometimes," she said, putting her cigarette out in the small dish he now left on the balcony, "I am happy to be born when I am. But other times, I feel it is all too complicated."

James smiled. "I think that's the sentiment of every generation. We look on the past with our rose-tinted glasses and imagine that living in a cave or tilling the land for some lord was a simpler life."

"You are a realist."

"Absolutely. There was no better time to live. Now is the best, and tomorrow will be even better. You couldn't pay me to go back before germ theory and the discovery of antibiotics."

She laughed. James loved the sound of it, so rich and uninhibited. "You are right. I would already be dead twice if not for antibiotics."

"Rough life, then, growing up in Belgrade?" he asked.

She looked pensive. "And New York. We've been going back and forth since I was a child."

"On account of your American mother?"

"My Serbian American mother. Her brother, my uncle, lives there. He has for years. My mother, originally we went so we could get our citizenship. We stayed for three years, but then she missed Belgrade. So we went back. But then Belgrade was too limiting. So we went back to New York. And so on. Each time she was dissatisfied with the place she was. It couldn't compete with the memories of where we'd just been. So we—my mother, brother, and I—are both Yugoslavian and American."

James decided to take a chance. "What's your real name, then?"

She looked at him, a ghost of a smile on her lips. "You don't like Jennifer?"

He shook his head. "It doesn't suit you."

"Jasminka."

"Jasminka," he tried out, his accent making it harsher than what had come out of her mouth. "Much better."

"I don't know why I use Jennifer sometimes," she said. "I should have picked something that didn't start with a J because the sound is so different in English. But Jasminka was so out of place in New York, and when I was younger, I just wanted to fit in. I read a play, *The Doctor's Dilemma*, with a Jennifer, and I thought it was nice. My mother loves the theater, and most of her books are the scripts of plays. Now, of course, the name is everywhere in New York. All the babies in the park are named Jennifer."

"I prefer Jasminka."

She shrugged. "It is a dual identity. Common for immigrants. We identify with the country we are from and the country we moved to and don't feel at home in either one."

James focused on his beer, letting the silence settle between them again. His instincts were telling him that this was the truth. Everything she had just said seemed authentic. The story was heartbreaking in the way that it was the story of the world.

It was also a terrible backstory for a spy, he thought. Yugoslavia wasn't behind the Iron Curtain, so it would be a lot to learn, that and being American.

Despite himself, he was curious. He was sure he shouldn't be, because he still didn't think meeting her was an accident. She didn't talk much and had yet to even casually mention what she was doing in West Berlin. They didn't spend any time in her apartment, and James had noticed some comings and goings out of her unit that suggested she knew more than a few people here.

But he liked her. He liked being with her. He didn't want her to go away anytime soon. Should he just shut up and enjoy it all, like he was usually wont to do? Or should he ask and risk blowing the whole thing up? He was used to being selfish in relationships, and selfish him wanted to keep enjoying what they had and not care about the rest. But he'd learned over the last year that if you ignore the rest, it can often come and bite you in the arse.

"How's your new romance?"

James was over at Jillian's for dinner. "Still something I don't want to talk to you about."

"You are no fun," Jillian said. "Look, I'm the perfect deployed officer at the moment. Everything is running well. The transmission through the consulate goes like clockwork. I'm keeping my head down and doing my job. I'm sorting paperwork for fun on the weekends. So I have to live vicariously through you."

"That's not going to happen. I'm not some girlfriend who's about sharing all the details."

"Will you at least tell me her name?"

"Jasminka."

"Jasminka. That's pretty. Where is she from?"

"She grew up shuffling between New York and Belgrade."

"That's different. I've heard Yugoslavia is very beautiful. What's she doing here?"

James shifted in his seat, starting to become uncomfortable. "I'm not sure."

"What do you mean, you're not sure?"

"We haven't talked about that yet." James waited, knowing what was coming.

"What she's doing in West Berlin—isn't that a first-date kind of conversation?"

"I haven't got around to asking yet."

"And she hasn't mentioned anything?" Jillian asked.

"We haven't been doing a lot of talking."

Jillian looked at him for a long time, and he felt like squirming. Damn it. She didn't have to say it. He knew he was letting her down.

"When I was first with Carlos," she said, "as I've told you, the attraction was real and deep. We had sex all the time. It was the anchor for the whole relationship. But afterward—or walking around before, or the moments in between—we still talked. Granted, it was all lies. But I did manage to find out most of his cover story, and I wasn't even looking hard back then."

James knew what her point was. "I'm sorry, then. I know I should be after asking what she does, even if it's just to find out the pretense."

"Why haven't you? I told you what's been going on for me. It's not a stretch to think she might be a honeypot."

"She's not," he said.

Jillian shook her head. "You can't know that."

"I've been over it a hundred times. Her backstory is too messy. A dual citizen Yugoslavian American? Working for who? The East Germans? The Soviets? If she's really one of them, then why not just have her be American?"

Jillian sat back, clearly thinking it all through. "And you know for sure, about her being from New York and Belgrade?"

"It's not like I've got a lot of experience trying to detect a honeypot, but I've been to both cities. Her story, the experiences she describes, it all rings true." Except it didn't. He knew that. Jasminka definitely had a story; he just didn't know what it was.

He looked at Jillian and forced himself to remember the day he'd helped rescue her from the Cuban. She had been covered in bruises, obviously beaten up badly. She hadn't eaten in four days and had shaken continuously for hours. And he'd never forget her eyes. They'd looked so large, so full of fear, the skin around them purple. He could never be responsible for putting her through something like that again. His friendship with Jillian, as complicated and unexpected as it was, was important to him. More important than an affair with Jasminka.

"Right, I'm thinking I should stop seeing her, then."

"No. You like her. That much I can tell. Maybe she's fine. You deserve something nice like this."

He felt worse. "I do think she's got something going on. I'm not sure what it is. I'm not sure if it has anything to do with me, or with you. She's never asked much about what I do. Never asked about my friends. Never seems after meeting anyone else in my life. But she's not exactly forthcoming either. Maybe because she doesn't like me enough to want to share. I don't really know."

"Do you want to know?" Jillian asked.

"I never used to. You keep asking about my romantic past, and the truth is, there's not much to it. I like women. I like sex. I've never been interested in any more than that. I don't want kids, and I have never had any desire to share my space or have someone in my life every day."

"Is she changing that?"

"No," James said. "You did. It turns out that I like having someone around to care about. And who cares about me."

Jillian just stared at him. "I don't know what to say."

"It would be better if you didn't say anything. This kind of shite makes me uncomfortable, but it needs to be said. You're a tough person to be friends with, at least in this city. That is just the way it is. So aye, let's look into Jasminka. We should find out if she's a threat. And if she's not, I'll just go back to enjoying the shagging."

"Okay. How are we going to do that?" Jillian asked.

"You aren't going to do a damn thing. I've no interest in watching you get in trouble again. I figure the best thing to do is just ask. Depending on what she says, I can verify how much is a lie."

"Okay. If you need my help…"

James shook his head. "I don't. I'll let you know what she says. Now, would you like another whisky?"

CHAPTER TEN

Frank had mixed emotions. And that was a rare state for him.

They'd rented a car from a local lot and driven an hour outside of Managua to this piece-of-shit bar. Frank and Veronica had ordered drinks and sat down to wait to see if Frank's hunch was correct.

After calling James in West Berlin and getting a detailed description of the CIA officer who'd interfered in the CBNRC operation there, Frank was convinced it was the same guy here in Nicaragua. He'd come after the Cuban. Why, Frank had no idea. And he didn't much care.

The situation was causing Frank an unusual amount of conflict. On the one hand, this CIA guy had almost blown Frank's extremely sensitive and complicated collection in West Berlin. For that, Frank wanted to punch him in the face. On the other hand, it was likely that here in Nicaragua, he would be Frank's best chance at finding Carlos. The West Berlin setup was part of the job he no longer had, whereas what he could learn about Carlos was part of the job he might have in the near future. Frank knew the smart thing to do was forget about what had happened in Berlin and focus on what was happening now.

But Frank wasn't the kind of guy who always did the smart thing.

"Do you think he'll show up?" Veronica wondered.

"I don't have a damn clue," Frank said, "but if he cared enough to threaten you, I imagine he'd prefer to meet in this dive than the street in Managua. At least the beer's cold."

Frank hadn't told Veronica about what he suspected. She only knew that Frank had got Mark to contact his counterpart at the American embassy and asked him to find someone to set up a meeting. There was a decent chance he was wrong about the whole thing.

They sipped their drinks for a while, not saying much. Then Veronica glanced at the door, and Frank saw her focus.

"He's here," she said.

The man took a seat at their table. "You wanted to meet. Here I am. You have five minutes."

Frank took a good look at him. He looked exactly how James had described. It had to be him.

"Quentin Foster," Frank said.

An eyebrow shot up at that. "How do you know my name?"

"I know enough to know that isn't your name, but I don't really care about that."

"Who are you?"

"I'm sure you have an idea. Frank Leachuk. Doing some work at the Canadian embassy. I work with Veronica here. But it's my old job that you're probably more familiar with—I used to be the director of access at CBNRC. I was responsible for setting up a little collection system in West Berlin. Jillian's old boss."

Frank could tell that whatever this Quentin had thought would come out of a meeting with two Canadians from the embassy, that wasn't it.

There was a pause as Quentin adjusted to the new information. "So why are you here looking for Carlos? To avenge Jillian?"

The scorn was a pretense that Frank could easily see through. It was clear that Quentin was throwing up a wall while he figured out what to do. Frank had wondered if this guy would give two shits about the Jillian connection. It was time to find out.

"I'm not in the avenging business. But if you're asking if I'm still pissed about you using my deployed officer to further your operations, in the process getting her kidnapped and coming damn close to comprising everything we had going over there, then yes."

Quentin got up and went to the bar. He returned with a Coke. "You were a fool to send her alone."

Frank leaned back and lit a cigarette. "I don't make all the decisions. We don't quite have the manpower that some other countries have."

"Regardless, she was unprepared for life in West Berlin."

Frank took in a long pull of smoke. "We all are. It's a hard business, to give engineers the right training for being in the field. It's not exactly a natural fit. Given what went down, I'm not sure anything I could have told her would have prepared her for getting hit on by a Cuban spy and subsequently getting used by the CIA."

Quentin looked at Frank. "Is she still there?"

There was something in the guy's face that suggested to Frank that he did care about Jillian.

"As far as I know." Frank shrugged. "Like I said, I'm not her boss anymore."

"They didn't like what happened with the Cuban?"

"No one at my agency has a fucking clue what happened with the Cuban. If they did, they'd have shut the entire operation down. No, I got put out to pasture because I brought James in to help her. He's my nephew and the only other person in that city I felt I could trust."

Quentin looked pensive as he drank his Coke.

"So how did you end up in Nicaragua?" Quentin asked.

Frank glanced at Veronica. She was following the conversation intently. How much she was able to put together, Frank didn't know. He had just let her in on two pieces of heavily classified information. By the end of the night, she was probably going to know a lot more. He realized he didn't care. He trusted her, and she needed to know this stuff to get the job done.

"Why are you here?" Frank countered. "From what I've been told, you were busy in Berlin. You certainly kept showing up where I didn't want you. I imagine there are a few other people who feel the same way."

"I'm on vacation."

Frank tapped the ashes off the end of his cigarette. "Taking a trip down memory lane?"

Quentin raised a brow. "What do you know about it?"

"What NSA shared with me when you started bothering my officer." Frank was bluffing a little. The truth was, his contacts at NSA didn't know much. They wouldn't, mostly being SIGINT engineers. The details of active CIA ops weren't in their purview unless SIGINT was directly involved. But there were always people who knew people, and Frank had found out that Quentin had a pretty big past in Nicaragua.

"So we're both in town looking for the same guy," Quentin said. "But if your reasons have nothing to do with Jillian, then I'm not sure why you're here."

Frank let the conversation lull while he thought for a minute. Carlos was always official CIA business, that much he knew because NSA permanently had him as a collection target. But there were millions of targets. Was there something specific going down now, or was Quentin really here on vacation? It was, of course, at least a vacation with an agenda, but it mattered if the whole thing was personal.

"I want to be the first to know if he goes back to Berlin," Frank said.

"He won't."

"And how do you know that?"

"Because I have no intention of letting him leave Nicaragua." Quentin finished his Coke. "Stop trying to find Carlos. It's a waste of your time."

Frank could tell the meeting was almost over, that Quentin was about to get up and leave. Frank also knew that if that happened, they weren't likely to see him again. He wanted the story on Carlos—he was starting to realize how badly.

"What are the British going to say when you accomplish what you came here to do?"

Quentin looked at him, clearly not expecting that question. "The British? Like MI6? What the hell are they going to care?"

"No," said Veronica, speaking for the first time. "The Home Office."

"What?"

"That's the reason we're here," Frank said. "To find out what Carlos is doing for the British diplomatic service."

Quentin looked at them like they had lost their collective minds. "What are you talking about? Carlos doesn't work for the British Home Office. He's never had anything to do with them."

"How would you know that for sure?" Frank said. "Have you spent every minute with him for the last ten years?"

"Damn it, I would know. Three years ago, I spent more than a year learning everything about him. I had access to his family, I followed him daily for months. I know everything there is to know. What beer he drinks, his favorite book of poetry, what kind of women he likes to sleep with. I know what sounds he makes in his sleep and how many teeth he's had fixed. I would've known if he had any contact with the British. He's a recruiter for the Soviets and whoever they sympathize with. No way he's done anything for an ally of ours. Whoever told you that is trying to lead you in the wrong direction."

"It was late 1969," Veronica said. "He was a guest at a reception honoring the new Home Secretary. So before you knew him, I think."

Quentin stared at her. "What?"

"He was photographed with three other diplomats, all men. They were dressed in tuxedos for the occasion. I haven't been able to identify them yet, but I did confirm that the event was guest list only."

Frank was impressed. He hadn't known she'd kept working on the photo.

"It wasn't him," Quentin said. "It couldn't have been."

"It was." Frank decided to light another cigarette. "One of our analysts ID'd him based on photos we got from NSA. We found it via a reprint in a diplomatic magazine. I had one of our facial recognition experts verify. It is most definitely a young Carlos Honouras having a swanky dinner on the Home Secretary."

"You're not joking," Quentin said.

"No, we're not." Frank took a long drag on his cigarette. "Look, we're not here to get in your way either. I know someone has to keep an eye on Carlos, and like I said, I want to know if he decides to go back to Berlin. I figure you have that covered and are better positioned than I am to make sure Jillian gets the heads-up. What we're really interested in is who Carlos had contact with at the Home Office and, of course, if the relationship is still active. Because that, to me, is an even bigger problem."

Quentin stood up. "I have to think about this. I'll be in touch."

Frank nodded. Quentin left a few córdobas on the table and walked out.

"That was interesting," Veronica said. "I take it he's who you were expecting."

"I can't tell you much more than what you've probably figured out. Jillian is our officer in West Berlin. She had the misfortune to have an affair with Carlos. Quentin tried to turn her into a honeypot and almost blew our whole operation."

"And the kidnapping you mentioned?"

"A damn disaster. There was another one from the CIA who misunderstood certain elements of the situation and ended up raising Carlos's suspicions. Not a hard thing to do. So Carlos took Jillian and beat the crap out of her. The one you just met, Quentin, he may have triggered that mess, but he also did a lot to get her out. He blew part of his cover to lure Carlos away from her. So he's not a total prick."

"Why do you think we can trust him? Because he's American?"

"Hell no. Why I've never liked your kind, regardless of nationality, is because you always work to your own agendas. We need to do some digging, but if he's really here for personal reasons, he might be easier to work with."

"You didn't answer my question really," Veronica said.

Frank took a final drag of his cigarette. "In Berlin, he did okay. He came through for Jillian. And he uncovered some rot in the CIA station over there. He's okay."

"Do you think he'll work with us?"

"I wasn't sure initially if he already knew about the British thing, but he didn't. And I think he hates Carlos and anyone who helps Carlos keep being the asshole that he is. I think that Quentin is going to want to find those Home Office contacts as badly as we do. So right now, because we both have information the other doesn't, working together is of mutual benefit."

"So," Veronica said, "I guess I really need to identify those other men in the picture."

"That," Frank responded, "is your first priority. Quentin will find Carlos. We need leverage to be included when he does."

CHAPTER ELEVEN

Frank was sitting at the desk enjoying a second cup of coffee and the one-week-old paper that had been lying on the table in the kitchenette. Every time he was at an embassy, getting the news from home weeks after it had happened, he reflected that news wasn't really news. He figured you could take a paper from any year, update the names to be current, and the headlines would still make sense. Leadership was always crap, and the world was always coming to an end. Which, of course, is why he'd always had a job. No matter what the state of the world, countries wanted to spy on other countries. He flipped to the crossword puzzle, hoping it hadn't been filled. That was about the only thing worth reading.

    He was trying to figure out a four-letter word for "cheese made backward" when Veronica came in and dropped her bag beside the desk. It was ten a.m., but he didn't really care. He wasn't her boss, and there were a few perks for being on an assignment that no one was interested in, like having a lot of freedom of movement. If she chose to use it to sleep in or do aerobics in the morning, good for her.

"Morning," Frank said.

"You'll never guess what came in this morning," Veronica answered.

Frank leaned back in his chair. "I figure you're going to tell me."

"Who else do I have to talk to?"

Frank waited.

"Anyway, I put in a request through external affairs for photographs from that Home Office dinner. They sent the request on. Apparently there was some digging, because although governments keep all that stuff, it was just sitting in a box in the countryside somewhere. They put them all onto microfilm for me. So guess what we're doing today?"

"And here I was, thinking I might go for a stroll. I'm out of cigarettes."

"You should just buy them by the case. Let me go get a coffee, and then we can get started."

Frank watched her walk away, feeling slightly smug that his instincts had paid off. She was good; she'd just never been given a chance—until now. She was both energetic and committed. He could see it in her attitude: she now felt like she was doing real intelligence work. And she was.

He was also sure that she trusted him. He didn't get the feeling she was hiding anything. She held back from Mark and Phillip, the defense attachés, even though they were essentially in her line of business. He was grateful, actually, that they were both military and not RCMP. That way there was no opportunity for conflicting loyalties.

Four hours later, Frank's eyes were starting to glaze over from looking at pictures of people posing for the camera. Whoever it was in whatever British department had sent all the pictures from the entire year. The dinner they were interested in was mixed in with a bunch of other dinners, with all the photos taken by the same government photographer.

"Why didn't they mark this stuff properly?" Frank grumbled.

Veronica was diligently labeling everything she could. "No, this is much better. We can see what other events the same people attended. I haven't seen Carlos in photos from any other events yet, but this man, with the funky eyebrows, he's cropped up in a few. It will help us identify him. Once we do, we can build up a better picture of who he is."

She was right. Of course she was right. He'd never really done this kind of intelligence work. Patience was something he had a lot of, so Frank kept at it until his neck started to throb.

"That's enough for today. I'm hungry. I'm going to that pork place."

Veronica looked up. "I'm okay for now. I'll knock on your door later if I find anything."

Frank nodded, leaving her to it. Hopefully she'd identify the three other people in that photo with Carlos tonight so he didn't have to do this again tomorrow.

When Frank got in the next morning, Veronica was already there.

"Have you been here all night?" he asked.

She looked tired, but she shook her head. "No, I went home around eleven and got back here at six. I'm making really excellent progress."

"Anything you want to share?"

"Yes." She stood and stretched her arms up. "My back is killing me. Also, the man with the funky eyebrows in the photo is Colin Edwards. He was a press secretary for the Home Office at the time. He's in a ton of photos. I got lucky—one of them was labeled. I've already called external affairs and asked for a report, including his bio. That's such a public role I'm sure we'll be able to get a bunch of info and maybe something we can use to identify the other two."

That was good news. "Are you looking for something to do for the rest of the day?"

"Well, I should probably keep going through these photos," she said.

"You could."

"Why do I feel like you have something else in mind?"

"Quid pro quo. I need help going through what we're intercepting from the Ministry of Agriculture."

"Going through it for what?"

Frank took a sip of his coffee. "At this point, just to evaluate if it's a useful feed. So far the cultural attachés are excited because it lets them know the party plans, but that's unclassified stuff they'd find out anyway. There's no point in sending it back to CBNRC for further analysis if it's just going to be more of the same."

"What will you do if it's just good for the event planners?" Veronica asked.

Frank shrugged. "They can keep it going. It's running from a tap we can access from the roof, so it's no big deal to keep collecting. But I'm not going to waste analyst time on that kind of stuff. I need to do a bit of triage, a preliminary evaluation of the potential intelligence use."

"Patience, right. Looking through all the haystacks."

"Welcome to the job. Go get a coffee, and I'll get us set up."

Over the next few days, Frank was reminded many times why he never went into analysis. Between Veronica's photos and the drivel coming out of the ministry, he was bored senseless. At least he could run search terms against the intercept; the photos were all manual. Neither were interesting.

"Hey, look at this," Veronica said. He came up to stand behind her. "I know it isn't much," she continued, "but it's a little weird."

Frank stooped to look at the printouts in front of her. As far as he could tell, it was just a series of references to the big shindig the ministry was planning. "Can you be more specific?"

"The stuff from the Ministry of Agriculture, all these phone calls. Well, I asked myself, where do I start? The obvious place is to identify the most senior people whose calls get routed on this cable and start with them. I did that. And there, we're in luck. We get the minister's calls. Only the official ones, which makes me think there's another line for more private stuff."

"Makes sense," Frank said.

"But even luckier, in my opinion, is we get his secretary's calls, and she doesn't appear to have a private line. So I searched all calls with her number. It's harder on the incoming, so I probably don't have everything."

"And?"

"There's a lot of talk about this party that the minister is hosting at his residence in December. Given the location, the secretary is heavily involved. Most of the conversations are just about booking things for the party, but there have been a few that were different. Apparently the secretary is receiving the invoices because she's coordinating the details—for food or flowers or whatever. Three times someone has called her saying she isn't routing them properly. The originals are supposed to go to a C. Fuentes in accounts payable. The secretary is insisting she's making a copy and sending on the original. But whatever is being received is a copy."

Frank leaned back against the windowsill. "That's not much."

"No," Veronica agreed. "It isn't. But it is an anomaly."

Frank thought for a moment. "We don't know that. It could be just part of a procedure that we don't have any insight into."

"Sure. Except the secretary has been around for a while, and apparently it's the first time it ever happened. And it's only invoices for that party they're planning in December. To me, it looks like someone is making an extra copy, and three times they've routed the wrong piece of paper."

"Why would someone need an extra copy of those invoices? It could be for the minister's wife so she can track what's going to happen in her house."

"Essentially, those invoices would be extremely useful for anyone who wanted to know exactly what was going to happen on the day of the party," Veronica said.

"Which could be one of a dozen people with a legitimate need." Frank stood up. "Okay, let's just track it for now."

"Should I run the search every day?"

"Yes," Frank said. "The secretary is a good target regardless. Otherwise, we keep going through the content in our spare time. We can compile a selection and send it home to see if anyone is interested in crop analysis or whatever."

"Sure," Veronica said. "I'll work on this for another hour. Then it's time to get back to my photos."

Frank was relieved it was the end of the week. He wasn't usually a "happy it's Friday" kind of guy, but after all the analysis of the last couple weeks, he felt a real need for a weekend. He had plans to take a drive out of town, south into the hills that surrounded Managua. It looked pleasant up there. Plus, signals were always better up high.

He wondered if he should take Veronica. She'd been going through the haystacks even more than he had, totally devoted to the cause. He appreciated the effort. They didn't have much yet, but identifying one of the men in the photo with Carlos would at least give them something to talk to Quentin about next time they saw him. Of course, knowing all three identities would be even better.

She probably needed a break too. Admittedly, it was handy to have her around. It was so much easier when they got stopped that she could jump in with her Spanish. But he didn't mind spending time with her. Maybe it was because she was a woman, the first female IO he'd ever spent time with. She wasn't as annoying as the rest of them. He didn't feel like he was being played, and he didn't feel like he had to be on his guard, which is what he usually felt around anyone from the RCMP. He thought they were working nicely together as a team. A surprise. And a lot more than he expected when he got exiled to this liaising assignment.

He looked up when Veronica walked in carrying two coffees. She crossed to their desk. "Here you go," she said, putting one of the coffees down in front of Frank. "Happy Friday."

"Thanks," he said. "Are you just trying to butter me up?"

She looked a little shocked. "No. What would I do that for? So you can let me go through even more intercept?"

Frank laughed. "Some people, you know, find it really interesting."

"Well, this woman isn't one of them. That kind of analysis isn't for me. Long-term, I mean. On this assignment…"

"It's fine." Frank waved away her hesitation. "You don't have to pretend to love it. I don't. I like finding the signals. I've never been as interested in the details they contain."

"I don't mind the work, though. Really. It's part of how we get to stay here. And that's important to me."

"I was thinking of getting out of the city tomorrow. Take a drive up around La Estrella. It's supposed to be nice, with a locally respected empanada stand, if you want to come with me. I think you need a break."

"What if the bio on Colin Edwards comes in tomorrow? And I'm almost done with the photos."

"Pace yourself."

She thought for a moment. "Okay. It sounds like fun."

Frank snorted. "Fun. We don't want to have fun. Fun attracts too much attention. This is a country at war with itself. We don't want to get noticed. It's just something to do."

"You're really selling it."

"You don't have to come."

"No, I want to. I want to see something other than Managua. Get a better feel for the country."

"Good. Be ready by nine. I've borrowed a car, so we'll be driving around with diplomatic plates, which might be good. Or it might not."

She sat down at the desk and flicked on the microfilm reader. "Phillip says that being affiliated with the embassy is good if you're dealing with Somoza's people. It can hurt if you have a run-in with anyone else."

Frank thought that made sense. Everything you did identified you with a side. It was a hard place to be neutral.

"How is Phillip?"

She looked at him. "What do you mean?"

"Do you think he's any good at his job?"

She glanced around the office as if to make sure the defense attachés weren't around. They were out until the end of the weekend. Some training exercise they got invited to.

"He's okay."

"That doesn't seem like a ringing endorsement."

"I don't think he's…curious enough. He's on top of all the defense files, and I get that there's a lot going on here, and we're small, but he doesn't seem to be particularly interested in seeing if those files connect to anything else. His contacts are mostly the obvious connections from the Somoza government. He's got some other contacts and claims to be looking for a connection within the Sandinista organization, but he's thinner on that front. Maybe I'm expecting too much. He hasn't been here that long either."

"Well, they don't usually send our A-team down here."

"What does that say about us?"

Frank smiled. "Everyone makes mistakes."

Veronica looked hesitant. "I hope so."

Jesus, Frank thought. He didn't know whether she was tenacious or just stupid, because whatever she'd been through at the RCMP, he was sure most people would have quit. "Look," he said. "You're no good to me if you doubt yourself. We're in uncharted territory over here. We don't know if we're collecting anything of value, we don't know if Carlos is going to pan out. We're trying to get some leverage over a guy on vacation from the CIA, which is going to be damn hard. We're trying to get involved in a situation that we weren't invited to, we don't have any real business in, and that no one in our chain of command is interested in. So I don't need you to bullshit it, but I do need you to believe in yourself."

"You make it sound so easy."

"No, it's not. I get that. But you have to start somewhere. You have a lot to learn, fine. But you have good instincts. Trust them, and trust yourself. You're all I've got down here in terms of HUMINT, and I'm damn well not going back to Ottawa empty-handed."

"Okay. I'm going to try to get through the rest of these photos before our day trip tomorrow."

Frank nodded. He didn't think he needed to say anything else. He hadn't worked with new recruits in a long time, dealing with their hesitancy and insecurity. He barely remembered what it was like to be new to the job. He remembered being paranoid about saying anything to anyone outside the office and locking his desk drawer when he went to the bathroom just in case building security walked by and saw his top-secret documents sitting on his desk. But he didn't remember not believing he could do the job. He wondered if it was like that for all of them now, if there were more expectations. Or at least for all of the women. It sounded like they were only grudgingly being admitted to the club of human intelligence.

Understanding some of what Veronica had been through made him think he'd been a little too hard on Jillian over in West Berlin. At first, all he'd focused on was that the collection kept running. It was such a unique setup, and he was damn proud of it. But he knew deep down he hadn't prepared her enough for working covertly overseas. He hadn't paid enough attention to the particular pressures a young female would face. It made him uncomfortable. That was no excuse.

Even though he hadn't held her back, in his own way he'd undermined her efforts. He hadn't set her up to succeed. He felt ashamed. If he was supposed to put the mission first, then he should have thought more carefully about how to protect Jillian when she was over there.

He wasn't too afraid to admit he was doing much the same thing now. As much as he might be supporting Veronica, it was ultimately because he was selfish. Her being on her game was better for him.

Frank had always believed it was possible to keep learning and stay relevant. He'd never wanted to be one of those people who got old because they stopped changing with the world.

Thus, he reflected, it was one of those moments where it was time to change. He'd let Jillian down. He'd like to not make the same mistakes with Veronica.

Maybe nothing would happen with the Carlos lead, but maybe it would. This was the man who had kidnapped Jillian and would have probably killed her if Quentin hadn't intervened. Frank needed to share everything he knew. He'd gotten lucky last time. No one had died on his watch.

He didn't want to rely on luck this time around.

CHAPTER TWELVE

James could admit that he was nervous. It wasn't every day that he confronted someone about being a spy.

He wasn't going to do exactly that, he acknowledged to himself. A fat lot of good it would do to ask Jasminka directly if she was involved in some covert espionage. If she was, she'd deny it. If she wasn't, she'd deny it. As would be standard protocol.

He might be able to tell the difference between a denial based in lies and one based in the truth, but probably not. He was fairly observant, but also emotionally involved. He really didn't want her to be a spy. He liked spending time with her. He didn't want to give that up. Or grow to hate her. Or have to be worried she was going to hurt someone he cared about.

He was, he reflected, bad at this stuff. He imagined he'd have to lead quite a different life to be any good at it. Confrontation was fine, but trying to figure out if he was the target of a honeypot was definitely outside his traditional milieu.

The aroma coming out of the pot wasn't half bad. He wasn't the greatest cook, but he'd invited her over for dinner in the hopes that the relaxed atmosphere would lend itself to encouraging her to be more forthcoming.

He was in the process of changing his shirt when he heard the knock on the door. He swung it open, dismayed at the way his heart started beating heavier when he saw Jasminka standing at the threshold.

She held up a little crate of beer. "Radegast. From Czechoslovakia. I'm not sure if it's exactly to your taste, but it is very good."

"Ah then, I can't say no to that." He stood back from the door. "Come in."

She smelled great. She moved great. James decided the whole situation was agonizing.

He opened them each a beer while they sat out on his balcony and watched the twilight roll in.

He served them dinner and spent too much time staring into her eyes.

And still he couldn't manage to start the conversation he'd been planning.

They ended up in bed, after which James fed them dessert. They talked about nothing important, and he gave up.

It would be too artificial now, he reckoned, to bring it up. It would make the whole evening seem like a setup. Which it was, in its way. But for some reason, he really didn't want her to think that.

They lay together in bed for a while, Jasminka slowly trailing her fingers all over his skin. There was nowhere else on this planet he'd rather be.

What was he going to do?

Jillian shifted her bag to her other shoulder. She'd started bringing her camera when she went to the garage to help Madeline. Some of the papers were beginning to fade, the paper becoming brittle. In order to have a complete record, Jillian was taking a photo of all the papers that appeared fragile. It was a ton of photos, but Madeline was paying for the film.

She was grateful Madeline had asked her to help out. It stopped Jillian from getting bored, and she got to spend time in a different part of the city. And it stopped her from thinking too much about Quentin.

She wondered if he was still in Nicaragua. If he had found Carlos. If he thought about her at all. On the last point, Jillian knew it wasn't a good idea to hope that he did. As much as she missed him, she didn't think they had a future. She couldn't work one out. Jillian didn't think that she could be with someone who was so enigmatic, who would disappear for months at a time and be in danger for most of it.

Technically they were in a very similar business, but for Jillian, human intelligence and signals intelligence felt light-years apart. SIGINTers had fairly regular lives. They went to work at the same place every day and decrypted signals or analyzed intercept, and then they went home and ate dinner with their families. It was a classified day job, but it was still a day job, and thus the lifestyle it afforded was similar to any other government employee's.

But Quentin was CIA. By definition that gave him a foreign intelligence mandate, and you can't run agents and gather intelligence on foreign targets and then go home every day to your house in the Virginia suburbs. To be an intelligence officer for a foreign intelligence service, well, you had to leave the country once in a while.

Plus, they weren't even from the same country. She couldn't permanently work for the NSA, and he couldn't work out of Ottawa.

She shook her head, embarrassed at the direction of her thoughts. Here she was, trying to work out logistics, avoiding dealing with the more pertinent fact that he was compelling to her in ways she didn't want to analyze. It was hard for her to hold two such separate emotions where he was concerned. How could she miss someone she wasn't sure she even liked? She worried that all her rationalizing would evaporate if she ever saw him again.

She sighed as she turned up Lindower Strasse. She had always prided herself on being such a clear thinker. This ceaseless churn about Quentin was so out of character. Jillian hoped that didn't mean anything more than she didn't have enough to do these days.

Jillian arrived at the garage, lifted up the door to her waist, and ducked underneath. She closed it quickly. The early November air was brisk tonight.

Madeline was already there, shuffling between boxes, clearly looking for something. "Ah, I've misplaced the last months of 1940. They must be labeled incorrectly."

"I think I saw notes from October 1940 in that yellow box over there," Jillian said.

Madeline peered in the box and moved some papers around. "Yes, here it is. These should be interesting to read. The end of 1940 was euphoric. The Nazis thought the Blitz was going to bring Britain to its knees. There was a lot of anticipation of setting up on British soil, knowing that Germans controlling London would end any resistance in the rest of Europe. Many thought the war would soon be over."

"Wishful thinking."

"Yes, well, obviously the Nazis had more than their fair share of that."

Jillian opened the next box in her queue. She was working on early 1941. They continued in silence for almost an hour. Jillian knew she wasn't being terribly efficient, caught up as she was in every third note.

Monika with Samuel, the U-boat lieutenant. He told her he hoped the war would soon be over or that he could get a posting to a ship. He hated being under the water. It scared him, the thought of being under all that pressure so far from the surface.

Christina with Peter, a banker from Bavaria. He spoke of how rich the war was going to make him. How he could afford dozens like her when it was all over.

Ingrid with Uwe, the engineer working at the rubber plant. He told her that victory was all but assured for the Germans. They were adapting to new technology while the rest of Europe was stuck in old ways of thinking. He was confident Hitler would not stop until there was no credible threat to his rule. He heard rumors that Russia was next.

It was fascinating for Jillian to read these excerpts from history. She also knew it was easy to get caught up in the intrigue when you knew the outcome. But these records captured a moment in time when the end of the war was far away. She appreciated how much one had to believe in order to fight for one's country. She also wondered how easy it was to stop believing once your country lost.

People in Allied countries could go on believing after the war was over that they had sacrificed for the right reasons, that their country did the right thing. Because they won, they were vindicated. But for many Germans, what they believed during the war would forever be in conflict with what they were supposed to believe after it.

Jillian stood up, her legs tingling as blood rushed into places that had numbed. "I'm going down the street to get a hot chocolate and one of those strudels that you've got me addicted to. Can I get you anything?" she asked Madeline.

"Maybe some warm milk, please."

"No strudel?"

"No." Madeline smiled. "I'm at the age where those types of foods are harder to work off."

Jillian smiled back. "Be back in a minute."

She let herself out of the garage, pulling the door down behind her. The sky was gray, and the wind had picked up. It was one of those November days that they sometimes got at home. The weather made the darkness start earlier, so all you really felt like doing was curling up with a good book.

Walking down to the pastry shop, she passed many people out on the streets. Very few West Berliners had cars, so the streets were always lively with people going about their lives. Jillian didn't mind the gloom of the day or the promise of winter ahead. There was something about this kind of weather that she found exciting. It lent itself to mystery in a way that endless sunshine on some tropical island did not.

She was standing in front of the strudels, debating about which flavor to choose, when she registered the tinkling of a bell as someone else entered the shop. A few moments later a soft cough sounded behind her.

"Hello again," said a voice.

Jillian turned around to see the man who had stopped by the garage the month before. Hans, she thought.

"Because you are here buying something," he said, "I think then that you are still working on sorting those memories."

Jillian smiled. "I have a feeling we'll be working on sorting those memories until the spring."

"That seems a lot for one person to have."

Jillian indicated the blueberry strudel to the woman behind the counter. "Well, they aren't all Madeline's. They are all the memories from about a dozen different women during the war. They all worked in a cabaret, one that was frequented by Nazis or their alleged sympathizers. Madeline's mom was in charge, and she kept a record of most everything that was talked about. Nothing is really earth-shattering, but Madeline has decided it should all be cataloged. She wants to write about it, then I guess she's going to give it to a museum or something to see if any of it has historical value."

"How…fascinating," Hans said.

"But really, Madeline is the one to talk to. I'm just cheap labor that can be bought with strudel."

"Yes, you said that before. I had every intention of going back, but I met a friend while I was here and got sidetracked. Perhaps I will stop in the next time I see the light on."

"I usually only come out at weekends, but I think Madeline comes during the week as often as she can. It's a big job."

"I can imagine. So far, nothing interesting that is making the effort all worthwhile?"

"Oh, it's all interesting," said Jillian, "but I like history. Original documents like these, written without the perspective of knowing how it was all going to end, are really fascinating. The men who visited the cabaret, mostly they didn't seem interested in talking about events or even what they did on a regular day. They talk more about how they feel. Excited, tired, defiant, scared. I guess the cabaret was like a sanctuary."

"All Nazis?"

"Yes, being in Berlin. I suppose one had to at least overtly support the Nazis in order to stay alive. I'm working on documents from early on in the war right now. At least then, it's fair to say that they mostly believed in Hitler and what he was doing. It'll be interesting to see if that changes as we get closer to 1945."

"I think you will find that the general attitude doesn't change much. Most Nazis were believers right to the end. They did a good job, you see, of getting people to believe. Their propaganda was…exceptional."

Jillian shivered a little. "It's been really wonderful talking to you. I'm sure you also have some interesting stories, but I must get back to my friend before her milk gets too cold."

"For better or for worse, my memories of the war are never far from my mind," Hans said. "Perhaps I will see you in here another day, and if you have more questions, we can talk again."

Jillian was both intrigued and unnerved. No doubt his stories would be just as interesting as Madeline's, but she got the feeling that his memories were a lot closer to the surface and that he was living some of the emotions from thirty years ago.

CHAPTER THIRTEEN

They were about an hour outside of Managua, driving through a bit of the Sierra. It was cooler, and the foliage was lush and thick. Giant trees grew alongside the road, and Frank was thankful he didn't get carsick as the road twisted and turned while it alternately climbed and snaked through deep ravines. It wasn't official business, since Frank didn't plan to find any signals to intercept out here. He went because he knew Veronica liked getting out of the city. Last weekend, at the empanada stand, they'd overheard some innocuous but interesting conversations. It helped her, Frank thought, to be around actual Nicaraguans instead of always the embassy people. Plus, it gave them a chance to talk more openly.

He'd filled Veronica in a little more about what had gone down in West Berlin. Not the details of Jillian's assignment or any details about the collection they had been copying, as that was still compartmentalized information. But he told her everything James had told him about Carlos: how Jillian had met him, why the CIA got involved, how she'd bugged Carlos's car and given the feed to Quentin. He also told Veronica everything he knew about the kidnapping and how Jillian had gotten out of that, plus everything he knew about Quentin's relationship with Carlos.

On that last point, it wasn't much. Everything James knew was pretty much the same as what Frank's friend at the NSA had told him. Quentin and Carlos had a previous relationship that had involved something that prompted Quentin to go rogue for a while, before turning up in Berlin. Apparently whatever it was had been accepted or forgiven. Frank didn't know if Quentin had been in trouble with the agency or his conscience. Usually Frank would have assumed the former, seeing as most of these guys had a pretty obscure definition of conscience. But Quentin had put himself on the line for Jillian in Berlin, and James seemed to think that under the façade, Quentin was a good guy. It was enough for Frank to reserve judgment and to see where it would take them.

"I've been through the Colin Edwards bio three times," said Veronica. "There isn't much there. He's a career public servant, has worked in a few different departments, and writes good press releases. There's nothing obvious that gives me an indication of who else is in that picture."

"What's your next step?" asked Frank.

Veronica tapped her fingers on the armrest. "I asked external affairs for a list of everyone he worked with at each department. They said they only keep current staffing lists. So I asked Marlene—you know, in records where I work—and she said I'd have to go to each department individually, but she offered to get me the contact info."

"You don't seem satisfied."

Veronica stewed a little bit more. "I think Colin Edwards is a red herring. He's a press secretary who was working for the Home Office. He was in dozens of the photos, always with different people. He's just a schmoozer who was working the room. I really don't think he's the guy who invited Carlos."

Frank thought for a moment. "Have you tried approaching it from the other end?"

"What do you mean?" asked Veronica.

"How would a guy like Carlos, a Cuban with a revolutionary background who sometimes works for the Soviets and East Germans, get to a dinner at the British Home Office? What would his life have to look like for that invitation to make sense?"

Veronica seemed to be contemplating. "Do you think whoever invited him knew who he was?"

"Maybe. Either way, it's a narrow set of possibilities. Let's say that John Diplomat knew that Carlos worked for the Soviets. That means one of two things: either John Diplomat has Soviet sympathies, or he's passing misinformation to Carlos. In both cases, Carlos must trust John Diplomat. So where in Carlos's past is there enough regular contact with a British diplomat to build that kind of relationship?"

"Or…," said Veronica.

"Or John Diplomat had no idea who Carlos was. Carlos was there under a fake identity doing something for the Soviets."

"We need more information."

"You know what," Frank said, checking the rear-view mirror, "I never did request anything from GCHQ on Carlos. After Quentin showed up in Berlin, I requested everything NSA had. It wasn't much, because the NSA reporting on him was for CIA targets, and a lot of it was marked NOFORN, so being Canadian I couldn't see it. But the diplomatic picture came much later, when I was halfway out the door. GCHQ might have something, or at least enough to let us know if the Home Office knew who they were dealing with."

Veronica didn't say anything. Frank glanced over and didn't know what to make of the expression on her face.

"Spit it out," he said.

"Nothing. It's not like I thought of it either. But requesting SIGINT reporting from your British counterparts on Carlos is a great idea and one that would have been a logical first step."

Frank laughed full on from the gut. "Are you trying to tell me that I'm not a good IO?"

Veronica's cheeks reddened. "I mean. It's just, we're trying to find out who he is. I assumed you'd already explored every avenue open to you."

"I didn't think of it. Too many years thinking about the signals. I got curious about Carlos, but I've never worked HUMINT. Ever. So, going forward, it's probably best if you don't assume a damn thing."

"Noted." Veronica let out her breath. "When we get back to the office, I'll write up the request for you. We should check on his known aliases as well and make sure the time line goes back a couple of years before the party. It seems like the British were involved with him before the Americans got interested."

"Good. Are you getting hungry?"

"Starting to."

"Okay. Next decent food place we see, we'll pull over. There's usually somewhere to eat in every town, and you seem to be enjoying all the local specialties."

Frank sat under a thatch umbrella enjoying a cigarette. Veronica was some distance away, shoes in her hand, walking along the shoreline outside of La Boquita. Looking out over the ocean, Frank thought this was one of the most interesting things about Nicaragua. The ocean was never very far away, and the coastline was littered with beaches. He lived in the middle of Canada, and although some of the lakes were big enough that they seemed like oceans, it was a couple hours by plane to actually get to one.

He was enjoying this assignment. Enjoying not being in the office and not having to play politics. The IO stuff he could do without. It was clear he was a SIGINT guy at heart. But maybe having a better appreciation for the other side would be useful for his career. Whatever was left of it.

He was wondering if he should go dip his toe in the Pacific, just to have something to tell his wife next time they spoke.

"Nice spot."

Frank started. "Jesus H. Christ. You scared the shit out of me."

Quentin shrugged. "Not on purpose."

Frank didn't bother pointing out that most people would have said something before sitting down.

"So," said Frank.

"So," said Quentin. "I've been thinking about this situation we find ourselves in."

"And?"

"And I want to know what your endgame is."

Frank took a drag on his cigarette. "You say that like I have one."

"You're putting in a lot of work, coming down here, just to look for Carlos."

He flicked the ashes into an empty Coke can. "You know, I can't stand intelligence officers. I don't know if James ever told you that, but you guys drive me fucking crazy. Nothing is ever direct. Everything is a probe. You don't have a damn clue how much effort got me here, or anything about what I do, or who I report to, or who might give a damn about what I'm doing here."

"I came here to put a bullet in Carlos. Are you going to get in the way of that?" Quentin said.

Fuck. How am I supposed to handle a guy like this?

"Tell me about Berlin," Frank said.

"What do you want to know?"

"Why did you keep turning up in the middle of my operation? I know NSA told you to back off Jillian right from the get-go. So why didn't you?"

"She was a good source," Quentin said.

"No, she wasn't. That's why I've never trusted your kind. You don't have allies. Not like we do." Frank could feel his blood pressure going up. "She was never your fucking source."

Quentin stared out at the ocean for a long time. "I know. Look, Carlos was important. He was recruiting for the

Baader-Meinhof gang, and they were kidnapping people off the street. At the beginning, all I wanted from her was information that she already had, but she kept on about that friend. I thought she should go home because it was likely she was compromised. But she kept it together, and after she realized her friend was in trouble, there was no stopping her."

Frank sighed. "I know Jillian took some unacceptable risks."

"She bugged Carlos's car," Quentin said, shaking his head. "You know, looking back, I think she did the right thing. With all of it. You may think she was crazy, or irrational, but how rational is it to not fight for what you believe in? We all wanted her to sit quietly and ignore her conscience, but that's not fair to her."

"Now don't I feel like an asshole. So what, you were just looking out for her the whole time?"

Quentin smiled. "I took information when I could get it. But yeah, someone had to. She wanted to do the right thing. It reminded me that once upon a time I did too. There are a few mistakes that I don't want to make again."

"Which is your roundabout way of saying what exactly?"

"I lost someone to Carlos once. When he kidnapped Jillian in Berlin, I thought it was happening again. I don't want to lose anyone else to that scum. Ever. That's why I'm here on vacation. Whatever your intentions are, you're just going to get in my way."

Frank didn't say anything for a long time. Quentin didn't seem to be in a hurry, and Frank needed to process. Maybe they should just walk away. Leave Quentin to do whatever he was going to do. The world would certainly be better off without people like Carlos.

"Do you want a Coke?" Frank asked. Quentin looked at him and nodded.

Frank could see Veronica had turned around and was heading back, so he went to the cantina and ordered three Cokes. Walking back to the umbrella, he handed Quentin his and set Veronica's in the shade by the pole. After popping the tab, he took a long swallow. There was something amazing about cold sugar in the heat.

"Here's where I get stuck. I don't much have a problem with you sending Carlos off into the next world, but there are some loose ends in this one that don't sit well with me. If there is a legitimate link with the British Home Office, then that's a problem. It could be a big one, depending on who is involved and how much they know about Carlos." Frank took another gulp of his Coke. "Whether or not his British handler is a double agent, Carlos is clearly connected with more people than we realized. You and I both know he plays a lot of sides, and one of his biggest pieces of leverage at the moment has got to be Jillian. He doesn't know about the SIGINT setup, but he's got to be wondering why kidnapping her resulted in a visit from you."

"All the more reason to put a bullet in his head," said Quentin.

Frank looked at him. He wasn't sure about what he was getting himself into. "Fine. I'm not going to stop you. But I think it would be…prudent to wait until we find out if he's told anyone else about Jillian."

Quentin seemed to chew through the logic of Frank's proposal. "That's all you want?"

Frank smirked. "I'd say that's about all I'm going to get."

Quentin didn't say anything as Veronica walked up.

"Hi again," she said.

"I got you a Coke," Frank offered. "Quentin and I were just discussing how to handle the Carlos situation."

"And did you reach any conclusions?" she asked.

Frank let the silence hang.

"Yeah," Quentin said. "We both want to find out who he knows in the Home Office and how strong the relationship is."

Veronica sat down and put her shoes back on. "I've identified one of the other men in the photo. Colin Edwards, a career government press secretary, but I don't think he's the one who brought Carlos in. I have a couple of new avenues to explore next week."

"I take it you haven't found him yet," Frank said to Quentin, "given that you're still here."

Quentin shrugged. "I burned a few bridges last time, so it's taking me a little while."

Frank finished off his Coke before it got warm. "We'll keep on the photo. Since you're here on vacation, how do we get in touch with you?"

Quentin stood up. "I'll find you. Don't bother with the embassy. I'm not reporting in."

Frank watched him walk away, feeling the guy was both honest and enigmatic. It was going to be hell for Frank to work with him in any capacity.

"So," said Veronica, "did he tell you anything interesting?"

"Yes. We mostly talked about Berlin. And it was interesting, because it gave me a clue about his motivations." Frank decided to light another cigarette. "At the time, I couldn't figure it out. I knew why he'd found Jillian originally, and really it was just a shitty coincidence. But he kept turning up."

"And?" said Veronica.

"And I think he likes her." Frank paused. "Or something like that. I don't mean he's in love with her or any of that melodramatic shit, but I think her not dying became important to him. I think he's got a lot of baggage that he's trying to get rid of."

Veronica sat quietly for a moment. "This is all so different than I expected. I don't know what I expected, not really, but something more like cleaner sides. This is messy."

"That's why I like signals. They're usually far less ambiguous. The HUMINT stuff, messy comes with the territory."

"I get the impression that you trust him."

Frank shrugged. "I'm not very complicated. Plus, everything he's said, it makes sense to me. Not that I would've made the same decisions, but his story seems to hang together. But you don't have to trust him. He should earn that from you, and you need to decide if you want to earn it from him."

Frank took a long drag on his cigarette. "I think he's our best chance of finding Carlos. The more I think about it, knowing who Carlos deals with is important. If the Brits have a mole, I'm sure they want to know. But on a more personal level, Carlos hurt my employee, and if he tells anyone on the adversary team what went down, there's a good chance he could hurt her again, and ruin the operation I set up in Berlin. I'm telling you, it's a damn fantastic operation. I don't want Jillian to get hurt, and I don't want that op to get blown. So I say we try to find out if he's told anyone about her."

"Fair enough," Veronica said. "It seems pretty square in the intelligence mandate anyway, and developing a contact at the CIA would be useful for me career-wise."

"I should let you know," said Frank, "that Quentin plans to kill Carlos after we find the info we need. His whole reason for coming here is to put a bullet in Carlos's head. I don't think he's kidding about that."

Veronica stared out into the ocean. "I guess we'll deal with that when we have to."

"Yeah," said Frank, "I guess we will."

CHAPTER FOURTEEN

James decided to button up his coat. It had turned to whisky weather. Berlin was experiencing an early November cold snap.

He hadn't seen Jasminka in over a week. Partly that was on him. There'd been a change of leadership in his unit, and the new major had wanted to go over all the current planning and priorities.

But also, he thought she was out of town. The same light was always glowing through the curtains, which remained closed on her windows. They'd gotten into some easy habits. Drinks out. Evenings in. She had not, however, mentioned anything about leaving town the last time he'd seen her.

She didn't owe him any explanations, but the suddenness of it had swayed James. He was determined to do what he should have done weeks ago: try to figure out if he or Jillian was in any danger.

He saw Jasminka approaching from the other side of the street. The evenings were getting darker earlier now, and the warm lights from the restaurants cut the gloom. James didn't mind the change in season. No winter here was as bad as the dampness in Inverness, where he'd grown up, and the early nights just lent the city a different kind of excitement.

Jasminka crossed the street, checking both ways as she jogged across, a bright red scarf trailing from her neck and getting caught in the wind. James noticed his attraction hadn't subsided.

She stopped in front of him, close enough that he could see the freckles on her nose. He kissed her, hoping it wasn't for the last time.

"Yes," she said, leaning her forehead against his cheek. "I've missed that."

His heart thudded, but he ignored it. "Good trip, then?"

"No," she said, not moving.

He put his arms around her briefly before pulling her away. "Jasminka," he said. "I like you. I've had a better time with you than I've had in a while. But this isn't a city for blindly trusting people. You don't owe me any explanation, but so you know, I'm not asking because I'm a jealous lover. Is there anything about what you do that could become a problem for me?"

He had been expecting one of two reactions, either defensive confusion or a smile and attempt at reassurance. What he got was the most hopeful expression he'd ever seen.

"I guess that depends on what you consider a problem."

He didn't know what to say.

"Let's go for a walk, okay?" Jasminka said, cupping his cheek briefly before letting her arm fall to her side.

"Are you working for the Soviets?"

She smiled. "If I were, I would not confess to you."

"Are you in trouble?"

"Aren't we all? Come, please, let's walk."

He fell into step beside her, keeping his hands jammed in his coat pockets and wondering what the hell she was going to tell him. He now realized how much he'd wanted nothing to come of asking her. But here it was—something.

Neither of them spoke until they were along the Spree. The path along the river was quiet at this time of night. Even though the trees offered some protection, the wind whipping around deterred most people from strolling along its banks.

"I did not expect that something would happen with you and me," Jasminka said, breaking the silence, "but it did. So now I will tell you my story, and at the end, you can decide if you want to help me or not.

"In Belgrade I am a journalist. Most of what I've told you is true. My mother is American, and I spent a lot of time in New York growing up. Because my English is so good, I was able to take assignments for English language newspapers that wanted to report on Yugoslavia.

"Lately it has been good in Belgrade—and the rest of the country. People's lives are improving. More goods, more education. The Western journalists like us because we are not Soviet. We are like, I don't know, friendly Communism. Diet Communism. Tito works hard to present to the West that he is their friend, a first line of defense against the Soviets. We are not friends with Russia, not really, but Tito does a balancing act there, too, reminding them that we are also Communist and therefore not a threat.

"Over the years I made many friends. A few enemies, but not much. Yugoslavs, Serbians, we are very comfortable in the West, Amsterdam or London. I have traveled a lot. Maybe because of my mother, but I enjoy a lot of Western culture. I also love Serbia and the dream of Yugoslavia, although I fear what will happen when Tito dies."

"I became known as someone who had good contacts in the West, someone who understood Western values and interests."

Jasminka pulled her scarf tighter around her neck and paused for a moment before continuing.

"Last year I was approached by a group. Well, at first it was just one woman, but there were three of them living in Belgrade. They were all Russian. They had been in Belgrade many years, but they all still had family living in the Soviet Union. They...they collected stories from behind the Iron Curtain. Specific stories. Two were nuclear scientists working on the Yugoslavian energy program. They all had relatives working in nuclear power plants in the Soviet Union, one in Chernobyl and two in Leningrad. They were worried about the Soviet nuclear program—worried that corners were being cut. The pressure to deliver on time, and to never admit problems, meant that serious concerns were going ignored. They asked me to publish what they told me."

James was transfixed. "And did you?"

"I couldn't. It was all verbal and secondhand, and I couldn't corroborate any of it. Yugoslavia is relaxed compared to the Soviet Union, but the arm of Moscow reaches far. My editor refused. He said the Soviets would accuse us of publishing

Western propaganda and would pressure the Tito government to shut us down. He was right.

"I broke the news to them but stayed in touch. Eventually we became friends. I even shared the story with a couple of American journalists I know, but they were in a similar situation. Without any complementary information, even just someone else to go on the record, it's impossible to print."

"So how do I fit in?" James asked.

"I was hoping you could help me find someone who could offer proof, or even just a firsthand account. Something that would wake the world up to what the Soviets are doing with their nuclear power facilities."

James had about a million questions but decided to start with the obvious. "And what are the Soviets doing exactly?"

"Just over six months ago, at the plant near Leningrad, there was an accident. There was trouble with one of the reactors. It hadn't been built to the right safety standards, and the materials—not the uranium, but for the buildings, the structure—were too low cost. In the rush to do it on some bureaucratic schedule, they didn't use enough materials. The Soviets, you know, they'd rather have it done poorly than be late. Done poorly becomes someone else's problem. Done late means getting fired or worse.

"Anyway, the accident caused a major radiation leak. Leningrad is not so far from the border with Europe. Accidents there affect more than just the Russian population. But the Soviets, they have completely covered it up—not just from the West, but from their own people. No one has been evacuated from the villages close to the power plant, and my friend says that her cousin who works at Chernobyl has never heard of the Leningrad incident."

Jasminka paused and took a deep breath. "I want to be able to tell this story. I want to help the Russian people, because I think, after all they've been through with their leadership, they deserve it. But I also want to warn Europe. I don't think what happened in Leningrad is an isolated accident. All Soviet nuclear power plants are being built the same way. A big accident could send radiation all over the continent and affect millions of lives."

James believed her, believed that she was telling the truth as she knew it. But there were a few more things he didn't understand. "How did you find me? How did you end up living in the same building?"

Jasminka offered him a tentative smile. "I moved here because I thought that Berlin, given its unique situation, might be a place where I would have a chance of corroborating my story. When I first came, I stayed on a friend's sofa. I listened to the radio, and I found your broadcast. Many people listen to the British station, and many people like your show. I do. I like your voice.

"After a couple of weeks, I began to think, well, I know this is hard, but the way you speak about the little things, like the cafés you like in this city, it shows a real affection. But also, the way you speak about Scotland, the UK, or the West in general, it also shows love for that too. I felt like, on your show, you were so honest. That you are doing this all because you want to make the world a better place. I thought someone like that might be able to help me."

"And ending up in the flat one floor below?"

She shrugged. "I'm a journalist. I have friends, including one who wanted a break from taking pictures of cheating spouses. You are not that hard to find, and I did need a place to live."

They continued to walk along the river. The darkness overhead was almost complete, and the temperature continued to cool. James was trying to process everything she'd said. He didn't know how he felt about it. It was flattering that she liked his show. It was unnerving that she'd moved into his building because of it. As to the rest, even if he wanted to, he didn't know how he could help her.

"Jasminka," he said, "I'm not sure what you think I can do to help. Not that I'm offering, mind you; I still haven't processed that part. When you imagined finally asking me, what was it you thought I could do?"

Jasminka fingered the ends of her scarf. "Your broadcast, it reaches easily into East Germany, yes? That's why you do it. I…I was hoping that you could ask, on your show, for information. Those power plants in the Soviet Union, they employ thousands of people who have thousands of family and friends. Someone in East Germany must know something."

As far as a plan went, James thought it wasn't much. "Even if that's true, and I suppose it might be, you've listened to my show. It's music and popular culture. More importantly, I broadcast on behalf of the military. I can't just start asking for people to phone in with tips on accidents at Soviet nuclear facilities. My superiors would yank me off the air before I had a chance to finish."

Jasminka looked disappointed, whether at his reaction or the result, he wasn't sure.

"I'm sorry," he said. "But there isn't anything I can do to help you."

"I understand," she said. "My seeing you, it's not contingent on that help. I do like you. Now you know what I do."

They turned away from the river, making their way back to their building. Neither of them said much, and James still wasn't quite sure how to process what she'd told him. They said goodnight at her door, and he couldn't help feeling like he'd disappointed her.

"You could help her, you know. If you want to. You just have to get creative."

James stared at Jillian over his beer. He'd told her Jasminka's story, mostly to reassure her that there didn't seem to be anything to fear on that front. Jasminka didn't know about Jillian at all.

"I'm sure I don't know what you're talking about," he said.

Jillian held up her hands. "Look, if you don't want to get involved, I'm not going to pressure you. I know how broadcasting rock music is your way of creating change, and you don't like to stray too far from that. But to defend her, because I can tell you feel put out about being asked, you do care a lot about that wall coming down. You care about the people stuck behind it. It's not such a far leap to imagine that you'd be concerned about them all dying of radiation poisoning."

James took a long drink from his beer. "Well, I'm happy you've noticed all that. Why don't you tell me, then: how would

I go about helping her without getting demoted and sent home, or causing an international incident?"

He knew he was giving her the impression that he was in it for whatever crazy idea was going to come out of her mouth. But part of him, a small part he hadn't dealt with since talking to Jasminka, was curious about what could be done. He didn't want to do anything, but he was starting to wonder if that was a problem. He never did do anything, and he wasn't sure how far it had gotten him.

Jillian rested her chin on her hands. "Well, I haven't thought it all through or anything, given that you just told me the story. But you're in psychological operations. There has to be some technique you'd use."

"My type of psyops is more like what the advert agencies do. Trying to convince people to buy the brand."

Jillian leaned back in her chair, chewing on her lip. "There's this idea in cryptography—I won't get into the details of what any given country may or may not be doing about it—but it's called asymmetric encryption. Do you know what that is?"

James shook his head.

"Regular encryption is symmetric, meaning that the same code that you use to encrypt your message, someone else uses to decrypt it."

"You'll have to take me back to the beginning," he said, hoping that it wouldn't involve two thousand years of secret messages.

"That's how code-making and breaking usually work," Jillian began. "Say I want to send you a message like 'Meet me at the pub on Friday.' Then I use a substitution cipher where every letter moves forward three in the alphabet. So 'meet' becomes 'phhw.' That cipher is our key. I make sure that you have the key, so you can decrypt the message. If someone else intercepts it and they don't have the key, the message is meaningless. Now, a three-letter substitution cipher is pretty basic and easy to crack. The principle is the same as the German Enigma from the war. If Berlin sent a message to a U-boat, then the U-boat captain would look in his codebook for the key that the Navy was supposed to be using that day. Then he'd decrypt the message."

"Okay, I'm following you," James said, "although it doesn't seem to have anything at all to do with my situation."

Jillian smiled. "Are you in some sort of a rush? Anyway," she continued, "symmetric encryption has always been limited because of the need to share the same key. People in the business even a hundred years ago wished they could have two different keys."

"And?"

"And lately some cryptographers—actually at GCHQ, you should be proud—have been coming up with ways to do just that. It's called asymmetric encryption. Instead of needing to share a key, there are two keys, one to encrypt and one to decrypt. The one to encrypt is public. Let's say I want to receive secret messages. I share my public key with the world, and anyone can use it to encrypt a message. But the decryption key, that's private to me. I'm the only one in the world who has it. So people can send me messages privately knowing that no one else will ever read them."

James was starting to get interested. "How can that work? Why can't everyone just use the encryption key to reverse the process?"

"Because the keys are different. They're based on a mathematical function that can be done by a college student with a calculator in one direction, but would take multiple computers working for multiple lifetimes to reverse engineer. Like, for example, if I have two numbers, 195483 and 109502, it's pretty easy to multiply them together. But if I asked you which two numbers multiplied together make 21405779466, well, it would be near impossible for you to figure out the exact two numbers that I have in mind because there are so many combinations."

"That sounds interesting and all. I confess, I've never really thought that much about cryptography. But again, I'm not seeing the connection. You aren't expecting me to figure out one of these asymmetric things and broadcast that I'm after information, but wait, encrypt it first. That sounds even more likely to get me arse shipped home."

He could see Jillian start to get fidgety. He knew she wanted him to jump on her bandwagon, but Jillian had a tendency to rush in to help while hoping for the best. If he was going to do anything for Jasminka, he was damn well going to think it through.

"No, I wasn't going to suggest that. But it's the idea of it. Could you put out a message that somehow encourages people to send information back to you? See, the asymmetry doesn't have to be mathematical. I'm just using it as inspiration. In fact, the original story that I heard was that someone thought of it in relation to the telephone. Let's say I call you, and I want to tell you something really sensitive that I don't want anyone with a directional receiver to pick up. What you can do is introduce noise on the line, like a radio frequency. You record our conversation, but it has all this noise in it. Anyone listening to it can't tell what I'm saying. But it's no problem for you, because the noise is yours. You know what frequency it is, so you can remove it." Jillian jumped up and began to pace around the room. "Of course, we couldn't do that, I don't think because it's not about having a private call with you. I'm not talking about true encryption, just the idea of asymmetry."

"I'm not sure I'm after doing anything, actually."

Jillian turned. "You can't know that until you know what your options are. The reason you're choosing do nothing is because you can't figure out a way to do something that's not going to compromise your career."

James tipped his bottle at her. "Fair point."

"This situation is just a puzzle to be solved. Thinking of an option doesn't mean you have to do it, it just means you can make an informed decision."

"Am I just meant to let you spin your wheels for a bit?"

"Probably. I usually solve problems by talking them out, so feel free to jump in."

"Christ, then. Let me get another beer."

James stood up while Jillian continued to pace. He could hear her talking to herself. "Jasminka wants information on Soviet nuclear reactors, especially the one in Leningrad. Anyone in the East who might know something about it needs a way to communicate that to her without getting caught. So Jasminka has to be connected with the information source securely."

She turned to James as he sat back down on the sofa, "Your role, if you have one, is to make it known to potential information sources that there is a journalist who wants to share their stories. But how to make that happen?" she said, turning away again. "You couldn't overtly ask for people to phone in with information on the nuclear power plants. So what could you do?"

He was getting dizzy watching her. It was also instructive. All he'd managed to do was stew about it and feel sorry for himself over the fact that the first woman he'd liked in ages wanted something from him that he couldn't give. Jillian was taking the situation apart piece by piece, looking for the requirements, setting out the parameters, exploring the potential conclusions of each option. James realized he'd probably never given her enough credit for her analytical skills.

Finally she stopped pacing. "Jasminka is a journalist. All she's looking for is a lead, right?"

"Sounds about right, but I don't know much about it."

"What I mean is, she's not looking for you to giftwrap her a box of proof. So you're not looking for anyone who's willing to go double agent against the Soviets. The most she can expect from you is some clues on where to look."

"I take it then that gives you an idea."

"Yes," said Jillian, smiling. "Why don't you run a contest? Like that one you did on coming up with rock-and-roll lyrics about Communism. Something fun. And something that would happen around nuclear power plants, especially ones that have leaked radiation. I mean, I'm thinking of details on the fly here, but what about something like, 'Tell me about the weirdest animals you've seen and how they ended up like that'?"

James didn't say anything. He hadn't really expected her to come up with anything realistic.

Jillian started to warm up to her idea. "You could kick it off with a story about how Spider-Man is your favorite superhero. He's just a regular kid, with regular life problems, who gets bit by a radioactive spider. And voilà—superhero. Then maybe something about a mutant squirrel that you once saw around a power plant. It's great asymmetry. You're putting something out there that people can easily respond to, but only you know the exact signal you're looking for." She turned to James. "What do you think?"

"You want me to run a contest asking for descriptions of strange animals on the off chance someone listening writes in about some two-headed goat they saw wandering a field outside of Leningrad?"

Jillian shrugged. "Stranger things have happened. Look, the way I see it, most shots are long shots. Do you know how much intercept we have to collect to produce one useful report?"

James didn't say anything.

"Let's say Jasminka is right about Leningrad, that there was a problem with a reactor and a bunch of radiation was leaked. There are physical consequences for that. And someone will have noticed them. Probably a lot of someones—one of whom might have relatives in and around East Berlin, or spend time here."

"There's a lot of assumptions there."

"Of course there are," said Jillian, sitting back down on the sofa. "It may all be worthless, and you'll be inundated with stories of crazy creatures. But it won't be a waste of time. First, we'll probably get a good laugh. But second, you'll help Jasminka. I think the act of wanting to help is more important than the result."

James just looked at her for a moment. "You would," he said. "It's that kind of thinking that almost got you in a lot of trouble earlier this year."

"True. But it's also the thinking that saved a friend and brought her home. You have nothing to lose here and a lot to gain. I can tell you like her."

"Aye, and our relationship shouldn't be conditional on me sticking my neck out."

"It probably isn't," said Jillian, "at least in the short term. But in the long run, James, all great relationships are great because the value of the relationship is worth sticking your neck out."

Ah, Christ, he thought. *She might just be right about that.*

CHAPTER FIFTEEN

Frank stared at the pile of photocopies in front of him. A great Jesus stack of the history of embassy events from the cultural attaché. It hurt him to look at it. Back at HQ he would never have to confront unfiltered information like this. That was an analyst's job, and Frank had never been an analyst.

But here, out in the field, he was a jack-of-all-trades. Their mission was nebulous, and their leads were flimsy. No support was forthcoming, either from the RCMP at home or the embassy staff here. He and Veronica were it. And she was busy going through the personnel files related to Colin Edwards. That left him having to sort through a pile of what he knew would mostly be junk because there might be one piece of valuable information that would make the effort worth it. He had requested everything related to the events the embassy staff had attended at the invitation of the Nicaraguan government in the last year.

For weeks he had been sorting through the traffic coming out of the Ministry of Agriculture. Agriculture wasn't usually a high intelligence target, so neither the CBNRC nor RCMP was overly interested in the raw intercept. Frank had been slowly collecting more information on the December party based on the anomaly that Veronica had first identified.

It seemed elaborate, not that Frank knew anything about event planning. But one day it was shrimp cocktails and the next day it was chocolate fountains. Plans seemed to be switching, and he didn't know if it was poor planning or the changing whims of the minister.

The problem with the invoices had happened for a fourth time. The minister's secretary got chewed out by accounts payable, and the secretary chewed right back. Frank imagined she was waving her photocopy around while she yelled down the line.

Frank thought the first thing to do was to establish a pattern, which was why he'd requested the information on events Canadian embassy staff had attended, particularly the ambassador. What was the setup usually like? Was this time any different?

He'd also spent an hour with the person who organized events here. He'd learned more than he ever wanted to about flag protocols and the loaded territory that was the final menu.

What he realized after that, though, was that events were one area where embassies were vulnerable. They had to go to local businesses, as they couldn't put on one of the larger events in-house. All the different people involved—caterers, entertainment, linens, and all the people in and out on the day of—it all added up to a lot of vulnerable points.

Stretching that line of thinking, Frank assumed it was the same for the Nicaraguan Ministry of Agriculture. If there really were Sandinista sympathizers everywhere, then an event would be the ideal time to infiltrate and cause mayhem.

Frank wondered if that was the reason for all the switching. The secretary had a mandate to make sure the minister got what he wanted, but there was obviously someone leading the security mandate, which would include vetting all suppliers to make sure the event wasn't compromised.

Frank wasn't sure if what he had was a legitimate lead that he should spend time exploring. He'd never worked intelligence like this. Figuring out what was important and getting into a report somewhere had always been someone else's job. Unfortunately, his partner, despite her enthusiasm, wasn't that much more knowledgeable about what was worth following up on when it came to Nicaraguan cultural events.

Frank started reading menus from events past. He'd given Veronica enough lectures about intelligence requiring patience to find the needle in the haystack. He wasn't above exercising some of that patience himself. He wasn't looking for a smoking gun. He was looking for enough information for Veronica to write a report about possible concerns. They could give it to the ambassador. Anything related to the event would be his call anyway.

"So," said Frank, sitting across from Veronica, "find anything interesting?"

"What are you eating?" she asked.

"Jalapeño roasted peanuts. If I'd have known the Nicaraguans made these, I would've come down here years ago."

"They sound…unique."

"You know, I appreciate how you think you have to be nice to me all the time, but your tone betrays you, so don't bother. I don't need you to concur with my snack choices. Did you find out anything interesting about that party?"

Veronica pushed a stack of menu cards across the desk. "Did you know that the number-one dish our embassy serves to high-profile guests is lobster? They fly it in from Nova Scotia to showcase Canadian cuisine. Consequently, we often fly in a chef at the same time, although they're not hard to cook. You just stick them in a pot and wait for the screaming to stop."

"Well, it's better than serving poutine."

Veronica shook her head. "Nothing is better than poutine."

Frank raised a brow. "That's interesting. You usually have so much green shit on your plate, I would never have guessed that weakness."

Veronica blushed a little. "French fries, cheese curds, and gravy. No one can resist it."

"Did you discover it at McGill?"

She shook her head. "No, although I ate it religiously every Saturday night when I was there. But actually, my maternal grandmother, she makes it sometimes. It's important to her to pick up those cultural norms. She likes to try to fit in."

"Where's she from?" Frank asked.

Veronica paused for a moment. "Northern Quebec. She's Cree."

"So that's where you get your black hair."

"Yes. Among other things."

Frank stared at her for a bit. "Do you like making things difficult for yourself?"

"I'm not sure what you're talking about," Veronica said.

"I may not have much time for the RCMP, but I know what goes on there. They aren't well liked on reservations."

"Which I've never lived on."

Frank didn't say anything.

"I learned a few other interesting things," Veronica said, clearly wanting to change the subject. "Security for these dinners is a nightmare. There's the night of, with everyone engaging their own protective detail and the host making sure everyone coming and going is vetted, which is almost impossible. There are always last-minute staffing substitutions, especially for waitstaff. So security has to be on full alert.

"But there's also the prescreening—making sure the caterer won't poison the food or the florist isn't putting bugs in the vases. And they clear all the people doing setup to make sure they go where they're supposed to and don't wander off to take pictures."

Frank nodded. He'd thought the same.

"So as far as the event at the ministry is concerned, it's safe for us to assume the same concerns. They have to be worried on two fronts: the usual international espionage angle, but also antigovernment groups. It's subtle, but I'm getting the feeling that support for the Sandinistas is growing, mostly by the fact that no one wants to talk about it. Anyway, high-profile events are attractive for precisely that reason. Anything goes down, and the attention will be easily focused. The only place we have to start with are these missing invoices. As you said before, it could be nothing, just something the ministry has set up uniquely for this event."

Frank munched on a few more peanuts. "You aren't telling me anything I don't already know."

"I realized that, as you constantly remind me," Veronica said, "we aren't doing a criminal investigation. We don't have to figure out exactly what is happening. The real question for us is if there is a legitimate explanation for what is going on with the invoices. First, I called the ministry and said I was from Cinqo florists and that I had an invoice to submit. I said I'd been dealing with the secretary—whose name is Carmen, by the way. I was directed to send the invoice directly to her. She makes a copy for the minister and then sends it on to accounts payable. They coughed this up when I expressed a big panic about not getting paid.

"So there should only ever be two copies of the invoices, which means somewhere in between Carmen and accounts payable, someone is possibly intercepting them and making a copy.

"Then I asked our cultural attaché Sally to make a call. I got her to call that C. Fuentes in accounts payable and say we were waiting for an invoice to get paid. Of course, there is no invoice, but since we want to know the routing anyway, she asked a bunch of questions, trying to determine where our invoice went astray. The Nicaraguan Ministry of Agriculture has a hub-and-spoke mail service for the building, like most big government offices. Anything that gets mailed internally gets sent to the mailroom and then redistributed.

"Thus, I conclude that if someone is making a copy of the invoices, they work in the mailroom. Which, if you think about it, we could have inferred without going to all this trouble. No one pays attention to the people who work in the mailroom, and they have access to the whole building."

Frank was nodding. "Them and cleaning staff. The perfect positions for spies." He stood up and started walking around the room. "You did good work. Now we have some decisions to make."

"Such as, do we try to get into that mailroom?"

"No," Frank said. "Right now that's not our primary interest. I'm thinking we have enough to get CBNRC interested in the intercept. We have reason to believe that the ministry has at least one vulnerability working in the building. There's enough overt anti-Somoza press that it's not hard to imagine thousands of invisible people supporting it. So it's not as much about lemons as it is getting a handle on when things are going to explode down here, which they most likely are. When is the party?"

"December 28," Veronica said.

"It's not enough time to rely on the analysts to produce anything. The next question is what to tell the ambassador."

"That we think something is going to go down at that party?"

Frank shook his head. "We don't have enough to make that supposition."

"But if Canadians are going to attend," Veronica said, "don't we have to say something?"

"No," said Frank. "We don't."

"Is that ethical?"

"It's not about ethics. It's about protecting the source." Frank sat back down and decided to light a cigarette. "Before you get all knotted up, I'll tell you that situations like this are why we're going to separate intelligence from policing at the RCMP, like the rest of our allies do. The way we're doing things isn't sustainable because sources keep getting compromised to support prosecutions, and pretty soon we're going to be out of sources."

"I've heard whispers of that around the building."

"I'm not surprised. But back to our situation here, which is a microcosm of the larger problem. The ambassador, like most people, is going to want proof. The good news is, I don't think an agricultural party is the highest profile of events. But still, it's a big deal. So for the Canadian delegation not to show and risk getting cut out or offending Somoza, well, the ambassador's going to want a good reason."

"Which we can't give him."

"Exactly. Right now we have a guess. To give him something concrete would have you and Phillip out there working every possible Sandinista connection we have. Which, given the timeline, isn't reasonable and not a good use of agents. Confirmation is unlikely. The most we're going to get is a moderate probability. If nothing happens, then we look like fools. The ambassador doesn't trust us again."

"But if we say nothing to him, or don't follow up where we can," Veronica said, "and something does go down, and the ambassador gets shot, and there's even an inkling we could have prevented it—"

"Prevented what, exactly?" Frank asked. "If you think about it, if something does go down and the Canadians are the only ones who aren't there, that's going to be very suspicious. In all the red flags that get raised as a result, there's a very legitimate chance our sources would be compromised. In the long run, that does no one any good at all."

"I don't know, Frank."

"Veronica, listen to me. The ambassador isn't going to be satisfied with an off-the-record statement that the upcoming event could be compromised. He's going to want to know why we think that. All we have right now is the thinnest supposition that someone in the mailroom is making a copy of a bunch of invoices related to that party. Saying it out loud makes me feel ridiculous. If I were working in that mailroom, why would I bother making a copy? Why wouldn't I just memorize the information and pass it on verbally?"

"You don't think it's worth trying to find out?"

Frank shrugged. "I'm not your boss. If you want to try to gather more intel, I'm not going to stop you. But I do think it's important that we step back and remember what we're doing here."

"Finding sources of information relevant to our agencies."

"Exactly. Not exploiting those sources the first chance we get to find out more about a party hosted by the Minister of Agriculture. Our situation here isn't mature enough—I mean yours and mine. You've done good work. We've validated a feed. Let's make the arrangements to get the intercept shipped home, pass on what we know to the defense attachés, and let them go to their agents if they want."

Veronica didn't look happy, but Frank didn't care. He thought it was important to focus on the bigger picture and not get sidetracked by one-offs. Knowing more about the party wasn't going to help the overall intelligence position here.

"What do we do now?" she asked.

"Same thing we were doing yesterday: look for sources and try to find the Cuban."

"Which are your priorities."

Frank shrugged. "You want to make a case for knowing more about that party, go ahead. So far you haven't."

Veronica was silent for a moment. "Fine. But gathering intelligence requires sources. My analysis of your SIGINT intercept suggests that there is a security compromise in the mailroom of the Ministry of Agriculture. If I were going to stay in Nicaragua, that would be a place to start developing my own agents. Because I don't know how long I'll be here, it's a missed opportunity if I ignore it."

"Right," said Frank. "A learning opportunity. It's not like you don't need the practice. If you screw it up and make them nervous and they call the whole thing off, well, then your conscience will be clear. You won't have compromised anyone but yourself."

"When you put it that way."

"That's the only way to put it. It's also not a terrible idea. Now"—Frank checked his watch—"I've got a call with GCHQ."

Veronica looked up. "A call? Are they sending a report?"

"They'll send something," Frank said. "I've got a lot of friends there, a couple of whom want to share some impressions that they aren't...comfortable putting into a report."

"Frank, it's been a while."

"Kelvin, good to hear from you." Frank was using the embassy's STU, the secure phone. The room that housed it was cramped on account of the size of the machine, but Frank was grateful for the ability to talk freely with one of his old colleagues at GCHQ.

They chitchatted briefly, filling each other in on the basic life updates. Kelvin was surprised to hear that Frank was in the field.

"How long has it been since you were out setting up the feeds themselves?" Kelvin asked.

"Not so long that I don't remember how it's done. You know what else? It's damn great to have a break from the bureaucracy. Makes me wonder why I ever went into management."

"Isn't that the truth. The further up you go, the further you get from the signals." Kelvin sighed. "Anyway. Thanks for calling me. I know it's not easy on those embassy STUs."

"It's no problem. I understand, not all information is good for reporting."

"We got your official request: any collection we might have done on a Carlos Honouras, dating back to the mid-1960s. Based on your information, your request got routed to the

Soviet desk. But they farmed it out, given that your guy seems to have been active in a lot of places. Now, normally I'd never see a request like this because I'm not usually bothered with intelligence requests. But with your name on it, a couple people got curious. You remember Dave from that satellite project we worked on? Well, he's running the entire intelligence portfolio now. Don't ask me why they've put an access guy in charge of the analysts. Something about wanting to make us more well-rounded."

Frank snorted. "I know. We spend twenty years building specialized knowledge but then can somehow transition to leading anyone."

"The HR department has to have something to do. Anyway, Dave sent me your request. Thought I could poke around for old times' sake. You'll be receiving a report that says Carlos Honouras became an official target of ours in 1964 at the request of MI6. He's got nothing to do with signals, so we've never been interested in him on our own account. The report is also going to tell you that we stopped targeting him in 1972 because he was no longer a person of interest."

"I'll tell you, Kelvin, it's starting to make me uncomfortable, all the places this guy keeps popping up. Do you know if your targeting overlapped with NSA's?"

"It looks like it. Theirs started in '70. Maybe '69."

"What I don't understand," Frank said, "is how a mercenary thug from Cuba became so interesting. My American contacts tell me that he popped up on their radar due to destabilizing activities in Nicaragua in the early '70s. But then he went to the Soviets, which is no surprise on account of both the Cuban and

Nicaraguan connection to Russians. It all seems like a typical story until you factor in that he was at a Home Office dinner in London in 1969. How'd he even get close to that?"

"I can't tell you that because I don't know," said Kelvin. "What I did want to tell you, which is not going to make it into the report, is that all MI6 requests came from Gavin Hoffsteader. Now, Gavin is an interesting guy. English dad, German mum. Grew up in the SOE during the war before moving over to MI6. Spent most of the '50s and '60s in West Germany. He's now Sir Gavin Hoffsteader. The reason he was knighted is publicly given as providing services to the crown, which is what everyone says. The real reason was his aggressive pursuit of ex-Nazis. He went after them with a vengeance."

Frank hadn't been expecting that. "Anything else you can tell me about him?"

"Nothing you can't find out from reading back issues of the *Times*. I'll save you the trouble and let you know that he's in that picture—the man beside Colin Edwards. And before you ask, no, we have no immediate idea who the fourth man is."

Frank sat back in the uncomfortable chair wedged in beside the STU, processing everything Kelvin had just told him.

"Hoffsteader, would he be close with Colin Edwards?"

"Anything's possible," Kelvin said. "Hoffsteader probably knows a lot of people. But I wouldn't think that connection would tell you much. Edwards is a career press secretary. Works at 10 Downing now. Events and photos are his job."

"Did Hoffsteader ever work in Cuba?" Frank asked.

"No. Strictly in West Germany."

"So the fourth guy," said Frank, musing out loud, "he has to be the connection between Honouras and Hoffsteader. Who would he have to be to connect a Nazi-hunting peer of the realm with a Communist sympathizing recruiter for hire?"

"Sounds like you have your work cut out for you on that one."

"You're telling me."

"Well, Frank, I'll keep digging in my spare time. I can send something through to MI6 and see if anything's shareable. But something about Hoffsteader—he's pretty…notorious in the community over here. Yes, he tracked down a lot of Nazis, and that's wonderful. But he made a lot of questionable allegiances to do it. Now, I'm not judging him, but Hoffsteader, he'd work with anyone if it meant bringing in a Nazi. Even other adversaries."

"Because of where he worked, I'm assuming you mean East Germans?"

"And Soviets," Kelvin said. "Hoffsteader is a 'the enemy of my enemy is my friend' kind of guy. That could be your connection."

"Where is Hoffsteader now?"

"Ostensibly retired."

"But you don't think so?"

"Blokes like that don't ever retire."

Frank smiled. "I guess they don't."

CHAPTER SIXTEEN

"Well?" asked Jillian.

"The results are in," said James, "and you've won the honor of helping me sort the entries."

"I seem to be doing a lot of sorting these days." She sighed.

"You intelligence types, always looking for the needle in the haystack." He dumped a pile of mail on the table. "Well, here's your haystack."

Jillian looked at the pile. There were easily a couple hundred letters. "Wow," she said. "I really wasn't expecting you to get so many entries."

"I think we can rest assured that most of them are barmy lies. The first one I opened swears they saw a red zebra whilst on safari in Kenya."

"Like I said, at the very least we get some entertainment out of it."

James had taken her advice and run a contest asking about weird animals that people had seen. He had prefaced his contest with the story of Spider-Man being bitten by a radioactive spider. He was smooth. Jillian had listened the day he launched the contest. He'd easily woven in the idea that radiation can do crazy things to animals. No one listening would be suspicious about why he was asking. But maybe, just maybe, someone had a true story to share about radiation poisoning.

Jillian picked up the first letter within reach and opened it. "'There is a place in the Black Forest," she read, "where the trees have stunted limbs that look like human hands and feet so it seems that whole bodies have become stuck in the trunks and are pushing to get out.'"

She put down the paper. "Wow. That would be creepy."

"I'm sure where you now want to go when you next get some time off," James said.

"It would be interesting to see." Jillian shrugged, picking up the next letter.

They spent two hours going through submissions. There was a seven-toed cat, picture included, as well as someone who was convinced the platypus they saw in Australia couldn't be real. Three people so far had written in asking for advice on how to find a radioactive spider because they thought being Spider-Man would be exciting.

"Contests, you know," James said, "are great for developing psyops. The range of responses you get, the connections that people make, gives a huge insight into how the mind works. Like this one, for example: 'My older brother likes to dress up in black and sneak around and spy on the people in our building. Sometimes I think he must have been exposed to some chemical that I wasn't, because he's very weird and sometimes I'm not sure he's human.' From a kid, sure, but it just goes to show how subjective most of our understanding of the world is."

James made them each a cup of tea as they continued to work through the pile. It wasn't a bad way to spend a Sunday afternoon.

"Oh, James," Jillian said. "Listen to this one: 'If Spider-Man was real, he would be from Leningrad.'"

James stared at her. "No bloody way."

Jillian looked up. "What?"

"No bloody way your bizarre plan worked. Is there contact info on that?"

Jillian checked the envelope. "No name, no address either. Just a phone number."

James took the letter from Jillian and sat back on the sofa. "What are the chances?"

"I'm not sure. But sometimes this stuff does work. I mean, if there really was a problem in Leningrad months ago, there would be quite a few people to know about it. Most of them probably want to talk about it, but none of them can."

"I didn't think it would work, you know," James said, shaking his head. "Your ideas, I guess because of your track record, I default to dismissing them. And I shouldn't. I've seen you pass electricity through a potato to show some bloke what you could do to his balls."

Jillian started a little at the memory but didn't say anything.

"What I'm trying to remember," James continued, "is when I stopped trying. Psychological operations, you know, there's a lot of trial and error there as well. Maybe not as much as in intelligence, but enough. You don't always know what story or what image is going to resonate. It's often hard to get the feedback to improve. But I used to work a lot harder than I do now. Ach, maybe I'm just getting old."

"Isn't that the value of experience, though?" Jillian asked. "That you get better at knowing what to do?"

"I got content. I'm not sure I got better." He stood up. "Let's get through the rest of them, then. I'll give what we've got to Jasminka and let her thank me."

"Does she know what you did?"

"We haven't talked about it, but she listens to the show often enough. I just didn't want her to be expecting anything."

"I'm sure journalism involves turning over a lot of stones and never expecting the first one you look under to be the one you were looking for."

"Is there a career in the world that doesn't require perseverance?"

Jillian smiled. "Not one I could imagine doing."

"Right, then. Did you want to meet her?"

"Maybe one day. For now, I'll let you have this moment to yourself. Just in case she wants to thank you in ways that would make me blush."

James grinned. "Aye, I'm damn well counting on that."

James checked himself over in the mirror. Jasminka would be here any moment, and he was strangely nervous. What set him even more on edge was that he knew why. Running that contest for her, that was about as big a declaration as he'd ever made. It scared him that he'd done it.

He wasn't used to wondering what would happen when they stopped wanting to be with each other. He knew they'd get there in the end, and usually he counted on it. Knowing there was an end made the rest of it interesting. He didn't want to think about the end with Jasminka.

He heard her knock at the door and gave his shirt a final adjustment. There wasn't much to be done with the rest of it, and he supposed she liked him how he was.

Trying to pre-empt another knock, he crossed quickly through the living room. The cushions were neat, the sauce on the stove making the place smell great. It was too bad his heart was pounding so hard in his chest. Otherwise, everything would be perfect.

Maybe he shouldn't have done it. Maybe he should have let her be disappointed in him and let the rest fade away. It was too late now.

"Hi," James said, opening the door. He took in her blue blouse and gray pants and her hair falling around her shoulders. "You look lovely."

"And you," Jasminka said, stepping inside. "You look like you got dressed up for me."

"It's the problem with wearing a uniform all the time," James said. "I've got these clothes that just sit in the closet otherwise."

"Well, you look lovely too." She smiled.

He took her coat, hanging it up in the hall closet and wondering why it was so hard for him to speak. Best to get on with it, then.

"Right. Would you like a drink?"

"A whisky would be nice."

He poured them both a scotch before settling in beside her on the living room sofa.

"Before, when you asked me to help you with finding someone who knew about the power plant in Leningrad…"

Her eyes widened a little as she nodded.

"Well," James continued. "I didn't think I could, because my role, it's too public, and I didn't think I could do anything that would be of much good. But then a friend of mine, well, she's the kind of woman who thinks there is a solution to every problem. Maybe she's right. Regardless, she came up with a plan to do something. It's based in some story she heard about disguising telephone conversations, but that's not the point."

James took a deep breath, feeling like he was getting off track. "Right, then. That bit doesn't matter. Anyway, to get to the point of it, I ran this contest on air, telling people about Spider-Man, ye know, that American comic book character who gets bit by a radioactive spider. Then I asked people to write in about the strangest animal they'd ever seen—so strange that they must have been exposed to radiation like Spider-Man."

Jasminka was staring at him. "Yes, I heard this on your show. You do contests a lot?"

"Aye. They're quite popular."

"It was fun, the results?"

"Some of them were right bizarre." He looked at her, wondering why he was having such a hard time getting it all out. "But that's not why I'm on about it right now. The idea that we had is that someone who knew something about the radiation leaks at Leningrad, someone who wanted to talk, might understand this as an opportunity to share what they know."

"Oh," Jasminka said.

"And, well, I got two responses you might find interesting. I'm not sure. There's a high chance they're probably nothing, but I figure you're used to following up leads that don't pan out."

The surprise was all over her face. "You did this for me?"

James was quiet for a moment. "Aye, partly. And partly because if you're right, the Soviets shouldn't be covering that shite up." He passed her the two letters that he'd left on the coffee table. "These are for you, and you can do with them whatever you want. If you want to talk to me, that's fine, but I'm not the type of bloke who needs to be knowing all the details of everything you do."

Jasminka opened up each letter and carefully read the contents. He could see her eyes light up with the excitement of new avenues to explore. As she looked them over, he took a deep drink of whisky to settle his nerves. There was nothing to be done about it at the moment. He liked her a lot.

She set the letters back on the coffee table and turned to him. "This is wonderful. It was so…kind of you to do this for me."

James was suddenly uncomfortable. "Well, I thought it was a good cause."

"Yes, you said that."

"It wasn't hard. It worked fine with my job. It was time to run another contest. Jillian and I had a good laugh at the others. I'm thinking the winner is going to be this one about a two-headed fish."

"I must be thanking your friend then as well."

"Ah well, that's true. She was the one who came up with it. To be honest, I didn't think it would work at all."

"Yet you did it."

He couldn't take his eyes off her. The space between them was becoming inconvenient.

"I did. Jillian, she was on about how it's the effort that counts. More than the result."

"She sounds very wise."

Not how James would describe her, but he was having a hard time thinking about anything with Jasminka staring at him like he was a better man than he knew he was.

"It was just something to try. Once we figured it out, it was easy. I didn't have anything to lose." Except that right at this moment, he thought that more had been on the line than he wanted to admit.

She leaned forward. "You are such a wonderful man that you tried."

How long he was going to let her believe that, he wasn't sure. But he wasn't going to try to change her mind tonight. He closed the remaining distance between them, settling his lips over hers. She wrapped her arms around him, pulling him against her.

She felt good. Everything about her felt good.

"James," she sighed into his ear.

He couldn't think anymore. Not a damn coherent thought. It was all sensation, all about how she felt. His hands were restless. He wanted to touch her everywhere. He thought he should slow down, but he didn't want to. She was all but vibrating against him. All he knew at this moment was that his body ached to be with her so badly he thought it might ruin him eventually.

Her fingers began to fumble at the buttons on her blouse, and he tried to take that chore from her, but he couldn't get his hands to stop touching the rest of her. What was building inside him was agony, but he dimly realized that he was rushing to a relief that might be short-lived.

CHAPTER SEVENTEEN

Frank sat on the little balcony smoking a cigarette. He was churning through information, thinking through his options. Veronica was off honing her IO skills, approaching Ministry of Agriculture workers and trying to develop an agent. He thought the party wasn't where they should be focusing their efforts. It was possible that something was going to go down at that party, but he wasn't convinced it was something he should care about. He supposed Veronica was interested because it was the first tangible thing they'd found here and thus more compelling than the traffic they were collecting about produce.

He was intrigued by the MI6 angle with Gavin Hoffsteader. With his signals background, Frank had a hard time understanding how Hoffsteader could have worked with Carlos. He understood it was possible, but it was territory that was difficult for Frank to appreciate. In SIGINT, the lines were clear. Sharing within the UKUSA community was fairly easy.

Sharing outside that select group of countries was hard, bilateral, and involved fifteen layers of approvals.

Carlos couldn't just be some agent in the field. He and Hoffsteader had developed enough of a rapport that he'd been invited to a Home Office dinner.

Frank inhaled and tried to think it all through. Not all mysteries needed to be solved. He didn't particularly care how Hoffsteader and Carlos got along. Frank thought it reasonable that the two were connected by the last unidentified man in the picture, a man that both Hoffsteader and Carlos would work with.

Frank's only real concern was if Carlos was still in contact with the unknown man, and if that man was in a position to harm either Jillian or the CBNRC operation in West Berlin.

Since he wasn't going to fly to London to interrogate a peer of the realm, Frank figured he was still on the original mission he came down here for: Find Carlos. Assess where his loyalties lay. Determine the potential impact to Canadian interests.

It was too bad he couldn't get anyone else to agree with him on that.

The embassy just wanted him to find new signals—which, to be fair, was all he'd told them anyway. Veronica had become obsessed with this party, certain that it was her job to verify the particulars. It sounded more like detective work than intelligence work to him, but he knew he wouldn't be able to convince her of that.

He wondered, if she did find out anything concrete, what they were going to do about it anyway? Would Veronica be able to make the decision to ignore the information in order not to compromise a source? Anything that was going to go down at a diplomatic party was going to be high profile anyway. The whole world would probably end up knowing what was going on.

He would just have to wait to see what was going to pan out.

The beer was cold, the music entertaining. Frank had made his way to a bar he'd discovered a few days earlier. It was on a side street, small and off the beaten track. He stood out a little, but no one seemed to care. It was about a fifteen-minute drive, but Frank didn't mind hiring a car for the back and forth.

After about an hour, Frank watched Quentin slide into the seat across from him.

"Nice to see you," Frank said.

Quentin gave him a wry smile before taking a sip of the Coke he'd bought before sitting down.

"This band," said Frank, "it's the second time I've seen them. They're good."

"The music here, it's usually good," offered Quentin. "Better than the Germans."

Frank smiled. "Better than the Soviets too."

"So," he continued, "found Carlos yet?"

Quentin took another quick drink of Coke. "Partly."

Frank merely raised a brow. The questions were obvious.

"The upside is he's here in Managua. The downside is I can't get anywhere near him. The locals are up to something—something big. There aren't many people willing to talk, even about the weather."

Suddenly Frank realized maybe Veronica pursuing this ministry party wasn't such a waste of time.

"We've identified another man in the Home Office picture," Frank said.

Quentin looked at him with interest. The questions were obvious there too.

"Sir Gavin Hoffsteader. Ex-MI6. Knighted for Nazi-hunting services to the queen."

"Jesus," Quentin said. "You're sure?"

"Yes. I got it from an old friend of mine at GCHQ. When I looked up pictures of Hoffsteader in the *Daily Mail*, well, even with a few more years on the face, it's a match."

"Anything else?"

"Only what I'm sure you've inferred. We've got one unidentified man left, one who somehow connects a Nazi-hating Englishman with a for-hire Cuban revolutionary. There can't be too many stories that will explain that."

"What are you thinking?" Quentin asked.

"Well, GCHQ told me that Hoffsteader made many, shall we say, questionable alliances in his pursuits. I assume Carlos was one of them, maybe through his links to the East Germans. Common enemies and all that."

Quentin seemed to ponder for a bit. "So this fourth guy, he's unlikely to be British?"

"That's my guess," Frank said. "My money's on German. Which side of the Wall, I'm not sure."

"Whoever he is, he could also be the one who brought Carlos to Berlin."

Frank shrugged. "Sure. He could also be a paper pusher in Leipzig or some officer they have out looking for Nazis in Argentina."

Quentin looked like this was all suddenly too painful for him. "Fuck." He sighed. "And the British don't know who he is?"

"GCHQ doesn't know because Carlos was their target. That's it. But MI6 obviously knows. They're your friends, aren't they?"

Quentin laughed, but there was no amusement in it. "I'm supposed to be on vacation."

Frank didn't say anything for a while. "While you're figuring out how to request information about a British knight while you're ostensibly supposed to be working on your tan, I think I know what's up with the locals, as you put it."

Quentin waited for Frank to continue.

"My partner, Veronica, has uncovered some indications of a big shindig hosted by the Minister of Agriculture at his house."

"And?"

"And she thinks the locals are planning to crash the party."

"That makes sense."

"You knew?" Frank asked.

Quentin shook his head. "No. Like I said, people are tight-lipped, and I don't have that many friends here anymore. But I have been hearing whispers—not even—about needing to take the fight with Somoza to the world. Those ministry parties, they don't just invite Nicaraguans. High-profile guests means high-profile coverage."

"Do you think Carlos might be involved?"

"I have no idea." Quentin shrugged.

Frank raised a brow.

"Seriously." Quentin almost smiled. "I know a lot about him, but I don't have some psychic connection with him. For all I know, he came back because he missed his aunt's cooking."

"Who pays Carlos's travel expenses?" Frank asked.

"Castro. But he sends invoices to the Soviets."

"Do the Soviets finance the Sandinistas?"

"Can't you get that from intelligence reporting?"

It was Frank's turn to shrug. "I can get it easier from you."

"Fine. Yes, there's some money flowing. Not directly, for the most part. The Soviets let Castro spread it around. Sandinistas get money and guns from Cuba, and they also go there for military training."

"I guess we should be hoping Carlos is here helping the Soviets."

"As opposed to eating empanadas in his family's kitchen?"

"As opposed to working for some mysterious, probable German who has ties to MI6."

Quentin finished off his Coke. "Yes, that would complicate things. Any indication that Carlos was an agent of Hoffsteader's directly? Or was it always through the mystery man?"

"I don't think GCHQ knows. Those are operational details. The kind of stuff you should put in your information request to MI6."

"Right. I suppose I can find someone to do that favor for me."

"In the meantime, we'll keep on about that party."

"How did you find out about it?"

"The party is public knowledge. The rest of it through old-fashioned signals and associated analysis. The underappreciated part of intelligence."

"You sound just like Jillian."

Frank hadn't expected that.

"By the way," Quentin said, "you should tell your partner to watch her back. I've confirmed Carlos is in Managua, and sooner or later he's going to hear about this supposed ex-lover who's out looking for him. You and I both know he's not a nice guy."

"I did fill her in on what he did to Jillian. I don't need him to kidnap anyone else who works for me."

Quentin stood up. "I'd remind her anyway. She keeps asking about him, he's going to get curious. And then he's going to get nasty."

"All the more reason to find him soon."

Quentin gave Frank a nod, then left the bar.

Frank sat there rubbing his temples and wondering if he should get another beer. Signals were so much easier. Tap a communication line, collect the traffic, do the analysis, produce a report. Most of which could be done from the relative safety of headquarters. Granted, the machine that collected and produced SIGINT was complicated, but it was linear. This IO shit was complex. Dangling all these threads, seeing who would bite, never telling the whole story to anyone—it made one vulnerable.

Frank hoped he was doing the right thing. Beyond the mandate, he hoped he'd made the right decision in bringing

Veronica here. She had no field experience, and they were up against someone who'd been working and manipulating in this territory for years. Frank knew Carlos was bad news. He'd kidnapped Jillian, for Christ's sake. Locked her up for four days and beat the shit out of her. All because he suspected she was an agent for the CIA or MI6. Five seconds looking into Veronica, and he was going to think the same thing about her. Except here was his territory. Here, Carlos had all the leverage.

He needed to have a talk with Veronica about how to proceed. And it had to be cautiously.

Frank got to the office early. He waved at Mark, who was on the phone, as he sat down with his coffee. He hadn't slept well. The air conditioner in his unit was temperamental, and last night it didn't show up for their date.

As he waited for Veronica to come in, he realized that was one thing that needed to change. He should have a better idea of what she was planning to do each day. She needed a schedule. When Jillian went missing, it took them four days to find out. He hoped there wasn't a next time with Carlos, but if there was, Frank wanted to have an earlier indication that things were going tits up.

Frank turned to Mark as he got off the phone. "What's Phillip up to these days?" He was too grumpy for chitchat.

"The same thing he's up to every day. Developing contacts. Looking for information."

"Yes, but on what exactly? How often do your priorities get updated?"

"The mothership updates them every three months." Mark laughed. "With only two of us here, there isn't a whole lot we can cover. I take the embassy files, which is essentially keeping on top of what everyone else is doing down here, who's supporting who, so if the military ever ends up on Nicaraguan soil, we have a good idea of what presence or interventions other countries might make. Phillip tries to get a handle on the Somoza government, what its plans are, who's on the friend list, the ever-evolving list of enemies. Again, so if we send our troops down, we have some idea of the environment they'd be operating in."

"How much does Phillip pursue relationships that are outside the Somoza government?"

"A little bit, and very cautiously. But it's important. Information from one source, information that you can't corroborate, is unreliable. Somoza lies all the time. If we relied on official information, we'd think this place was Shangri-la—which, as I'm sure you've noticed, it isn't. Phillip isn't covert. He's not looking to infiltrate anything or do any disruption. He isn't in so close with anyone that he's got the Sandinista passcodes for the next six months. He's just a Canadian embassy worker, a low-level diplomat, sympathetic to the cause of democracy. He's careful, because he has to work both sides. But if you want to know what's really happening in Nicaragua, you have to make friends outside the Somoza government."

Frank mulled this over. Sometimes being a defense attaché was a cover for intelligence officers, but not in this case.

Mark and Philip were true defense attachés, at the embassy to represent military needs and priorities.

That meant there was a gaping hole. CBNRC collection was thin. RCMP didn't have anyone until Veronica showed up. And that meant there wasn't anyone looking to develop an intelligence presence here. He felt briefly irritated that Nicaragua was so neglected but knew that it was because Canada was small and so had to divide and specialize.

The Soviets and their Iron Curtain sucked the life out of everyone and didn't leave room for much else. Canada was all over Cuba but didn't have capacity to have the same coverage all over the region, so it relied on American coverage of Nicaragua.

Frank sighed. It was time to go to the Americans.

"Feel like coming to the American embassy?" Frank asked Mark.

"I always like getting out," Mark said. "Any particular reason?"

"I need to talk to someone in the CIA. I want to know if they have any interest in the Ministry of Agriculture."

"Agriculture? Is that on anyone's priority list?"

"The Minister of Agriculture is hosting a fancy party at his personal residence next week with a very high-profile guest list. I'm curious if it's on the CIA's radar for any reason."

"Why is it on yours?" Mark asked.

"You know their phone lines run over our roof, so I was able to tap them. Veronica and I have been dipping into some of the conversations so I can give CBNRC an intelligence estimate. They're talking about this party a lot, more than you'd think for a suit-and-gown dinner hosted by Agriculture. But, you know, I don't get invited to parties that often."

Mark rubbed his chin. "Sure, a trip to see the Americans is always fun. But Frank, if this party is on their radar, they aren't going to tell you until after it's over."

"What other choice do I have? Plus, Veronica should get to know her counterparts."

"There's probably about fifteen of them." Mark smiled. "Not that they'll admit it to us. They'll probably send in the junior one to meet with you."

Frank sat back in his chair, nursing his coffee. "You know, it's a mystery to me why human intelligence operatives are so difficult to deal with. I've said it a million times. Information is only useful if you can get it to someone who can do something with it."

"Why don't you set it up to talk SIGINT?" Mark said. "They might have someone from NSA on-site. But unless you have any information to exchange, I can't see any of them jumping at the chance to share anything with you."

Frank thought for a minute. "Except if the party is on their radar, we've got a full, unencrypted copy of some high-level discussion at the ministry. A lot of traffic we haven't been able to go through."

"Not to be a killjoy, but are you authorized to share raw traffic, even if it is with the Americans?"

Frank scowled. "That's exactly my point. I have a lot of traffic that I can't do anything with. This party is not a priority for CBNRC analysis, and the RCMP has already got one IO on it, which is all we've got. But if the CIA is interested, it's better than that traffic going to waste."

"How much do you care about them looping you into what they find?"

"None at all, unless some Sandinistas are planning to assassinate everyone who attends. In that case, I care enough to warn our ambassador."

"What's your angle here, Frank? Why try to engage with them at all?" Mark asked.

Frank hesitated. He didn't want to tell Mark about Carlos. Not unless he had to. "Look, there's a large chance nothing at all is going to happen at that party except a bunch of diplomats drinking too much and puking in the bushes. But we have this slim possibility that's not the case. We also don't have the access to verify our hunch either way. The CIA is better positioned on that front. Like I said, it's no big deal unless there's some rebel plan to make it a huge, all-over-the-news deal. We'd be remiss to not do all we could to validate that our ambassador, and the other attendees, are going to be okay."

"Fair enough," Mark said. "Let me know when you're going."

"Sure," Frank said. "I'll get Veronica to set it up. She's more their counterpart. Like you said, I'd rather talk with someone from NSA."

"Maybe that will impress them," Mark said.

Frank barked out a laugh. "Yeah, I'll be in my grave before anyone in human intelligence is impressed by SIGINT."

"Bring me up to date."

Veronica looked startled. "Can I put my bag down?"

Frank waved his hand. "Of course."

He watched her as she got settled. She was getting a nice tan. It didn't hide the fact that she was tired.

"How's your infiltration of the Nicaraguan Ministry of Agriculture going?"

"What's wrong, Frank?"

"Nothing."

"Then why are you on me as soon as I'm in the door?"

"Just curious."

Veronica didn't say anything, just sat down with her coffee and gently blew on the top. "It's been a week."

"It's hard work."

"Yes, it is. In a lot of ways. There are a lot of people here who are angry and scared and who have lost someone they love."

"If there wasn't some sort of conflict, we wouldn't want to be collecting intelligence. No one worries about Agriculture parties in France."

"No," she said, "I suppose they don't."

Frank knew he was probably going to screw up the rest of the conversation, but he jumped in anyway. "Look, I think it's important that you communicate your plans with me more. Where you are going, the contacts you're trying to develop. We're partners."

"I'm spending time trying to figure out who works in the mailroom at the ministry. I'm also having lunch or drinks with the one Nicaraguan woman I know, the one Phillip's friend introduced me to. We talk about clothes mostly. Sometimes she invites a friend, and then the conversation switches to poetry and the Nicaraguan arts culture. Neither of these women know anything about the Ministry of Agriculture. At least not that they're telling me."

"Are you still asking about Carlos?"

She shook her head. "I have no one to ask. Now that we've connected with Quentin, I thought I should calm down a little on that front."

"Quentin dropped in on me the other day. Confirmed that Carlos is in Managua."

"Does he know where Carlos is?" Veronica asked.

"Maybe. But he can't get to him." Frank paused for a moment. "Look, Veronica, I know you don't report to me, but I'm sure you appreciate that no one else is looking out for you down here."

"I know."

"When Carlos took Jillian, it was four days before I found out. It took her not showing up for work. Even then, it was a chain of phone calls across half the goddamn world's time zones before I got the message. He hurt her bad. And he liked her. He doesn't know you. He'd rape you, then put a bullet in your head."

"What do you want from me, Frank?"

"I want you to be careful." He sighed. "None of this is worth losing your life over."

Veronica was quiet for a while. "I don't imagine you worry about it too much doing signals intelligence, but they do brief us on the...range of potential consequences. I think it was awkward for the RCMP when they started sending women to the embassies. A whole new set of possible consequences to consider."

Frank just listened.

"Sometimes I think they scare us because they're hoping we won't go."

"You want to have the same opportunities, I get that," Frank said, "but it comes with the same risks. Plus, the added vulnerabilities of being a woman. It's ridiculous to pretend otherwise."

"Torture is torture. Whatever part of the mind or body gets violated."

Jesus. Frank rubbed at his eyes. *What a fucking minefield this conversation was.* "Okay. For a minute forget about the RCMP and official business and even your career. This is your first foreign assignment, and we haven't exactly been set up to succeed. What I'm saying is that I would prefer you not to die while we're down here. If you do die, I would prefer it not be my fault. So I'm telling you, based on the intelligence we collect out of Cuba, rape is a distinct possibility with Carlos. Based on my knowledge of him, death is also a likely option. So call me selfish, but I'm asking you to share your contacts and general fucking plan everyday so I can at least convince myself I did everything I could."

Veronica smiled. "You're such a sweet guy."

"I'm serious."

"I know. And I appreciate your concern. I really do." She shifted in her chair and pulled out a paper she'd tucked into one of the desk drawers. "I've spent most days this week drinking too much coffee at the various cafés and restaurants that have at least a partial sightline to the ministry building. I'm trying to get a sense of who goes in where. I've also gone into the building a few times and have begun to capture a layout of the first floor and how it's run. There isn't much security, but what there is I've taken note of. Truthfully, I don't think it would be that hard to get into the rest of the building, but I don't see a need for that at this point. I've also started flirting with one of the security guards. He seems lonely, and he's very receptive. We had coffee this afternoon while he was on break."

"Did he tell you anything useful?"

Veronica shook her head. "I didn't ask. Too soon."

"The advantages of putting women in the field."

"Damn right," she said.

Frank took a look at her floorplan. "The party is in a couple of weeks."

"So I've taken your advice. I'm not going to develop contacts, let alone agents, in that time, unless someone gets misgivings and really wants to talk. Really, I just want to see if Agriculture is the leaky ship I think it is. But Frank, I have to tell you, I'm uncomfortable that we aren't telling the ambassador anything. He can't make an informed decision if we don't say something."

"And so," Frank said, leaning back in his chair, "I've taken your advice. I'm not going to give the ambassador our hunch. But if we can corroborate the legitimacy of our hunch, I'm willing to go to him off the record."

Veronica looked curious. "How do you plan on doing that?"

"If anyone knows what's going to happen, it's the CIA."

"You're just going to ask them?"

"We are. They aren't going to tell us anything, but we can gauge their reaction. If they jump all over our collection, then I figure that's enough to tell the ambassador. You get the honor of setting up the meeting. They're your kind. Hopefully they offer us a decent whisky, or at least some premium bourbon."

"What if they decide to reciprocate?"

"They won't. There's no real incentive. I can't give them the raw traffic from the ministry forever. They'll go back to waiting for NSA reporting, just like everyone else. But maybe we'll learn something about Carlos."

Veronica's eyes sharpened. "Do you think he could be involved?"

"Honestly, I have no idea," Frank said, "but he's got to be involved in something. Or else why is he here? And if the Sandinistas are planning something big, where else is he going to be?"

"What does Quentin think?"

Frank shook his head. "Who the hell knows. The way I figure it, finding Carlos is about finding out what antigovernment activity is going on. That's the most likely place he'd be. Here on familiar turf, he's likely to have a lot of, if not friends, then contacts. He'd have to be making himself useful somehow. Otherwise, why come back?"

"And if we find him?"

"We get him to tell us who he works with in West Germany. Then we follow that lead to make sure our collection and deployed officer are safe. Then we determine if there are any other risks we're not aware of."

"That's it?"

"Well, and then Quentin will probably shoot him. In the meantime, you've gained excellent field experience, we've improved the collection in Nicaragua, and we've tied up a major operational loose end. I'd say that isn't bad for your first field assignment."

"I like working with you, Frank."

These conversations with Veronica, they took him across such a spectrum of emotion. Frank thought that might be what made it all so interesting. "Ditto. You're the first IO I haven't wanted to punch in the face."

Veronica smiled. "So let me get on that call to the American embassy."

CHAPTER EIGHTEEN

Jillian juggled her two grocery bags while searching for her keys. Her hands were cold, and she was starving. She'd just spent three hours sorting documents for Madeline and had limited herself to one strudel. She wanted to get into her apartment and have some dinner. How come keys in a purse always managed to migrate to the exact opposite location of the hand? She went to put down a bag before she ended up dumping her vegetables all over the street.

"Here, let me hold that for you."

Jillian started. How had she not noticed someone had come up right beside her?

"I'm okay thank…" The words trailed off as she focused on the man standing with his hand out.

"I know you," she said, her heart beginning to knock around in her chest. "From the café beside the garage. Which is in a completely different part of the city."

He gave her a little smile. "I introduced myself before, but I see I did not make much of an impression. Hans Gohl. I take it you do not believe in coincidence."

"Not in this city."

He tipped his head in acknowledgment. "Perhaps you could invite me up to your apartment."

Jillian's nerves were taut. She understood it wasn't a question.

She nodded and turned to the door.

"Here, I will hold one of your bags. To make it easier for you to find your keys."

She gave him a bag. Holding her groceries would make it harder for him to pull out a gun.

God, was that really where her brain went? She didn't know what to think. She didn't feel in imminent danger. But who was this man? How did he know where she lived? What did he want? And always, underlying everything, did he know about her SIGINT mission?

She went through the door and led him up the stairs. "I'm sure you get how I'm feeling really nervous right now," she said. "This old guy I chatted with a few times shows up at my door. It doesn't make me feel good." She was looking for some indication he wasn't going to murder her in her apartment.

"Of course. In your position I would feel the same," Hans replied. "You are handling it very well. Your reaction, it says to me you have a certain expectation for the unexpected."

Jillian swallowed. Who was he? Because he was right. A normal person, a regular student, would have been more taken aback, would have demanded more out on the street. Yes, she had been surprised to see him. But once that registered, it hadn't surprised her that he wanted something.

She opened the door of her apartment without saying anything else. He crossed the threshold and offered her groceries back. She went behind her kitchen counter, determined to put the perishables away. No need to panic. Jillian watched as Hans cleaned his boots thoroughly on the mat before shutting the door and stepping fully into the apartment.

"I will admit, from what I have been able to see, you are quite a curiosity. Very sedate for a student. Although your visa application says you are completing a PhD. Maybe that is why you are so quiet. But it is quite clear that you are not a woman who wants to draw attention to herself."

Jillian forced a small smile onto her face. "I've always preferred puzzles to people. And I like exploring the city. It's very different from Ottawa."

"Yes, I did check. You are Canadian. From what I can tell, nothing you are doing is helping the East Germans or the Soviets."

"I'm a student," Jillian said. "Why would I be involved with either of those countries?"

"As you said, in this city there is much that is not typical," Hans said. "But I don't think, whatever it is you are doing in Berlin, it is something that should worry me today."

Jillian's head was pounding. "Why are you here?"

"I think maybe you are someone who can help me. I have not had the chance yet to work with a Canadian, and I find myself needing someone of your national background."

"I think you have the wrong person for whatever it is you need. I study underwater earthquakes."

"So many things to study these days. Let's not waste time playing around. It will be very easy for me to demonstrate how serious I am, and in the meantime, you would have to deal with consequences I'm sure you would prefer to avoid. I suggest you not make things worse for yourself just to prolong us agreeing on what we both know to be true. I would like to ask you, are you curious about how I found the garage?" Hans asked.

Jillian took a breath. "You said you lived across the street."

"You have a good memory. But that was a lie of convenience."

It was suddenly hard to swallow.

"You brought me there, Jillian," he continued. "I have been following you for a while. Trying to get your attention. You didn't engage with any of the men I put in your path. I thought I chose some attractive ones." He chuckled a bit.

So she hadn't been paranoid. Who was this guy?

"Why were you following me?" She knew she had to ask. She was terrified of the answer.

"I know many people, and I hear many things. It was suggested to me that you might be a person I should pay attention to."

"Who suggested that to you?"

"Oh, just a friend," Hans said.

Jillian's mind was racing. Who had pointed this guy in her direction? Technically, there weren't too many possibilities, unless she was on a list somewhere that she didn't know about. Which was all too probable.

"Who do you work for?" she asked.

Hans shook his head slightly. "There is no need for you to know anything about me in order to do me this favor."

It seemed to her the only way she had a hope of resolving this situation was to get as much information out of him as she could.

"What favor is that?"

Hans gestured toward her living room. "Come, sit down. No need to look so nervous. It is a small thing I ask of you, really."

Jillian went to sit on her sofa. She needed to play nice until she understood better what was going on.

Hans settled in the chair opposite her. He carefully took off his gloves, laying them across his knee. "I will leave my coat on if you don't mind. I find it a little cold in here."

Jillian was so tense her muscles had begun to ache. She wished he'd just get to the point.

"What I am interested in, it goes back to the war," Hans said. "You know the highlights, I think, and you seem to have a certain appreciation for what went on in this country. But there is so much more than has been talked about. Millions of people. Millions of actions. More than could ever be accounted for."

He looked down at the floor for a moment before raising his eyes to hers. "Have you ever heard of a company named IG Farben?"

Jillian shook her head. Her knowledge of war history tended to the military and espionage side of things.

"They were a great German company," Hans continued. "They had many products. Some were very valuable. The company started as a dye manufacturer, but the system they created could produce many things. They became interested in pharmaceuticals, eventually producing the world's first antibiotic, a sulfa drug. Their research saved many lives. Even today, although IG Farben itself was broken up after the war, one of their components, Bayer, is the world's largest manufacturer of aspirin.

"During the war the company became beholden to the Nazis. Like all manufacturing companies, their infrastructure and personnel were expected to produce for the war effort. Now, if they had carried on developing and making pharmaceuticals for German soldiers, they would be like so many others in this country: guilty but not responsible. But IG Farben did not simply divert their production. There was a group of them that worked to create new tools for Hitler."

Despite her misgivings about Hans's presence in her living room, Jillian was intrigued by his story. "What did they do?"

"IG Farben made the gas for the chambers in the concentration camps."

In all that she had ever learned about World War II, Jillian had not once considered the manufacturing effort that had supported what went on in the camps. She felt her heart pound with this new awareness. It wasn't just soldiers obeying commands but scientists and businesspeople who thought it was okay to make a gas solely for committing genocide.

"I see you are not unmoved by my story."

"It's horrific," Jillian said, "but I still don't understand how you think I can help you."

"I have made it my life's work to discover every person who worked on the gas project and bring them to some sort of justice. There are a few who have remained elusive. One, Helmut Radsch, left Germany in 1946 for Halifax, where he is said to have died in 1947."

"But?"

"I think he was given a new identity by your government. This is what you are going to help me find out."

Jillian stared. It was not at all what she'd been afraid of. Nothing to do with signals intelligence, or the Soviets or East Germans, or anyone she cared about. She also didn't see how she could help him at all.

"That's an amazing story, but I really don't see how I can help. If it is what you think, no one is just going to hand over that kind of protected information. I mean, how do you know he didn't die?"

Hans gave a small shrug. "I don't. It does not matter. You will do me this favor, and we will see."

"What is it that you think I can do?"

"I don't know exactly what you are, but I have been told you have friends in the CIA. That makes me suspect that your work is in a similar vein."

Jillian shivered. He was so calm, almost nonchalant, but she was beginning to understand that he had all the leverage.

"I can't get those records for you, even if they exist."

"I do not expect you to do this. I want you to ask the people you know. I want you to make many transparent inquiries for information about Helmut Radsch. Your justification for such inquiries, I leave up to you."

"In return, you will do what exactly?"

"I have been looking for these people for a long time. Over the years I have discovered many who want to help me. I've made some…interesting friends. I have no interest in what you do with the CIA. But here, in West Berlin, I am a rarity."

And that was that. Jillian knew her first job was to protect the SIGINT mission. People getting interested in her was a bad idea—the Stasi or the Soviets, for sure, but even West German intelligence or the French, who still controlled a part of this city. Her mission was of the most sensitive kind, making her vulnerable to pressure from allies as well.

What Hans Gohl was asking, it wasn't impossible. Sure, it would be a little out of character, and she'd have to do it clandestinely through her contact at the embassy. But asking for that information wasn't going to make anyone suspicious about a covert signals intelligence operation.

"In return you will keep your mouth shut?" Jillian asked.

Gohl smiled. "Yes. As long as you help me find Helmut Radsch, I will not let anyone know you are anything more than a science student."

She wanted to ask what happened after Gohl found Radsch, but she figured she knew the answer. She would be on this man's list of friends until the leverage he had over her didn't exist anymore.

"What if Radsch really died?"

Gohl frowned. "Then I will have the information I need. But if he didn't, then your actions, they might help drive him from his hiding place."

"What if he's living a quiet life in Nova Scotia and doesn't really care about his past coming to light after all this time?"

"There are ways to make a man care," Gohl shrugged. "Justice takes many forms."

Jillian chilled at his answer. This man was an enigma. Courteous. Soft-spoken. But she sensed that it would not be wise to get in his way. At this point she felt she had no choice but to agree to help him, at least to buy herself some time to figure out what to do. It sounded like he had access to a fair number of resources, and she had too many secrets here she wanted to protect.

"It will take me a few days to figure out the best way to submit those inquiries," she said.

"I am a patient man."

Jillian didn't doubt that.

"And now I will leave you," Hans said, standing up. "I will check in with you again soon. Now you may get back to preparing your dinner."

Jillian stood and followed him to the door. He disappeared down the stairs without another word. The smell of his subtle cologne lingered in her apartment.

She made herself a coffee and sat back down on her sofa. She needed to plan her next moves very carefully.

CHAPTER NINETEEN

Frank adjusted his tie. It was probably a little formal, and it probably made him look uptight, but he wasn't trying to be anyone's friend. He was trying to get business done. To impress that fact, he'd chosen to wear a tie. He met Veronica in the hallway and noted that she looked equally no-nonsense, dressed all in black.

"Nervous?" he asked.

"Yes and no. You seem to be keeping your expectations low. I figure I should do the same."

"But they're your own kind."

"Right. All the more reason not to expect much."

Frank held the front door open. "Well, it's something to do. Let's see what happens. You never know, they could treat us like we aren't the junior reps at the national sales conference."

"At the very least," Veronica said, "you'll probably get your bourbon."

"Fingers crossed," said Frank. "Fingers crossed."

They took a taxi to the American embassy. It was swanky, as befitted the most powerful nation on earth—better crown molding, better security. They met up with Mark in the lobby.

"Someone named Joe is on his way down. I've arranged to meet my counterpart, Ronald, afterward, since I'm here and all. He's a good guy."

"You said he fought in Korea?" Frank asked.

"I think so. We've never talked about it."

"I started out in military SIGINT with the Navy collecting signals on subs. I moved to CBNRC in the middle of that war, so I saw it from both sides."

"I didn't know that about you, Frank. That was before I started. Did you spend any time there?"

"Enough to wonder if it wasn't all going to come and bite us in the ass someday. Another dividing line between east and west."

"One day we'll finish dividing the earth, and then aliens will come and we'll realize it was all for nothing," Veronica said.

Mark stared at Veronica like she was from another planet. Frank laughed. Hard. He was really beginning to appreciate her.

A man whom Frank could only conclude was Joe came up to the desk. "Showtime," Frank said.

They followed Joe into the bowels of the embassy.

They got to some kind of boardroom with four men seated at a large table. Joe did introductions of his group as they all sat down, complete with basic titles and areas of interest so general as to be almost useless. Trust was not easy to come by in this field.

When he was done, Frank waited for Veronica to take the lead. The men were Americans, and none of them looked like engineers. Veronica introduced herself, then explained Frank was her CBNRC partner. She told them about the new joint agency effort to develop intelligence sources that matched the priorities of both SIGINT and HUMINT.

"Part of my work down here has been to improve the embassy's collection," Frank said. "To that end, I'd love to compare notes with any access guys from NSA who may be down here."

He noticed that everyone twitched at that. Even among intelligence types, embassy SIGINT collection was a sensitive subject. He wasn't too bothered, as NSA was one place he had a lot of friends. He'd worked on a lot of multinational technology projects and had no doubt it would take him less than a day to find out all about NSA collection out of the American embassy in Managua. He was trying to gently remind them that he knew what he was talking about. Despite HUMINTers being the more cagey and controlling of the intelligence workers, signals intelligence had a bigger moat around it. Frank thought it likely that he had better access to NSA than any of the Americans sitting at the table.

"Well, Frank and I have been getting to know the city," Veronica picked up the dialogue. "Interesting place. The impact of the earthquake a few years ago is still so visible. The Canadian embassy wasn't too affected, but no one had checked the signals access in a while. It turns out, from our roof, we can tap a few phone lines."

Frank watched for interest but didn't get much as she spoke. He stopped himself from rolling his eyes. These guys. No matter how many SIGINT reports they read, you had to spell it out for them.

"We've got a lot of traffic coming from the Ministry of Agriculture," Veronica continued.

Still not much, but Frank thought he saw the young guy, George something or other, perk up a little.

"I know Agriculture isn't usually a high-priority target," Veronica said, "but it gives us a good glimpse into how the Somoza government works. The minister is planning this big party. We were wondering if you knew anything about it."

There was a moment of pause around the table.

"We can't confirm anything right now," said Joe. "Of course we know about the party, because our ambassador will be attending."

"Have you heard anything interesting about that party that you could share?" Veronica asked Joe.

"As far as we know, it's a regular party."

This was such a useless conversation. "It is going to be a regular party from the minister's point of view," Frank said, "but we wondered if you'd heard of any antigovernment groups expressing interest?"

"There are anti-Somoza groups everywhere," said Joe.

Frank wanted to rip his own eye out. "Yeah, I get that. But we think there might be some particular interest in this party. We've picked up some anomalies as we've been sorting through the traffic."

"We don't have any NSA reporting on that."

"Well," Frank said, "we have a lot of raw intercept from the ministry that we don't have the manpower to go through."

No one flinched. "We'll look into it. If we want your collection, we'll let you know."

Frank pinched the bridge of his nose. At moments like this he wasn't sure why he didn't retire. "The party's in two weeks."

"Like I said, we'll look into it."

"Then what? You get interested, and I'm just going to drop off months of collection as a fucking Christmas gift?"

The tension ratcheted up around the room, but Frank didn't give a shit. What a waste of time this was. He'd been hoping for some off-the-record concurrence that he and Veronica hadn't been wasting their time. Instead, he'd been dismissed. He pulled out a cigarette. He wondered who was going to speak next.

Everyone looked up at a knock on the door as it swung open. A woman stuck her head in. "Frank Leachuk and Veronica Raeburn?"

Frank had never seen her before. He looked over at Mark, who looked equally mystified, but the Americans were sitting up a little straighter.

"I'd like to meet with you before you go. I'd like to say when you're done here, but I have fifteen minutes starting now. So unless you're on the verge of creating world peace?"

Joe stood up. "No, ma'am. We were just finishing up."

"Great. Frank, Veronica, walk with me. I'll escort them to the lobby when we're done." She directed this last at Joe, whom Frank guessed was responsible for making sure they didn't wander into an awkward situation in off-limits rooms.

Veronica looked at Frank, clearly waiting for his lead. He'd thought the whole effort of coming here had been wasted. Now he was curious to see if this woman would prove that untrue.

Frank stood up. "Gentleman, thank you for your time." He was going to add something about being open to information exchanges, but then decided he'd said enough for them to figure it out. No need to come off as desperate. He put away the cigarette he'd never got a chance to light and waited for Veronica to stand before crossing to the door the woman still held open.

She barely waited for them to get close to her before she turning and sweeping away down a hallway. "Follow me," she said. "I'm serious about only having fifteen minutes, and my office is the best place for us to have a chat." Despite wearing heels tall enough to stab someone, she moved fast. Frank worked to keep up with her.

They finally reached a solid wood door without any identification as to who its regular occupant might be. The woman stood back to let them enter, closing the door behind them.

"I hope that wasn't too dramatic, but it's convenient to just grab you when you're here. Amaya Perez." She extended her hand to each of them. "I'm a special advisor to the ambassador."

Frank had no idea what to say.

"Look, I know you're wondering what's going on, so I'll get right to it. I know Nicaragua well. I won't bore you with the details, but I've been around a long time and developed many relationships with the people who've worked here."

Frank was lost. He figured it was best to just listen.

"Without going into particulars," she said, "one of those people was Quentin. We have a good relationship. He's asked me to help you both with any information we might have on an upcoming party at the Ministry of Agriculture."

It was all clicking now—and totally unexpected. "And you agreed?"

Amaya smiled. "We go way back. I trust his judgment."

"Of course," said Frank.

"Look," she said, holding up her hand, "there are only a few people who know he's in Nicaragua, and I'm sure he doesn't talk to the other two."

"Is it because they're some of those assholes we just got out of a meeting with?"

"They're just doing their jobs."

"Not all of them know about Quentin?" Veronica asked.

"No. He's here on vacation, so just the chief of station and the deputy. You can see where the problems are. But Quentin, he was in touch a couple of days ago. First, I've sent off a very interesting information request to MI6 that I'm hoping I won't have to answer too many questions about. Quentin said that whatever I got back, I needed to give to you. I think you can appreciate how that's not going to happen in an official capacity, so I'll invite you over for a drink and you can read whatever happens to be sitting on my desk.

"Second, about this party, I'd like a little quid pro quo. Why has it come up on your radar?"

Frank didn't see any reason to bullshit this woman. "The ministry's telephone lines go over our embassy, so I was able to tap them. We were going over the intercept to determine if it was worth sending it all home for analysis when we noticed a couple of anomalies with respect to this party. Without going into all the details, there's something about the invoicing that's made us suspicious."

"The invoicing?" Amaya asked.

Frank turned to Veronica. "Like I said, it's just an anomaly at this point."

"We think someone is making a copy of every invoice that has to do with the party," Veronica said. "Caterers, florists, the entertainment. But we don't have any other access, nor do we have anyone in the building, as Nicaraguan agriculture wasn't high on our priority list. We don't know if it means they're just trying out a new process that's confusing everyone or if someone wants those invoices to be able to know the party plans intimately. But if something is going to go down, then we'd like to at least be able to give our ambassador a heads-up."

Amaya thought for a moment. "What if it's just some rebel planning to expose the excesses of the Somoza government?"

"Fine," said Frank. "Nothing to get worked up about. Like Veronica said, we're just looking for a sign in either direction so we can unofficially tell something to our ambassador if it's warranted. We're trying to avoid him getting shot and thus getting blamed for a massive intelligence failure on our watch."

"Okay. Up front, I know nothing about the party, so I can't tell you what you should report. But I can share that we've been getting indications that the Sandinistas are getting very organized and are planning something big—bigger than anything they've done so far."

"Define big," Frank said.

"Sure. Indications are that the Sandinistas want international attention. The only way they think they can get help with Somoza is to reveal all of the gory details of his leadership. Whatever they've got planned, or are trying to plan, has to involve something that would make the international community listen."

"It's possible then," said Veronica, "that they could use this party to get people to listen. There will be attendees from more than a dozen countries."

"But the party itself won't be on anyone's radar," Amaya said.

"So they'll have to put it on the radar."

"Which they could do in a few different ways."

"Like take hostages," said Veronica. "That would get people to listen."

Amaya contemplated this suggestion. "It's possible, but no one would be listening clearly. It would be a circus."

"So would shooting the guests," Frank said, "which wouldn't do much to distinguish them from Somoza."

"Now, Frank," Amaya said, "the Somoza government has the support of the United States in dealing with this rebel faction."

Frank shrugged. He wasn't getting into the politics. "Any indication of when this epic event is supposed to happen?"

"Sometime before the end of the year."

"That would fit with the timeline," Veronica said. "The party is in two weeks."

"Look, I offered your boys a copy of the intercept we're getting from the ministry. We don't have time to go through it all. They didn't seem to want it. The offer stands. The American ambassador is going to be a bigger target than ours—unless you have some contacts who will confirm or deny all this for you."

"Obviously I can't tell you that. Let's just say that if I was getting my nails done with any Sandinista sympathizers on Saturdays, I would know a lot more."

Frank smiled. "I'm sure you've got people you can ask. Like you said, you've been in Nicaragua a long time."

"I might, somewhere," she said. "Now, I've got to run. I'll get my secretary to escort you back to the entrance. I'll ask around about that party, and if I think it's warranted, I'll be in touch."

"Do you have an idea about when that report might arrive from MI6?"

"If it's warranted, I'll be in touch about that as well. In the meantime, I'd like to call in one of those favors you're going to owe me."

Bold. But she didn't get to such a senior position by being a wallflower.

"Look out for Quentin. He's a good guy, but I'm not sure about his intentions being back here."

Interesting, thought Frank. "I thought he was here on vacation?"

Amaya shook her head. "I don't believe that for one second. He's here on his own time, yes, but he's not spending his days on the beach."

"You think we're in a better position to look out for him?" Veronica asked.

"I think he needs all the help he can get."

That is probably true.

CHAPTER TWENTY

"And he gave you no indication at all who he worked for?"

Jillian shook her head. "No. But given what he said about going after the gas makers at IG Farben, who would be supporting that?"

She watched as Jean-Marc shook a cigarette out of the pack he kept in his jacket pocket and lit up. It was clear he was as stumped as she was.

After Gohl had left the other day, Jillian had done two things. First, she had prepared an information access report on Helmut Radsch that she sent along to CBNRC with the intercept she collected. That was a long shot, as it was a thirty-year-old file that likely had nothing to do with CBNRC and signals intelligence, but it technically fulfilled her initial commitment to Gohl. She could honestly say she'd done as asked when he next showed up at her door, whenever that would be.

Second, she had used her emergency contact number for the Canadian embassy in Bonn and told her intelligence contact that he had to meet her in West Berlin immediately. The last time she'd met with him had been when her friend Lisa had disappeared, and Jillian had needed a new method for sending her intercept back home. Jean-Marc Belanger was RCMP, not CBNRC, and he wasn't in West Germany under deep cover like Quentin, but he was whom Jillian was supposed to go to if she had any concerns about her operation. He was technically responsible for all Canadian intelligence activities in West Germany.

Meeting up with someone from the embassy was risky. How many exchange students hung out with embassy officials? And despite Jean-Marc's official title as a defense attaché, it was likely that anyone watching embassy staff suspected he was something else. So they tried never to meet. These were, however, exceptional circumstances.

"How did he even find out about you? Shit, I'm the only person at the embassy who knows what you're doing here."

Jillian wasn't about to tell Jean-Marc about her affair with Carlos, her relationship with Quentin, or her helping Lisa escape from East Berlin. The truth was, when she looked past her guilty conscience, she knew that her past might have nothing to do with it.

"Well, at least we know he's not a Canadian double agent," Jean-Marc continued. "If he had someone that deep in one of our intelligence organizations, why bother even approaching you?"

"He could work for an ally. The CIA found me last year."

"Chalis," he swore with Quebecois exasperation, "as if I don't have enough to do here. Look, you have to find out more about this guy. Your cover is semi-compromised with him anyway. We need to know how far this thing goes and if he's going to surprise us with any more ultimatums. Then we need to figure out how to neutralize him."

Jillian had no problem following Jean-Marc's logic. She couldn't be indebted to this man forever. Any help she could get on that front would be welcome.

"What do I tell him about Radsch? That all the reports came back negative?"

"I'm not sure," Jean-Marc said. "It depends on if you think he's testing you. I had someone look into Radsch, and it turns out we do have files on him. He came over after the war, wanting to share information about chemical weapons. I got two reports from the '40s sent to me. Nothing so far about a new identity, but it's not impossible. It happened. Some people wanted a fresh start."

Jillian thought for a while. "You think Hans Gohl might already know that?"

Jean-Marc shrugged. "Maybe. You say he knew Radsch went to Halifax and that he supposedly died in 1947. That's too specific for a guess."

"And Radsch wanted to share info about chemical weapons. That fits with the gas thing at IG Farben during the war."

"There was nothing about that in the two reports I got on his original debriefings. But yeah, it fits."

Jillian was quiet for a moment. "I get that this situation is a problem, that Hans Gohl is a problem, and that you have some responsibility to figure out how much of a problem. But there is only so much I can do. I have a SIGINT operation to run, and I don't know how to, like, tail this guy, or whatever it is that you HUMINT types do."

"I know. You're an engineer." The way he said it made Jillian think he didn't feel it a very useful profession. "Look," Jean-Marc said, "we're spread thin. There's no one who can just dump their current files and rush in to fix whatever the hell is going on here. I get that you're SIGINT, and at home we've all got our roles. But here in the field, we don't have that luxury. So you can do your best to find out something we can use to make this guy back off, or CBNRC can cut their losses."

"They aren't going to want to do that."

"Above my pay grade. I'll report up. I'll try to find out what happened to Helmut Radsch. And I'll try to find out who Hans Gohl works for."

On top of whatever else he was handling, Jillian realized she'd dumped a huge amount of work in his lap. He was right—she didn't want to shut down the operation and go home, but she knew it wasn't her call. Risk analysis would happen somewhere. In the meantime, if she wanted to stay in Berlin, her best bet was to find out more about Gohl.

"Okay," she said. "It's elicitation, right? I try to give him what he needs in order to trust me."

Jean-Marc raised a brow. "Elicitation, huh?"

"Isn't that what they call it? I'm sure it came up in an intelligence brief."

"Do you have any idea how to do it?"

"Well," Jillian said, thinking on the fly, "I'm sure the first step here is to not fight him. Make him think that I've come over to his cause, that I'm not angry but happy to help." It had an element of truth. It wasn't a stretch for her to want the people who made the gas for the chambers to pay for what they'd done. Gohl's idea of payment might not be hers, but she would have to deal with that later.

Jean-Marc nodded. "That's what I would do. Get him to open up. I'll send you those old reports. You can give them to him as a show of good faith. Build some trust." Jean-Marc put out his cigarette. "What's your boss like?"

"At CBNRC? I don't know him actually. Frank Leachuk was in charge when I came over, but I got a note saying he'd moved to a new position. I've never really met the guy who's there now."

"So you don't have a guess on if he'll want to pull the plug once he finds out you've been threatened?"

"I have no idea. Why?"

"Because if you go, we have almost no way of finding out who Hans Gohl works for, and therefore if he might be a threat in the future."

"You're saying you don't want to bring in CBNRC on this potential threat to their operation?"

Jean-Marc hesitated. "In the field, there are always threats. If an IO went home every time they got nervous, there'd be no one doing intelligence. The way I understand it, the operation itself hasn't been threatened. Gohl only thinks you're connected to the CIA. My bet is he thinks you work for the Canadian version. You said yourself he didn't appear to know anything about the SIGINT mission."

"He could have been holding back," Jillian said.

"Maybe. Until you know for sure, I think you should stay the course. They pull you back now, we're never going to know how vulnerable we really are here."

Jillian thought back to what Frank had always told her: put the mission first. The problem was, she didn't know if it was better for the mission to pull out before it was compromised to their adversaries or to keep collecting in the face of increased risk. She knew the intercept was valuable; the setup had come about as a result of a rare opportunity. She also knew that if they pulled out because of what might happen, then a lot of reports wouldn't get written—reports that helped save lives.

She sighed. Collecting SIGINT overseas was always risky. If it wasn't, she wouldn't have needed a cover story. It wasn't her call to decide when the risks were too much for the CBNRC; it was only her call to decide when the risks were too much for her. After all she'd been through in Berlin, finding some information in old war records didn't seem that risky.

"Okay. I won't say anything. For now. Until I get more information, I'll keep on with what I'm doing."

"Get in touch if you need me, but try not to need me. You can put any information you get about Gohl in your dead drops." Jean-Marc stood up, shrugging into his nondescript brown coat. "Good luck."

Jillian only nodded. No doubt she was going to need it.

CHAPTER TWENTY-ONE

Frank's head hurt. He didn't know what to do.

"What are you thinking, Frank?" Veronica asked.

He didn't know what to tell her. Stalling for time, he finished a third of his beer in one drink. Christ, this was not the kind of field work he was used to.

"Do you want to know what I think?"

Yes, please. Frank nodded for Veronica to continue.

"We need to go to that party."

Frank choked on his beer. "What? That's not the conclusion I was coming to. Have you lost your goddamn mind?"

"Frank, think about it. You want to get to Carlos; Quentin can't find him. So we have to think about where he's going to show up. The most likely place is wherever the antigovernment activity is really active. The most likely place for that is the party hosted by the Minister of Agriculture."

Frank rubbed at his eyes. "No way. An Agriculture party? Christ."

"Maybe that's why the Agriculture party is getting attention. Did you think of that? Because it's on no one's priority list. Totally easy to fly under the radar. We got lucky with the phone lines."

She was right. The truth was, luck happened in this business all the time. "Fine. Okay, let's say I agree that the Agriculture party might be something that should be on the intelligence radar. I don't see how you make the leap to either one of us attending."

Veronica shook her head. "No, not go to the party. Just be in the vicinity on the evening it happens."

"No fucking way," Frank said. "If you're right, there will be people all over the place, with no one really knowing who's on whose side. The potential for disaster is huge. And, fuck, I'm not trained for that kind of stuff. I've spent the last fifteen years doing paperwork."

"Then I'll go."

Frank drank more of his beer. "I can't stop you, but I'm telling you it's not a good idea. You are an intelligence collector. There is no intelligence to be had there, just a lot of angry people with guns."

Veronica was quiet. "I don't want anyone here to die."

Frank looked at her. "You've got to let that go. People know the risks associated with their job, just like you. It's not about saving people today. What we do, it's about the long game. Democracy everywhere. At the rate we're going, it's looking like a hundred-year project."

Veronica gave him a small smile. "Nothing like a bit of perspective."

"This party fell into our lap, which has been great, because it's given us something to trade. If Amaya Perez gets back to us with something tangible, we'll go to our ambassador. Other than that, you've got to let this damn party go."

"But Frank, we only started caring about the party because you were convinced it would help us find the Cuban."

Frank took another sip of beer. "I've been thinking about that. Carlos Honouras isn't going to be at that party. He's a setup guy: recruiting, logistics. When he was helping the Red Army Faction, he wasn't involved in the execution of anything they did. He might have helped set something up, but he's not going to attend."

"Things might be different on his home turf."

"I've been thinking about that too. It's not actually his home turf. He's Cuban. He's got some family here, an aunt and presumably cousins, according to Quentin. But he's not going to be prominent in the Sandinistas. It's not his cause. He's a survivor, and you don't survive by putting yourself on the front lines."

"What do you want to do?" asked Veronica.

"I say we keep going through as much intercept as we can. The party is in ten days. I agree with you that it's our job to find out as much as we can to prepare the ambassador. But I just don't think there's anything else for us to find. Not in the time that we have."

Veronica was quiet for a long time. "Okay. I'm going to defer to you on this one. But I'm going to work overtime in the next ten days to find out what I can."

"Fair enough," Frank said. And it was. He wanted some better assurance either way. It was their job to get some indication when things were going to blow, and here in Managua, things most definitely were going to at some point.

Frank's eyes were crossing, but he was making the effort to go through as much intercept as he could. He figured he could take a few days off the Cuban to support Veronica. She was dividing her time between the collection and the security guard she'd befriended in the Agriculture building.

He was scanning through another batch of outgoing calls when his phone rang. He jumped a little; he and Veronica hadn't gotten many calls since they'd been here.

"Frank Leachuk," he said, picking up the phone.

"Amaya Perez here. How much of that information we talked about before can you send to me?"

It only took Frank a second to catch up. "I've got three months' worth."

"Can I have it all?" she asked.

"Sure, but the recent stuff looks to be pretty useless. You'd want to focus on when all the planning was happening. So at the front end of what I can give you."

"Okay. I'll send someone over now."

"And then we'll compare notes," Frank said. It wasn't a question.

"Come over for a drink on Thursday, after work. Say, eight p.m. If I don't have anything for you by then, I'm not going to."

On Thursday, after shutting down for the day, Frank went back to his apartment to shower and put on a fresh shirt. He then met Veronica in the lobby to catch a cab to the American embassy.

They were quiet in the car, their driver paying them the usual amount of interest. "It is nice? Where the Americans are?" he asked.

Frank shrugged. "We only see one boardroom. We're trying to put together a multinational deal for lemons."

"You work for farmers?" the driver said.

"We write policy," Frank replied.

That was the end of that conversation. Nothing killed unwanted curiosity like saying you worked in policy.

They pulled up close to the embassy, entered, and went through the standard screening process. Amaya met them on the other side. "Let's go to my office."

They followed her. No one said another word until they were seated on the sofa in the conversation area beside her desk.

"Coffee? Bourbon?" Amaya offered.

"Americans do good bourbon," Frank said.

"I'll take that as a yes. And technically," Amaya continued, "only Americans do bourbon. It's similar to the distinction between champagne and sparkling wine."

Something he hadn't known.

"Coffee for me, please," Veronica said.

Amaya brought them their drinks, poured herself a bourbon, and sat down. "Well, it's been a week. But here, it always is. Thank you for that collection from the Ministry of

Agriculture. I'm obviously not giving you any sources, but we followed that invoicing thing and were able to confirm that the copies being made were destined for rebel hands. That was good intelligence work, noticing that anomaly, but you don't need me to tell you that. Why they want the invoices, I have no definitive answer, but it's safe to say that your hunch is likely correct. The Sandinistas, or at least one group of them, are interested in that party. It's an international event, but not high profile enough to demand excessive scrutiny. We don't know what's going to happen or even how they are going to use the information."

Frank had been listening carefully. "What are you going to brief your ambassador?"

"That he should leave early."

Frank sat back and sipped his bourbon. He liked working with this woman. She was direct and no bullshit. Would that everyone could be the same way. "Any objection to us giving our ambassador the same advice?"

Amaya smiled. "None at all."

"Why are you telling us this?" Veronica asked. "Why are we not hearing it from someone representing the agency?"

"Miss them, do you?"

Frank watched Veronica unsuccessfully try to hide her smirk.

"I probably should have gone through more traditional channels." Amaya sighed a little. "But it would involve more paperwork, and since you didn't want an official report…" She paused for a moment. "To get them involved would interfere with the other reason I asked you both here. I haven't heard from Quentin in a while—too long. He's supposed to check in with me on a somewhat regular basis, and he hasn't."

Frank was surprised. Certainly she had some better people to talk to about this. "Shouldn't that be an agency file as well?"

Amaya tapped her fingers along the arm of her chair. "When Quentin was here before, he did a lot of good work. But the end of his assignment was less than spectacular."

"I heard he went rogue," Frank said.

"Okay. It was an unmitigated disaster. He got what he needed, got the agency what it wanted, then blew up half the relationships we had down here, seeking revenge for a woman who had gotten caught in the cross fire."

Frank hadn't been expecting that.

"The agency had a lot of cleanup to do. I wasn't privy to the details, but I do know people were moved—fast. Quentin was not well regarded by some of his peers."

Frank began to understand where this was going. "Let me guess, the guys who are here now are among those who didn't approve."

Amaya nodded. "The chief of station in particular. There are no neutral opinions when it comes to Quentin. Some people think he's a great intelligence officer, and I heard he did some excellent work in Berlin. But others can't forgive him for the way he went off here."

"Who was the woman?" Veronica asked.

"One of his agents. If she was anything else to him, I have no idea." Amaya shook her head. "We pretend there are two sides to every battle, the good guys and the bad guys. The truth is often much more nuanced. I'm not even sure she knew who she was helping."

It sounded complicated to Frank—too complicated. "I'm not sure we can help you. I assume if you had an address for him, you'd be looking for him yourself."

Amaya regarded them both for a long moment. "Why does he trust you two? You aren't American, you've never worked together, and you"—she pointed at Frank—"aren't even HUMINT. So how do you know him well enough for him to pull favors with me?"

Frank didn't know what to tell her. He thought for a moment. Fine, he'd like that MI6 reporting, but maybe Veronica could get that on her own. Yes, he'd like to find Carlos, and it was pretty clear he'd need Quentin for that. The question was, did he need a relationship with a special advisor to the American ambassador in Nicaragua? He didn't know, but it was clear she was well connected down here. That might come in useful. Even if it didn't, he liked her. He got the feeling she was doing the right thing in looking out for Quentin. Because of Quentin's past and the nature of his work, she didn't have a lot of people to ask for help.

But the truth was, he wasn't sure why Quentin did trust him.

"He showed up in the middle of an operation I was running in West Berlin. He, well, it's not something I can really get into."

"Were you in Berlin?" Amaya asked.

Frank shook his head. "No. In fact, I hadn't met him until we ran into each other here."

"That doesn't sound like much."

"It isn't," Frank agreed. "Look, I'm surprised by all this. I was surprised when you pulled us out of that meeting the first time we met you. I was surprised he asked you to loop us in on the Agriculture party and the MI6 request. I don't know him at all, and I've spent most of our relationship cursing him. I don't usually give two shits about human intelligence officers, although my opinion of some of them is improving slightly. But I think he and I came to an understanding about what happened in Berlin. He ended up doing a lot of good there—for both our countries, sure, but also for some people who otherwise might not have made it home."

Amaya took a slow sip of her bourbon. "Do you know what he's doing in Nicaragua?"

"I have some idea."

"Do I want to know the details?"

"Probably not," Frank said.

Amaya sighed again. "He's never been great at meeting the requirements of the administrative overhead. And he technically is here on vacation. But it's going on a three-month vacation, and I know the agency folks are starting to get uncomfortable. I asked him to check in with me because he's got a lot of history here. I know he's not checking with his colleagues here. He doesn't know most of them, and the ones he does—well, I explained that situation. Plus, he's not usually based out of embassies, and to contact them could compromise his cover. The only way he's in this country is on one of his covert identities. Which leaves me with the two of you. An unusual situation, to say the least. So I have to ask, do you meet with him regularly?"

"Not really," Veronica said. "He finds us."

"Why?"

"Because we're pursuing a target of mutual interest," Frank said. "The reason he's in Nicaragua is one of the reasons we are as well. In our case it's related to some loose ends from that Berlin op."

"And for Quentin?"

Frank was uncomfortable. He couldn't believe he was feeling obligated to protect Quentin's interests. If someone had told him that six months ago…"You understand, we aren't best buddies. But my impression is that it might have something to do with that unmitigated disaster you mentioned."

Amaya shook her head. "I was afraid of that. Look, I know I can't force you to do anything, but next time you see him, tell him from me that he needs to wrap things up. Otherwise, the agency is going to do it for him."

CHAPTER TWENTY-TWO

Jillian watched James wash the dishes. She had cooked for them—pea soup, nice and warm for December. Walking back from Madeline's today, Jillian had appreciated the Christmas decorations that were all over the city. It was charming and festive, and she wished she could enjoy it instead of feeling the stress and worry of churning through what she was going to do about Hans Gohl.

She and James had talked about their usual subjects: his work, music, books. He'd gone off for a while about some rugby match, but when he was unable to penetrate her blank look, he had given up and moved on. She asked him if he was going home for Christmas, and he said he'd always left that for the people who had kids. He could visit his family anytime, and plus, Inverness was not all that attractive in December.

She knew she was prolonging the moment when she'd tell him about the visit from Hans Gohl. He was going to be upset. Another situation. Another potential mess with her cover on the line.

Jillian had thought about not saying anything. Not only did she trust James, she cared about him, and she thought that maybe it would be kinder to not involve him. Just let him avoid the inevitable stress and worry that was going to come with her news. But she couldn't. Aside from the fact that she needed someone to talk through the situation with and he was all she had, keeping him in the dark made her more vulnerable. What if something happened to her? What if she got picked up or detained—or worse? If James didn't know what was going on, he wouldn't be able to help her.

She felt bad about this role he had to play for her. He'd never asked for it and wasn't trained for it. It also put him in an awkward position in terms of his job, to say nothing of the potential dangers he had to deal with.

Jillian sighed. One day she hoped she could make it up to him.

"Do you want something else?" she asked. "Tea?"

James nodded. "Aye. And let it steep properly this time. Last time it was colored water."

Jillian smiled. "Isn't that what tea is?"

"Aren't you a cheeky lass. As I've told ye before, in a proper brew, the spoon should near stand up on its own."

"Ah, so like tar, then." Jillian put on the kettle while James dried the suds from his forearms. "So, James, I have something to tell you."

He hung up the dishcloth and regarded her with a steady look. "Why do I get the feeling I'm not going to like what's about to come out of your mouth?"

She really didn't want to keep doing this to him, but there wasn't any choice. "Yeah, well, one day, you know, I'll be back in Ottawa. Then we can get together and reminisce about all the crazy adventures we had."

"Out with it, Jillian."

She filled their cups with hot water and mashed the teabags around to darken the water more quickly. Crossing to the fridge, she pulled out the milk. As she poured it into the cups, she started to tell him the story of Hans Gohl.

His eyes widened at a couple of points, but he didn't interrupt. He sipped at his tea as she finished with her discussion with Jean-Marc.

"So that's where I'm at," she said. "At the mercy of someone of unknown background and allegiance who will sink my operation and toss me over to the Soviets if I can't help him find some long-lost chemist from the war."

James stared at her for a long moment. "Christ Jesus, Jillian. How is it that stuff like this happens to you?"

"I don't know. It's not even regular intelligence activities. This guy, Hans Gohl—probably not his real name—I'm not sure who he works for or how he found out about me. But what he's asking, it's old information. It's not state secrets or intelligence capabilities or anything I was trained to be sensitive to."

"It can't always be bad luck."

"Maybe it is. I've been thinking, given that he mentioned the CIA, maybe it was Victor who sold me out, a little retribution for blowing his sideline theft operation. So maybe Hans Gohl is just one of those ripple consequences of past actions. I don't know."

"Are you thinking you'd have been better off staying in Ottawa?"

"Right," Jillian said, "just like you should have stayed in Inverness. Living comes with risks, James."

"That it does. But the worst that most of us risk is clogged arteries or a broken heart. That said," he continued, "some of us risk a fair bit more. One doesn't have to look very far into history to see that."

She sipped at her tea. "I'm sorry I keep dragging you in. I know it's not the kind of thing you want to be doing."

"Jillian," James said, "I know helping you doesn't mean sending you home. That's a fair bit more patronizing than I want to be. But I've never wanted my life to be quite this exciting. That, and as you well know, I don't want anything bad to be happening to you either."

She smiled. "I'll do my best. In all seriousness, James, I will. I don't want to die. If I think it's heading in that direction, I'll put myself on a plane home. Right now there doesn't seem to be an immediate threat. This guy Gohl's after, Helmut Radsch, he did go to Canada, and he might have done some really bad things during the war. My conscience is clear at the moment."

"Right, then, so are you needing my help?"

"Well," Jillian said, "I was wondering how much you knew about IG Farben."

James drifted over to the window for a moment, evidently collecting his thoughts, before settling on the sofa. "I don't know anything you couldn't find out in some old papers, but they were bad. The worst kind of organization, I'd venture. They jumped on Hitler's bandwagon with conviction and didn't look back until Nuremberg." James rubbed his hand on his face. "They're still around actually. What I know is mostly the same as what you got from that Gohl bloke. They were a giant pharmaceutical conglomerate. Given what happened later, funny enough, in the 1920s they did the world a huge public service by discovering the first antibiotic. Scientists there found that sulfa could kill strep bacteria when ingested. It was momentous. The number of women who died from infection after childbirth fell by about 98 percent.

"But after Hitler came to power, they shifted their R&D to causes the regime was interested in—none of it pretty stuff. Not only did they make the gas for the chambers, like Gohl told you, but scientists from IG Farben participated in the human experiments the Nazis conducted. They also used slave labor from Auschwitz to churn out war materials. Their whole effort was horrific."

Jillian stared at James. "Oh my God."

"Yes, well, some of those IG Farben chemists could have a go for worst war crimes."

"How did I not know that?"

James shrugged. "Not many people do. After the company broke up into parts, no one was saying the name 'IG Farben' anymore."

Jillian felt slightly nauseous. "What happened at Nuremberg?"

"A couple dozen men went on trial. About half the company's executives were convicted of war crimes, but they were all out by the mid-fifties. There are more than a few people who think what IG Farben did was worse than the Gestapo."

"Why did those executives get released?"

"It was all part of the effort to heal. By then the Cold War had started. Communists were the new enemy, so it was easier to let the fascists repent. Put that chapter of history into the past. And, well, you can't put a whole country in prison. Nuremberg only went after the leaders. There were enough of those. But is the man who follows the order any less guilty than the man who gives it? And with IG Farben, these weren't soldiers. I've read Hannah Arendt. I've studied totalitarianism. I know what a bloody mindfuck it is. And still, you think about the people in that company, and you wonder how it's possible that there were enough of them willing to go along with what they did."

Jillian was silent for a while. "So, Hans Gohl, what he's doing, it's not so bad."

"Ah, Jillian," James said, "I've no way of knowing that. Where does justice end and retribution begin? One can't go eliminating every Nazi or everyone who helped them by looking the other way. The sad truth is, there wouldn't be many left if ye did that."

"At least I know enough to try to convince Gohl I'm on his side. Although after listening to you, wanting to protect my job seems a little shallow."

"You want to protect your life, and there's nothing wrong with that. If ye learn anything from this, I'd say it's more about knowing what moral compromises you're unwilling to make along the way."

"And if part of me doesn't care that Helmut Radsch is about to answer for his crimes?"

"I'd say that makes you human," James said. "After all, if we can't agree that making gas to kill millions of people deserves retribution, then I'm not sure what we have left."

"Thanks, James. For everything."

"Just remember that it's a slippery slope. Focus on what you need to do to get Gohl out of your life so that any future retribution can be on your own terms."

Jillian was watering her plant and tapping her foot as "Band of Gold" blared out of her speakers. James was great for playing a variety of songs on his show. She supposed it kept the Stasi on their toes, trying to figure out the hidden messages in everything that came over the airwaves. In this case, she couldn't imagine what they'd make of it. Underneath the insanely catchy beat was the saddest song.

She heard the knock on her door and turned her music down. Looking through the peephole, she felt her heart start to thud when she saw Hans Gohl on the other side. He looked so innocuous, like someone's harmlessly doting grandfather. Putting her guard up, she undid the bolt and opened the door. She'd been expecting him, and she was ready for this.

"Jillian," he said. "I hope it isn't too soon. I find myself excited about our new connection."

She said nothing, just stepped back and waved him inside. She led him over to her living area and sat on the sofa. He took the chair across, as before. Again he took off his leather gloves but remained in his coat.

Jillian motioned toward the papers she had placed on the coffee table. "These are for you," she said. "Two reports on Helmut Radsch's interaction with the Canadian government in 1947."

She saw Gohl's eyes ignite. She had the feeling she was feeding an obsession. He was like a beast who was never sated.

"So soon," he said. "It is more than I expected. I had no idea you would have access to such impressive resources."

In other circumstances Jillian would have been pleased to over-deliver. In this case, she knew it would just serve to increase his expectations. "Don't be. It has nothing to do with my resources and everything to do with how seriously the Canadian government takes recordkeeping. As you can see, these reports are heavily redacted. I have a friend at external affairs who was willing to spend a couple lunch hours in the records department."

Without redaction, the reports were classified SECRET. Even after thirty years, information on old defectors was held tight—especially if those defectors were alive. That's why Jean-Marc was still hunting for more information.

"Can I expect anything else?" Gohl asked.

How much would be enough? "I've done as you asked. I've made four different requests to three different organizations. I spent a lunch hour last week getting the third degree from someone in the RCMP about why the hell I was asking."

"What did you say?"

Jillian shook her head. "Nothing that involves you, but also nothing that I'm going to share. You and I, we're not at a high trust level. I will do as you asked so that you'll fulfill your end of the bargain."

"Ah, yes. I suppose I cannot complain," he said, dropping his eyes to the reports.

Jillian let him read. There wasn't much, but since she didn't know what other information Gohl had, then she didn't know what would help him.

"What did you do during the war? Were you here?"

Hans shook his head. "No. I was near Frankfurt for most of it."

"Did you fight?"

"I was not a soldier. But all Germans were expected to fight in whatever way they could."

Jillian was curious about the distinction. "So I take it you weren't a Nazi?"

"Oh, we all had to pretend. Those of us who despised them had to pretend the hardest. Many Germans were inspired by Hitler. They thought his theatrics were compelling. But I saw them for what they were: the posturing of a tyrant. If what one is doing is great, one should not have to try so hard to convince people of it. And, of course, as the '30s wore on and the war got closer, dissent was silenced and dissenters banished. That is never a sign of good things to come."

Jillian felt so strange. Despite the fact that he was manipulating and threatening her and she didn't trust him at all, she agreed with him.

"How many have you found? These IG Farben people you're looking for?"

"Not all. That's all that matters. There is no victory in half measures."

"What do you do when you find them?"

Gohl shrugged. "Whatever is appropriate to the situation. In all cases they are exposed for the monsters they are."

Jillian suppressed a shudder at the expression on his face. His convictions ran deep. She got the feeling there were a lot more targets on his list than a small group of chemists. She wondered what his parameters were. "I've done some research on IG Farben. They were a large company."

"Ah. You are wondering if I've decided to punish them all, if there are hundreds of dead bodies strewn across the path of my past." Gohl chuckled. "On my deathbed I will confess all. But not until then." He picked up the reports, folded them neatly, and tucked them into his coat. "Hitler degraded Germany. He turned us into the dark tale of history. A country full of ignorant masses who followed a leader bent on destroying everything he led. Hitler did not care about economics, about prosperity, or even about power. He created a system that bankrupted itself both morally and financially and so could do nothing but implode. He did not care about Germany. All of these imbeciles who followed him could not see that. I don't have the time to worry about the followers. I care only about serving justice to the enablers, the ones who helped him tear Germany apart."

Gohl stood up. "No need to see me out. I shall come back in a week or so, and we can see if you've managed to shake loose anything else about Radsch."

Jillian simply nodded, watching Gohl's back as he let himself out and closed the door. One thing she'd learned from today's visit, if Gohl was employed by an intelligence service, she'd be surprised. He was not executing a mission; he was on a quest. One that seemed very personal.

CHAPTER TWENTY-THREE

Frank watched the television with a mixture of curiosity and dismay. Like the rest of the country and most of the world, he was closely following the hostage situation at the Minister of Agriculture's residence in Managua.

Thirty-six hours earlier, as the party at said residence was beginning to wind down, a group of approximately thirteen people fighting for the Sandinista cause against the Somoza government of Nicaragua stormed the building and took everyone in it hostage.

The news coverage was instant and international, which was the presumed intention of the hostage-takers. After twenty-four hours of intense negotiations amidst threats from the government, all party staff and household servants had been released. According to those who had been held, the Sandinistas were being pleasant to and considerate of their hostages. No one was injured, and everyone had enough to eat and drink. No one was happy, but no one was terrified. It was clear the Sandinistas wanted to distinguish themselves from the tactics used by the Somoza government. On that front, Frank thought they were doing quite well.

It seemed like the city had shut down. All focus was on the developing hostage situation, and not much else was getting done.

Among the hostages were a couple of ambassadors and other high-ranking officials, but both the American and Canadian ambassadors had already departed before the takeover of the residence began.

Frank and Veronica were now basking in the glow of successful intelligence reporting and the gratitude of their ambassador and his wife. The CBNRC was asking for all embassy intercept to be sent home, since the situation in Managua had raised the profile of the country in terms of intelligence priorities.

Of course, no one at HQ knew Frank had given the Americans a copy of the intercept they'd collected. Hopefully that didn't come to light, as Frank didn't relish the idea of another sit-down with personnel security about his avoidance of official sharing protocol.

Veronica had yet to hear anything from the RCMP, but the ambassador's gratitude would go on her file. That would be worth something.

It meant, though, that they had nothing to pursue in the current situation. No Canadians were involved. There was no immediate need for intelligence related to the hostage-taking.

They were free to keep looking for the Cuban.

That effort, however, was completely stalled. They had no leads. They hadn't heard from Quentin, and the situation in

Managua made it hard to make new contacts at the moment. He stood up, stubbing out his cigarette and grabbing his jacket. He tapped Veronica on the shoulder.

"Come on, you can't spend the whole day glued to the television. Get your purse."

"Where are we going?"

"For a drive. Let's go."

"What is this?" Veronica asked.

Frank glanced at her quickly. "It's an amplifying dish. You can use it to listen to what people are saying—if you're close enough and have somewhere to hide so they don't notice you. But that's not what we're going to do today."

Veronica played around with the dish, flipping the switch and surreptitiously trying to point it out the window. "Let me guess, we're going to try to pick up some other signals. Radio?"

Not bad. "Not quite. We're going to use it to try to find out what other people are intercepting."

"How are we going to do that?"

"With a lot of patience," Frank said, "because it's not going to work most of the time. However, some of the embassies around here are really small. Their intercepting equipment is on the roof, but those aren't very high on a two-story house. We're going to aim this at their dishes and see what and who they're picking up."

Veronica thought about this for a bit. "Presumably we're not going to try to permanently collect anything we find today."

"Unfortunately not." Frank sighed. "Although, just so you know, that's my dream. I love intercepting others' SIGINT feeds. But this is still a valuable exercise in building a record of what access other countries are likely to have. And it's a good time to do it. A lot of people are busy dealing with the hostage situation."

Frank set the car up across from the back entrance of the Polish embassy. "You get behind the wheel now. Anyone starts walking toward us, you drive away. They have no power to stop us here, and they aren't going to be able to trace the car."

Veronica continued to drive them around while Frank pointed his dish at various buildings around the city.

Three hours later they were down the street from the side entrance of the Turkish embassy.

"You're having fun," Veronica said.

Frank smiled. "A little. I used to do this all the time when I first joined CBNRC."

"You guys go around the world doing this?"

"We go some places where it's operationally feasible. For instance, there's not a chance in hell of doing this in Moscow. But a team goes around Ottawa once in a while. If we think anything important of ours is vulnerable, we can redirect it or scramble it. It's like evolution. Everyone is constantly adapting to the changing environment."

"You know, I've been thinking. I'm surprised we're the first joint team to be deployed like this. It seems to make a lot of sense, having the access of both agencies supporting the intelligence priorities. It's complementary and saves a lot of time."

Frank didn't say anything. He was slightly uncomfortable, because he could see her point, and he knew that he'd done more than his share to make collaboration between the two organizations difficult. "We're very used to our silos," he offered.

"I know. Believe me, I see that all the time in the RCMP. But out here, off Canadian soil, it's pretty easy to share. Those embassy meetings we sit in, where everyone shares what they've learned, it helps them be so much more functional than if everyone protected their information. It makes me wonder why the RCMP and CBNRC don't do more of it, more broadly, especially at home."

Frank held up his hand. "Before you go off on the potential for it being all sunshine and roses, as you've noted, it's easier here. It's easy when you're all on this little metaphorical island in a different country, all on the same team, looking out for one another. It's a lot harder when priorities conflict and sources are at risk."

"I get that, but it's not all or nothing. I'm just saying, this assignment wasn't such a bad idea."

Frank woke up to a pounding on his door. *Christ, what time was it?* He glanced at the bedside clock. 1:43. *Okay, not quite the middle of the night, but close enough.*

Damn, I'm getting old.

He shuffled to the front door in his pajamas. Whomever it was knocking at this time of night could damn well deal with him in his sleepwear. The door was barely open a few inches when Veronica shoved her way through.

"Get dressed," she said.

"What?"

"We're going dancing."

What the hell is she talking about? He gave her a look that communicated exactly what he thought about her showing up with such an idea.

"Frank." Veronica looked him directly in the eyes and held his gaze. "I want to go dancing. It's Thursday night. Almost the weekend. And you need the exercise. So let's go."

His brain woke up a fraction. He belatedly realized she needed to talk to him about something that couldn't be discussed in an unsecure environment.

At two a.m. Whatever it was better be pretty damn earth-shattering.

He left her and went to throw on some clothes. He didn't even bother to ask her what this was all about until they were well out of the way of the apartment.

A couple of turns and a couple of side streets later, he figured it was safe to talk. "Okay, Veronica, what the hell is going on?"

She turned to him. He could barely see her face in the dark, what with Managua being not that well lit at night. But he could feel her excitement.

"I got invited to a poetry reading earlier this evening. It was interesting. It seems like a lot of Nicaraguans are pretty pissed about what's happening in their country. A couple people were discussing how foreigners needed to back away, let the people here make their own decisions without foreign interference."

Frank waited, knowing there would be more.

"Surprisingly, it wasn't just anti-American. It was intervention generally. So anyway, I was there, not saying much, just listening. Then coffee was served. I was up, pouring myself a cup, when this woman started talking to me. She said she knew I was looking for an old lover and where Carlos might be. I asked her why she was helping me. I didn't even know her. She said her country would be better off without people like him."

Frank was shocked. He supposed he shouldn't be. Veronica had been out trying to develop contacts from day one. She'd planted seeds and spread information. This was how intelligence was supposed to work. You put out enough connections, eventually you got something back.

But it wasn't a guarantee. Ever.

"Did she give you an address?"

"Yes. It's just south of here. A small village called Santa Rosa."

"You trust this woman? You aren't being set up?"

Veronica shook her head. "No, and I have no idea. I've never met her before. She could be legit; she might not be. But what would the setup be? Carlos wants to find out more about this woman asking around about him? The way Quentin talks about him, he'd more likely just yank me off the street."

She had a point. Carlos presumably had a lot of friends in Managua. There were other, more direct ways of getting to Veronica.

"What did she mean, where he 'might be'?" Frank asked.

"It's his aunt's house."

Frank deflated a little. "He does have an aunt here. That much I got from Quentin. But Carlos can't be there. Quentin would have looked there."

Veronica was silent for a moment. "You know that Quentin knew where the aunt lived?"

"No," Frank said.

"And—" Veronica paused. "Well, we have no reason to assume Quentin told us everything. He said he couldn't find Carlos. Maybe he did, and that's why Amaya hasn't heard from him in a while. Maybe he found Carlos and figured he'd just recap the whole thing for us. Maybe Carlos doesn't spend a lot of time at his aunt's, but it could be his base in Nicaragua, where he goes when there's nowhere else to go."

Frank pressed his fingers together and rested them on his chin. "So we go to the aunt's house."

"Yes," Veronica said. "Reconnaissance. We can watch it for a while. See if we can identify Carlos, see who else is there. Maybe his aunt can't stand him either."

Frank smiled in the dark. "Wouldn't that be nice."

Frank's ass was getting sore because he'd been sitting on it for almost three days. It was like a damn stakeout. Brutal. Thank Christ he'd never become a cop.

They'd been eating takeout food and taking turns sleeping in the back seat. They moved the car occasionally, but they always had a good view of the turquoise front door. Veronica had gone poking around and discovered there was a back entrance, but they couldn't sit on both. Frank had decided to give it three days on the front. If they didn't get anything, they could go back to their apartments in Managua for a much-needed shower, then come back for a few days on the other entrance.

He watched Veronica come around the corner with some coffee and something that had already stained the paper bag she was carrying with oil.

The windows were down because it was hot, even parked in the shade. Frank knew that he stank. The whole thing was fucking miserable. It certainly wasn't how he had planned on spending New Year's. He did not understand how Veronica seemed so chipper.

"Here you go," she said, handing him his coffee as she slid into the passenger seat. "It's fresh. I can't say the same for the food."

He took a sip of the coffee and burned his tongue. "Jesus Christ," he said, almost dropping the cup.

Veronica took a small sip of her coffee. "It is hot."

"Yeah, no shit."

"Feeling okay, Frank?"

"Do I fucking look like it?"

"No."

"Then why did you ask?"

She shrugged. "In case maybe you wanted to talk."

"Talk about what exactly?" Frank snarled. "How my ass cheeks are so painful I think I'm getting bedsores?"

"A bit dramatic, no?"

"Shut up."

Veronica leaned back against her seat and closed her eyes. "Next time I'll come by myself. Or bring Phillip. He'd be up for it."

"I'm up for it," Frank said, grabbing a flaky something out of the bag.

Veronica didn't say anything.

Frank jammed the food into his mouth. It tasted like fat. His gut rumbled in protest. *Who'd've thought I'd be craving a carrot.* He supposed he should make conversation, but they'd covered everything easy, and he was tired. Even though he'd been sitting for most of the last sixty hours, he was tired.

"Any of your children plan on following in your footsteps?" Veronica asked, breaking the silence.

Frank shook his head. "Not a one. They all take after their mother—more artistic. None of them like playing around and taking things apart."

"Does it bother you? Like you had no influence on them?"

Jesus, did she ever cut to the point. "I can see why people have trouble with you. You jump right to all the uncomfortable parts."

Veronica blushed a little. "Sorry."

"It's fine. It's the same reason people can't stand me." Frank paused to drink some of his finally almost cool enough coffee. "I had some influence. Tavia, she's the oldest, she loves problem solving, like I do. She chose math instead of engineering, but I think she's driven by similar questions. Cleo, she's the pure artist. Loves making beautiful things, she says. She's in Toronto, trying to break into costume design. She got my work ethic. Selene, the youngest, she's still in university studying architecture. She and I watch football and debate communism. She wants to make the world a better place, so we fight about the best way to do that."

"Three girls. You sound like a good father, Frank."

He shrugged, slightly embarrassed. "I did okay. My wife gets most of the credit. Livia was always there. I couldn't be, not all the time, but I tried."

"I think the most important thing you can give kids is the support to help them figure out the kind of person they want to be. Too many parents dump their expectations and unfulfilled dreams on their kids. Then those kids end up where they don't want to be, and the cycle continues."

"Which one are you?"

Veronica smiled. Frank noticed it was a slightly sad one.

"A Métis woman in the RCMP? That's not anyone's unfulfilled dream," she said. "My mom, actually, she was really opposed to me joining. Family dinners are still a little awkward, especially because I couldn't quite hide how frustrated I was at work. But my dad, he supports me. He doesn't think it's a good idea, but he supports me. I think he's hoping that it proves to be a disappointment and that I find a new dream. In the meantime, he keeps my mom off the ledge."

Frank wondered if he should stop there. "Where are you at about your decision now? Brave or stupid?"

"Often the same thing, right?" Veronica looked out the window for a while. "I want things to get better. Not just lifting the Iron Curtain and securing global democracy, but at home. For Aboriginal Canadians, they're systematically disenfranchised by the government and misunderstood by the general public. There's so much pain in those communities but also so much possibility that is never realized. I don't want it to be easy for us to keep trying to do all this good in the world and giving out all this foreign aid while ignoring what's going on in our own country."

Frank had a feeling that he was one of those people who had no clue. "So why the RCMP?"

"I know that one person can't fix everything, but the first step to treating people—any people—better is to stop seeing them as others. The RCMP goes on reservations and sees the people living there as different, as not like them. It's like persecution anywhere. You have to pretend the people you're persecuting are somehow not like you, not human, they don't feel as much, or they aren't as intelligent, or whatever. I wanted to work in intelligence. I thought it sounded interesting. And I thought that seeing a Métis woman doing intelligence work, having people in the RCMP interacting with me as an equal, well, it would have to help break down that barrier of otherness."

Frank thought about how hard it had been to send Jillian to Berlin because none of his superiors could imagine a woman doing the job. He thought about how the only people of color at CBNRC were the linguists. He thought about how everyone he'd ever dealt with at the RCMP was white and mostly male.

"It's a slow fucking process, isn't it?"

Veronica smiled, a genuine one. "Yeah. But one we need."

Frank was saved from further discussion in uncomfortable territory by the turquoise door opening across the street. He watched as a woman came out. She was older. They'd seen her a couple of times. He figured she was Carlos's aunt, out to do some shopping or whatever.

She stopped outside her door and turned to look in their direction. Frank and Veronica just sat sipping their coffee. The woman started to walk toward them.

"Is she coming here?" Frank was unnerved.

The woman got closer. She was definitely headed toward their car.

"It looks like it," said Veronica.

The woman went up to the passenger side window and leaned down.

"You are watching us," she said. "Who are you? We don't want any trouble."

Her English wasn't great. She had clearly rehearsed the words.

Veronica answered her in Spanish. The woman looked surprised and slightly relieved. Veronica smiled and put down her coffee on the dash. She gestured to Frank and then herself. The conversation seemed to take off. The woman continued to visibly relax. She waved her arm in the direction of her house.

Veronica turned to Frank. "This is Carlos's aunt Claudia. She'd like to invite us in for coffee."

Frank considered the situation for a moment. "You feel confident it's a good idea?"

"I do," Veronica nodded. "I think she has some interesting things to tell us about Carlos and about Quentin. And then I think she wants us to get the hell off her street."

Frank could get behind that, desperate as he was for a shower.

He unbuckled his seat belt. "Let's go, then."

The interior of the house was small but pleasant. Someone was a good artist. There were colorful pictures of landscapes hanging on the walls. Claudia gestured for them to sit at the round, lace-covered table beside the kitchen. She started heating up water for coffee and then began chopping something.

Veronica was asking the odd question, but they seemed to be innocuous. About the house, or maybe the art.

After a few minutes, Claudia placed a platter of fruit on the table with small plates and forks. She returned to the stove to attend to the coffee, then sat at the table with them while it brewed.

Claudia started speaking, and Veronica alternated between follow-up questions and translating for Frank. An interesting story started to emerge.

Carlos was indeed Claudia's nephew, and she did not know where he was. He had come to the house months earlier to say that he was back in Nicaragua. Frank assumed that he'd come right from Berlin.

She didn't want him here. She'd told him to get out and never come back.

Veronica asked why.

Claudia got a look on her face that Frank had seen a few times. A sadness so deep it would never go away, not completely. "Mató a mi hija. Mi Isabella."

Frank could figure out what those words meant. He also wondered who Isabella was. Wondered if she had something to do with Quentin and his past in Nicaragua.

Veronica placed her hand on Claudia's. "Lo siento."

The silence hung for a while. Claudia had just opened her mouth to continue speaking when the front door opened. A man entered. Younger. A son? "Mama…" was all Frank caught in the rapid Spanish that followed.

The conversation was clearly heated. Frank also caught "Canada" as Claudia gestured toward them. He was grateful Veronica could follow what was going on.

Abruptly, the man pulled out a chair and sat himself down at the table. He looked angry, but he had clearly agreed to stay and at least monitor the exchange.

Claudia introduced him as Luis. Her son-in-law.

The husband of her dead Isabella.

Luis's eyes changed from angry to being as sad as Claudia's.

"What do you want from us?" Luis asked.

Frank appreciated his switch to English but figured Veronica should keep doing the talking. He wasn't exactly known for his charm.

"We are looking for Carlos," Veronica said.

"Why?" Luis asked.

"A friend of ours may be in a lot of trouble. Trouble that he put her in. We need some answers about who his friends are."

Luis scowled. "He has no friends. He is a parasite sucking the lives of others in order to survive. We have nothing to do with him. Like my mother-in-law said, we don't know where he is, and he won't come here. So you can leave us alone."

"We are also looking for another man, an American. His name is Quentin. Has he contacted you?"

The scowl on Luis's face deepened as his cheeks colored with anger. "He is not welcome here either."

Claudia spoke up, directing her words at Veronica.

"My mother-in-law is more forgiving than I am. The monthly checks from the American are guilt money. Nothing more. He wasn't the one who put a bullet in Isabella, but he put her in its path."

Frank studied Luis. This was, apparently, the situation in Quentin's past that Frank had learned about all those months ago, when Quentin had gone off the rails. And it was the reason he was back to put a bullet in Carlos.

"Why'd she get involved with him in the first place?" Frank asked, speaking for the first time.

Luis shook his head. "Isabella just wanted the world to be a better place. She thought the way to fight was with words and books, building a community that wanted to change. Carlos, he's always been violent, the kind who throws a grenade for fun, just to watch the carnage. She thought people like him would undermine what she wanted for our country. So she worked with the American. I told her not to. Carlos would come to a bad end on his own, and we can't trust Americans. But she believed that the American would help, and that journalists always want to tell the truth. He could be one to bring the story of the suffering in Nicaragua to the world. She was wrong."

To Frank, it sounded like a typical intelligence cock-up. In all fairness, being an agent was a dangerous volunteer position. There were lots of examples of it not ending well.

"We are sorry to be bringing this up for you. I know how painful it is to relive something so sad," Veronica said. "If you haven't seen either of them, then you can't help us, and we won't bother you anymore."

Luis looked at Veronica. Frank saw hesitation in his eyes.

"The American was here. Parked where you are now."

"When?" Veronica asked. "Recently?"

Luis shook his head. "Months ago. Not long after Carlos showed up."

"What did he say to you?"

"Nothing," Luis said. "He came for a few days and then never came back."

Frank didn't know what to make of that. Guilt? Regret? Whatever it was, there weren't any words Quentin could offer these people that would make it right.

There was a long pause, but to Frank, Luis looked like he had something else to say.

"I don't know who I hate more," Luis said eventually. "Isabella was nothing but a pawn for both of those men. But the American, he wrote to us once. He said he was sorry. Isabella was a beautiful person, and he was sorry that we had lost our wife and daughter, and that my son had lost his mother. Carlos has shown no remorse. No feeling. He just showed up here expecting to use whatever we had left. What will you do when you find him?"

"Beat the shit out of him until he answers our questions," Frank said.

There was a ghost of a smile on Luis's face.

"If we can find Quentin, he'll be with us," Veronica said. "He came back to Nicaragua on vacation. To put a bullet in Carlos."

Luis sighed. "That might be some justice." No doubt this man understood how unfulfilling that kind of justice ultimately was. "Carlos stays at a compound in the western part of Managua, deep in the barrio there, an old school. It's where people hunted by Somoza go too. There are many people in there. I don't know how many. It's well guarded. But he is not one of them, not really."

Frank stared for a minute at Luis and Claudia. It looked like the nightmare was a long way from ending for the both of them.

"Gracias," Veronica said.

As the door shut behind them, Frank looked down the street to see someone lounging on the hood of their car.

"Unbelievable," Frank said.

They crossed the street, not saying anything until they were close enough to not call too much attention to themselves.

"You certainly have a knack for showing up," Veronica said.

"Now you know all the sordid details of my past," Quentin said.

"Among other things," Veronica responded.

"Where've you been?" Frank asked. "Amaya's worried about you."

"Costa Rica," Quentin said.

"Doing the full tour," Frank said.

Quentin shrugged. "While I'm here."

"We're heading back to Managua because I need a shower more than salvation. After that, it's the coldest beer I can find. Where can we meet you?"

Quentin was staring at the house they had just left. After a moment he refocused on them. "I'm coming with you."

Frank was nonplussed. He wanted time with Veronica to come up with a game plan in the car. He didn't see any way of avoiding bringing Quentin in, given what they'd just found out. They were going to need him to get to Carlos. But hell, he wanted to process everything he'd just heard.

"You don't have a car?"

"No," Quentin said.

Frank gave it a pause, but elaboration wasn't forthcoming.

"Christ. Get in, then. And keep your window down. We haven't showered in two days."

They all got in the car. Frank pulled out and turned to head back to Managua. Glancing in the rearview mirror, he saw Quentin looking at the turquoise door until his neck wouldn't bend any further.

CHAPTER TWENTY-FOUR

"Did you have a nice Christmas with your family in Dresden?" Jillian asked as Madeline draped her coat on the back of a chair.

"Ah, you know. I have told you before. Visits with my family in East Germany are never easy. The further we get from the war, when we were all the same, the harder it is to find things in common. It saddens me so deeply, what they are told by their government. How they do not understand that it is not needed to live in so much fear. As much as I try to focus on the good memories—the people we know, who is getting married or having babies—the pressure of where they are living, it makes things so hard. Then I remember I can leave. I can come back here and enjoy my freedom. So I help where I can and make sure I go often enough that they are always reminded there is another way."

Jillian had a lot of admiration for Madeline's desire to spend time with her family in East Germany. The couple times

Jillian had been over, well, it wasn't an easy place to be. She knew it would be so much simpler for Madeline to stay away.

"And you, my dear Jillian, how was your Christmas?"

Jillian shrugged. "Pretty boring. Although, I love this glühwein you serve at this time of year. It definitely made me feel more festive."

Madeline smiled. "Yes, it is a good drink. You do not have this in Canada?"

"No, sadly. Canadians don't know what they're missing."

"Did you miss your family?"

"A little," Jillian said, "but Christmas is a pretty quiet time for us anyway. My parents are thinking of coming for a visit. I told them to wait until May because the city is really beautiful then."

"Very true. We are very blessed in Berlin to have so many trees now. After the war there weren't many left, between the bombs and the need for firewood in the cold winters. Here in the West, we started planting trees as soon as the city began working again, so now there are many beautiful trees that have been growing for decades. And of course, we protect those that made it through the war."

Jillian looked down at the papers in her hand: the history of the cabaret in wartime Berlin. She looked at Madeline and realized that here was an opportunity that she'd almost missed. Madeline would no doubt have some perspective to share on IG Farben during the war; it couldn't hurt to ask. Hans Gohl wasn't going away anytime soon, and Jillian had been in SIGINT long enough to know that it wasn't a good idea to ignore a potential source.

"Madeline, I wanted to ask you, I've been reading some history—you know, to understand Germany better—and in this one article about the war, they were talking about how much of the manufacturing sector was repurposed in support of the Nazis, companies that are pretty famous and still around. As I was reading it, I made the connection that those were the kind of people who would have probably come to your mother's cabaret. It was, I don't know, kind of a revelation."

"Yes, I suppose it is a bit abstract for you, these records," Madeline said.

"Kind of. What I mean is, what do you remember about the men who came? Not as individuals, but as a group? Like, how did it work? Were they dropped off? Told to go?"

Madeline sat back and thought for a moment. "Do you know, I don't remember much of that, of how they got to the cabaret. I remember my mother saying that I always had to be respectful, because all of these men were important to the Nazis somehow. Like I said, not the most important, but still very useful. The Nazis needed them all in some way. Of course, all claimed to be Nazis as well, so I can see how that is confusing. But yes, there were many businessmen who came to us. Scientists also."

"Anybody famous?" Jillian asked.

Madeline laughed. "No household names. But there was the man who designed the Volkswagen Beetle. And the man who created the first Fanta. It became very popular during the war because we could not get American drinks like Coke. It was very different from the Fanta today, though."

Jillian started to laugh. "Every time I think you can't tell me anything more surprising than what you've already shared, you manage to come out with something incredible. The guy who developed Fanta? That's amazing."

"In many ways," Madeline said, "they were remarkable times. Living them, there was very little that was good. But to survive it, after a while one can appreciate some of what made it such a powerful moment in history. Without, of course, being nostalgic for anything that happened."

Jillian understood that. To share about the cabaret, to be able to do that now, was to tell a truly unique story. But she knew that there was no way Madeline would ever want to go back to that time.

"What about a company named IG Farben? Do you remember anyone from there? I read an article about them, how they invented the world's first antibiotic, but then did terrible things during the war." It was a shot in the dark, Jillian knew. But if the cabaret hosted car people and soft drink people, surely people from other industries wouldn't be outside the realm of possibility? The truth was, she was starting to think having something to trade Hans Gohl might be one way to get him out of her life. Madeline's documents wouldn't constitute evidence in court, but Gohl didn't seem too bothered about keeping everything above board.

"That is a name I have not heard in years," Madeline said, shuddering slightly. "They were such a bad company. I remember, after the war, when people started to look around and try to understand how it all happened, they were one of the first indications of how deep the pain was going to go."

She paused, looking around at the boxes. "Yes, I suppose there must have been some men from IG Farben who came to the cabaret. They employed thousands of people and were very involved in making some of Hitler's dreams a reality. They worked on many things that were special to Hitler. Some of them must have been very good candidates for our cabaret, but I do not remember anyone in particular."

"Would you mind if I kept an eye out as we are looking?" Jillian asked. "I find it helps me concentrate, to be looking for something specific."

"Not at all. If I see anything, I will pull it aside for you so you can see a whole piece." Madeline shook her head. "You know, when I made the decision to start going through all these documents, I thought the hardest part would be the memories they brought back. Now I realize there is so much more to contend with. I'm not sure anymore how to organize all of the stories."

"If it were me, I'd do it by dancer. If anyone deserves to come alive from all of this, it's the dancers themselves. I think that would be the most compelling. If you're worried about protecting identities, you could always do, like, a composite character."

Madeline smiled. "Maybe you are right. But there is so much information. I am beginning to think that I am not the right one to handle all of this in the end. Perhaps I should do what you suggested before, go to a museum or a university."

"You could, and they might help. But they also might just put the boxes in storage and forget about them."

Jillian wondered what Hans Gohl would make of all these records. No doubt he would go through them all very carefully. It's too bad he wasn't someone she could trust, on account of being ruthless and possibly a little unhinged. He'd probably be a great help to Madeline with all of this old information.

"Yes. I guess I will just focus on finishing the organizing."

"I'm not really sure, as I'm not a writer," Jillian said, "but maybe it would help to just focus on one story at a time. That way it doesn't get overwhelming. That's how I do it as an engineer. Focus on one problem at a time and try to avoid creating new ones."

Madeline smiled. "That does make sense."

"I wouldn't wait. Sometimes changing your perspective can rejuvenate a project. We've sorted through so much already. You could pick a stack and try writing something. That way you might find out if it's even something you want to do."

"You are very wise." There was a stretch of silence as Madeline contemplated the boxes stacked around the room.

She stood up and moved to one of the newer boxes that contained the color-coded files they were using. "My attention to this project has begun to flag, but I cannot bear the idea of just closing the door again. So I will start with Monika. She and I were very close. She had such a wonderful laugh. Even at the end, when things were clearly falling apart and everything began to crumble around us, she could still make me laugh."

Madeline pulled out a set of files and sat back down, opening the first folder. "And you? You have done so much; I am grateful that you keep coming back. If there is anything that would make it easier for you, then please, go ahead."

"I think I'm going to focus on seeing if I can find out anything about IG Farben. I confess, the story of that company has completely intrigued me. I don't understand how a group of people can go from discovering antibiotics to making gas for the chambers in the space of a few years."

"You are not the only one. That is why they had to be broken up after the war. Not only were there so many employees that still needed jobs, but buildings and technology and products that belonged to the company. Too much to get rid of and too much that the new Germany needed. But no one wanted to say the name IG Farben. So it was taken apart and the parts rebuilt under their old names, and we all forget that those parts were once a much larger whole."

"How do you feel about that? Like every time you take a Bayer aspirin? I mean, I get that it's hard. I hope it doesn't seem like I'm judging, but the more I'm learning, the more I'm realizing that many of those old Nazis didn't go away. They resurfaced after a few years and started rebuilding."

Madeline sighed. "Yes. There is a lot of unrest still. Some people feel that too many of the Nazi leaders were not made to pay for their crimes. So many of the young people now, they look at who their grandfathers were and they are ashamed. I can only say that in 1946, it was not nearly so clear. The country was in ruins. Leaving us all to starve would have been hypocritical. Many were afraid to sow the seeds of discontent again, like had been done after the First World War. The truth was, many who had the knowledge and the skills to rebuild the country had also been members of the Nazi Party. The culture of fear was so pervasive during the war, it is hard to know who acted out of belief, and who was just closing their eyes and waiting for it all to end."

Jillian reflected on Madeline's words. "For what it's worth, that's why I think what you're doing here is so great. The stories you have in these files, they're real. I think, if you can find a way to share them, they'll be one more piece that shows people how complex it all was. Going forward, to avoid it ever happening again, well, we have to understand all of it—even the parts that make us uncomfortable."

Madeline smiled. "On this we are agreed. So let's get to telling our stories, then."

"Yes, ma'am," Jillian said, returning Madeline's smile. She knew it was a long shot that these records contained anything that might be useful to Hans Gohl, but she was looking through them anyway. It couldn't hurt to keep in mind. They were original documents from the war that hadn't already been explored by historians, and they had the added benefit of being unclassified—which made it very lucky, really, that they had fallen into her lap.

CHAPTER TWENTY-FIVE

"So what are you going to do?"

Veronica was staring at him. She wanted an answer. Frank didn't know what to say.

"Because he's going to walk into this bar in about five minutes, and you know what he's going to ask us," she continued. "He's going to ask for that location."

"And it's my decision?" Frank asked.

Veronica took a sip of her drink. "Yeah, it's your decision."

Frank scowled. "Fine time for you to start deferring to me."

"You know why, Frank. The whole reason we were looking for Carlos was so you could protect your setup in Berlin and the woman running it. So you're the one who needs to decide. Will giving Quentin that location for Carlos help or cause more problems?"

The damnedest thing was, Frank didn't know. Part of him wanted to give the location to Quentin and just be done with it. Carlos dead was better for everyone—especially Jillian. But

Frank knew that taking that route wasn't the long-term choice, because then there would be a giant loose end. And it would eat at him until it got tied up.

Veronica sat up suddenly, surprise flickering across her face. Frank turned in his seat as Amaya sat at their table. He almost didn't recognize her. Her hair was down, and she was wearing a long blue cotton dress and flat sandals. She looked like a local.

"We have a lot to talk about," she said. "Thank you for telling me where to find you."

Veronica shot Frank a questioning glance, but he'd explain to her later. He'd called Amaya to let her know they'd seen Quentin alive and well. She told him she had some information to share.

"About eight hours ago, a report landed on my desk," Amaya said, motioning toward the bartender to order a drink. She yelled something in Spanish, resulting in a wide grin from the man behind the bar. Frank didn't doubt her drink would be arriving at the table soon.

"It was the response to my request to MI6 for information on Carlos Honouras and who he might have been working with on behalf of those in Her Majesty's service."

Amaya paused for a few moments as her drink was delivered. She exchanged a few words with the bartender, who had brought over the drink himself. Frank thought the State Department would be crazy to move her from Managua. She quite clearly was comfortable in her influence in this city.

She took a sip of the gold-hued liquid. "Not that it will shock you, but the report was empty. Nothing to report on Carlos Honouras."

"That's bullshit," said Frank. "At least one person in MI6 worked with him for years."

"Hmm, yes," Amaya said. "It did surprise me. But on the other hand, it didn't. I'd say it's very likely your boy never made it into reporting. Not under his real name, anyway."

"But we have the report from GCHQ," Veronica said. "They confirmed Carlos was a target of theirs on behalf of MI6."

Frank felt his beer had gone sour. "GCHQ targets only foreigners. It would have been a typical targeting request, given who Carlos is. Whoever was running things at MI6—and I have to imagine it's Hoffsteader—could have easily decoupled the reporting from the cover name."

"Why would he do that?" Veronica asked.

"Maybe he didn't want to advertise who he was working with."

"You didn't come here to tell us that," Veronica said, turning to Amaya. "You could have shared the info about an empty report in a phone call tomorrow morning."

"Well, I do like getting off campus for a drink. Mixing up the company and keeping up foreign relations and all that. But yes, you're right. I have something much more interesting to share."

Frank and Veronica waited expectantly.

"Funny you should mention that name Hoffsteader," Amaya said. "Right after that report showed up, I got ordered to the ambassador's office. Seems someone had made a complaint that I went to MI6 directly. The station chief was there, suitably pissed. Apparently he'd received an earful from someone in London about targeting British citizens."

"Where does Hoffsteader come in?" Veronica asked.

"I'd say he's right in the middle of it," Amaya said, "because my original request didn't mention Hoffsteader. I only asked about shareable MI6 reporting on the activities of Carlos Honouras since 1965. I figured I was more likely to get something if I didn't start with an ask on one of their most esteemed citizens."

Frank smiled. "He tipped his hand."

"Yes, especially because I have it on good authority that he's planning a trip to Nicaragua in the next couple of days."

"What?" Frank started.

"It seems Gavin Hoffsteader has decided to take a vacation and visit Managua."

"How do you know?" asked Veronica.

Amaya tapped her fingers on her glass. "I've been working here for a long time. I know a lot of people."

Frank sat there, trying to digest the information. The obvious question was, why was Hoffsteader on his way to Nicaragua? To shut Carlos up? To protect him? What was in their relationship that was worth that kind of risk?

Suddenly Amaya's face broke into a wide smile. "Quentin."

Frank looked up to see Quentin's features lighten momentarily before the neutral guard slipped back in place.

Quentin sat down, distributing beers to both Veronica and Frank. Frank looked at his in surprise. It was an unusual gesture from Quentin. He didn't know how to read it.

"You look...not well, but not any worse than the last time I saw you," Amaya said.

"I appreciate you looking out for me."

"Someone has to. You don't have many friends left here."

Quentin drank his Coke. "Is this your attempt at being inconspicuous?" he said in Frank's direction. "Drinking with the special advisor to the American ambassador?"

"It's a damn full-time job, finding places where nobody gives a shit," Frank said. It was true. They couldn't meet like this in any official capacity, so embassies were off-limits. Official residences would likely be bugged and monitored. So the only hope was bars like this, too dark and too noisy for anyone to overhear them.

Silence filled the table, and Frank couldn't figure out which conversation to have first.

"Shit," said Frank, turning to Quentin. "Amaya's just told us that despite MI6 reporting nothing on Carlos, Gavin Hoffsteader is about to get on a plane to Managua. Sir Gavin fucking Hoffsteader."

Quentin's eyes narrowed. "Tell me where Carlos is."

Frank didn't know what to do. Quentin's hands clenched around his Coke bottle so hard Frank thought it might shatter.

"We just need to think this through," Frank said.

"There's nothing to think about. I told you not to get in my way. I'm not going to sit by while Carlos gets bailed out again and parachuted somewhere else. Tell me where he fucking is, or I'll go back to Isabella's and beat it out of her husband."

"You don't know why Hoffsteader's coming here," said Amaya.

"And I don't fucking care. This has to end. Now."

Frank was hardly surprised the situation was turning into such a mess. So much of it had been a long shot from the beginning. He could see now that it was going to be hard to get anything out of the Cuban with a guy like Hoffsteader watching his back.

"It doesn't matter if we tell you where Carlos is," Veronica said. "You aren't going to be able to get near him."

Quentin stared at her. Frank could see his jaw clench. "You know this how?"

"I drove out there as soon as we got back from the aunt's house. I had to park and do a lot of walking. It's an old school in the middle of the barrio. It looks like a homeless shelter, but they have lookouts. You aren't going to be able to get in there, let alone find him. So it doesn't matter."

Frank was stunned. When they'd got back from the house in Santa Rosa, Frank had spent twenty minutes in the shower and another twenty brushing his teeth. Veronica had gone out and done reconnaissance.

"Why didn't you tell me you were going?" Frank asked.

"I left you a note. And I think we can talk about this later."

"I know what I'm doing. I'm not going to just fucking walk in," Quentin said.

"I know. You'll have to spend days watching them, learning the routines, finding the opening. There's no other way to do it. Which means you're not going to get to Carlos before Hoffsteader does."

Quentin looked ready to explode. It was the most emotion Frank had ever seen from him. "Then I'll take out Hoffsteader."

Amaya sat up straighter as the tension rippled around the table. "No, Quentin. Please. You can't."

"Why not? It sounds to me like Hoffsteader has a loyalty problem."

Amaya looked at Quentin for a long moment. "You would never be able to come back from something like that."

Frank thought that maybe he should just share the location, drink his beer, and stay out of the whole thing. He was starting to lose track of what he and Veronica were supposed to be doing.

"That's not a good idea," said Veronica.

"Why the fuck do you care? About any of this?" Quentin looked ready for a fight.

Veronica sighed a little but maintained her composure. "I don't care who you kill. That's your choice and your life. We don't work for the same people, and how you live your life—what's left of it—is of no concern to me. What is important to my country, and by extension to me, is that we have a sensitive operation in Berlin that could be compromised by Carlos Honouras. My job as an intelligence officer is to confirm if he has made the Berlin operation or the woman running it vulnerable to any of our adversaries. I need to get information out of him, not kill him. You can do that when I'm done with him."

Frank stared at Veronica. She was becoming damn good at her job.

"So what's your plan? If he's so protected inside that school, you're not going to be able to get to him before Hoffsteader does either," Quentin said.

Veronica paused for a moment. "The Hoffsteader thing doesn't change anything. After I went by today, I realized that we have to flush him out. We have to get whoever is protecting Carlos to kick him out. In that moment, he'll be vulnerable."

Frank noticed that Quentin was looking interested. Skeptical maybe, but interested.

"How are we going to do that? Spread rumors and hope for the best?"

"We don't need rumors. We have the photo. Carlos is clearly recognizable, along with three other men, two of whom we can prove are British and members of the UK government. He's holed up with a bunch of people on the run from Somoza, some of whom have to be Sandinistas who get their funding from Castro and the Soviets. That kind of connection is a deal-breaker. My hunch is that Carlos isn't exactly the prodigal son around here. His track record suggests that he's burned a few bridges in his time. It stands to reason that whoever he's with now doesn't trust him completely. The picture is just the straw to make his reputation collapse."

Frank drank some of his beer. Her logic was sound. It could work.

"Actually, I think Hoffsteader coming here does change things," Amaya said. "It helps you. A photo is enough for suspicion. But one of the British men on a plane to Managua— that says a lot about the relationship. I could easily make Hoffsteader's travel plans more…public knowledge."

"How do you plan to deliver the photo?" Quentin asked.

"I'll just walk up to the door. Someone will stop me."

"And you're going to tell them what?"

"The truth. That they can't trust this man. No one can."

"What's to say they don't just shoot you?"

Veronica thought for a moment. "Why would they? I'm not going to stay around for a chat. I've got information they need. The photo is going to do the convincing, not me."

Frank wasn't sure he liked this part of the plan. "What if they haul you inside?"

Her eyes narrowed at him. "That's a risk I'm willing to take."

"We should explore options."

"There aren't any, Frank. We've got less than twenty-four hours to pull this off. It's possible Hoffsteader has intentions that we haven't thought of, but the worst-case scenario is he's here to intervene on Carlos's behalf. That's the situation we have to prepare for."

Damn it. She was right.

"Fine. We go in three hours. Just after sunset," Quentin said. "I'll go with you and watch. If something happens, I'll contact Frank. When you're done, you walk away. If Carlos leaves the building, he's mine." He turned to Amaya. "You have three hours to tell everyone you know that Sir Gavin Hoffsteader is on his way to Managua to protect his asset Carlos Honouras." Quentin looked around the table. "Does anyone have a problem?"

Frank shook his head. "If anyone in MI6, including Hoffsteader, wanted to protect that relationship, they shouldn't have sent a bullshit report. As far as I'm concerned, that connection isn't classified."

Amaya stood up. "I'm off. I've got some people to see."

Quentin waited for her to leave. "I'll pick you up," he said to Veronica.

"At the apartment?"

He finished his Coke. "Three hours." He got up, following Amaya out the door.

Frank didn't say anything for a moment. "I guess we've got some pictures to copy."

"Please tell me I'm not going to get shot tonight," Veronica said.

Frank hoped not, but it scared him that he couldn't be sure. "You don't have to do this," he said. "Berlin isn't your operation."

"It's not yours either. This is the job, Frank. Everything I've said, it's true. And hey, if I decide the risk isn't worth it, I can always sit in a room by myself doing media monitoring."

"So you could."

"Let's go get ready."

Frank finished off his beer. "After you."

CHAPTER TWENTY-SIX

Jillian stepped out of the America Memorial Library. Even though it was only four thirty in the afternoon, it was winter dark, and West Berlin was lit up with the lights of buses and windows, streetlights and billboards.

She wrapped her scarf tighter against the wind. The area was quiet, as if everyone was resting after their New Year's celebrations. She supposed all the glühwein vendors were closed up as well. The mulled wine was one of her favorite parts of the holiday season in West Germany, and she'd had her fair share over the last month.

As she joined up with the sidewalk along Blucherplatz, Jillian wasn't paying much attention to her surroundings. She had initially planned to U-Bahn to Madeline's garage to keep reading through the war memories, but now Jillian thought she should head over to see James. She'd discovered something at the library that James wasn't going to want to hear. Just once she'd like to bring him good news, or at least something positive to justify the friendship on his end.

She was so deep in thought that she was unprepared for the arms that grabbed her and pushed her into an opening between two buildings and up against a concrete wall.

"Why are you asking about Helmut Radsch?"

The voice stayed behind her. She twisted, but couldn't turn around. Whoever was behind her was pinning her to make sure they stayed hidden. A million questions tumbled through her mind.

"Who are you?" she asked.

That earned her another push against the wall, scraping her cheek. "Answer my question." The voice was male and the accent definitely German.

"How do you know I'm looking for Helmut Radsch?" Another shove. Jillian felt sweat break out in a line down her back. Time to try to end this. "A man named Hans Gohl approached me. He knew I had friends in the government. The Canadian government. In the foreign relations department. He said he would hurt me, and then my parents, if I didn't help him."

"What else are you doing for him?"

"Nothing. He just wanted me to ask questions. He knows Radsch went to Halifax after the war. He wants to find him."

"Why?"

"I don't know." Jillian forced her voice to break. It wasn't hard. As much as she had anticipated this moment would arrive, it was still terrifying to be pinned and interrogated like this. "Look, I really don't," Jillian said again as she was given another shove. "I don't know anything about Hans Gohl. I don't even know how he found me. I've contacted the Canadian embassy and asked for help. My parents are working with the police back home."

It was all made up, of course. Something else Jillian had prepared. It fit her cover. If this guy had been following her for a few days, he'd seen her go in and out of the institute. If he poked holes in her story, that would tell her a lot about whom she was dealing with.

"Stop asking questions about Radsch. I can do a lot worse than just hurt you. Now sit down and face toward the back of the alley. If I see you following me, you won't be going home tonight."

Jillian nodded, sinking to her knees, which were like Jell-O anyway. As the man released her with one last shove, she braced herself on her hands and shifted to rest against the wall. That was not an experience she wanted to repeat. But at least Gohl would be happy. His plan seemed to be working.

"You look like shite."

Jillian unwound her scarf and took off her coat. "Nice to see you too. It's been a rough night."

James just shook his head. "Go get cleaned up, then, and you can tell me all about it."

Jillian went into the bathroom and looked in the mirror. Her left cheek was scraped a little, so she cleaned it carefully. She knew she looked exhausted and scared, and no amount of soap and water was going to fix that.

She rejoined James in his living room to find he'd poured her a whisky. She took a sip, still not quite the connoisseur that James was trying to turn her into. But she could admit there was something centering about the fire that burned down her throat and into her stomach.

"I got accosted on the way home. Some guy shoved me up against a wall in an alley by the America Memorial Library and demanded to know why I was asking questions about Helmut Radsch."

James regarded her. "Were you scared?"

Jillian took a deep breath. "Yeah. I figured if Gohl was on to something, it was bound to happen. But yeah, it was pretty damn scary."

"So, what did you tell him?"

"I gave him Gohl's name and how he was threatening to hurt me. The supporting details weren't true, but the gist of it was."

"Right, then. Do you think that's the end of it?"

Jillian tried more whisky. "No. How can it be? Gohl can't be the guy's real name, so what use is that going to be?"

James sat drinking for a while. "I would well imagine that there's the added problem of how this person found out about you anyway. It appears you've made someone in your own government right nervous."

Jillian had thought the same thing on the walk to James's. Someone connected to Radsch knew she was asking questions. That someone had to be in the RCMP. External affairs would stick with official channels, and someone at CBNRC could just pressure her boss. Plus, Jean-Marc had done the most poking around, so it would stand to reason he would start with his own turf.

"I'm so surprised," she said. "Really. This is a thirty-year-old file."

"Long memories. But—and I've been thinking about this—if someone cares enough to seek you out, that likely means one of two things. One, someone in your government did something to or with Radsch thirty years ago, and they're now trying to protect their own arse."

"Or?"

"Or two, Radsch is alive and well and living a life that would fall apart if his activities during the war came to light," James said. "I can't help but think, if he's just someone's old granddad living in Halifax, sure, he'll be embarrassed, and maybe it might ruin his relationship with his family or something. But a man like that doesn't have the resources to track you down in West Berlin. Someone with those resources is a man who has something to lose."

Jillian shivered. "Well, when you put it that way."

"Like what?" James said. "Like you've opened a great bloody can of worms?"

"Except I didn't open them. Not willingly. After tonight, well, maybe they'll start ignoring me for a while and focus on each other."

"Aye. But how long is that going to last?"

"Hopefully long enough to get him off my back," Jillian said.

"Just how do you plan to do that?"

Jillian took as large a sip of whisky as she could manage. "Remember how I said I was at the library this afternoon?"

"And?"

"Well, one of the reasons I go once in a while is they have current newspapers from all over the world."

"Right."

She took a breath. "You know that Quentin is a journalist." She held up a hand. "Among other things, I know, but part of maintaining his cover is that he actually files stories once in a while."

James didn't say anything. Somehow it made Jillian feel awkward and ridiculous.

"Don't look at me like that. It's natural that I'm curious. He and I have unfinished business, and—"

"Nevermind, lass, you don't have to be justifying yourself to me."

She sighed. *This is only going to get worse anyway.* "So, because I was there, I decided to look up Jasminka's articles. I just wanted to satisfy myself that she wasn't a honeypot. Because, well, also, I don't want you to get hurt."

James's expression didn't change, but she noticed his hands tighten around his glass.

"Jasminka is definitely a journalist. I found a few of her articles. It seems like she's mostly independent. Somewhat gracious toward the Soviets, but I imagine in Yugoslavia there's probably a line to toe somewhere. Based on the kinds of articles she writes, it's possible that she's legitimately looking into suspicious Soviet nuclear reactors."

"You wouldn't be acting so nervous if that's all you had to tell me."

"I also found three articles published in the last two years about the activities of ex-Nazis in Yugoslavia."

Jillian felt like she'd just dropped a bomb into the apartment. The seconds ticked by as she waited for it to explode.

"Bloody bleeding Christ."

"James."

"Jesus, Mary, and Joseph."

"Look. I'm not going to pretend that it could be a coincidence. I also don't know exactly what it means. And you know her better than I do."

James leaned back in his chair and closed his eyes. "I knew it was too bloody lucky, her showing up and renting an apartment in the same building. Her story about hearing me on the radio and thinking I could help. Aye, I wanted to believe it. But I guess some part of me's always been knowing there was more to that story."

Jillian felt horrible. "I'm so sorry, James."

"Ah, don't be. I've never been one much for relationships anyway. It would've ended sooner or later."

"We should go talk to her. I mean, I can go with you."

"No. I know what information you'll be needing. No sense in making you any more vulnerable. I'll go confront her myself."

James could feel the disappointment churning away in his stomach. He wasn't disappointed in Jasminka. She was who she was. Nor was he disappointed that their relationship was a sham. He'd been with women on much flimsier pretexts. No, the disappointment was entirely in the fact that he cared.

Ach. He rubbed at his face. *A bit asinine, isn't it.* Lowering to admit that he was mostly irritated that he just wasn't ready to end it.

Now he had to go talk to her. Wade through the emotions that were hovering around and try to figure out what best to say. He usually ended relationships when the feelings were all gone. This time it was a proper mess.

He knocked on Jasminka's door.

James heard the chain slip off before the door opened. He looked at her face and let the attraction rip through him. Not a damn thing he could do about that anyway.

He walked past her into the apartment and waited until she shut the door behind him.

"James?"

He turned and met her eyes. "Are you a spy?"

Jasminka paused for a moment. "Why do you ask?"

And isn't that a telling response. "You disappear for days at a time, and journalism is a great cover for intelligence work, so I'm told."

Jasminka sat down on the arm of her sofa, regarding James with a steady gaze. "You do not trust me."

The funny thing was, he did. And it made him feel naive. "You know," he said, "I wouldn't have cared. I'm not bothered about how people make their living. I'm only bothered about being manipulated."

"Then, for what it's worth, I will tell you that I'm not a spy. I am a journalist. Sometimes I feel like I'm doing the same kind of work, but everything I find, I am trying to make public."

"So tell me, then, how did you get interested in publishing what old Nazis did during the war?"

Jasminka smiled sadly. "You want to know about Hans Gohl."

James suddenly felt tired to have it confirmed. "Not really. Not for myself. But I feel obligated to ask what you are doing for him and how much longer you're going to use me to get it."

"I do not work for Gohl." She sighed. "To survive, I take no sides. I'm just as likely to critique the West as I am those behind the Iron Curtain."

"It's not enough, Jasminka. He sent you in my direction. I'm a radio announcer with the British Army. Everything I do is pretty transparent. So what did he want?"

"If you will listen, I would like to tell you what I know. I do not work for him. He is a source." She paused for a moment. "He contacted me for the first time years ago. There were two old Nazis in Belgrade. Gohl couldn't touch them, not really. So he gave me the information, the evidence, to run stories on them about what they did during the war. It ruined them. One committed suicide."

"And you've stayed in touch, then," James said.

"Yes. Not often. But when the people he finds are in Yugoslavia, I help, if it's a story he wants. And I don't mind. He provides evidence, and the crimes, they are real."

James could understand that. It was becoming more complicated than he had anticipated, because he understood that journalists ought to be bringing stories like that to light. "How come you came to Berlin? Did he ask you to?"

Jasminka shook her head. "No. I came for the nuclear power plant story and to see what else I could find here. But Gohl, he knew I was here. I don't know how. That's when I started to become uneasy. I have many sources, but none who track my movements across Europe."

James felt his irritation with himself rising all over again. He didn't want to feel sorry for her. Or worried. The whole point of this exercise was to find a way to stop caring. "So then he just contacted you out of the blue, and what? Asked you to sleep with me?"

For the first time Jasminka looked angry. "No. Becoming intimate with you was my own choice. One you seemed to agree with."

"Aye, that I did. It wasn't hard."

"He only suggested to me that you might know interesting people. That there might be a story."

"And is there?"

"No." She shook her head. "You are not a story to me. I do not sleep with my sources."

James filed that away as something to process later. "So what have you told Gohl?"

"Nothing. I have not heard from him since."

James arched a brow. "That's right hard to believe. Why would he set you in my direction, then not even bother to follow up?"

Jasminka began to wind her hands together, obviously frustrated. "I do not know. He is not a friend. I know nothing about him. And I've tried. Because I do not like this—how he pointed you out then disappeared. I'm not here to do his bidding."

"Then why did you say yes?"

"I only said yes to finding out more about you. If I hadn't liked you, it would have ended almost immediately. There is no story with you."

"And now?"

Jasminka looked at him. "And now I am worried. Because what I know about Gohl, he always has a motive. I cannot figure out how you fit. Also, I don't want you to."

James wished he didn't like looking at her so much. It was hard to remember that he wasn't supposed to want to see her again after today. "So this is the first time he's asked you to do something like this?"

"Yes," she nodded. "Before now, it was a relationship of clear—how best to say it—mutual benefit. He needed a trusted journalist to bring to light the crimes he'd uncovered. Whatever else he is, he is a man who likes to stay in the shadows. He could not publish those stories himself. Hans Gohl is not his real name."

Jillian had thought the same thing, but James was curious. "How do you know?"

"I am a journalist," Jasminka scoffed. "Of course I checked. Everything he gave me I independently verified. It all checked out. But I reached a dead end when I tried to look into him."

James sat down. "I don't suppose ye have a beer, then?"

Jasminka went to her kitchen and returned with two. "You do not know what to do with me now," she said, sitting next to him.

"Christ, what a mess. I don't well know what to do with myself."

They sat for a moment in silence.

"I like spending time with you, Jasminka," James said. "And I can't be bothered with not trusting people. It takes too much work."

"What are you saying?" she asked.

"I'm saying I know I should feel betrayed, but I don't. Whatever else this bloke Gohl wants, I'm grateful that he sent you in my direction. I don't have any secrets."

She leaned her head against his shoulder. "I like you too, Jamie Murphy."

James closed his eyes for a moment, letting his cheek rest against her hair. "But it's not just about me. I have friends who do have secrets they want to keep. And to me, it has to be that Gohl is interested in one of them."

Jasminka sat up and cupped her hand on his face. "But I am not. If I do not have my integrity as a journalist, I have nothing. I owe Gohl nothing. Whatever debts are incurred are immediately repaid when I print his stories. He may be how I found you, but he is not why I'm still here."

James let his eyes roam around her face. One day this attraction would run its course, and then none of this would matter anyway. "If he comes back to you, I want to know."

"I can do that. As I said, I am uncomfortable with his knowledge of my life. I have been thinking that it is time I try to learn more about him in case his involvement becomes more problematic in the future."

James sat back, picking up his beer. "Where are you going to start?"

"There isn't much. He has never revealed anything about himself. But the information he's given me over the years, some of it was very precise and very private. He is not a man who gets his stories from the library. I have thought to start by going back to those sources. Some of them might be sympathetic. I gather his methods are not always friendly."

"He's interested in a group from IG Farben," James said, "the ones who developed the gas for the chambers during the war. He's pressuring a friend of mine to help find one in particular, a bloke named Helmut Radsch. I was thinking, I wonder if there's anything to be learned from the particular Nazis he's going after. There were loads of them. Does his crusade have a certain focus?"

Jasminka looked thoughtful. "The three stories I published for him, they were all about businessmen. No politicians. No military. They had all worked in companies that manufactured items for the Nazis."

"Right. The problem is, every company in Germany was making shite for the Nazis. Krupp. Siemens. BMW. The list is long and covers thousands of people if you factor in everyone who worked for them."

"IG Farben was a conglomerate, right?"

James nodded. "Aye. Bayer. BASF. A half dozen other chemical companies."

Jasminka's eyes brightened. "One of the men in my stories worked for Bayer, and all were involved in chemical manufacturing. Pharmaceuticals. Synthetic materials."

James felt a little shot of adrenaline rush through his body. "So it would seem your Gohl is selective."

"He's not my Gohl, but yes. And being selective usually means you have a particular niche of experience or resources."

"Does it give you some ideas?"

"Yes, it does." She smiled. "More than you might think. It also gives me the idea that I should have learned by now what an amazing man you are. I am so used to having to hide things from people. There are so many who are uncomfortable with the questions I ask and the sources I have to protect. But you, you are different. You don't spend time on the insecurities that many men do."

"Ah, Jasminka, you flatter me. But I'm not a man you want to be falling for. No one could live up to those expectations forever."

She leaned over and kissed him lightly on the lips. "They are not expectations. They are observations. I'm a journalist."

He let the kiss linger. Let her lips move to his cheek, to his ear. Let her hands slide up under his shirt.

"I can't think properly when I'm this close to you," he said against the skin of her neck.

"James," she whispered. "It's too late anyway. But we can fall together. If only for a little while."

That was good enough for him.

CHAPTER TWENTY-SEVEN

Frank paced around the apartment feeling like he was waiting for his wife to give birth. The anxiety. The worry. Would everyone be okay? Would he be able to handle his life tomorrow?

He hadn't gone with Veronica to meet Quentin. There had been no point. He would only have been a liability. So he stayed behind. Standing by his open window and working steadily through a pack of cigarettes.

None of this had been his decision. He wasn't in charge here, but he'd gone along with it. It had seemed like a good idea. From all their limited options, it came off as the best one.

What nagged at Frank was those options were only limited if talking to Carlos was the goal. They could've just ignored him. He turned it over a thousand ways. Walk away from Carlos here, but then if something happened to Jillian in Berlin, he'd regret not doing everything he could. So Veronica here or Jillian there. Someone had to take the risk. And possibly, Veronica was the better choice for that. At least she was trained. Inexperienced, fine. But trained.

Long term this kind of work wasn't for him. He missed his signals. He missed their clarity. A signal either gave you information or it didn't.

That was his biggest worry. Even if Quentin got to Carlos, Frank had a hard time believing Carlos was going to open up. Then Quentin would shoot him, and all this risk would have been for nothing. Jillian and the Berlin setup would still be in jeopardy.

He grabbed his jacket and headed into the office. The embassy was open twenty-four hours, and he needed to distract himself.

"Frank. Wake up. Come on."

Frank felt someone shaking his shoulder. He sat up, wiping away the moisture in the corner of his mouth. "What?"

"Wow, Frank, you planning on sleeping here all night?"

He looked up into Mark's grinning face.

Mark stepped back. "You look like hell."

Frank rubbed a hand down his cheek. If he looked as bad as felt, he wasn't surprised. His mouth was like a graveyard in the desert, given that all he'd consumed in the last little while was nicotine. He tried to clear his throat, but his voice got stuck around his tongue. "Christ, what time is it?"

Mark looked at his watch. "Ten thirty. How long have you been here?"

Frank took a drink of the stale coffee sitting on his desk. "A couple of hours. Have you seen Veronica?"

Mark shook his head. "No, but I just got here."

Shit. He couldn't believe he'd passed out. "Yeah, but up until thirty seconds ago, I was sleeping."

"You expecting her?"

Yes. No. Thoughts ran through his mind. Would she come in? Was she sleeping in her apartment? Was she lying in a ditch somewhere with a bullet in her head? Frank needed some fresh coffee.

"She was going to a meet tonight. It was risky. Can you do me a favor? Can you check the entrance log while I call her apartment?"

Frank saw the worry jump onto Mark's face.

"Sure. But Frank, if she's not in this office, where would she be in the embassy at this time of night?"

His gut tightened, but he refused to jump to conclusions. "Just check it. Tick the box before I raise the alarm."

He watched Mark walk off, wondering what the hell he was going to do if Veronica wasn't in the building or didn't answer her phone at her apartment. Whose problem was it going to be to track her down?

Fifteen minutes later, Frank was sitting with Mark, smoking a cigarette. Food could wait, and his throat couldn't get any worse.

"What the fuck am I supposed to do?" Frank asked.

"It depends," Mark said.

"Depends on what?"

"How worried you are. She's an IO, Frank. They're known to go off the grid once in a while. If you call in the cavalry, her cover will get blown, and that'll be the end of her career here."

Jesus Christ. What a situation.

"How long would you wait? If it were Phillip? How long would you give him with no contact?"

Mark exhaled. "There's no right answer here. You must get that. It's context specific. Where was she going? Who was she meeting? Could she have gotten any leads? Is she in a position to run them down?"

"A Sandinista stronghold. Whoever happened to be guarding the door. She might have gotten a lead on a sociopathic Cuban. And I don't know what the fuck she's prepared for."

"Then give her time."

"And if she's tied up in a chair somewhere with a broken nose and blood pooling on the floor?"

"Shit, Frank, I don't know. Can she take care of herself?"

Frank stubbed out his cigarette. "A female Métis in the RCMP? That's all she's been doing since she joined. She's as tough as they get. But everyone breaks eventually."

Mark thought for a moment. "Okay. My take is, she knows you're going to be worried, so she's going to contact you as soon as she can. I'd give her twenty-four hours. If she can't get to a phone in that amount of time, I'd assume she's in trouble."

It was logical, and Frank appreciated logical. He realized that although Veronica might be inexperienced, so was he. He'd never partnered with an IO before. He really had no idea how to support her, what the protocol was if things went south, or what south even looked like.

He felt this huge anger welling up inside him. They'd been thrown together because no one knew what else to do with either of them. No training, no tools, just a vague joint mission and a washing of the hands. He knew that a lot of that anger was directed at himself. Get the signals. Pursue the Cuban to protect a SIGINT mission. He was still working for the CBNRC. He'd treated Veronica the same as everyone else at the RCMP. Fine, he hadn't ignored her. But he'd used her. Now something had happened, and there wasn't a damn thing he could do about it.

He thanked Mark for his advice and went in search of a coffee and a sandwich before he returned to sit by his phone to sit and hope that his selfishness hadn't gotten Veronica killed.

Three hours later, Frank was staring out the window. It was raining. He could see the drops reflecting on the night lights. It suited his mood, frustration and anxiety growing in equal measure in the pit of his stomach.

He jumped two feet when the phone rang.

"Defense desk," he growled into the headset.

"Frank."

It was Veronica. Thank Christ. She was whispering and the connection was shit, but he could tell it was her.

"Where the fuck are you? Do you need help?"

"You need to come here now. I've messed up my ankle, and I've got a nail embedded in my arm. So bring some antiseptic and a bandage. And a weapon, like a gun, if you have one."

Holy Christ. What the hell was going on?

"Where are you?" he said, dredging up some calm from a place he didn't know existed.

"Claudia's. Carlos's aunt. Or I will be. Now I'm two streets over at a bodega using their phone."

"What the hell are you doing there?"

"No time, Frank. Just get here. I can explain everything later. Park beside the fountain, remember? At the end of the street. I'll meet you there. Stay out of sight of the house. I'll figure out something while you're on your way. And don't forget the antiseptic."

Frank had a million questions, but the connection clicked off. Talk about no training. A gun? He didn't have one, nor would he bring one, given that he wouldn't know how to shoot the damn thing. He picked up the nine iron Mark kept by his desk to practice his chip shots on the carpet. This he could do some serious damage with—if he had the element of surprise. He hoped he'd have that.

Grabbing the keys to an unmarked embassy car, Frank raced out, hoping there was still time to influence the outcome of whatever the hell was happening at the aunt's house.

The rain had only become heavier on the drive to Santa Rosa. Frank splashed through puddles as he navigated increasingly poor roads. Finally, he made it to the rendezvous point and pulled up a block away from the fountain in the opposite direction of the aunt's. He rummaged around for the first aid kit he'd demanded from the admin desk on his way out of the embassy. He wasn't sure what to do with the golf club.

There wasn't anyone out on the street, the weather and the time of night keeping everyone in who didn't have a reason to go out. Frank grabbed the club. It wasn't like he was going to blend in anyway.

He cautiously made his way down the street toward the fountain. He could see the splashes blending with the rain when Veronica fell into step beside him, limping slightly.

"What's with the golf club?" she asked.

"I couldn't find a gun. What the hell is going on?"

He stopped and looked at her. She was soaking wet and in obvious pain, but her eyes were alert enough for someone who hadn't slept in a while.

"Short version. I did the drop. I had a long conversation with the guy guarding the school entrance. He had a lot of questions about Carlos. I didn't think it would take long for them to show Carlos the door, so I stayed. Quentin popped up to remind me to stay out of his way. I didn't go far. I'd arranged a car, so I was able to follow them. Here."

There were so many parts missing from that story.

"Why here? And how did you get injured?"

She pulled him into an empty alcove beside a closed storefront. "Where's the antiseptic?"

He handed her the first aid kit. She shook her head and turned around, pulling half her shirt up to reveal her left arm. "I got the nail out," she said, "and I'm up to date on my tetanus shot. But I'd appreciate you dumping half that stuff on it."

Frank put down the golf club and opened the kit. He soaked a bandage in the antiseptic solution and pressed it on the gaping hole in the back of her arm. He could hear her wince. He used the bandage as a towel and poured some more on for good measure. Then he tied a roll of gauze around it.

"What about your ankle?" he said.

"I'll live." She turned around, pulling her shirt back down. "Frank, I don't think this is going to end well."

"Why did he bring Carlos here?"

"I'm sure he's got a reason, and I'm sure it doesn't matter now."

Frank watched the rain for a moment. "Well, Quentin did say he was here to kill Carlos. We've known that since the beginning."

Veronica put her hand on his arm. "That's not it, Frank. I don't know what Quentin was hoping to accomplish, but it's not working out. Quentin's tied up. Carlos is in control."

Frank was unprepared for that news. "What? How the hell did that happen?"

"I don't know, but the husband's there. Maybe he's playing both off each other. Maybe he hates Quentin more than Carlos. Maybe Carlos has some leverage. In any case, Quentin's not going to last the night."

It all made sense to Frank now. If Quentin had been in control, Veronica wouldn't have called him here. She'd be observing, not getting involved.

"Do you have a plan?" he asked. Now wasn't the time to speculate how this clusterfuck had come to pass.

"Yeah," she said. "We have to light the house on fire."

CHAPTER TWENTY-EIGHT

Frank stood back from the house, the smell of gasoline filling his nostrils. *If I ever get back to a desk job, I'm going to appreciate it. Appreciate how I'm not in danger of dying from the job. Appreciate how I get to go home at the end of the day and kiss my wife. Because I'm sure as shit ten thousand miles from that now.*

Veronica had found gasoline in a neighboring lot. They'd doused the back of the house. It was going to light up. Frank didn't know if it would burn down, what with the rain, but that was out of his control.

"Listen, Frank, I can't do much. My ankle's doubled in size."

Frank fingered the lighter in his pocket. "Last chance to walk away."

"Do you really want to do that?"

Let Carlos kill Quentin. Let Carlos live to go back and settle things with Jillian. "No."

"Okay. So I go untie Quentin. You deal with Carlos."

"Where's the husband?"

"He's sitting in the corner looking like he's watching a nightmare. I don't know what's going on there, but I don't think he's putting his life on the line for either of the other two."

Frank thought for a moment. "And the fact that we're burning down his house? Is anyone else at home?"

"No one else is here," Veronica said. "Yes, he's an unknown. I'll prepare for him as well. You—you can't worry about anyone other than Carlos."

Frank took a deep breath and ignited the flame. It was the right thing to do. *Oh, hell.*

He watched as the tree went up first. Fast. Sparks shot out, catching where they'd tossed gasoline. It wasn't easy to light a house on fire, but there was enough wood, old enough and dry enough that the flames caught and spread. The backdoor. The pergola. Flames reached up to the roof. They were climbing up the walls, looking for a way in. The shutters caught. Smoke billowed and flames hissed in the rain. They'd spilled an entire tank, and it showed.

Frank and Veronica launched rocks at the windows, shattering the glass and offering another path for the fire. Frank hoped that Carlos didn't shoot Quentin just to cut his losses before he ran out the front door.

Time to get going.

Wielding the iron like a baseball bat, Frank broke the door and launched himself inside.

The situation inside the house was a freeze frame of horror. Quentin was tied to a chair in the small living area, hardly recognizable under the blood covering his face. Frank dimly registered Luis, the husband, on the far side of the room back toward the kitchen, seemingly frozen in place. But the bulk of Frank's attention was on Carlos, who had turned in his direction with a knife.

Frank took two steps into the room. The heat from the fire created a haze. There was smoke everywhere and the steady hissing of the rain as it fell on the flames above them. He was only going to get one shot at this. He turned his body perpendicular to Carlos, lining up.

"Saving the—"

He heard the Spanish accent. He didn't meet Carlos's eyes. Didn't engage. Just looked down at the floor and imagined a little white ball. He lifted the club and swung, swiveling his hips and following through.

Frank heard the crunch as it connected with Carlos's jaw. The Cuban crumpled to the ground. The power of centrifugal force.

He stood over Carlos, the bruising from the contact of the golf club rising to the surface of his skin already. The Cuban was unconscious—probably not for long, but Frank hoped for long enough.

He turned to see that Veronica had liberated Quentin, who was able to stand despite the injuries.

They were a mess. Her with her ankle barely able to support a portion of her weight and her left arm bleeding through the gauze wrapped around her bicep. Him with a cut along the left side of his face, his right eyelid almost swollen shut, and his collar bright with his own blood.

The heat and humidity were making them all sweat, and everyone's face was further distorted by the smoke and flames.

The house had properly caught fire now, and Frank knew there wouldn't be any salvaging it. He looked around. An entire lifetime of memories up in smoke. And for what.

They had to get out. Get to the car and get far away from this place. It was sad, and it was also dangerous.

Veronica appeared to read his mind as she led Quentin to the front door. Frank stepped over the Cuban to follow them.

Luis abruptly stood up. "You killed her," he yelled over the sounds of the house falling apart around them. "You both killed her."

Frank didn't care. Not about any of it. He just wanted to get out. It was starting to feel like hell itself was trying to devour him. Why it had all come to this, he still wasn't sure.

His quest for the door was stopped when Luis pulled out a gun. Frank froze. So did Veronica. Luis wasn't pointing it at anyone in particular. Instead, with tears streaming down his face, it appeared he was letting out everything he'd bottled up since his wife died.

"You are taking everything from us," Luis screamed. "First Isabella. Now the house. Everything. My life. I have nothing left."

The gun was flailing, and Frank didn't know what to do. Instinct told him that Luis wouldn't need much of an excuse to start pulling the trigger.

The gun steadied at Carlos, still unconscious on the floor. Frank could see that Luis couldn't pull the trigger. The man was angry, and scared, and so close to being desperate. But even with all that churning through him, he couldn't shoot Carlos.

Frank didn't know what to do, what could resolve this impasse. The fire was everywhere now, and soon the roof was going to collapse in on them.

Suddenly Quentin pushed away from Veronica. He staggered to Luis, stopping when Luis's gun hit his chest. "I'm sorry," Quentin said. "I'm sorry for everything. I loved Isabella. I shouldn't have, but I did. And I'm sorry."

Luis looked at Quentin, the words colliding with his confusion and pain.

Quentin gently took the gun from Luis, who stared at it like he didn't know how his life had come to this.

Then so fast Frank could react only after it was over, Quentin turned and shot Carlos in the head.

Frank jolted at the sound. He looked at Carlos dead on the floor and felt it had happened too fast to process. Nothing but a body now, when minutes ago he'd been alive and seething with viciousness.

Quentin tucked the gun into the waistband of his jeans before almost collapsing into Veronica.

The two of them made it to the door and swung it open.

Frank grabbed Luis and pushed him out into the night in front of him. Luis stumbled and sank into a heap. Frank assumed someone would help Luis, as they didn't have the time.

Frank barely registered the people on the street, the hose that had been lined up to start dealing with the fire. He pulled Veronica's arm over his shoulder, taking some of the weight off her bad ankle. He all but dragged her toward the car, trusting Quentin to keep up. He passed the fountain, grateful that everyone was too preoccupied with the fire to think about following them.

He opened the back door, motioning for Quentin to get in before Veronica. Once they were settled in the back seat, he got behind the wheel, started the car, and turned in the direction of Managua.

No one spoke for a long time as the car sped through the darkness.

"Thank you," said Quentin, breaking the silence. "That didn't go according to plan. Obviously. I…well…I wouldn't have made it out of there on my own. So thank you."

Frank decided there were things he didn't need to know. Why Quentin had brought Carlos there. What the original plan had been.

"What about the body?" Frank asked. Given all that he had to process, he wasn't sure why that was his first concern. "And the gun. Christ. You should throw the damn gun out of the window."

Frank watched Quentin lean his head back against the top of the seat. Blood was still trickling out of the cut on his jaw, but he wasn't doing anything to stop it.

"And the house." Frank knew it was the adrenaline making him babble, but he couldn't stop it. These people had been through so much. And now their house was gone. *What a fucking mess.*

"Luis will get rid of the body, whatever is left of it after the fire stops. He'll put Carlos in an unmarked grave. He'll do it for Isabella."

"Great. And is he going to tell anyone who burned the house down?"

The silence pulsed in the car. It seemed no one knew the answer to that.

"Maybe not," said Veronica.

Frank wasn't sure if that was good enough.

"I mean, one way to look at it," Veronica continued, "is, who would he tell? I'm not sure there's anyone who'd do anything about it."

There was a pause as more countryside sped by. "Besides, we've got other problems," Quentin said.

Of course they did. Two of them could barely walk, they'd just committed arson and murder, and now they were trying to get back into Managua without getting shot by the Sandinistas or Somoza's men.

"Carlos compromised Jillian."

Frank felt a dark hole open in his stomach. "To who?"

"He wouldn't tell me. But once he had me tied up, he took pleasure in describing the various ends Jillian might come to now that he'd passed on his suspicions about her cover. He said he knew powerful people who would be very curious about her and who had the means to make her disappear to satisfy their curiosity."

Frank's head began to pound so bad he thought his skull was going to split open. He forced himself to think. There was no point in giving in to the anger. No point in wallowing in it until it churned into guilt about all the things he should have done. He couldn't go back and fix any of it. He needed to focus on his next series of decisions.

"Do you think it's that fourth man in our picture?" said Veronica, pain edging her words.

"I don't know," said Quentin, sounding equally rough. "It could be. But Carlos was connected to so many people who'd be interested in Jillian: Soviets. East Germans. Even the Red Army Faction would see an opportunity for leverage."

Frank kept his attention on the road while letting the possibilities run through his brain. "Okay. It seems bad, but I'm going to talk this out. First, Carlos wasn't the type to sink Jillian because of his principles, which means it's more likely he gave her up for specific leverage rather than broadcast her situation just because. We know he was in West Berlin before he left for Nicaragua. Maybe he had a stopover in Moscow or Havana. But if he gave her up to the Soviets, it doesn't connect with then departing for Managua. What would he have gained to use in Nicaragua? If he gave her up to the East Germans before he left, well, she's already on some Stasi list somewhere, I guarantee it. And again, it doesn't help him in Managua."

"And the Red Army Faction connection?" asked Veronica.

"I'm not sure there'd be much for him to gain from that either," Quentin said. "He was only helping the RAF because the Soviets think what they're doing is interesting. The leverage idea, it makes sense. That's the kind of guy he is. Was. And I don't think anyone in the RAF would have anything that Carlos was interested in. He had a lot better connections than most of the people left in that group."

"So the fourth man is the highest probability," Veronica said.

"Yeah," said Frank, "especially if he's in West Germany. That's where Jillian is most vulnerable. If this guy, whoever he is, was powerful enough to connect Carlos to Hoffsteader, then he probably had a few other things he could offer in exchange for interesting information."

"How do we find out who he is?" asked Veronica.

"*We* don't. You are going back to the apartment to ice your ankle, and you?" Frank looked in the rearview mirror. "Where am I taking you?"

The blood had stopped trickling down Quentin's face, but he still looked horrible. "I don't suppose I could go with you?" he said to Veronica.

There was a brief moment of silence. "Okay," she said, "I think I have enough ice for the two of us. And you, Frank?"

"I'm going to go shower because I smell like a fuel truck. Then I'm either going to smoke, sleep, or do some combination of the two until I can get into the American embassy."

"To do what?" Veronica asked.

"To ask Amaya to set up a meeting with Gavin Hoffsteader so he can tell me who that fourth man is."

CHAPTER TWENTY-NINE

Jillian slipped out the back door of her apartment building. Her breath was rushing in and out of her lungs on account of her mad dash down the stairs. Turning right, she raced down the narrow alley between the buildings. She slowed as she came up to the street, not wanting to burst out and draw attention to herself.

She quickly scanned the street, looking for Gohl amidst the steadily falling snow.

She saw him across the street to her left, making his way north. His head was bent slightly into the oncoming wind, but she recognized the gray hat he'd been wearing as he'd left her apartment.

Jillian hung back at the opening of the alley, trying to figure out how far ahead she was supposed to let him get. She had never tried to trail anyone before. The only thing she knew is that she had to be as inconspicuous as possible so that if he turned around, he wouldn't see her.

The snow helped, and the fact that her coat was dark blue. In the fading light, it looked the same as the majority of black and gray coats around her. The streets were busy enough that she wouldn't stand out just by being on them.

Gohl didn't appear to be in any rush. His walk was steady but unhurried. Jillian waited until he was a few blocks up, then started to follow him, sticking to her side of the street. She'd left her hat and scarf in her apartment, thinking they were too colorful. She hunched up her shoulders against the snow and tried to keep an eye on Gohl.

After another block he turned right down Alt-Moabit. When he was out of her view, she raced across the street and up to the corner where she'd last seen him. Slowing again, she made the turn—just another person joining the commuters heading home at the end of the workday.

Alt-Moabit was busier, with its shop fronts and restaurants. Light spilled from windows, reflecting off the snow and creating pools of moving shadows. More people were out on the sidewalks. Jillian walked as fast as she dared, trying to get a glimpse of Gohl before she ran into him.

She thought she saw his hat up ahead. She wasn't sure if she should stay behind him or cross the street. Was he constantly on the lookout? Did he suspect she would try this? Or was he so wrapped up in his goals that he was oblivious?

Her heart was pounding, half from exertion and half from nerves. She felt stupid and out of her depth, but she also knew that she had to try whatever she could to shift the balance of power between them, because after today, she knew it wasn't going to end.

He'd grown excited about her run-in with the unknown man outside the library. His eyes had lit with what Jillian could only describe as obsession. He'd said his plan was working. She was to stay the course.

"What if next time they put me in the hospital? Or use a gun?" she'd asked.

"Much more has been sacrificed in the pursuit of justice," he'd replied. "Not all means can be protected in the pursuit of such noble ends."

So she was just another tool for him to use, and he was prepared to lose a few along the way. Which was why she was out here trying to get some usable information. It was clear he would just keep using her. If she went home, he would just start again with whomever they sent to replace her. So the only real way out was to shut down the entire operation running out of the West German Science Institute, and Jillian wasn't going to give that up without a fight. No way this man should be able to dictate Canadian SIGINT collection and compromise valuable intelligence to fulfill a personal vendetta.

Jillian noticed that the gray hat had slowed, so she stopped in front of the next window, pretending to check on the selection of cured meats. She dared a glance up the street. *Damn it.* She couldn't see the hat anymore.

She started to walk again, moving as fast as she could without breaking into a run. The hat was nowhere to be seen, and it seemed like everyone was wearing a dark coat. She kept going, not sure what else to do, looking left and right, trying to see if he'd crossed the street or gone into one of the restaurants.

After what was probably a minute but felt like an hour, she slowed down to a trudge. She had lost him, whether by design or because she was completely crap at this, she had no idea.

Jillian turned to go home and found herself looking at Gohl's face. He grabbed her elbow and pulled her out of the flow of people into the doorway of a store that was closed for the evening.

"Now I wonder who you really are, because you are not very good at what you just tried."

She forced herself to breathe through the constriction that had just assaulted her throat. "Can you blame me for wanting to know more about you?"

Gohl tipped his head. "I expected nothing less. However, I knew you left your apartment right after I did."

"I got curious. It wasn't planned," she lied.

"I will not be filling your curiosity today. Perhaps next time you will have better luck."

"I don't want there to be a next time. I've done what you asked. I confirmed your suspicions about where Radsch went after the war, and I got the attention you were looking for. I don't feel like getting assaulted in an alley again. I want you to leave me alone."

Gohl smiled. "You work with the CIA. What I am asking you to do is simply toss one more ball in the air. You will manage. Now, perhaps you should wander the streets a little longer to give Radsch's people more time to approach you again. I will see you soon."

Jillian watched him walk off. What was she supposed to say? Him thinking she was CIA was better than him knowing the truth. And wasn't that an ironic situation to be in.

"So you trust her."

"Aye, that I do. You're paranoid, as well you have a right to be. But not everyone can lie and manipulate without blinking an eye. I've gone out and looked up her other stories, and she does seem to be a proper journalist."

"And you think she's hot," Jillian said.

"If all I liked was sleeping with her, I could well do that without getting involved."

"So you are attached, aren't you?"

James sighed. "Would you like it better if I was just shagging her and didn't give a rat's arse?"

"No. You're right. I like you because you care despite the fact that you don't want to. About me. About the East Germans. And now about Jasminka. It's really actually charming."

"Right. We all have our patterns, I'm guessing. Back to my point: I do trust her, but just with my life, not yours. I'll not be saying anything about what you do. I haven't, and I gave you my word on that."

"That's good enough for me."

"Glad to hear it."

"Besides, from what you've told me, she doesn't seem like she has some hidden agenda, at least not one involving me. Gohl seems to have not said anything about what he's asked me to do or who he suspects I am. The fact that she's never asked about me, and you've been with her for three months, well, Quentin never would have waited that long if he was looking for specific information. If she's playing a game, it's certainly a long one."

"Maybe she'll find out more about Gohl, or at least who he really is. That information would help you."

"It certainly would."

"Now tell me, what's all this, then?" James said, nodding to the small hardware store she'd dumped on her dining table.

Jillian looked down at the table and couldn't keep the frustration off her face. "Nothing. It's absolutely nothing."

"It doesn't look like it."

"Fine," Jillian said, leaning back in her chair. "It's my wishful thinking. I've been playing around for hours, trying to figure out how to get a signal on Gohl. As you can see, it's a problem I haven't solved."

"Ah. Don't have the right parts?"

Jillian shook her head. "No one does. I can't make anything small enough. Tracking devices can easily be hidden on a car, but not a person. Gohl doesn't appear to drive, like most everyone in this city. There's nothing I can make that would be light enough, inconspicuous enough, to slip into his coat pocket or something."

"Don't they make devices small enough to fit on rabbits to follow them around wherever they get to hopping to?"

Jillian sighed. "Yes, but the equipment on the receiving end is large, and the signal needs to be triangulated. I can't set that up here."

James smiled.

"What?"

"You should see the look on your face," he said. "Proper disgust."

"Yeah, well. Mostly it's just impatience. The way things have reduced in size in the last fifteen years, it'll keep going. Moore's law. In ten years the woman in this situation is going to have a ton more options. Me, I'm stuck wondering if I can get good enough to try to tail him again next time he drops by."

"That you probably cannot."

Jillian pushed back her chair and stormed into her kitchen. "Want a beer?" she called out.

"I'll not be saying no."

She returned with a bottle for each of them. "So then, any bright ideas on how I can get the upper hand here?"

"What would help you?"

"I've been thinking, if I could just find where he stays. Or does his business. Or both. He's not sleeping on the street, and I'd bet he's not staying at a hotel either. Once I know, I can build a basic voice receiving dish and angle around the building to see what I can find."

"Would that work?"

"It worked well enough last year when I was trying to find out more about Victor and what he was doing in East Berlin." She took a large swallow of beer. "At least it would give me something to do, something that I could at least pretend was going to be useful instead of waiting around for Gohl to keep using me as bait."

James was quiet for a while. "Ye know, Jillian, ye can't always be pushing to sort everything out."

"You're saying I should just keep doing whatever Gohl wants?"

"No," James said. "I'm saying that you need to recognize when you don't have enough pieces of the puzzle yet. And I'm also saying you can ask for help."

Jillian felt one bit of anxiety dissipate only to be immediately replaced by another. "I didn't want to ask you for anything. You've already done so much for me."

"Aye, that I have." James grinned. "You're going to owe me your firstborn pretty soon. Lucky for you I've never been wanting any wee ones."

Jillian laughed. "If I ever have kids, you're first in line for godfather. But what are you proposing exactly? Are you going to follow Gohl for me?"

"Nay, I don't think that's the best idea. I imagine he might already have a fair idea of who I am. But I have many friends, Jillian. I'm sure I can sort out a few people who will help us on this."

Jillian stood up and walked around the table, leaning over to give him a hug. "You're the best."

"I know, Jillian. I know."

Jillian's eyes were threatening to shut permanently in protest. She didn't know if she could process any more Sütterlinschrift. She stood up, stretched, and wondered if some strudel and caffeine would help her persevere. She felt like Hans Gohl was weaving a net around her and, like a dolphin swimming through a tuna fishing area, at some point, she'd find she was too big to escape through the fine mesh.

These records of Madeline's were her best bet at finding something to trade for her freedom from Gohl. Once he had Radsch, so he didn't think he could keep using her again and again, she would need something to set him off on a new path of inquiry—one that had nothing to do with anyone in Canada. And one that was compelling enough that he'd agree to leave her alone forever.

So far she didn't have much.

But she had a few things, which, she admitted, surprised her a little. Jillian felt like she was pursuing this path due to a lack of options. Part of her was skeptical that it would work. After learning everything she could about the makeup of IG Farben during the war, she had a list of keywords she was looking for: names of the member companies and their main products, a few key factory locations, and some key players in the company.

She'd almost fallen off her chair the first time she'd come across a relevant bit. It was from a man who talked about the work he was doing on synthetic rubber. He didn't say where, and although IG Farben was the obvious contender, without the reference the man could have worked somewhere else.

Then there was another one about the presentation of the Magnetophon. In the note, it said the man, Frederick, worked at IG Farben. Jillian had been perplexed, because she was familiar with the device, given that it was the first reel-to-reel tape recorder. She'd learned how to build those in school, and she was sure the machine was built by AEG. The next time she went to the library, she'd researched the story, discovering that the

IG Farben connection was the magnetic tape on the reels. They contained a coating that had been developed in a BASF lab.

It was another document to add to her small pile. But Gohl didn't seem interested in anything other than the gas division, which meant Jillian had to keep hunting for the tiniest of needles in this great, giant haystack.

She sighed. The truth was, she knew almost nothing about Hans Gohl. Maybe he was pursuing multiple vendettas. Maybe there were many wrongs that he wanted to see exposed. Maybe he was going to try to kill her after he was done with her. She really had no idea.

Jillian was in the information business. Information had value.

She didn't know enough about Gohl to know if it was the same for him.

She looked at the boxes around her. The only alternative was to get something on Gohl, but her last attempt had failed spectacularly. So until James's friend came through or Jillian saw another opportunity, her best course of action was to keep trying to collect enough from these files to get him out of her life.

CHAPTER THIRTY

Frank stood staring out the window. The rain had cleared off, and it was a beautiful day in Managua. He hadn't slept much, but a few aspirin had made his headache marginally better.

He heard the door open. Turning, he waited for Amaya to speak.

"Well, the meeting is arranged. He'll be at the hotel bar at two."

"Thank you," said Frank.

"Don't thank me yet. At this point it's all diplomacy."

"What did you tell him?"

"That I was facilitating an unofficial request from a friend, someone who wanted to share something about a mutual contact, Carlos Honouras. I gave the impression my friend was Nicaraguan."

"That's great. He'll be curious, but he won't be concerned."

Amaya tapped her foot. "Should I be?"

Frank turned back to the window for a moment. "No. You have plausible deniability. You aren't going to be there, and he's not going to find out who I am."

"That's good. I don't feel like dealing with any angry British diplomats today."

Frank shook his head. "You won't. Hoffsteader has been keeping his ongoing relationship with Carlos off book. He's not going to want any of it to become public. He may be retired, but he was MI6. He's not giving anything up to the diplomats. He also knows that Carlos is of perennial interest to the CIA, so it's not going to be out of possibility that you were asked by them to facilitate the setup. I'll put a little drawl on my vowels and watch how I say 'about.' He's not going to guess that I'm Canadian and you're acting without official support."

"So," she said, sitting down behind her desk, "you're hoping that he'll tell you what you want to know because Carlos is dead?"

"I'm hoping that Carlos was an anchor around his neck. Someone he had to protect, not someone he wanted to protect, so he won't mind giving me some information to clean up his mess."

"It might work," said Amaya, "as long Hoffsteader isn't afraid of this mystery man."

"If that's the case, the mystery man doesn't have to know about Hoffsteader. It can be Carlos who gave him up."

"That ties it together nicely. And Quentin?"

Frank paused for a moment. "Whoever it is, Quentin will be the one to follow the lead. He's in a better position to do something about that loose end."

Amaya nodded. "Well, that's better than him hanging around here making everyone at the agency nervous."

Frank hadn't told her how Carlos had died. He was aware that Amaya hadn't asked either. "You'll have one less thing to worry about."

One corner of her mouth ticked up. "Which usually just makes room for about two more. How much longer are you staying in Managua?"

"Assuming I get the answers I need today, not long."

"Well, good luck today," she said. Frank took the hint that it was time for him to be on his way.

"Thanks for everything," he said, walking to the door.

"No need to thank me." Amaya smiled. "I consider it more a quid pro quo. One day I might need to call in the half dozen favors you owe me."

Frank returned her smile. Such was the nature of the business.

Frank sat in the lobby of the Intercontinental Hotel, folded newspaper in his lap, watching the door for Hoffsteader. He smoked a cigarette, playing through some scenarios for how the upcoming conversation was going to go.

He had no real sense of how to approach Hoffsteader and could imagine the situation unfolding in a number of ways. Denial, anger. Defense, attack. Frank still couldn't quite figure out the history necessary to get Carlos to a Home Office dinner, so it was hard to predict what kind of relationship he had to

Hoffsteader. But Frank wasn't interested in the skeletons in Hoffsteader's closet. He wanted a name for the fourth man and information Jillian could use to protect herself.

Hoffsteader showed up right on time. He didn't look nervous. A little hot maybe, his linen suit a bit crumpled, but calm. Frank watched as he took in all the people in the lobby in an easy gaze that betrayed nothing. His eyes didn't stop on Frank. No doubt he was looking for someone less white.

Frank's eyes followed him into the lobby bar. He stubbed out his cigarette and picked up his paper. It was time.

Frank took a breath to steady his nerves. He was at the disadvantage, this not being his type of intelligence work and Hoffsteader being ex-MI6. Ultimately they were on the same side, and all Frank had to do was make Hoffsteader see the importance of the present.

He eased himself onto the stool beside Hoffsteader, placing the newspaper between them.

"Are you the one who asked to meet?"

"Yeah," said Frank. "I'm curious about one of your friends."

"A conversation, then, that can be had over a drink."

"Fine."

Hoffsteader motioned the bartender over. "A scotch, please. The Glenfiddich you have over there. And for my friend here?"

"Cerveza," said Frank.

The bartender nodded and moved away to get their drinks.

"Open up the newspaper," Frank said. "There's a picture of you at a Home Office dinner about six years ago."

Hoffsteader opened the paper and glanced down at the photograph Frank had put inside. "Ah, I remember this affair."

"Good, because I need you to tell me who is with you in that photo."

Hoffsteader looked up as the bartender returned with their drinks. "The Scots really do know how to make whisky."

Frank didn't say anything.

"Official parties are great for developing contacts, but the photos are most annoying. I suppose I shouldn't be surprised that despite my efforts, one of them has surfaced."

Frank just waited. He was going to have to explain himself in some context. He waited to see what Hoffsteader wanted to know.

"The question for me is, what are you going to do with that information?"

Frank shrugged. "Does it really matter? You're retired. And have been rewarded for your services."

"One never burns good contacts, no matter how many hours one spends rusticating in the English countryside."

"Except you're not rusticating now. It makes me wonder how retired you really are, given that you're in Managua. And so is someone else in that picture."

"Nicaragua is lovely at this time of year. What's to say I'm not here on vacation?"

"We both know that isn't true. The thing is, I also don't care about that. I know you're here for Carlos Honouras. I'm not sure what someone who gets paid by the Soviets did to get invited by you to a Home Office party. I'm also not sure what he kept doing to get you on a plane to Managua all these years later. But none of that's important to me. What is important is that Carlos got involved in an operation I have running in West Germany. Whatever allegiance he owes you, that doesn't seem to extend to your allies. He's compromised it, and not to the Soviets. This picture makes me wonder who else he knows."

Hoffsteader looked thoughtful. "An official operation?"

"Yes. The kind where we work with GCHQ and collect a lot of very valuable intelligence."

Hoffsteader paused. "The problem is, I'm not here by what you'd normally call choice. There are certain exchanges I made that put me in a bit of a bind when it comes to Carlos."

"Would it make a difference if I told you he was dead?"

Hoffsteader's eyes widened before he smiled slightly. "Yes, actually. That would make quite a bit of difference. Are you sure?"

"Yes," said Frank. "I was there when the bullet lodged itself in his head. Carlos Honouras is no longer anyone's problem. But as I've said, there are a few loose ends of his I need to clean up."

Hoffsteader tapped his finger on the picture. "This party was so long ago, and I've been to so many, you would think I'd forgotten it. I had to host him in order to get the information I needed. He loved parties. I knew he was networking, or at least trying to, but one can only fight on so many fronts. I made sure to keep a close eye on him while he was in the country in case any of his efforts were successful. But he was important. The information he could get sometimes was truly unique."

"You were after Nazis. Someone else could deal with the Communists."

"Not quite. I wasn't going to give him the opportunity to recruit another Philby, if that's even what he was after. With Carlos, I was never really sure. A Home Office party isn't quite the same as working alongside him. It's always a balance, as I'm sure you must know. Manageable risks and all of that."

Frank wasn't sure anymore about manageable risks. Or maybe he just wasn't sure today. If he wasn't going to risk anything, he should start rusticating himself.

"I understand," said Frank, "that there's a big, wide gray area between the good guys and the bad guys populated by people I don't want to spend much time with."

"Yes." Hoffsteader nodded. "It's hard to keep track. I find the only way to do it is start with a known bad and see where you end up. Carlos was dark gray, I'll give you that, but he wasn't exterminating Jews and Gypsies."

Frank sighed. "No, he wasn't. He was, however, helping Brezhnev make sacrifices to prove Lenin right."

"Détente may be irritating, but it's certainly working. The world is more stable now than it was thirty years ago."

But at what cost? Frank didn't want to get any further into it. He wasn't about to argue who was worse, Hitler or Stalin.

"Carlos was very dark gray," Frank pushed, "and if he thought you were going to bail him out every time he got in trouble with the Five Eyes, then maybe he wasn't as careful as he should have been about who he shared information with. I know about the Soviets. I know about the Red Army Faction. What I don't know is who this is. Not Colin Edwards, but this man right here." Frank jammed his finger down on the picture.

He was trying not to let the impatience seep into his voice. It would just be leverage for Hoffsteader.

"What will you do with the information?"

"Protect my operation. So it's very dependent on who he is and if he's in a position to harm the people involved."

Hoffsteader took a long swallow of his scotch. "The truth is, I'm not sure how much I can help you. He approached me years ago, right after the war. He was disgusted by Nuremberg. Embarrassed that everyone was making excuses, as if Hitler had personally held everyone at gunpoint. I had made it known that I would be continuing to pursue Nazis to hold them accountable for their crimes. He shared a similar sentiment."

"Who did he work for? BND?"

"Run by an ex-Nazi? No," Hoffsteader said, shaking his head. "He doesn't work for anyone. He works for himself."

"What? Just as a concerned citizen? He decided to hunt down ex-Nazis for the rest of his life?"

"Remarkable, but yes. He never told me much about himself, but I learned over the years that there was a great deal of family money that had been significantly augmented during the war. It seemed to me that he was atoning, but for what I never knew. When it was expedient, he shared information with me. But I was not his only means of pursuing retribution."

Frank found the story unsettling. It was harder to judge someone's motives when they were acting on their own. There was no overarching mission, no guiding principles.

"How did he hook up with Carlos?"

"I have no idea," said Hoffsteader.

"You bring them both to a Home Office party, and you don't know how they're involved with each other?"

"I never needed to."

Frank sighed. *Jesus Christ. Couldn't any of this be simple?*

"How do you get in touch with him?"

"I don't. He gets in touch with me."

"Every time?"

"Yes, because that's how it was useful. Once I had unearthed a Nazi, I had the ability to do something. I didn't need him for that. I also didn't need him for evidence or any other information gathering. He brought me avenues of exploration. Not the other way around."

Frank sat for a moment and thought. What did he really need to know? Carlos likely suspected Jillian was either American or Canadian intelligence, or that she could be used to get close. If he'd given that up, then what?

"Does he do anything else besides go after old Nazis?" Frank asked.

"Like knitting or golf?"

"Like helping the Soviets or the East Germans."

Hoffsteader shook his head. "Not that I know of. But as I've said, I don't know very much about him. Maybe he summers in Moscow."

That old feeling of wanting to punch intelligence officers in the face was returning to Frank. "If he has information that is of no direct relevance to hunting down Nazis but that could be used as leverage, then who would he go to?"

Hoffsteader appeared to think for a moment. "I got the impression that all of his contacts were one-offs, like me. See, he didn't work for the British. He wasn't interested in our goals or ideology. He just wanted to find Nazis. When he intersected with people who could help him, because they had information or were interested in the same, then he worked with them. He never asked me about anything beyond our mutual goal. He wasn't interested in MI6 or our relationship with either of the Germanys. He treated Carlos the same way. The few times we were all together, he made it clear that discussions of communism or capitalism or democracy were irrelevant to the business at hand. I assume that he was like that everywhere—meaning that he wouldn't go to the Soviet government, or the East German government, but he would share information with particular people to meet his own ends."

Frank drank some of his beer, giving himself time to think. He wasn't sure what to do with the information he was getting. And he was less sure about the fourth-man connection than he'd been when he sat down. Maybe Carlos hadn't told him anything about Jillian. Maybe he had sold her out to the Soviets, because the Soviets were guaranteed to be interested. This mystery man was only interested in old Nazis, and as far as Frank knew, Jillian had nothing to do with that.

"I can see I've only complicated matters for you," Hoffsteader said, motioning the bartender for another whisky.

"A Nazi-hunting private citizen wasn't high on my list of possibilities," Frank said. "Is he West German or East German?"

"It's a bit of an artificial divide, isn't it?" said Hoffsteader. "But let's say West German. He often flew in from Frankfurt and seemed to have an ease of movement that would be unusual for an East German."

"Why isn't he working for the Stasi? Aren't they always complaining about the West being run by Nazi-sympathizing capitalists?"

"I really don't know. I never got the impression he was anti-capitalist. I think he quite appreciated all the money he had."

The bartender brought Hoffsteader another scotch.

"Look," he continued, "if Carlos compromised your operation, he probably did it to save his own skin, and not because anyone was asking."

"So I just need to hope, then, that this friend of yours doesn't need anything from the Soviets in the near future?"

"It's a reasonable hope. They don't spend many resources looking for ex-Nazis. But why do you think it's him? Carlos knew a lot of people."

"The timing," Frank said. "Let me ask you, what are you doing here? What were you planning to save him from?"

"You've got that all wrong. I was planning to save myself."

Frank considered Hoffsteader for a moment. "So is there anything you can give me?"

Hoffsteader smiled. "There is one thing I can give you. His name. His real name. It's Arlo Morris. That should be enough to keep him away from your operation."

"I take it that name isn't one he uses often."

"Not since the war."

"What did he do?"

"I have no idea. Nothing that ever made it into an intelligence report or a newspaper. But everything he does, it goes back to the war, so I'll give you a tip. If you want to protect your operation, don't underestimate the resources he has at his disposal. He's made many friends over the years. There are many people who are supportive of his efforts."

Including the man he was looking at. "We shifted to the Communists pretty fast after the war," Frank said. "I appreciate how some people may feel like there were too many loose ends from the Nazis."

"Germany needed to be rebuilt," Hoffsteader said, "and the Soviets certainly were taking the opportunity to take over as much as they could. I am not unaware that compromises had to be made. I made my share of them. But you should know, those kinds of nuances are not understood by Arlo. If and when you ever have to deal with him, do not expect any compromise or an appreciation of competing agendas. Only share with him what can be exploited. Because that's what he does."

Frank stood up, knowing Hoffsteader had given him all he was going to. "Thanks," Frank said.

"My pleasure," said Hoffsteader. "And thank you for the update on Carlos. Now I can spend the rest of my time here by the pool."

After saying good-bye, Frank decided to walk back to the apartment, needing to think. What Hoffsteader had told him, it didn't hang together in a clear narrative. Despite being forthcoming with a few details, there were obviously a lot of holes. Frank knew he wasn't going to be able to fill too many of them.

What now? He had a name that he couldn't do much with. He could ask that it be targeted, but that didn't seem likely to turn up much. How was Jillian supposed to protect herself—or the operation—from a ghost?

It unsettled Frank, the notion of a Nazi-hunting private citizen mixed in with intelligence operations. When personal agendas got too close to intelligence, the result was usually a moral compromise.

Frank didn't think there was any way to handle this via the RCMP or CBNRC because there was no corresponding agency to lean on, no state-sponsored adversary to target.

He supposed he should be grateful that he had Quentin. Quentin, who could go warn Jillian, was very familiar with the mess created by personal agendas.

CHAPTER THIRTY-ONE

Jillian was balancing her muffin on the coffee cup, trying not to soak one with the other. She shoved her change into her pocket, grabbed her papers, and transferred the muffin to her other hand. She munched as she walked, appreciating the late-January afternoon sun that was streaming in through the windows of the institute. She'd just taken a break from her transcription duties, needing both the coffee and the brightness. Maybe she could leave while it was still light out and head over to Madeline's. They were making good progress through all the documents, and Jillian thought that Madeline would be able to write an unbelievable story once everything was sorted.

Lost in thought as she was, she didn't notice the man coming up beside her until he was close enough to whisper in her ear. "Know anyone who can bug a car for me?"

Jillian spun around. Quentin.

The shock came and faded. In its place came a stillness as she stared at him, not sure if she could trust what she saw.

Then he touched her briefly and said, "Where can we go to talk?" And she knew it was really him. She wasn't hallucinating.

Jillian led him to her lab, really the ex-utility closet that had all her recording equipment. She put down her coffee and muffin, staring at them as if she couldn't remember how she got them.

Looking at Quentin again, she didn't know what to do. Part of her had assumed she would see him again, and part of her had wondered if he'd disappeared out of her life forever.

"When did you get into Berlin?" It was the first thing she could think of to say.

"A few days ago," he replied.

She kept staring at him. He was here. He seemed different somehow. Maybe because he'd just been in her imagination so long, the physical presence felt incongruous.

"What happened to you?" she asked.

His face was a mess of healing bruises, and he had a large, ugly cut along his jawline that still looked raw.

"Carlos is dead."

Jillian started, not expecting that. "Is that where you got those injuries?"

Quentin paused for a moment. "Yes. But…it all worked out."

"Did you kill him?"

"Yes."

Jillian just looked at him, still trying to catch up with the fact that he was here, let alone that he'd killed Carlos. "I hope you didn't do it for me."

"In part, yes," he said. "But that's not on you. I also did it for Isabella. And her son."

"So did it work? The amends you went to Nicaragua to make?"

He shrugged, but Jillian could see the pain behind it. "I can't bring her back. At least this way, he won't kill anyone else."

Jillian was having trouble swallowing past the lump that had suddenly formed in her throat. In the last few months, she'd indulged in these ridiculous, idle thoughts about what a relationship with Quentin might be like. She'd allowed herself to daydream about a man who didn't really exist, because the one standing in front of her had so many complications she couldn't imagine where she'd fit in.

"Well," she said, "thanks for coming all this way to tell me."

He tilted his head down, raising a brow. "I had other reasons to come back."

Jillian realized she didn't know what she wanted from him. It was almost surreal, talking to him like this. No prep. No heads-up. He just appeared. And she knew how easy it was for him to disappear. What was she supposed to do?

"Can I ask about Carlos? About what happened?"

Quentin shrugged out of his coat and sat down in Jillian's chair. "Yes, but can we go through it some other time? There are more important things to talk about. Are we going to be undisturbed here?"

Jillian felt her skin tingle with apprehension. Of course there was another reason for him being here at this moment. "Yes. My advisor only visits once every couple of weeks. No one else has any reason to interact with me. Plus, I have to switch tapes every twenty minutes for the next two hours."

"Perfect," Quentin said. "Can I have some of that coffee?"

"So, what did you want to talk about if not Carlos?" Jillian asked, handing him the coffee before leaning against the edge of her desk.

"Well, it starts with him, but there's something more interesting. I wasn't the only one looking for him in Nicaragua."

"Given what I know about him, I'm not surprised."

"Well, you might be surprised to know that I spent a lot of time with your old boss Frank."

Jillian couldn't believe there was something more shocking than everything that had happened in the last ten minutes. "Frank? My Frank? Frank Leachuk from CBNRC?"

"It's a good thing we have two hours," Quentin said. "Can I have some of the muffin too?"

Jillian passed it to him soundlessly, waiting for him to speak. Then she spent the next hour listening.

"I really can't believe that one misguided affair just keeps causing trouble," Jillian said.

"Frank said he would look for Arlo Morris, but given that Gavin Hoffsteader, with all of MI6 at his disposal, was never able to put together much, he's not optimistic."

Jillian took a sip of the now cold coffee. "He doesn't have to. I'm pretty sure I know Arlo Morris."

A ghost of a smile played around Quentin's mouth. "Why am I not surprised?"

"You say that like I had something to do with it."

"What does he want with you?" Quentin asked.

Jillian leaned her head back for a moment. "It all makes sense now. My God. I had no idea how he found me, so I didn't know how much of a threat he was. I thought maybe he'd gotten his information from Victor. I mean, Carlos did cross my mind, but it seemed more unlikely somehow."

"Why?" Quentin asked.

"You should see this guy. He's polished, soft-spoken, and quietly fucking crazy."

"What's going on, Jillian?"

Whatever else he was to her, Jillian was immensely grateful that Quentin was back, because he was the best person she knew to help her figure out this mess.

Recognizing that it was her turn, she started with Gohl—now Morris—approaching her on the street. Laying out every detail she could remember, she ended with her thwarted attempt to follow him.

When she had finished, Quentin regarded her for a long moment. It was an old look, one that suggested half disbelief and half admiration. "What were you planning to do now?"

"Wait for his next move," Jillian said. "James said he'd try to find someone to help, but I don't know if he did. I don't exactly have a ton of options. What about you?"

"Me?"

"It was a long plane ride over here. You must have thought about something on the way over."

"I thought about a lot of things."

"Regarding the information you were coming over to share."

"Oh, that," Quentin said. "I hoped it wouldn't matter. Then I hoped we could figure out how to protect you from him."

"But you're a worst-case-scenario kind of guy," Jillian said. "What were you planning if Arlo Morris had already made contact?"

Quentin smiled slightly. "We all fall to our experience, Jillian. There are certain things I'm very good at."

He was, she realized, smart and somewhat ruthless. For the moment, it was a combination that made her feel somewhat hopeful. "Why do you think Carlos did it? Why did he think Morris would be interested in me?"

"Because I think Morris is interested in everyone. He's a private citizen on a quest. He's not bound by formal agreements or treaties. He likely collects every bit of information he can, not knowing what might be valuable in the future."

That makes sense.

"Tell me about Jasminka," Quentin said.

Jillian's thoughts stuttered a bit before catching up. "I...I think I told you everything, at least that I know. Maybe James has more and he's holding out, but I don't think so. He's been adamant about keeping me away from her."

"You believe she really is a journalist?"

Jillian sighed. "James does. And if she isn't, can't you find out?"

"Maybe. But for the record, I think you're probably right about her."

"Gee, thanks."

"Do you think she'd be willing to help you?" Quentin asked.

Jillian tilted her head at the unexpected question. "With what?"

"Well, and maybe I should talk to James, but if his assessment is correct and now Jasminka's looking for Morris to get him out of her life as well, it would seem that the two of you have a mutual goal."

"Okay," Jillian said.

"And that goal has a much better chance of being reached if she has his real name."

Jillian smiled. "I did help her find some contacts in East Germany about Soviet nuclear power plant issues."

Quentin raised a brow. "How did you manage that?"

"We'll make that one of my stories for another day. But yeah, I think you're right. Even if she has another agenda, it's not to protect Morris, so I could give her his name. See what happens."

"Hopefully nothing that makes him paranoid."

Lovely. "So, are you working here?" she asked.

Quentin leaned back and sighed. "This, maybe, is yet another conversation for another day. But yes, technically I'm working. I just spent almost six months in Nicaragua, where I filed stories for the *Chicago Tribune*, but not reports for Langley. They're a little pissed. And since the access they provide is useful to me, I thought it best to make amends. So I do have some official duties here."

"The access they provide? That doesn't sound like someone committed to the cause."

"Like I said, it's a story for another day. And the work here is not difficult."

"Is that what you've been doing since you got here?"

"Partly. I've also spent a lot of time following you."

Jillian started. "Following me?"

"I came over here to warn you about some Nazi hunter with ties to Carlos. Aren't you wondering why we're talking here instead of your apartment?"

Jillian's stomach clenched. "I am now."

"You're being tracked, Jillian."

She breathed out a little. "I think I knew that. By Gohl's men. Morris's men. He wants me to flush Radsch out of the weeds, so he must be following me in case his plan is successful."

"I think it already is. Because there is someone else."

She felt the momentary peace disappear. "What?"

"There are two different people following you, and they do not appear to be working with each other."

Suddenly she had trouble swallowing. "You know this for sure?"

Quentin only raised a brow.

Of course he knows it for sure. This is what he does. "So what do I do?"

"You're asking me?" Quentin said.

"Why not? I really don't know what to do with that information."

He regarded her for a moment. "I'm just surprised. It seems out of character for you."

Jillian began to gently tap her fingers on her desk. "The truth is, Quentin, you have a very narrow understanding of my character."

He again raised a brow.

"Last time we were together, I was helping a friend who was in trouble. It was important to me."

"You're wrong, Jillian. I know you quite well."

The space around them seemed to fill, and Jillian realized that having Quentin back came with its own set of difficulties.

She met his gaze, waiting for him to continue.

"I can see," Quentin said, "that you didn't start any of this. But these events were partly set in motion because of your past. That means you have a part in it all, and you've been trying to resolve things in accordance with your values. I also know that you will fight for what you value, even when it comes into conflict with what most people call basic self-preservation."

"And you think I'm an idiot because of it."

"No." Suddenly he looked as serious as she'd ever seen him. "Isabella was like that."

Jillian swallowed. "She's dead."

"She died fighting for something she believed in. It's sad, but it's not tragic because if no one does, then eventually the world falls apart. You just have to be prepared for the potential consequences."

"I don't know what to do, Quentin."

"What do you want to do?"

"I want to do my job." She sighed. "I want Arlo Morris to go away. I don't want to die."

"And delivering justice on the people who made the gas during the war? Because I can tell you're not unmoved by that story."

"The funny thing is, if Morris had just asked me to help, I probably would've. What he's doing, I get it. It's not right that people do something so awful and then get to walk away and never have to own up to it. But his blackmailing, I can't do that. This SIGINT operation, it's important too. Radsch isn't the only bad person in the world."

"If you had to choose between the two?"

Jillian let out a breath. "It's not a choice. I have to choose my job. Maybe there might be other options in the future, but right now I don't have a choice."

"You could walk away," Quentin said. "You could go home. You could quit your job. You could go run a little restaurant on a Greek island. You have options."

"All of which involve me giving up my life," she said. "Plus, it's not going to change anything. I've thought this through. Anyone sent to replace me is going to be in the same position with Morris. Me leaving would be both selfish and shortsighted." Jillian rubbed at her temples, trying to avert the headache she could feel building. "It seems that everyone else in my life, they just push on me what they think I should do. What a woman should do. What a SIGINT engineer should do. Or whatever it is that will help them. I don't know if this is a good thing, or even real, but before, even though you disagreed with most of what I did, you still seemed to pay attention to who I was. And now you seem to understand who I am."

"Does that scare you?"

"I find it terrifying. Especially because I don't seem to know you at all. But I would like your help."

Quentin stared at her for a while and seemed to sort something out for himself. "I'm not a very good person, Jillian. I got into this job for all the wrong reasons. I've spent most of my life being selfish and hurt a lot of people in the process. I spent a lot of time in Nicaragua wondering if it was just best for you if I disappeared. For a long while, I wasn't that much better than Carlos. The sad thing is, I didn't think anyone was. Not really. Isabella changed that. It was her gift to me. Sometimes you remind me a little of her. Not so much that it should worry you, but enough. I want to be honest with you: I haven't changed completely. Let's sort this out. I'll help you. And then…well, we'll see what's left."

Nothing with him was ever going to be easy, but that was something to worry about in the future.

"So, what next?" she asked.

"I'll follow your followers," Quentin continued. "We can't make a plan until we know who we're dealing with."

She had so many questions for him. How he had met up with Frank. If Carlos had said anything about her. What the story was in Nicaragua, and what had happened there all those years ago. She wanted to know more about his job, about the regrets he had about Isabella. Jillian wanted to know if Quentin was worth waiting for.

It seemed there wasn't time for that. Not now anyway. It appeared her current mess was far from resolved.

CHAPTER THIRTY-TWO

It had been ten days since Quentin had shown up at the institute. Ten days of knowing she was being followed. Ten days of knowing that if anyone tried to attack her again, well, at least Quentin was likely to be watching.

She'd seen Gohl/Morris once. He's dropped by just to say hi. "Don't worry, Jillian, you will not have to act your part much longer. Radsch is coming out of the shadows. He has made a mistake. But you must keep on for a while yet."

Jillian assumed that meant that Gohl/Morris was now aware that someone else was following her. Hopefully that meant he'd seen Radsch's man and not Quentin.

It wasn't like her to sit still like this. She wanted to confront everyone involved. Start screaming until they all went away. But Jillian knew that wouldn't solve anything. The second she became a liability, she was useless to them all.

She watched as James entered the bar. It was his favorite whisky hangout—small, selective, and refined. The booths were private, the atmosphere muted. A place where businessmen went to make deals and politicians went for privacy. The smoke alone made the air almost translucent, obscuring any sharp edges. The dim lights did the rest. It was as private as they could get in a public place.

James slid into the booth beside her. He was out of uniform, but not entirely inconspicuous. He was too big and had too much presence. He did not, however, stand out in this bar full of high rollers. She, in her jeans and black sweater, was the one who didn't quite fit.

He ordered whiskies for both of them before turning to her. "So, what are we here for, then?"

She looked at him. "You're the one who chose this place."

"Well, your spook dropped off a note asking for somewhere nice and quiet. It was the best place I could think of."

She looked around. "It is that. No one here looks like they want to be noticed. Hopefully they'll do us the favor of not noticing us."

He took a drink of his whisky when it arrived. "And how're you doing, then?"

Jillian shrugged. Her stomach couldn't get any more knotted. Other than that, "Fine." She knew James was worried about her. She could see it in his expression every time they saw each other.

"Right, then."

"I just hate being inactive," Jillian said, fighting the urge to squirm in her seat. "I'm the one in the middle of this, and I can't do anything about it."

"You know, it's a proper pain, watching you feel sorry for yourself."

She scowled at him. "What are you talking about?"

"You're not a victim, Jillian. You never have been. You've got that contact of yours searching all over Canada for what happened after the war, you've got Quentin running around getting you more information about what in Christ is going on, and now you've dispatched Jasminka to somewhere in West Germany to track down the history of this Morris bloke. You're like a bloody music conductor at the moment, getting everyone to play to your rhythm."

Jillian was sure her jaw had hit the table.

"And don't be denying it," James continued. "You really want to get out of this mess, own up to your part in it. Then figure it out."

She decided to take a large gulp of her whisky. "You sound pissed."

"Aye, with Jasminka gone, I'm not getting a regular shag. I'd been getting quite used to it."

"Well, if that's all. Sorry I've been such an impediment to your sex life."

James smiled. "I've been through worse. But I am serious, Jillian. The sooner you stop thinking of yourself as a pawn in all of this, the sooner you'll be out of it. I've not given you proper credit over this last year for how good you are at sorting through puzzles. Play to your strengths, lass. You're a tenacious pain in the arse when you want to be, as I've said before. I'm sure if you put your mind to it, you can figure out what you need to resolve this."

She sat for a moment, considering his words. "James," she said, "how did you become my best friend?"

"Ah, I see you're in the mood to heap on the responsibility."

"No." She leaned over and kissed him on the cheek. "You're right. I can sort this out. You don't need to do anything other than be my friend."

"Right." He laughed. "Famous last words coming from you. We'll just see what the future holds. In the meantime, your spook has arrived."

Jillian looked toward the door to see Quentin walking toward them. He settled in opposite James, taking off his coat and looking alert.

It was different now somehow, Jillian thought, watching him. She wasn't sure why. Maybe because they were working to the same purpose, or because no one's intelligence agency was involved at all, but he didn't seem as unreachable.

"Whisky?" James asked, motioning to a waiter.

Quentin shook his head. "Coke."

"Not bloody likely, seeing as you're after staying under the radar. No one in here would be caught dead having a Coke."

Quentin shook his head. "I'd forgotten what a pleasure you are to be around." He turned to the waiter. "Coffee," he said.

"Well, I suppose that'll do," James said.

"Coke, my friend, is more ubiquitous than clean water. Everywhere in the world you go, you can always find a Coke."

"And a sad sentiment that is."

They were quiet for a while, waiting for the waiter to return with the coffee. Jillian reflected that the last time the three of them had been together was when they'd gone over to East Berlin to get Lisa. It seemed like a lifetime ago.

"So, then," James said after the waiter had left, "Jillian tells me you've spent the last six months in Nicaragua. I'm not after believing it, seeing as you've not got much of a tan, even under all those fading bruises. Still pale as a bloody ghost."

Quentin smiled. "I burn. So I avoid the sun."

"Ah, more a vampire, then."

"Lovely to see you two catching up," Jillian interjected, "but shouldn't we move on?"

"Aye, lass. To the hot item of the night."

"You're not going to like where we're moving to," Quentin said.

Jillian sighed. "Just tell me. I wasn't expecting it to be any good."

Quentin shrugged, as if he was so used to delivering bad news that it didn't bother him at all. "The second man following you around is a private investigator. He's good, but probably more used to insurance fraud. He stays on you most of the time. That's his mistake. Whoever hired him thinks that you're important, which you're not. He should be following Morris's man, but I'm not sure he's really noticed him."

"And Morris's man, does he know about the PI?" James asked.

"Yes. I assume because he knows you're just bait," Quentin said, pointing at Jillian, "so he's been waiting for someone else to show up."

"Unimportant bait. Your flattery is incredible, you know," Jillian said.

Quentin ignored her. "I followed the PI around for three days. He sends a telegram every day at five p.m. to a Lily Hahn in Saarbrücken."

"Lovely town, that. Saw a memorable football match there," James said.

"Did you go to Saarbrücken?" Jillian asked Quentin.

"Yes, on the assumption that Lily Hahn wasn't the end of the line. She is definitely female, so is very unlikely to have ever been Helmut Radsch." Quentin suddenly looked uncomfortable.

"What is it?" Jillian asked.

"I bugged her phone. It wasn't hard. I think it's the first time she's ever played a role like this. The rest of her day was spent playing bridge and shopping."

"So not exactly a proper spook, then," James said.

"After she receives the telegram, she places a call to an exchange in Frankfurt. She reads out the contents and hangs up."

"Who does the exchange connect to?" Jillian asked, trepidation suddenly squeezing her chest.

"The private residence of Kurt Richter."

The name didn't mean anything to her. "Who is that?"

"The president of the Handelbank," James said. "Jesus Christ, Jillian, you're caught in a bloody brutal cross fire if that's true."

Quentin drank some of his coffee. "It fits. Of course, I didn't have time to verify all the details. The number was unlisted, but I found it easily enough. Someone who can afford to have his past remain buried isn't going to be a clerk in a retail store. The twenty-four-hour surveillance by this PI isn't cheap either."

Jillian sat there trying to process everything she'd just learned. So Helmut Radsch, who worked on the team that developed the gas for the chambers in the concentration camps during the war, had become Kurt Richter, head of one of the largest banks in Germany. For some reason he'd gone to Canada after the war, and for an even more obscure reason, he had been given a new identity there. He'd used that identity to come back to Germany, where he amassed wealth and power. There were enough ex-Nazis running various enterprises in West Germany that Radsch might have been okay if he'd stayed and kept his head down for a while, but he'd gone for a new identity instead. Was that what he was worried about now? Not only about what he did during the war, but also the fact that he'd deliberately taken steps to cover it up?

Whatever the reason, Kurt Richter obviously wanted to protect his new identity. And just as clear, Arlo Morris would have no moral qualms about bringing down the head of a bank.

"If Morris's guy is following me, then presumably they've got someone on the PI as well. I mean"—she turned to Quentin—"I know you're good, but wouldn't they have found Lily and Kurt too?"

"What do you think?" he asked her.

She thought for a moment. "I don't think he has—Morris, I mean. If he'd figured out that Helmut Radsch is now Kurt Richter, he would have hinted something to me, if only to gloat that his plan worked. But he can't be far behind you, I don't think."

"Well, Jillian," Quentin said, "it's a little humbling to know you think my talents are so pedestrian."

"What's your guess, then?" James asked. "How close is Morris to finding Lily Hahn and Kurt Richter?"

Quentin shrugged. "That depends on a bunch of factors that I have no insight into. His background makes him less than predictable, and I have no idea what his resources are. But I did have a chat with Lily. I explained that the government was doing a land survey, the ones for that area being out of date. Once we discovered a mutual love of *Derrick*, last week's episode being particularly memorable, it was no problem to stay for a coffee. I was the first unexpected visitor she'd had in a while. It's been a little lonely for her since she retired from the Handelbank, but her daughter was planning to relocate to the area, so soon she hoped to be busy with her grandchildren."

James grinned. "You sound like you enjoy it, then, coffee and biscuits with old ladies."

"Anyway," Quentin said, "it's impossible to know if her phone had been tapped before I got there, but there wasn't anyone else sitting on her house."

Jillian tapped her fingers on the table. "So I've got a name with a short shelf life. Sooner or later Morris is going to catch up with us, and then this info is going to become useless."

"I'd say that gives you one opportunity to get Morris off your back," James said.

"Yeah, but how to do it? If I give him the name, it opens the door to more of these supposed favors."

"You could go the other way," said Quentin. "You can walk right up to the PI and tell him about Morris. Let them fight it out."

"I could." Jillian sighed. "It might get them to leave me alone. Or maybe Morris will just add me to his 'deserves retribution' list."

"To say nothing of the fact that Richter may not answer for his crimes."

Jillian rubbed at her temples. "Don't put that on me. It might be that the right thing for me is the right thing for Morris. I just have to think for a bit."

"I'll come find you soon," Quentin said. "In the meantime, be careful. I won't be able to watch out for you for the next couple of days. And both of these men are still following you."

Jillian reached out and put her hand on Quentin's. "Thank you. For doing all this for me. For going to Saarbrücken and Frankfurt and finding some answers. I really, really appreciate it."

"When you figure out what you're going to do, well…Let me know if I can help," Quentin said.

"Okay."

Quentin's eyes lingered on her for a moment before he stood up. Nodding at James, he turned down the hall that led to the kitchen, evidently planning to slip out the back.

"Another drink?" James asked.

Jillian refocused her attention. "Sure. Isn't alcohol meant to be the gateway to creativity or something?"

"I do think it improves my singing voice." James smiled.

"Maybe it'll help me, then."

"One never knows. But Jillian, same for me—if you need me, just ask. You don't have to be sorting the rest of this out on your own. Christ, everyone else has been doing something interesting. I might as well join in."

"Thanks. One of these days, I'll be doing you a favor, I promise."

"Ah, lass, you already have."

CHAPTER THIRTY-THREE

Jillian went out as little as possible now. It was unnerving, knowing she was being followed by Richter's man as well. She wondered how long both parties were planning on keeping it up. Morris, no doubt, would go forever, given that he'd been patiently chasing phantoms for thirty years. Richter was a larger unknown. Was he patient as well, protecting his decades-old secret? Or impatient to make sure it was buried again?

After meeting with Quentin, Jillian had included the information about Kurt Richter in her next dead drop marked for Jean-Marc's attention. She hoped that sharing it would give her some sort of protection. She also hoped it would give Jean-Marc some ammunition to keep poking around the RCMP. Surely someone had to know how the chemist became the banker. Someone had approved that paperwork all those years ago.

The problem was, she was starting to feel like a prisoner, or a sitting duck. She didn't want to make herself an easy target. One thing she wanted to get across to Arlo Morris is that although he might have all the leverage now, he shouldn't imagine that situation was going to last forever.

She began to pace around her apartment. She'd already gone over everything a thousand times. She didn't have enough to turn the tables. Not yet.

Before Jillian could think it through and come up with all the reasons Quentin or James would tell her it was a terrible idea, she threw a set of clothes and her toothbrush into the bag she usually took to work. Anyone watching her was going to assume she was heading to the institute and possibly not bother to follow too closely.

Walking down the street to the U-Bahn, she acted like it was just another day. She passed a bunch of kids sledding down a mountain of snow that had been piled up in a park. Shops were open, and she resisted the urge to get a coffee. Instead of turning toward the institute, she took the U-Bahn to Tempelhof.

Five hours later, Jillian was sitting on a train that was making its way to Saarbrücken from Frankfurt. It hadn't been hard to get a same-day ticket for the flight to Frankfurt. The East Germans only allowed West Berliners to fly to three destinations, and the West Germans made sure those flights were running frequently.

Arriving at the airport, transferring to the train station, Jillian only had to wait forty-five minutes for a train to Saarbrücken, close to the French border. It was dark now, so Jillian couldn't see anything other than the lights that dotted the view from the train. It was too bad. She'd have liked to see more of the German countryside.

She wondered where her followers were. Had they managed to get on the flight? Was one of them now sitting in the next car over, poking their head out at every station to see where she got off? Or were they in a panic in Berlin, frantically wondering where she'd gone?

Either way, she didn't care. Either way, they'd be shaken up. And if one or both of them had managed to follow her here, it should make them even more nervous. And people made mistakes when they were nervous.

The train began to slow down as it approached the city. She made her way off the train and into the station, a three-story building whose bricks were illuminated to a dark gray by the station lights. It was too late to visit Lily Hahn, and Jillian wasn't entirely comfortable wandering a strange city at night anyway. Not given the situation she was in.

She exited into the forecourt and headed for the first hotel she saw. The Eurohaus announced itself in large, garish, glowing-orange letters. Perfect.

Jillian checked herself into a single. Pulling out the food she'd bought on the train, she settled in to watch *Derrick* and wait for morning.

Lily Hahn lived in a pretty three-story apartment building close to a park that bordered the Saar river. It was a nice neighborhood to retire to. Jillian watched her breath frost in the air as she waited after pressing the bell. February meant that mornings were still crisp, even this bit farther south.

Jillian had formed a loose plan during the night. Shifting the flowers she'd bought to her other hand, she pressed the bell again. Jillian saw a couple of other people on the street walking to the park. Lily Hahn couldn't be far. Quentin said she passed on a daily message from the PI in West Berlin to Richter in Frankfurt.

Finally the intercom cracked. "Ja?" said a disembodied voice.

"Blumen," Jillian responded.

"Blumen?" the voice asked.

"Ja. Fur Lily Hahn."

The door buzzed to let Jillian in. Step one complete. Now she just had to go scare an old woman enough that she'd go running to her boss.

Jillian had been expecting an older woman, probably because Quentin had said she was waiting for her grandchildren, so Jillian had automatically gone to wrinkles and gray hair. She'd assumed sharp eyes—otherwise, Lily would never have been asked to play a middleman—but in an elderly face.

The woman who opened the door was no one's stereotype of a doting grandma. Her blond hair was carefully braided to frame her face. She had on subtle eyeshadow and bright red lipstick, and looked ready to walk on some Hollywood set.

"Lily Hahn?" Jillian asked.

"Ja," the woman responded, holding out her hands for the flowers.

Jillian pushed the flowers at the woman, causing her to take a couple of steps back and allowing Jillian to step into the apartment so the door couldn't be shut in her face.

Lily Hahn looked past the blooms with an expression of confusion.

"It was the least I could do," Jillian said, motioning to the flowers, "considering I've come to ruin your day."

Shock rippled across the woman's face. "Who are you?"

"Actually, you know a lot about me. Where I live. Where I work. What I get up to every day. I'm the woman in West Berlin you pass on messages about."

Lily turned and carefully placed the flowers on a small table by the door. "What do you want?"

At least she wasn't denying it. "Just to have a chat. Mostly to know why you're doing it. Kurt Richter, is he paying you? Threatening you? Or have you just been in love with him for thirty years?"

"He is an old friend who has asked for a favor. That is all. But I don't suppose that is enough to get you to leave."

"No," said Jillian.

"I could call the police."

"But you won't," Jillian stated, moving into the living room that was visible from the entranceway. "Nice view. It seems like a nice town. Along a river, but much quieter than Berlin."

"You seem very sure of yourself. What are you, American?"

Jillian felt anything but confident, with the nerves dancing around her stomach. But whatever, she was here now. "Do you know why Kurt Richter is having me followed? Did he tell you?"

Lily was quiet for a moment. "No. I did not ask. It was simply a favor between friends. We have done many for each other over the years."

"How long have you known him?"

"I worked for him for over twenty years."

"Did you work for him at IG Farben when he was Helmut Radsch, or have you only known him as Kurt Richter?"

Genuine confusion settled on Lily's face. "I do not know what you are saying. He hired me as his secretary when he first started at the bank. We worked well together, so I went with him as he changed positions. I retired last year."

"So you don't know what he did before the bank? During the war."

Lily's jaw clenched slightly. "No. I do not. It is a time I have never seen the point in revisiting. They were terrible years. If you survived, it was best to just get on with it."

"Yeah, if you survived."

"You think you are in a place to judge us?" Lily's words sprang out coated with anger. "Yes, the Americans, who stopped Hitler and saved everyone. I know what you think, what you all think. So horrified at all the Germans who gave Hitler a place and let him do whatever he wanted. Well, you were not here. Germany got better for a time, and it was a relief to have someone trying to make it better, to give us a purpose after it had been stripped from us. My parents lost everything after the first war. When I was growing up, it was hard to eat, to have hope for a better future. Hitler gave us that."

"Then he exterminated twelve million people. He tried to wipe out all the Jews. Was that how you got your hope back?"

Lily waved her hand as if dismissing all that happened in the end. "Hitler went too far. He did not live up to his promises. He ruined us again. If the world disliked us after the first war, it was nothing compared to what was felt after the second. We were reviled everywhere. My brother was in the Gestapo. He killed himself in 1948. It was our childhood all over again, as if to be German was to be a mistake of nature. But my brother did not need to die. There was nothing to be ashamed of."

Jillian knew she should stop being amazed by now. Every story from the war was different. The broad brushes painted by history faded under an examination of the details.

"Kurt Richter is having me followed because I know what he did during the war. He was a chemist at IG Farben. He worked on the team that developed the gas that Hitler sent to be used in the chambers—the gas that killed millions of innocent people."

Lily pursed her lips. "And you are telling me this why?"

Jillian shrugged. "I'm not entirely sure."

"Are you planning to put it in the papers?"

"Would it matter?" Jillian asked. "You seem to think that what happened during the war has no bearing on the present. I'm sure there are others like you."

"Yes. But there are also many who want the self-flagellation to continue. The young people. The Jews, especially the scholars. How many times can one country apologize?"

"I guess it depends on who you ask. Some people think there is no place for immunity from war crimes. In Richter's case, no one gets to be absolved from that kind of action."

Lily narrowed her eyes. "It is so easy to judge after the fact. As if all the bad people in the world were in one country.

Maybe when you are older, you will have the courage to admit it can happen anywhere. Look at what you did in Vietnam. I read about this. It does not seem so heroic to me."

Jillian knew, despite taking sides every day to go to work, that Lily Hahn was right. Moral principles only existed if there were people everywhere willing to uphold them.

"Just tell Richter I was here when you call him today. Tell him that I'm sick of being followed. That his secret is out, that I wasn't the one looking for it, and that I'm not the one he's going to have to answer to." Jillian turned and walked the short distance to the front door. She could let herself out.

"Who is it?" Lily asked from behind her. "Who wants to know about Kurt?"

"I don't know," Jillian said, "but I guess there are some people who think there are things to be ashamed of. That need to be addressed. From the war."

Jillian took her time walking back to the train station. The weather was cool, but the sun was out, and the next train to Frankfurt wasn't for a couple of hours anyway. For a moment, with the sun on her face and not a breath of wind in the air, Jillian felt far away from the problems winding their way around her. It was almost possible to forget them for a moment. After all, it seemed so long ago. It was almost possible to believe that none of it mattered, that the past had sorted itself out and put itself to rest.

But she knew that wasn't true. She was about to go back to a city with a giant wall dividing it. The watchtowers and the concrete reminded everyone every day that there was no forgiveness for being different. You were on one side or the other. There was no room to straddle both.

As much as she hated to admit it, she struggled with ambiguity. Life was easier when the lines were clear. Jillian despised what Radsch had done during the war, and she agreed that the statute of limitations should never run out on a crime like that. But she was grateful she didn't have to extract the justice. Arlo Morris would not allow Helmut Radsch to escape to a different place. She wondered at the toll a lifetime of seeking retribution took.

CHAPTER THIRTY-FOUR

James exited the base and pulled up his collar. Spring seemed forever away. He didn't mind so much, winter being part of why spring was so lovely. He knew that he'd enjoy the day when the linden trees started to unfurl their leaves, made all the more rewarding from the months of cold they'd had to endure.

He turned the corner, heading to the S-Bahn station. It never ceased to amaze him that a man from a family who'd not much left Inverness could feel so at home in Berlin. He went home on some of his leave and enjoyed seeing his mum and his sisters. There were plenty of nieces and nephews to keep him well entertained on the visits, and it was a proper treat to slip back into the expressions of his childhood and be around people who understood them. But he never felt like going back permanently. Even growing up he'd never felt much like he fit there, and he knew that the restlessness that characterized his youth would come back full force should he try to resettle in that place he'd left long ago.

James was content in Berlin. He had another two years left on this tour, then it was likely time to retire from the military and sort out another adventure. These days there was no shortage of them. *Especially if I continue to spend time in Jillian's company.* Lord knew how she managed to get herself in the middle of so much intrigue.

Perhaps because joining the military and getting posted all over the globe was an adventure, James had never wished for more. Leaving Inverness had felt right. Finding a career in the military that didn't involve shooting people had been appreciated. He enjoyed what he did. Partly because it was fun, and partly because he believed in it with all he had. Societies only changed when beliefs changed. And beliefs never changed under force. They only changed when people were given the freedom to explore new ideas. James loved putting ideas out there. Every time he was on the radio, he imagined some fourteen-year-old boy in East Berlin, hiding out on a rooftop, a small transistor radio stuck up to his ear. That boy didn't want to hear about politics or ideologies. He wanted to listen to rock.

But James knew it wasn't a far step from loving a piece of music to being curious about the people who made it. And that curiosity was the first step in developing an open mind, beginning the search for answers other than the ones you were force-fed.

It had started to drizzle by the time he climbed the steps exiting the S-Bahn station closest to his flat. It was too much like Inverness for him to mind, or even notice.

As much as he gave Jillian a hard time—sometimes to play devil's advocate, but also because he really did care about her—he could admit that he found her drama a mite interesting. Before her, his day-to-day had been significantly less complex. He tended to spend most of his time amongst people who thought in a similar way. The good guys and the bad guys were well defined.

Being friends with Jillian was letting him glimpse a world that was harder to define with precision. It was making his history books come alive in a way that he found intriguing.

And now, too, he had Jasminka. Not completely, and maybe for just a short time, but she was definitely not on a side that he normally interacted with. He wondered how much of that was part of the attraction.

Climbing the steps to the front door of his building, he noticed that her lights were still out. He expected her back at some point, but he thought it was for the best that they'd both got a little space. He wasn't quite sure what to do with her. And, of course, it might all be out of his hands anyway.

James hadn't even gotten his coat off when a knock sounded on his door. At this point not sure who to expect—and realizing that made for an interesting life—he opened it to find Quentin. The man was looking better than the last time James had seen him, his bruises continuing to fade and the cut on his jaw looking a little less raw.

He smiled as Quentin entered, supposing that he had to add this relationship to his list of ones that were adding unpredictability to his life.

"Miserable night for a walk," James said.

Quentin shrugged like he hadn't much noticed it. "I grew up in Chicago."

"Ah. Like me, then. Days like this make one feel at home."

James hung up his coat and got them both a beer. Quentin sat on the sofa, elbows on his knees, staring around at nothing.

"Thanks," he said as James handed him the Radegast. He looked at the label and raised a brow. "On account of the new girlfriend?"

James scowled. "It's a fine beer. Don't be doing your spook shite on me."

Quentin leaned his head back. "It's not like I can turn it off. And you're right, it is a good beer. She has taste."

"Right, then," James said, settling into his armchair. "Is there something else you want to be saying on that front?"

"Such as?"

"How once I found out she was a journalist, or a Yugoslavian, or had been put onto me by this Morris bloke, I should have been moving my arse in the other direction."

Quentin drank more of his beer. "I'm not saying any of those things."

"Aye, but you're thinking them. That I should have been making things less complicated for Jillian."

Quentin barked out a laugh. "Right. Because either of us can do that. She's still in Saarbrücken, isn't she."

James couldn't stop a chuckle himself. "Christ, yes. Tell me, what are the chances you think she's going to go a stretch with some peace and quiet?"

"With Carlos dead, I'd say we're at an even fifty-fifty. Because there is her job."

James was curious about what had happened in Nicaragua. Jillian had told him the gist, but he had his own questions.

"Was your trip to Nicaragua satisfying, then?"

"Do you mean was it satisfying to put a bullet in Carlos?" Quentin asked.

"More did it exorcise those demons that were following you around?"

Quentin was silent for a while as he drank his beer. "I don't know. I did it for this woman I knew there. Isabella. Carlos was her cousin, and he killed her. She was a wife, a mother, a daughter, and, well, a beautiful person. He took her away from everyone who loved her because he was a selfish, inhuman prick. And I thought it might give her family some peace instead of him showing up every once in a while and rubbing their faces in it."

"Killing someone. Not the easiest good deed to perform."

"Yeah, well, one more stain on my conscience isn't going to matter."

"There I think we might have to disagree," James said. "It seems to me that it's one more thing for you to carry around."

Quentin rubbed at his eyes. "Christ. Talking to you, I can't figure out if it helps or just makes everything worse."

James smiled. "I figure you need it. We all do sometimes."

"You know, Carlos wasn't even conscious when I shot him. In my mind, all those months I'd been imagining what it would be like, wondering if I'd do it when I got the chance, I never thought it would go down like that. It was a mess. I was all cut up. I'd miscalculated and got lucky that someone got curious enough to rescue me. The house was on fire, smoke everywhere. I was just going to walk away, because everything was falling apart anyway. But then Isabella's husband, he was hysterical. Said Carlos had taken his son. And I was like, fuck, I can do this for her. So I shot him. It was just one more moment that made me realize I should have made better choices a long time ago."

James took it all in and let it sit for a while. If anyone had told him a year ago that he'd develop a friendship with this man, he would have thought they were mad. At the beginning, all he'd thought he'd seen was selfishness and manipulation—mostly of Jillian. He'd thought Quentin was just someone who used whatever was available to meet his own ends.

Over time that had changed. It was rather a tightrope that this man was always walking. Most remarkable to James was the self-doubt that seemed to underlie everything Quentin did. James knew he himself was the opposite. He didn't doubt for a minute the value of broadcasting Queen or Aretha Franklin as far as he could into East Germany. To be that unsure that anything you're doing is at least the right thing to do, James didn't think he'd be able to stand it.

That, more than anything, was why he opened his door to Quentin.

"Well, not that she would've ever asked you to do it, but I imagine Jillian is quite grateful as well that Carlos is no longer around to make trouble for her. After she sorts out this mess, that is."

"I don't want her gratitude."

"What are you wanting, then?" James asked.

"Tell me about Jasminka."

James let the change of subject go. A man could only confront so much in one night.

"She's gone to track down the history of Arlo Morris."

"You trust her?"

"Aye, that I do. I can't promise that the right thing for her is always going to be the right thing for Jillian, but I don't think Jasminka is working for Morris. I know you're thinking my judgment's compromised, and that it most definitely is. But if I thought she was lying to me, there wouldn't be any compromise."

"Wanting to believe in someone doesn't make you an idiot."

James raised his beer. "I'm happy you agree. I'm not going to lie to you, I like Jasminka. Probably more than I should. But I'd not be doing anything if I thought it was going to hurt Jillian. She's had enough of being caught up in other people's priorities."

"She's lucky to have you."

"She's lucky to have both of us. She missed you, you know. Lord knows why, with a face like that. But she did. Even went to the library to read your articles for the *Tribune*."

"When's she coming back from Saarbrücken?"

"Tonight," James said. "She can't be away from her duties for too long."

"I wish she'd let me gather more intel. She's likely stirred up the situation by going there. I know that's what she wanted, but I can't help thinking there's a piece we're not seeing."

"Like what?" James asked.

"What do you think? Do you really think some Nazi who did some bad shit during the war would be all that nervous about having it come out now? Can't he just say he's sorry and get on with it?"

James thought for a moment. "I guess it depends. Making the gas for the chambers, that's as bad as it gets, isn't it? Not only is he responsible for killing millions, but without the bollocks to get up close. Maybe he's afraid about being unmasked as a coward. If he were just a regular bloke living out his life somewhere, he could just apologize. But he's the head of the second-largest German bank. How's that going to pan out?"

"Yeah, you're right." Quentin sighed. "It could be just that. Being exposed as one of humanity's worst assholes is something he wants to avoid. What a thing for Jillian to be caught up in."

"I'm not sure what she's going to do," James said.

"I am," Quentin responded. "She's trying to be smart, to get leverage over Morris so he doesn't bother her again. But in this instance, she's not going to let anyone get away with not paying for those kinds of crimes. She'll watch her back, but I've got no doubt she'll help Morris if it comes down to it."

"Aye. And I'm sure this time, I agree with what she's doing. Not that I think she should put her life in jeopardy over it, but I understand why she's not gone directly to Richter. Why she's walking that line, so that Morris doesn't lose him."

"Yeah, me too. That's one thing I was reminded of back in Nicaragua. There is some satisfaction in making assholes pay."

James laughed. "That there is."

Before he could ask Quentin if he was staying for another beer, there was a soft knock on the door.

"Expecting anyone else?" Quentin asked.

"I wasn't expecting anyone this evening at all."

James crossed to the door and looked through the peephole. His chest lurched when he saw Jasminka on the other side.

"It's Jasminka," he said, turning to Quentin. "Are you staying or taking your leave out the fire escape?"

Quentin thought for a moment. "Staying."

"And who should I say you are?"

"The me you know so well. Quentin Foster, journalist for the *Chicago Tribune*."

"Right, then. I hope I'm ready for this."

CHAPTER THIRTY-FIVE

James made them all coffee. Thank goodness they all took it black, as he seemed to be out of milk. He watched Jasminka and Quentin make small talk as he got the mugs out. There was no doubt but Quentin was a good actor. All of the heaviness of moments earlier had disappeared. Instead he looked animated, chatting about deadlines and working in West Berlin.

"Thank you." Jasminka smiled up at him as James handed her a coffee. "It is nice to meet someone else in the business. And such a small world. We have both worked with Peter Slater, a wonderful editor."

"Makes me think I should have introduced you two a long time ago," James said. "But Quentin has just arrived back in town."

"Even reporters get vacation," Quentin said, not volunteering where his most recent vacation was.

"That they do." James understood. The less said, the better.

"I must try to take one soon. It is so easy to always keep working because I love my job, but one time it might be nice to take a break. Go to a Greek island and spend some days being a tourist."

James thought that sounded lovely. Jasminka in a sundress. The two of them with nothing to do but be together. He imagined her freckles getting darker in the sun, her smiling at him as they sat across from each other in a little restaurant on a beach. Suddenly he wished he'd thought of it before.

"But for now," Jasminka continued, "we are in West Berlin, which has its own charms. We are, I think, not here to talk about geography. Shall I tell you what I found out about Arlo Morris?"

"Aye, please do." James gestured to Quentin. "I've told him most of the story, so you don't need to bother catching him up."

"It was not so hard, really, once I knew what I was looking for. Arlo Morris is not so common a name. There was only one in West Germany who fit the age and the connection to chemicals.

"He and his brother are the sole shareholders in FP Deutsch, a basic chemical manufacturing company. It started in 1888 as a soda manufacturer. Over the years it became very successful, supplying products to many companies, including those in the IG Farben conglomerate, like BASF. They are still in business and do very, very well. Their products are used in things like pesticides and fertilizers."

"Let me guess, then," James said. "Something they manufactured was also used in the gas for the chambers."

"It would take much more digging for me to prove that, but yes. In Zyklon B maybe. Or something we do not know of.

Early in the war, the Nazis used carbon monoxide, like in the mobile gas vans. But Zyklon B was much more deadly, and we do know that IG Farben manufactured it and promoted its use for the chambers."

They were all silent for a moment.

"That's his motive," Quentin said. "Morris's family company sold product to IG Farben that they used to make the gas."

"Aye. And he's been wanting revenge for it ever since."

"It does make sense," Jasminka continued. "Or rather, it fits what you told me about him, how he is determined to expose chemists from the war, and a certain kind. I looked further into the men he asked me to report on before. They all had ties to IG Farben. It is hard to know how many others he has found, because his name does not appear in connection to any of it."

"What are his weak spots?" Quentin asked.

Jasminka looked a little startled. "I must ask why you want to know?"

"You aren't the only one he's using," James said. "Quentin and I have a mutual friend, and Morris is using her as well. Though his ends might be morally correct, his means most definitely are not. She needs help, information, so Morris can't manipulate her anymore."

"It would seem that your friend and I have much in common. Perhaps I should be talking to her. Is this the woman who figured out the contest about the radioactive spiderman?"

"Yes."

"I would like to meet her one day."

"I'm sure she'd like that, given that she won't shut up with questions about you anyway. But she's out of town right now, and her situation with Morris—well, it's a little more complicated."

Jasminka thought for a moment. "What does she want from Morris? Does she want him dead?"

"No," Quentin said. "She wants to be able to deal with him on her own terms."

"She's a fair bit sympathetic to his cause, our Jillian. I don't think the story of what happened in those gas chambers is one that she wants to see forgotten. But, ah…"

"One of these war chemists doesn't want his secret to come out. He doesn't know about Morris. Only Jillian. So that's who he's going after," Quentin finished.

"Yes, I see. Your friend Jillian, she does not have a choice." Jasminka gave James a small smile. "I will keep all my questions for another day. For now I will tell you what I think.

"Arlo Morris's company profited greatly from the war, and so the war made Arlo Morris very wealthy. From my dealings with him, I understand he was never sympathetic to the Nazis. During the war the company was run by his father. Arlo did not have a say in the support that was given to the Nazis or the products that were sold to IG Farben. It is probable that any resistance he offered would have been wasted anyway. Whether he was willing to go to a concentration camp himself for his beliefs, we will never know.

"But I think he is ashamed, both of what his family did and what IG Farben used them for. I think his way of making it right is to use his money to shine a very bright light on everyone involved in the chemicals used on civilians. The chambers, yes, but also the experiments. I believe that it is his way of apologizing for not doing anything during the war itself.

"I also think that being Hans Gohl for him is a way of distancing himself from his past. It is interesting that he takes no credit as Arlo Morris. It is also telling that he does not do any of this as Arlo Morris. So that I think is his weakness. There is no real reason for the alter ego. Arlo Morris is not famous. His name is not known to his enemies. There is no reason not to use it. I think his shame runs deep. He does not want the world to know what Arlo Morris and his FP Deutsch company did during the war either."

It struck James as a logical assessment. "To do it under his own name would just invite counteraccusations, and it's probably true that there are no clean hands here. So Morris exposes the crimes of others but has yet to come clean on his own."

Jasminka turned to Quentin. "If you are looking for a weakness, I think this is it. Arlo Morris does not want anyone to know that his family company contributed in any way to the gas used in the chambers."

Quentin didn't say anything. Silence descended on the room. James felt like he was trying to navigate in a snowstorm.

"Come, then," he said, standing. "I think my friend here needs some time to think."

Jasminka took his hand and pulled herself up off the sofa. "I hope I have been able to help your friend. I'm not sure what she can do with this information, but maybe knowing where Arlo Morris is vulnerable will help."

"And you?" James asked. "What are you going to do the next time he comes asking for a favor?"

"So far his favors have been of mutual benefit. I think he is not a man to threaten lightly, but I know now that I can refuse him if I need to."

He leaned down and kissed her until he heard her breath catch. "Thank you, Jasminka."

She smiled up at him. "I am home all night, if you are free later."

"I damn well will be."

He watched her walk down the stairs before shutting the door and turning back to Quentin.

"How did he meet her?" Quentin asked. "Morris and Jasminka."

"She said he approached her. Said it was based on the content of her journalism, the kind of articles she wrote, and her credibility. I don't suppose that's enough for you."

"But it's all I'm going to get."

"Right," James said. "And you should be asking yourself, even if you knew the details, would it really matter? You're going to be suspicious anyway. Nothing is going to make you trust her but time."

Quentin smiled. "Okay, I'll leave your girlfriend alone."

James almost rolled his eyes. "We've got enough to worry about with Jillian. I don't see how this information helps her all that much. She could threaten Morris, but then what? Presumably he's not just going to walk away with her knowing his big secret."

"What do you think's more important to him? Keeping his past buried or revealing everyone else's?"

James shook his head. "How in the bloody Christ am I supposed to know? I've never met the man."

"I guess we wait for Jillian to get back from Saarbrücken."

"Aye. She's the one who has to sort this out."

Jillian let herself into her apartment. The flight from Frankfurt had been delayed due to high winds. It was now past eleven at night, and she felt like she'd done five days of living in the past thirty-six hours. She wanted a book and a blanket and some tea.

She almost tripped on the envelope lying just inside her door. It had been hand-delivered, because the only thing on it was her name. She picked it up, turning it over while she put the kettle on. It was fairly thick; no way it had fit under her door. Since her lock was intact, the envelope had been delivered by someone who had a key or who knew how to pick locks. She wouldn't know until she opened it, so she leaned against her counter and slowly peeled back the flap.

Scanning the contents, Jillian realized the envelope was from Jean-Marc. Maybe not directly, but he'd put it together.

Jillian,

You never know where you're going to find a mess. I went looking for Helmut Radsch and found a bunch of purged files. Since that pissed me off, I tracked down the man who gave him a new identity. William Dawson, ex-RCMP, now retired. Dawson lives well in Sydney, Nova Scotia. Maybe he's good with his money. Maybe he invested well. But I got a friend to pull three months of bank statements. Dawson receives a monthly deposit from a bank in

Germany. I wonder how far those go back. We have to tread carefully with Dawson. So far we're exploring an investigation under the Official Secrets Act. I don't know if he's the one who purged the Radsch files, but something's not right. Hopefully you know more about this Gohl who's got you twisted up over there. It looks like this all goes back to the war. Stay alert, but I think you're safe for now.

J-M

Jillian felt her heart rate speed up. She hadn't expected this from Jean-Marc. She thought he'd let the paperwork make its way through the system. She never thought he'd uncover some answers.

She looked through the rest of the papers. There were copies of the three bank statements, as well as the file numbers on the purged files. There was also a summary of William Dawson and the history he had at the RCMP.

She shook her head. Had it really just come down to money? Dawson gets a war criminal a new identity so he could retire in style on the ocean?

Before she could organize her thoughts, there was a knock on her door.

Her heart rate sped up for entirely different reasons as she let Quentin in.

"I thought it wasn't safe to meet at my apartment," she said.

"The PI's gone, and it's shift change for the other ones," he replied, stepping up to her. "How was Saarbrücken?"

"Sad. Lily Hahn didn't care that her old boss was an evil chemist during the war. She thinks it's better to not look back at any of it."

Quentin shrugged. "Some people do. It's how they cope. But I'd say you gave Richter an open invitation to come here himself."

"Now I just have to find something on Morris."

Quentin didn't say anything. There wasn't more than a foot between them. She could feel his breath on her cheek. Her heart was now pounding so loud she was sure he could hear it.

"Jasminka might have come through for you," he said, abruptly turning away.

Jesus, she was having trouble keeping up. "What are you talking about?"

Quentin leaned up against the counter. "She found out Arlo Morris's big secret. His family company supplied some of the ingredients used to make the gas."

"What?"

"You wouldn't happen to have a Coke, would you?"

She blinked. "No. Um. I have a Fanta if you want."

"That'll do."

Jillian got the Fanta out of the fridge and handed it to him. He took a long drink before setting the bottle down and telling her about his recent conversation with Jasminka and James.

"I don't trust her, not completely, but James thinks it's because I don't trust anyone new."

"Is he right?" Jillian smiled.

Quentin ran a hand through his hair. "Maybe."

"For the record, I think she's okay. She's complicated in a way that makes no sense for a cover story. Plus, I think James deserves a little happiness."

Quentin looked at her. "You're too soft, Jillian. You can't trust people just because you want them to be good."

"It worked with you."

He sighed. "What do you want to do now, about Morris?"

"I've got some ideas."

"Anything you want to share?"

"Well, Quentin, like you once told me, we all fall to our experience."

He finished up the Fanta in one long drink. "I'll check in with James every day. If you need me for anything."

"Okay." It felt weird to be able to rely on him, however tangentially. She was more used to him coming and going unexpectedly, without any pattern. For the first time since Jillian had known him, he didn't appear to have an agenda with her. He was almost like a friend.

"I don't suppose," Jillian said, "I could have a way to contact you directly. I mean, I don't even know where you stay when you're here."

"That's not a good idea, Jillian," he said. "I'm still CIA. You're still here on a SIGINT mission. It's better to keep those things far apart."

"Is it always going to be like this?"

"I don't know."

Before she could say anything else, her phone rang. "Hello," she said, picking up.

"Ah, you're back then."

James.

"The flight out of Frankfurt was delayed a bit. I just got in about twenty minutes ago." Already it felt like hours what with all she had to process in that time.

"I don't know if this will do much good or just get you into more trouble, but I have Morris's address for you. That favor I called in. It came through. He's at 7 Klausenerplatz in Charlottenburg."

"Someone followed him to there?"

"Aye, a friend of a friend. Needed some practice at that sort of thing and was more than willing to help. I don't know if you still want to do your thing with him, but I thought it best to tell you that result had come through."

She didn't know if she could fit it all in her head at the moment, but she appreciated the effort. "Thanks, James."

He paused. "Are you okay, lass? You don't sound excited."

"It's been a busy evening. But really, that's amazing. Please, tell your friend thank you. If I can ever repay the favor."

"Ah now, you don't want to be offering that, seeing as it might get you involved in more shite that won't be good for you. I will, however, tell him you'll be buying them all a couple of rounds at the mess next week."

Jillian smiled. "Okay. I'll, um, talk to you tomorrow."

She hung up, wondering how to fit in this new piece of information.

"Good news?" Quentin asked.

"Maybe," she answered, rubbing her eyes. "James called in a favor and had someone trying to figure out where Morris was staying here in West Berlin. We started it before you came back. Or before I knew you were back. I'd forgotten about it actually. Anyway, he got an address."

"What are you going to do with it?"

"Originally I was going to try to inconspicuously hang around and see if I could pick up any voice signals. But now, I'm not so sure. I just…have to think. Or something."

Quentin came near and ran his hand down her arm. "Get some sleep, Jillian. You're not going to be able to put all the pieces together tonight."

She didn't say anything as he left. Locking the door behind him, she leaned her head against it for a moment. *That was really good advice.*

CHAPTER THIRTY-SIX

She couldn't do it. She couldn't steal from Madeline. Even though Madeline would likely never miss these particular documents, Jillian couldn't steal from this woman who'd become her friend. She worried that if she did, if she justified it to herself, there'd be no end to what she could justify doing.

Then she'd end up like William Dawson, or worse. Hadn't she been learning over the last few months just how slippery the slope of self-justification was?

Jillian looked down at the documents she'd collected through hours of eye-numbing search. There was some interesting stuff here. Maybe not anything obviously earth-shattering, but still, there were enough names and references to IG Farben that Arlo Morris should be interested. Even though Jillian was sure she had the means to get Arlo out of her life with what she'd learned from Quentin, she didn't want to make an enemy of the man. This information was part of the package to trade for Arlo to forget about her.

Now all she had to do was ask Madeline to share them, without being able to fully explain why.

Jillian kept working away until the door opened with Madeline's arrival at the garage.

"Jillian," said Madeline, "I did not expect to see you here so early."

Sighing inwardly, hoping the words she'd rehearsed were the right ones, Jillian put down the papers in her hand and turned to face Madeline.

"I have a favor to ask you," she started.

"After all you have done for me, I owe you many favors. What can I do?" Madeline said.

"You remember last year, when I helped Lisa, that friend of mine whose dad was in the Stasi in Dresden?"

"That is something that is not easy to forget."

"Yeah, well, apparently the Stasi have taken an interest in me. Which, I guess, was to be expected. It makes me nervous, but I guess maybe the Stasi are interested in a lot of people. Anyway, that man who introduced himself to us, back in the fall, Hans Gohl? Well, he doesn't live across the street. He was looking for me for reasons that I don't completely understand, but that came about in some sort of information exchange. He thought I might be a person who could help him. My friend, she worked for the Canadian government, and he assumed I did too. He approached me for information that I had no way of even finding. But he told me his story. And, well, it's pretty interesting."

"You have me very intrigued, Jillian," Madeline said.

"He's not in the Stasi, or at least he says he isn't, and I believe him. He's a West German businessman who works with whomever he can. He's really most interested in shining a light on the activities of German pharmaceutical companies during the war. It was him who got me interested in IG Farben."

"That is fascinating. Do you know what he did during the war?"

"I'm not exactly sure, but I do know his family was involved in things that he is not proud of. I think he's trying to make amends."

"What is it you would like from me?"

Jillian gestured to the folder on the table beside her. "I would like to share with him the documents I've found that might relate to men who worked for IG Farben."

"From my collection here?"

"Yes."

"That seems simple enough," Madeline said. "I have more than I can handle, I think."

Jillian let out a breath. She should have known Madeline would be so understanding.

"But I am curious," Madeline continued, "about what he is doing. Would it be possible for me to meet him again and give him the papers myself?"

Jillian felt her pulse skitter a bit. She hadn't anticipated that request. "I…I can ask him. He seems very private." Her thoughts continued to stumble over themselves as she quickly thought through what Madeline was asking. "But, oh, Madeline, I should warn you. He's…different. I'm not sure that he's not a little bit crazy. This pursuit of his, it's like a quest. I get the impression that he believes it's his only chance of salvation or something."

Madeline was quiet for a while. "One thing I have always appreciated about you, Jillian, is your willingness to listen. You are genuinely interested in history, and it gives me hope, because the more young people who learn, the better the chances of never repeating it. But there are some things that are impossible to explain. If you've never lived them, you will not understand them in the same way." Madeline looked around the garage. "What am I doing here if not atoning? For what, I'm not sure. Sometimes I feel like it's just for surviving when so many didn't. So maybe I am curious about what this Hans Gohl is doing, and wondering if he's successful, or if he finds peace."

"I don't want anything bad to happen to you."

"Do you think something would?" Madeline asked.

"I'm not sure," Jillian answered. She thought for a moment, recalling her interactions with Morris, how she felt around him, what he seemed to be capable of. "I think he's fine, unless you get in his way. But I'll warn you, if he wants something from you, be prepared to give it to him. On that front I'd say he's completely relentless."

"I suppose you think it unwise to want to meet somebody like that," Madeline said.

"I'm in no place to judge. I get that the unexpected can be compelling sometimes. So if you want, I'll ask him. I just suggest you watch out for yourself."

"I appreciate it, how you are so concerned. Perhaps you can just send him to me for the papers you want him to have, and I will decide if there is anywhere to go from there."

"Sure. And Madeline, thank you."

Jillian couldn't quite suppress her misgivings about the situation. Arlo Morris wasn't someone she trusted, and Madeline knew nothing of the real reason why Jillian was in West Berlin. The thought of the two of them together made her uneasy in many ways.

It was too late now. Jillian had decided the documents were worth sharing, and Morris knew about Madeline anyway. He could approach her without Jillian's introduction if he was curious. He could tell her anything about Jillian. There was nothing Jillian could do to stop him. She could only hope that the two of them had enough history to talk about that neither would be all that interested in discussing their mutual connection.

CHAPTER THIRTY-SEVEN

Jillian looked over her apartment. She'd done well. It wasn't perfect, but it was good enough that no one would notice from a casual inspection. She grabbed her jacket. She just needed one more part, then it should all work perfectly.

Three hours later, she was sitting in the middle of her living room floor with a screwdriver in her hand when her doorbell rang. She shoved what she was working on under the sofa and ran to her bedroom, flicking the switch.

The doorbell sounded again, impatience coming through in the noise. Jillian looked through the peephole and paused. She didn't recognize the man standing on the other side. She watched his fist come up and pound on the door. She could feel the force of the knock on her hands.

"Jillian Meyers," the man said, "open this fucking door or I'll shoot the lock out."

Not hesitating, Jillian ran to her phone and made a call.

James had to stay late queueing up songs for the night shift. Half the unit was out sick with some cold that was sweeping through the base. So far James had avoided it, but it meant he'd had to cover some shifts. He was almost done putting together enough songs to last through the wee hours so he could go home and get some sleep.

He supposed he wasn't missing much anyway. Jasminka was gone again, tracking down another potential source on her nuclear power plant story, and Jillian had holed up in her apartment trying to figure things out. So far she'd only asked for one small favor, and since it didn't inconvenience him at all, he'd had no problem saying yes.

James was tense, though. He wasn't sure why, but it seemed this situation with Jillian was like one of those state changes they talk about in physics class. It was an analogy they used all the time in psyops. Often the overall picture looked the same for ages, like adding one grain of sand to a pile. But one day a critical mass is inevitably reached, and the whole structure changes. You can't see it happening, and you never know which grain of sand or which radio broadcast is going to send the current structure toppling, but one day it does.

Things hadn't seemed to change much for Jillian. But with all the pieces falling into place, with all the grains of sand being added by people asking questions, the structure was no doubt becoming precarious. The critical mass couldn't be far off.

Jillian wondered if she should let the man shoot. *It would probably bring the police, which wouldn't help at all.* There was also the added problem that the bullet might hit her. She took a deep breath, knowing it was next to useless in terms of slowing her racing heart, but she hoped an outward veneer of calm might defuse the situation.

She opened the door before the man could make good on his threat. "Who are you?" she got out before he pushed her inside and slammed the door behind him.

"Who the fuck are you?" he snarled at her. "Jillian Meyers. You aren't anybody I could find."

She stumbled back and caught herself on the kitchen counter. "You showed up at my door."

The man looked around the apartment, obviously expecting to see something and just as obviously disappointed at what was there. "You started a shitstorm. You requested information on Helmut Radsch from the RCMP records department. Now I've got IOs crawling up my ass and the criminal branch poking around. I want to know why. How did you ever even hear of Radsch?"

Because the language felt so normal, it had taken her a minute to process this man was Canadian. "You're William Dawson, aren't you?"

The man's eyebrows shot up. "How the fuck do you know that?"

"One of those IOs crawling up your ass is a friend of mine. He sent me a heads-up. Does the RCMP know you've left the country to threaten a fellow Canadian?"

Dawson started to look nervous. "Why were you asking about Radsch? It was thirty years ago. Why now?"

"Why did you give him a new identity, then purge the files? Who was he to you?"

"It's none of your fucking business."

"Do you know what he did during the war? Do you know what you helped him cover up?"

Dawson stared at her. Five, ten seconds passed. "How do you know all of this?"

Jillian swallowed the bile that had risen in her throat. "So you knew? What he did? The gas for the chambers. The chemical process to kill millions of innocent people."

"Is that what this is all about? You're what, twenty-five? How are you even involved?"

"Did you never think it would catch up with you? Your role in this? What Radsch did, that's not a crime that time heals."

Dawson sneered at her. "I don't know how you found all this out or what you hope to achieve, but you're not going to get a chance to be an avenging angel."

"What, is Kurt Richter going to put even more money into your account if you get rid of me?"

The mention of Richter's name had an effect on Dawson. Up until then he'd been somewhat collected. Jillian surmised at one point he must have been an IO himself. But at soon as the name Richter left her lips, Dawson paled and his left hand began to shake slightly.

"Maybe you were good at your job once," Jillian continued, "but retirement and easy money have made you soft. Surely you must appreciate that this goes way beyond me. There are people looking for retribution that you've never heard of. Getting rid of me isn't going to stop them."

With absolutely perfect timing, a knock sounded on the door.

"Who is that?" Dawson snapped. "Get rid of them."

"I don't think so. If you really want this to be over, you should meet the real avenging angel."

Jillian opened the door and let in Arlo Morris.

"Jillian. I have come as you asked." Arlo looked at the other man in the room. "And who is this?"

Jillian stepped back. The three of them made a triangle connected by tension.

"This is William Dawson, the Canadian who arranged for a new identity for Helmut Radsch thirty years ago."

Morris smiled in the manner of a wolf finally cornering his prey. "Ah. Finally. It is as I expected."

"Yeah, William here did it for the money. Kurt Richter has been paying him well for the last thirty years to keep his secret."

Morris turned to Jillian. "Kurt Richter? Of the Handelbank? Yes, that does make sense. Many investments in pharmaceuticals over the years. Directed by Richter. It fits. Nicely."

Dawson looked really nervous now. Jillian wasn't sure what he'd thought. That she'd come across some old info from the war and got curious? That she was conspiring with someone to make a quick buck by blackmailing an ex-RCMP officer about missing files? Whatever it had been, he seemed to realize now that he'd overstepped. He'd failed to anticipate the full scope of the situation.

"Who are you?" Dawson said to Morris.

"A friend of the German state. One who believes that we will never realize our true greatness by allowing old filth to bring shame on the German identity. Tell me, was money enough when the stories of Auschwitz and the other camps came out? Did it help you sleep at night as the Jews told their stories of the forced labor and the conditions? Did Kurt Richter increase your compensation when they found the mass graves of those who had been gassed?"

"What do you want from me? Do I think it's right, what happened during the war? No, of course not. But by the time I met Radsch, it was over. Nothing was going to change what had happened. The world wanted to move on. I saw that, everyone saw that, after Nuremberg."

Morris's features hardened in hatred. "Nuremberg was an embarrassment. A stain worse than the war."

"Radsch was one guy. The Nazi machine was so large, one guy didn't matter. That was the problem," Dawson stumbled out.

"One man always matters," Morris said, rage outlining his words. "The Nazis were not a machine. They were made up of men, and all men have choice. Radsch needs to answer for the ones that he made."

"What are you going to do? Go after everyone who did something wrong?"

Morris looked at Dawson with contempt. "And you, who once represented your country. You would have been very happy in Nazi Germany. But no," he continued. "I must be…practical in my endeavors. Radsch was not merely a worker bee, as you say in English. Heinrich Hörlein was the head of research and development for IG Farben. It was he who proposed the gas solution to Hitler. And it was Radsch who convinced Hörlein that it could be done, that IG Farben could make the gas."

Oh my God. Jillian could hardly process what Morris was saying. It was too awful to contemplate. Radsch hadn't just been a guy in a lab making a product. As awful as that would have been, what he'd done was much worse.

"Heinrich Hörlein died before I could arrange for him to pay for what he did, but I have a copy of this IG Farben company memo. And now I have you to prove that Radsch is now Richter. Richter will answer for his crimes in one way or another, and his story will be yet one more to make sure the memory of Hörlein is reviled for the rest of history."

"I…I'm not going to talk to you about Richter," Dawson said.

Jillian wondered if he knew how pathetic he sounded. "Not quite sure who to be more afraid of, are you, Dawson?" She turned to Morris. "Here are copies of his most recent bank statements, with a direct monthly deposit from a Handelbank account. Here's his bio, including the name of his wife and kids in Canada. The RCMP has opened an investigation into the files he's purged. All, I'm assuming, related to what he did for Radsch."

"I'm not going with you," Dawson said, starting to panic.

Morris removed a small object from his pocket. Holding it up to his lips, he blew quickly. At the sound, Jillian's door opened, and two well-built men entered. Morris pointed at Dawson. "He will be coming with us. Please subdue him."

Jillian watched as the men walked up to a now-sputtering Dawson and each gripped an arm. Dawson began to fight, but one of the men jabbed him in the leg with a syringe, and the resistance stopped. Supporting him on each side, they walked him out the door. To anyone seeing them, it would look like two men supporting their drunk friend.

She took a deep breath and let it out slowly. She wasn't sure if she'd done the right thing, but there was no going back now.

"Now I must thank you, Jillian," Morris said, turning to her. "Our relationship has been very fruitful."

"Do I have to worry about Richter showing up here too? I have to assume that he and Dawson have been in contact and that he instructed Dawson to confront me."

"Kurt Richter will not be a problem for you. By the end of the day, he will know that Dawson is in my possession and that I am the one he should be concerned with."

Morris's tone was chilling. Jillian had no doubt Richter was going to be a broken man at the end of this.

"That is all for now," Morris continued.

Jillian held up her hand. "Wait. Before you go. I'm happy that you found Radsch. What he did, during the war, I have to agree with you that it should not disappear in history. I do believe that the only way to not repeat humanity's worst moments is to shine the light on them. But I can't agree with your methods. Our relationship has to end. I won't be doing you any favors in the future. So please, don't ask."

"I respect what you have done for me, but I cannot promise I won't need your help again. There is much evil in this world that has to be addressed."

Jillian nodded. "I understand. Believe it or not, you and I have similar goals. But our association, it has to stop. Arlo."

The shock seemed to reverberate through the apartment as his eyes widened in amazement. "How do you know my name?"

"I'm not going to tell you that. But I will tell you that I found your place in history. I know why you're so interested in these IG Farben chemists because I know what your family did during the war."

Morris started, the greatest look of sadness coming over his features. "Ah, so you know my great shame: that my father was one of the enablers."

"You told me before how you hated the Nazis from the very beginning. It must have been awful for you then, with your father. Did he know what he was doing?"

"Does it matter? It was no secret what the Nazis were like. Even in our small town outside of Mainz, we could see what was happening, the fear and the indoctrination. I wanted to leave at first. I am ashamed of that now. But at the time, I could see no other way. It was only later that I realized that there were other things I could do, other ways to stand up to them. Direct assault was not possible by the time the war began. Too many had become blind followers. But I did what I could. I sabotaged many shipments to IG Farben. I helped people escape. And I rejoiced when the Nazis lost the war. I thought the world would expose them all for what they were. Then I watched the trials, read about the pardons, saw so many of these evil men regain their positions in society. So I vowed to continue on, destroying them all one by one until there was nothing left."

Jillian didn't know what to say. What could she? She didn't think she'd ever come across such a complex set of motives in her life. There was no doubt Morris thought his ends justified his means. He was singular in his purpose, and the morality of his results outweighed the immorality of the steps he used to pursue them. In some ways he was no better than those he was punishing. But it was hard for her not to sympathize a little. Men like Hitler or Stalin, they wouldn't be able to achieve anything if they didn't have support. Something like the Holocaust couldn't happen only through the actions of one man. People needed to remember that, to remember that there is always a choice to reject inflicting the worst kind of fear and pain. If not for men like Morris, it might be too easy to see that pattern repeat itself.

"Your secret is safe with me," she said finally.

"It seems I underestimated you, Jillian," Morris replied. "We have come to an understanding. Your secret is safe with me also. I will not ask you for more favors."

Jillian exhaled slowly. It seemed she was safe again. The power of that swept around her like a cocoon. For the first time in months, she felt at peace.

"I have something else for you," she said, crossing to the counter to write something on a piece of paper. Turning, she handed it to him. "When you first introduced yourself to me, I was helping a friend sort through some old war documents."

Morris took the paper. "Yes, I remember."

"Her name is Madeline. Here's her number. I've told her a bit about you—about Hans Gohl, and how he's interested in the activities of IG Farben during the war. In my spare time, I've been searching through her papers, and I've found a few references about men who worked at the company. She's agreed to share them with you."

He stared at her for a moment. "I thank you. This is very generous."

"She doesn't know anything about what I'm doing in West Berlin beyond being a student. That can't change. But she's a really wonderful person who's taught me a lot about this city and the war, and it's partly because of her that I understand a little about what you're doing."

"Why are you giving this to me?"

Jillian was quiet for a moment. "I want to leave on good terms. And so you know, in my way, I support you."

"You are a very interesting woman. I wish you a good future," Morris said.

"Good luck with Dawson," Jillian said.

"I do not need luck." Morris smiled a little. "Well, Jillian, perhaps our paths will cross in the future."

"Not too soon."

"Yes. For you, I understand that. Well, good day to you." He tipped his head and turned to exit.

Jillian closed the door behind him, leaning her head against it as she turned the lock. She let her heart rate steady while she thought over what had just happened. She supposed she should have asked what he was going to do with Dawson, if only to pass it on to Jean-Marc, but she couldn't find it in her to care. The man had misused his position for decades of profit, and to her that was unforgivable. Not as bad as what Radsch had done, but still beyond forgiving. Morris was too smart to kill him. No doubt in the next few days, Dawson would realize he had a new master.

Turning into her kitchen, Jillian picked up the phone and dialed.

"All right, lass?"

"Yeah," Jillian said. "Did you hear it all?"

"Not all of it. I got home late. But I went to check that it was recording like you instructed. When I put the headphones on, you were already in the middle of it."

Jillian closed her eyes. "It worked out. I mean, I didn't expect Dawson to show up. If anything, I thought it would be Richter at my door, but it all seems okay now."

"Are you going to come over, check out the tapes for yourself?"

"Yeah," she said, "in a little bit. First I think I'm going to go for a walk. Without an agenda, without worrying who is behind me. Find some strudel, go take a look at the Wall."

"Want some company?" James asked.

"Sure." Jillian smiled. "That would be lovely."

CHAPTER THIRTY-EIGHT

Frank sat in the car waiting for Veronica. It was sweltering. February in Managua was too hot for him. It seemed like every month in this country was too hot for him. He didn't know how people did without seasons. He missed his wife, and he missed being cold once in a while. He was ready to go home. But he had a few loose ends to tie up first.

He and Veronica were going back to Santa Rosa, hopefully for the last time.

It had been a whirlwind few weeks since they'd last been there. Frank had watched Quentin go off to Berlin to help Jillian. He hoped that what he'd got from Hoffsteader was enough for Jillian to protect her operation. He'd found out from James that Morris had made contact with Jillian. To what end Frank had no idea, because he couldn't imagine what a man who was interested exclusively in ex-Nazis could want with someone like Jillian, but Frank felt vindicated that he'd done the right thing by pursuing the Cuban in the first place.

One day he'd get over to Germany and take his nephew out for a drink so he could hear the whole story. He'd received a postcard from Jillian that simply said "Thanks." Given all that he'd been through over the last few months, it was enough to know that things over there were okay.

It was a much more beautiful day than the last time he and Veronica had been here. They had the windows down. Veronica's hair was whipping around, and she'd turned the music up loud. It was nice to not have to talk and still be comfortable.

Frank slowed the car down as they neared the village. The same colorful doors. The same determined-looking fountain. The bodega was busy. The streets were quiet. The only thing out of place was the burned-out carcass that had been Claudia's house. They pulled up in front.

Veronica got out of the car. "Someone has to know where she is. I'll ask around."

Frank was content to sit and wait.

After a few minutes, Veronica returned. "We can walk. She's at a friend's just down the street. That orange door there."

Frank got out of the car and followed Veronica. The woman who opened the orange door regarded them with suspicion but finally relented to getting Claudia.

"I told her we were here to apologize."

Claudia came to the door looking profoundly sad. This was a woman who kept losing what she loved. Frank was sorry to have contributed to that.

Veronica took the lead in the conversation. Frank heard the Spanish words for "sorry" a half dozen times.

After the words seemed to be slowing down, Frank cleared his throat and put his hand on Veronica's arm. "Translate for me, would you?" Then he turned to Claudia. "I'm sorry about your house. I'm sorry that we couldn't find another way to save our friend."

He waited for Veronica. "She says if the house was what she had to give up to see Carlos dead, for her it was a fair deal."

Frank thought that was the one silver lining to this situation—Carlos couldn't hurt this family anymore. He handed Claudia an envelope. "Tell her this is from me and my wife. I know how important it is for a family to have a home."

Claudia looked at the envelope in confusion while Veronica translated. She reached out slowly and took the envelope, gently lifting the flap. Frank saw her eyes widen in astonishment. She looked shocked and grateful and panicked all at once.

"Tell her there are no strings attached. It's a gift from someone who can afford it. Tell her I'd just spend it all on cigarettes and beer anyway, so she's doing me a favor by accepting it."

After listening to Veronica, Claudia turned to him. "Gracias," she said.

Veronica laughed as Claudia continued. "She says thank you. The money will be well spent on a new home she can share with her grandson. She also says she hopes never to see any of us again."

Frank smiled. "I don't blame her."

Veronica said good-bye for the both of them, and they got back into the car. Frank pulled a U-turn on the dusty street and headed back to Managua.

"So, how much was in the envelope?"

"You know, that's not really any of your business."

"We're partners, Frank. It'll give me some idea of how much I have to save for the next time I burn down someone's house."

Frank laughed. "Fine. About ten grand Canadian. That should be enough to get them something decent."

Veronica was silent for a moment. "That was really generous of you, Frank."

"Yeah, well." He shrugged. "What else do I have to spend my money on? All I do is work and smoke, and now my wife sells her paintings for more than I make in a month."

"Really?" asked Veronica. "When we're back in Ottawa, I think you should have me over for dinner. I was curious before, but now…"

"Speaking of," Frank said, "do you want to go back?"

"To Ottawa? I, well, I'm not sure if I have any option."

"There are always options. I'm asking you what you want."

Veronica looked forward out the windshield, clearly thinking about how she wanted to respond. "What I've done here, this is why I joined. I feel useful. When we helped the ambassador, that was a good day for me. I know it's not always going to be this exciting. There's not always going to be a nasty Cuban hanging around. More of it is going to be the information gathering and relationship building I've been doing. But I like it. I don't know if I want to stay in Nicaragua forever, but it's interesting. And I know what's waiting for me back in Ottawa."

Frank thought about that. He'd been thinking a lot about what he wanted, about what would be good for him, for

Veronica, for CBNRC. He'd also thought about how much his wife would put up with.

"You know," he said, "when I was the director of access, I didn't think there was any better job in the world. Access—where all the taps go. The people who find all the signals. It seemed logical that I was there, that it would be the culmination of everything I'd done in my career.

"There are a lot of good things about that job. But, like with any job, there were also a lot of tedious things. Being a director is middle management. You're squeezed in both directions. It got so I stopped noticing all the corporate requirements and all the political maneuvering. Being here, I can look back with a clearer eye. It was a good job, but it wasn't the best job, or the only job. At first, when I got assigned this liaising gig, all I could think about was finding something here to get me back there. But now, I think I'm ready for something new."

"What are you saying, Frank?"

"I think we're a good team. I think we've proved our agencies should work together overseas more. I'd be interested in doing more of it—but only with you. If you're interested." He glanced over to find Veronica staring at him.

"Really?"

"Really." He smiled. "Now, I'm not going to be able to do back-to-back assignments. My wife doesn't mind a break once in a while, but I don't think she'd be happy if I was gone eleven months of the year. But I think I can sell it to my boss. Every division needs a leader, and they're still paying me to be a director. You can report to me to start, and we can see where it goes. I mean, Christ, there's enough untapped targets for us to be busy for the next ten years."

"By which time I'll be ready to apply for your job."

Frank barked out a laugh. "Yeah, you damn well will be."

"I appreciate it, Frank. I know you're not doing it for me, but I appreciate how you're giving me a chance anyway."

"You've earned your chance. You did good work here. Really good work. There's no benefit to wasting talent. You go back, that idiot boss of yours is going to put you back in media monitoring, and that's not good for you or the taxpayer."

Veronica smiled. "You remember when we first met, and you told me that the day I got assigned to you was going to be either the best day or the worst day of my career? Well, I've got my answer."

Frank felt an awkward combination of pleasure and embarrassment. "I'm just putting the mission first. Like I always do. Sometimes, though, putting the mission first is a win-win."

Veronica rolled down her window and tipped her head back. "Works for me. Just for the record, I wouldn't mind going up to the Arctic one day."

Frank laughed. "Hell no. You'll have to wait until you're the boss."

"I can do that."

Frank rolled down his window as well. When he'd first been assigned this liaising gig, he'd looked at it like it was the punishment it was meant to be. It was amazing to him that over the course of the last few months, it had come to feel like an unexpected gift. He felt energized, like the rest of his life wasn't neatly mapped out. There was something to be said for dwelling a bit in the unknown. In the right structure, it was invigorating.

He had no doubt there would be battles ahead of him. Anything requiring joint funding was always a challenge. And lord knew he hadn't made a lot of friends at the RCMP. But the results from Nicaragua were good. Veronica would push from her end. And maybe, just maybe, they'd get the chance to do something great.

CHAPTER THIRTY-NINE

Jillian sat in her lab checking the signal strength. She'd noticed in the last couple of days that the BND feed was flickering a little. She was sure some of what had been copied would be useless and that there might even be spaces of time that were empty. There wasn't much she could do about feed problems upstream, but she could probably augment the signal on her end. It looked like this week's task was going to be how to not raise any flags while she did that.

She looked up at a knock on her door.

Quentin stepped inside as soon as she opened it, maneuvering to quickly close the door behind him.

"Hi, Jillian. Hard at work, I see."

As if he would know anything about the work she did. But she smiled. "Always. The very unglamorous part of signals intelligence."

"You have to tell me, then, because I've never been able to figure it out: what's the glamorous part?"

That made Jillian laugh. "Probably the interesting reports that someone gets to wave in front of the prime minister once in a while. Certainly not the electric pulses traveling across the wires."

Quentin leaned his hip up against the desk. "So you had a good result then, with Arlo Morris."

"You've been talking to James," Jillian said, sitting back down in her chair. It didn't bother her that he went to James first. She supposed that his way of gathering intelligence was too ingrained by now to take the direct approach. "I think we understand each other enough for him not to be a problem for me in the future."

"Plus, you like him. Or at least like what he's doing."

Jillian shook her head. "I'm not sure it's that easy. It's not a binary. He's confusing to me."

"So you don't want to see him again anytime soon."

"No. Not at all."

Quentin regarded her for a long moment. "What did you tell your superiors about Dawson?"

"Enough that if and when he ever gets back to Canada, he's going to have a lot to answer for. I recorded the whole thing, you know. I'd like to keep Morris out of it, because I don't think the RCMP can do anything about him anyway, but I told Jean-Marc that I have proof should anyone ever need it."

"This kind of stuff, it never makes it to a court of law."

"It's also way outside my area of expertise. Someone else will figure out what to do about Dawson."

"So that's it, then," Quentin said. "It's all wrapped up."

"It would seem like it," replied Jillian, and they were both silent for a while.

"Do you ever think of yourself as Tom?" Jillian asked.

Quentin looked startled at the question. "Sometimes," he said slowly. "It technically still is my name, although I don't use it much anymore. But when I need to remind myself who I am, that's the name I think of. Why do you ask?"

"I suppose I'm just curious."

"Names are just labels. I don't think of Quentin as being all the different from Tom. They're like, I don't know, different jackets that I put on. I'm still the same person, no matter what I'm wearing."

"Do you regret killing Carlos?"

"Jesus, Jillian." Quentin's hand shook a little as he ran it through his hair. "These are some serious questions."

"I've got them saved up," she said. "It seems like we're always in the middle of something, that what's going on in the moment needs to take precedence, but we're at the end of something now. I figure now's the time to ask."

"No, I don't regret killing him. In that I don't regret that he's dead."

"But?"

"It's not an easy memory to have, pulling that trigger. No matter how awful he was, it feels like something that I'm going to have to live with forever."

"I'm sorry for that."

Quentin shrugged. "It's better than the alternative. Either way, the day he killed Isabella, I knew I would never be rid of him. It just came down to what kind of pain I wanted to live with."

"Carlos killed her? Why?"

"She was in the way. His own cousin, and he shot her to get to me."

"You loved her."

Quentin was silent for a while. Jillian could feel her heart beating in time to the whir of the tapes as she sat waiting for his response.

"I did. At least, at the time I thought I did. Looking back, I'm not sure it was love."

Jillian didn't know what to say.

"It was unrequited, by the way," Quentin continued. "She was devoted to her family. Everything she did, she was doing for them. I wonder sometimes if that was what I was attracted to."

"Attraction is a funny thing, isn't it?" Jillian said after a while. "I'm still so ashamed that I was attracted to Carlos, that at no point did I pick up on what a monster he really was."

"The problem is, no one is a monster a hundred percent of the time. Carlos could be charming. And he was human. No doubt he had needs like the rest of us."

Jillian swallowed past the lump in her throat. "Yeah. For whatever that's worth."

"We all make mistakes, Jillian," Quentin said, and she saw the compassion in his eyes. "I know that better than anyone. I might not have pulled the trigger that killed Isabella, but it was my fault she was there. I've made so many mistakes I'm starting to lose track."

Jillian supposed it was impossible to get through life without making mistakes. The really bad ones, they were supposed to hurt and haunt. *That's how you stop yourself from making them again.*

"What's next for you?" she asked.

"I'm here," Quentin said, "and I'm staying for a while."

"Lots of intelligence to collect?"

"A business that never dies. But also, lots of stories to write." He paused for a moment, looking somewhat hesitant. "When I was in Nicaragua, well, I realized I liked filing stories for the *Trib*. It's funny, but I only got into journalism because it was convenient for the rest of it. But it turns out I find it rewarding."

"Your stories are good. I liked reading them."

"James said that you went to the library sometimes to read them."

Jillian could tell he didn't know what to do with that. She almost didn't know what to do with it herself. "I wasn't sure about you. I mean, I trusted you, as in you know all my big secrets. But you didn't seem real to me. I thought reading your articles would help me understand better who you are."

"And did they?"

Jillian smiled softly. "A little. I learned that you care. Like James does. It comes out differently, obviously, and you don't care about the same things. I'm still not sure Somoza is the right answer for Nicaraguans, but you do care. The articles you write, they're not propaganda. It's good journalism."

"I guess I should say thank you."

"It's just my opinion. Not that I know much about reporting. But your stories, they were engaging."

Quentin was quiet again for a long while. "And you, Jillian? What's next for you?" he asked.

"I have some things to work out. I've been neglecting my job a bit lately. I've been more in maintenance mode. I think there are some elements I can improve. That kind of work, I know most people find it boring, but I really love it. Every time something takes me away from it, I'm reminded of how much I actually love solving engineering problems."

Quentin smiled. "The world needs all kinds."

Jillian let the silence fall and hang for a moment. "I can't figure out how our relationship is supposed to work. You disappear, and then you come back. I can't contact you. But you seem willing to help me if I need it. We aren't friends, but we aren't strangers either."

Quentin took a deep breath. "What is it you want?"

"Really? I'm not entirely sure. I think, for now, it would be nice to have the chance to get to know you a little better. That, or you have to go away completely. It's too hard for me, this idea of relying on a ghost."

Quentin folded his arms across his chest. "What if you don't like what you find out?"

Jillian smiled. "I'm getting pretty good at being open-minded. If I decide I can't stand you, that's fine. I'd rather know either way."

"Fair enough," Quentin said, returning her smile. "I can come visit you here sometimes. The campus is an easy place to be invisible."

"That would be nice. Next time, you can show up with a coffee and try to explain to me why baseball is such a great game."

He shook his head. "That I'm not sure you're ever going to get."

"Well," Jillian said, "better to know that about me now."

Quentin's grin flashed across his face before his features settled into serious. "I've been thinking, too, that if you need me for something, well, I would like to be able to help. You seem to get into conflict with enough regularity that I might be of some use in the future. I share a desk at the West Berlin office of *Zeit*. I'm not there every day, but someone does take messages. You could contact me there if something came up."

"Thank you," Jillian said. "I appreciate that."

Silence filled the room again, but it didn't seem so awkward this time.

"Take care, Jillian," Quentin said, moving to the door. "And I'll see you. Soon."

"Back to work?"

"Actually," Quentin said, "I'm off for a drink, just soaking in the atmosphere of the city, like any good reporter. James is on me about never having been to Land's End pub."

She smiled. "Maybe when you're being a journalist in the next little while, you can find a place that's worth going to that he's never been to. Just to, you know, shut him up."

"That's the best mission I've been given in a long time."

She watched him leave, then got up to lock the door behind him. She didn't know if it was going to lead to friendship or something else, if the attraction was always going to simmer away in the background or if it was real enough to turn into something they could build on, but she was okay with this step. Jillian had realized that if she and Quentin were going to ever have a relationship, then she had to spend time with him without drama or conflict. Without being hunted or manipulated, without having her life in danger.

Perhaps what she felt for him was real, but it was also possible that there wasn't any substance behind it. If she was only intrigued by the enigma, better to take that apart and be able to move on.

Maybe there was something worth caring about under all the mystery.

Jillian smiled to herself as she slipped her headphones on. It was going to be a lot of fun to find out.

Jillian got off the bus, appreciating the unseasonably warm March day. She was sure spring would come in its usual fits and starts, but she wasn't grumbling about the surprising warmth. She figured, when it came to weather, it was better to be teased than ignored.

It seemed like all of West Berlin was out enjoying the day. There was something about early spring that swept in like a promise of adventure. The renewal in nature was accompanied by a corresponding renewal in possibility. New things of all kinds would be growing soon.

Jillian made her way to James's apartment, the haggis she had bought wrapped in the package she held carefully under her arm. It hadn't been easy to find, but she had located a butcher shop in Wedding that made it. When she had gone to pick it up, the woman behind the counter explained her grandmother was Scottish, and there were enough Brits in the city that they sold out on a regular basis. Jillian had no idea if James liked haggis, but even if he didn't, he probably had a story about it. Most important was the idea of doing something thoughtful for him, because she really didn't know what she'd do without him.

James was sitting out on his balcony as she walked up to the building. The woman with him, Jillian presumed, was Jasminka. Jillian was looking forward to finally meeting the journalist. She had about a million questions for Jasminka, everything from her impressions of Arlo Morris over the years to how she went about finding information on Soviet nuclear reactors. Plus, she had to admit curiosity about the woman James had fallen for.

Jillian knew that she would still have to be careful. Her SIGINT mission precluded relaxed and open honesty. But she was more than her day job, and she hoped that she and Jasminka could connect on one of the thousand other topics Jillian was interested in.

James swung open his door before Jillian could knock.

"I'm right nervous about this, you know," he said.

"I brought you haggis." She held up the package to him.

His laugh boomed around the apartment. "Have you ever tried it?" he said, stepping back to let her in.

"No. And, to be honest, I'm not sure I want to. I asked the butcher to tell me how they made it just so I could act like I knew what I was getting into, and, well, I'm not sure how it became your national dish. It sounds disgusting."

"Ye have to thank Robbie Burns for that. Plus, there's something to be said for embracing the odd with gusto. But really, cooked properly it's quite good."

Jillian nodded, hoping he was right. Detecting movement out of the corner of her eye, she turned her head to see Jasminka stepping into the living room from the balcony. "Hi," she said.

"Hi. Jillian, yes? I am so happy to finally meet you."

Jillian smiled, shaking the hand that Jasminka had held out. The reality was never going to match the expectation, but she noticed immediately Jasminka's genuine smile and direct blue eyes. "Me too. James has told me the most interesting stories about you. I really want to hear more about how your Soviet nuclear story is going."

"Yes. Well, getting information out of the Soviet Union is never easy. There is such a culture of fear there from Stalin that I think will take generations to undo. But no one wants to see their loved ones die from radiation poisoning, so I am slowly finding people who are willing to talk to me."

They settled down in the living room with James bringing them each a beer.

The next hour passed smoothly. Jillian was interested in what Jasminka had to say and curious about the kind of life she led. It was also fun to watch as James moved from uncomfortable to resigned as she and Jasminka developed a rapport.

It was easy. Whether by intuition or instruction from James, Jasminka refrained from asking Jillian any questions about her position at the West German Science Institute. Instead, they talked about cities Jasminka had been to that Jillian wanted to visit, what it was like in Belgrade, and Jasminka's wildest adventures as a journalist.

"It is nice, getting to know this very good friend of James. It is important, I think, to meet the people that someone cares about. It helps to understand someone, knowing who they choose to spend time with."

Jillian couldn't agree more. "I know. As much as I've shared with James, it's fascinating for me to meet his girlfriend."

Jillian saw James choke a little at the word.

"Ah, so I am the girlfriend?" Jasminka smiled.

"It seems appropriate," Jillian said.

"And have you met many?"

Jillian grinned. "Nope. You're the first. I've never seen him smitten before."

"Christ Jesus," James said.

"I think I am equally smitten. It was a very fortunate day when he came and knocked on my door."

Jillian really liked Jasminka. She liked her confidence and her stories. She was a woman who seemed comfortable in who she was.

"One of the things I wanted to talk to you about," Jillian said, "was Arlo Morris. I wanted to tell you how grateful I am that you found out who he was and that you were so generous in sharing it with me. It helped. More than you know maybe."

"You and I, we were in a similar place, I think."

"Yeah. It was a bit crazy for me. The more I got to know him, the more I, well, appreciated what he was doing. I think there are some things in history that we should never, ever forget. The Holocaust is one of those things. I hope something like that never happens again. To hold people accountable for their part in that, I understand why he does what he does. But I didn't want to be beholden to him anymore. So thank you for helping me with that."

Jasminka reached out and put her hand on Jillian's, giving it a light squeeze. "You are very welcome. I ask you to think no more of it. I feel similar to you. I will continue to help him if he brings me a story I can verify, but I do not like the idea of being a pawn in his game. This time it worked out, because it brought me to James. I suppose because Arlo got to you, he didn't need James in the end. But I knew it might not work out so well the next time. To be a good journalist and to live how I wish, I need to be independent from those kinds of manipulations."

Jillian breathed a sigh of relief. She felt like Jasminka understood. "So, James tells me he's taking you to Mykonos next month."

Jasminka raised her brows in surprise. "I did not know this."

James took a long drink of his beer. "It was just something I was tossing around. Looking into flights and all that. I thought it would be nice."

"I think it would be more than nice." Jasminka smiled, her eyes crinkling at the corners as she looked at James. "I would love to."

Jillian was so happy for James. He deserved to be in love for a while. Jasminka was cool and different and totally perfect for him. After all Jillian had put him through, everything she asked of him, every time he was there for her, she was happy that he had something to offset all that.

Jillian put on her most fun dress, really the only cocktail dress she had, fiddling with the zipper and making sure the tag wasn't sticking out. Nothing like trying to be sophisticated, all the while having that little white square showing. She so wanted to be a little sophisticated tonight. Madeline had invited her to a reunion of the cabaret dancers.

She was so excited. After months of reading all those memories from the war, she was getting to meet some of the women behind the boxes of papers. She had so many questions and couldn't wait to hear the stories that would undoubtedly be shared.

Flicking on the light in the bathroom, she checked her hair one last time. It looked good. More importantly, she felt good. Although she'd be one of the youngest people there, Madeline had assured her that she wouldn't be out of place. Some of them were bringing their daughters, and the evening was about sharing and sorting through it all. Madeline was going to tell them about the work she and Jillian had done with the documents, and ask for their input on the next steps she wanted to take.

Deciding she was ready, Jillian flew out of her apartment, heading to the U-Bahn. She'd probably be early, but she didn't care. She couldn't remember the last time she'd been this excited about going out.

Arriving at the restaurant, Jillian made her way to the private room Madeline had booked.

She stepped in hesitantly, taking in the chatter that was already filling the room.

"Jillian," Madeline said, stepping up to greet her. "I'm so happy you could make it. I hope it will be interesting for you to meet some of the women you have been reading about for so long."

"It's amazing. I wouldn't have missed this for anything."

ABOUT THE AUTHOR

Rhiannon is a writer of both fiction and nonfiction. Her first fiction release was *Alone Among Spies*. A sequel to that thrilling adventure, *The Wrong Kind of Spy* continues the action in Cold War West Berlin.

She is also the co-author of the successful book series, *The Great Mental Models*. Covering models from physics to systems, this series explains how you can use fundamental knowledge in non-intuitive situations to improve your thinking and, ultimately, your outcomes. *Volume 1: General Thinking Concepts*, was a *Wall Street Journal* bestseller.

Rhiannon also occasionally helps others make their book ideas a reality (because she loves bringing beautiful, insightful content into the world.)

She lives and works in Ottawa, Canada.

You can find out more at rhiannonbeaubien.com, or on her Instagram (rhibeaubien), LinkedIn (Rhiannon Beaubien), or TikTok (@rhiannon.beaubien).

HISTORICAL NOTE

Although *The Wrong Kind of Spy* is a work of fiction, numerous real historical events inspired my writing.

During the mid 1970s, tension between the Somoza government and the Sandinista National Liberation Front escalated. One of the most fascinating accounts I read of this time in Nicaragua is Gioconda Belli's *The Country Under My Skin*.

In December 1974, a group associated with the Sandinistas seized control of the Minister of Agriculture's house in Managua. They kept everyone inside as hostages to negotiate the release of several imprisoned comrades and to bring attention to their cause. By all accounts the hostages were treated well. The American ambassador had already left the party when the Sandinistas arrived.

IG Farben was a real company. I first came across it in the book *The Demon Under the Microscope* by Thomas Hager. The book chronicles the story of the invention of the world's first antibiotic by scientists working for IG Farben under the direction of Heinrich Hörlein. Their work saved millions of lives, especially women who got strep infections during childbirth. The lead scientist Gerhard Domagk won a Nobel Prize in 1939.

During World War II, the company switched to producing materials to support the Nazi war effort. IG Farben scientists, also under the direction of Heinrich Hörlein, did develop the gas for the chambers. This work resulted in the killing of millions. I found the juxtaposition of these two efforts to be incredible and devastating.

ACKNOWLEDGMENTS

There are so many people who support the writing of a book, adding their feedback and helping to shape the final product. Any errors, whether by omission or deliberate, are mine.

First, a thank you to my early readers. Dave Langner, your knowledge of history always astounds me. The details you contribute help make the story come alive. Tina Cantrill, your thoughtfulness is remarkable. I quite appreciate that you took the time to make sure a friend of yours would never release something bad. Vicky Cosenzo, your willingness to jump into anything is fantastic. I love how you're always looking out for me and my characters.

Thank you to Christine Beauchamp for the title. It's great having friends to fill in one's weak spots.

Thank you also to Justin Beaubien, who continues to thoughtfully answer all my emails asking for advice.

Thank you to Kristen Hall-Geisler, my amazing editor. You are so great to work with, and I appreciate that you give all parts of the story your diligent attention, even though you are firmly on "Team James."

To my proofreaders Melissa Ousley and Jenn Kepler, thank you so much for being able to do what you do, giving the manuscript the final polish.

To the two designers I worked with, thank you to Auni Milne for creating a beautiful cover, and to Yvonne Parks for a wonderful interior design.

I also want to acknowledge the amazing Ottawa Public Library. This book required a lot of research to make the setting and story authentic, and the cost of that research would have been prohibitive if I'd had to buy all the books I used. It was so wonderful to have an effective library at my disposal. Public libraries are a gift to the communities they serve.

I am very lucky to have the most amazing support system. My parents, Roland and Angela, thank you for staying enthusiastic about my writing dreams. My husband, Sylvain, thank you for being willing to engage on whatever plot point I need to untangle. My children, Mylo and Zane, thank you for your questions and interest—you both keep the writing fun! I love you all.

Manufactured by Amazon.ca
Bolton, ON